Ice Cream Man

VOLUME TWO

• STRANGE NEAPOLITAN •

WRITTEN BY **W. MAXWELL PRINCE**
ART BY **MARTÍN MORAZZO**
COLORS BY **CHRIS O'HALLORAN**
LETTERING BY **GOOD OLD NEON**
COVER DESIGN BY **SHANNA MATUSZAK**
INTERIOR DESIGN BY **GOOD OLD NEON**

IMAGE COMICS, INC.
Robert Kirkman: Chief Operating Officer
Erik Larsen: Chief Financial Officer
Todd McFarlane: President
Marc Silvestri: Chief Executive Officer
Jim Valentino: Vice President
Eric Stephenson: Publisher / Chief Creative Officer
Corey Hart: Director of Sales
Jeff Boison: Director of Publishing Planning & Book Trade Sales
Chris Ross: Director of Digital Sales
Jeff Stang: Director of Specialty Sales
Kat Salazar: Director of PR & Marketing
Drew Gill: Art Director
Heather Doornink: Production Director
Nicole Lapalme: Controller
IMAGECOMICS.COM

"...all knowledge is a borrowing and every fact is a debt. For each event is revealed to us only at the surrender of every alternate course."
–**Cormac McCarthy,** *Cities of the Plain*

What's your emergency?
Email wmaxwellprince@gmail.com

ICE CREAM MAN, VOL. 2: STRANGE NEAPOLITAN. First printing. December 2018. Published by Image Comics, Inc. Office of publication: 2701 NW Vaughn St., Suite 780, Portland, OR 97210. Copyright © 2018 W. Maxwell Prince, Martin Morazzo & Chris O'Halloran. All rights reserved. Contains material originally published in single magazine form as ICE CREAM MAN #5-8. "Ice Cream Man," its logos, and the likenesses of all characters herein are trademarks of W. Maxwell Prince, Martín Morazzo & Chris O'Halloran unless otherwise noted. "Image" and the Image Comics logos are registered trademarks of Image Comics, Inc. No part of this publication may be reproduced or transmitted, in any form or by any means (except for short excerpts for journalistic or review purposes), without the express written permission of W. Maxwell Prince, Martin Morazzo & Chris O'Halloran, or Image Comics, Inc. All names, characters, events, and locales in this publication are entirely fictional. Any resemblance to actual persons (living or dead), events, or places, without satiric intent, is coincidental. Printed in the USA. For information regarding the CPSIA on this printed material call: 203-595-3636 and provide reference #RICH—824503. For international rights, contact: foreignlicensing@imagecomics.com. ISBN: 978-1-5343-0876-3

Chapter Five

Ballad of a Falling Man

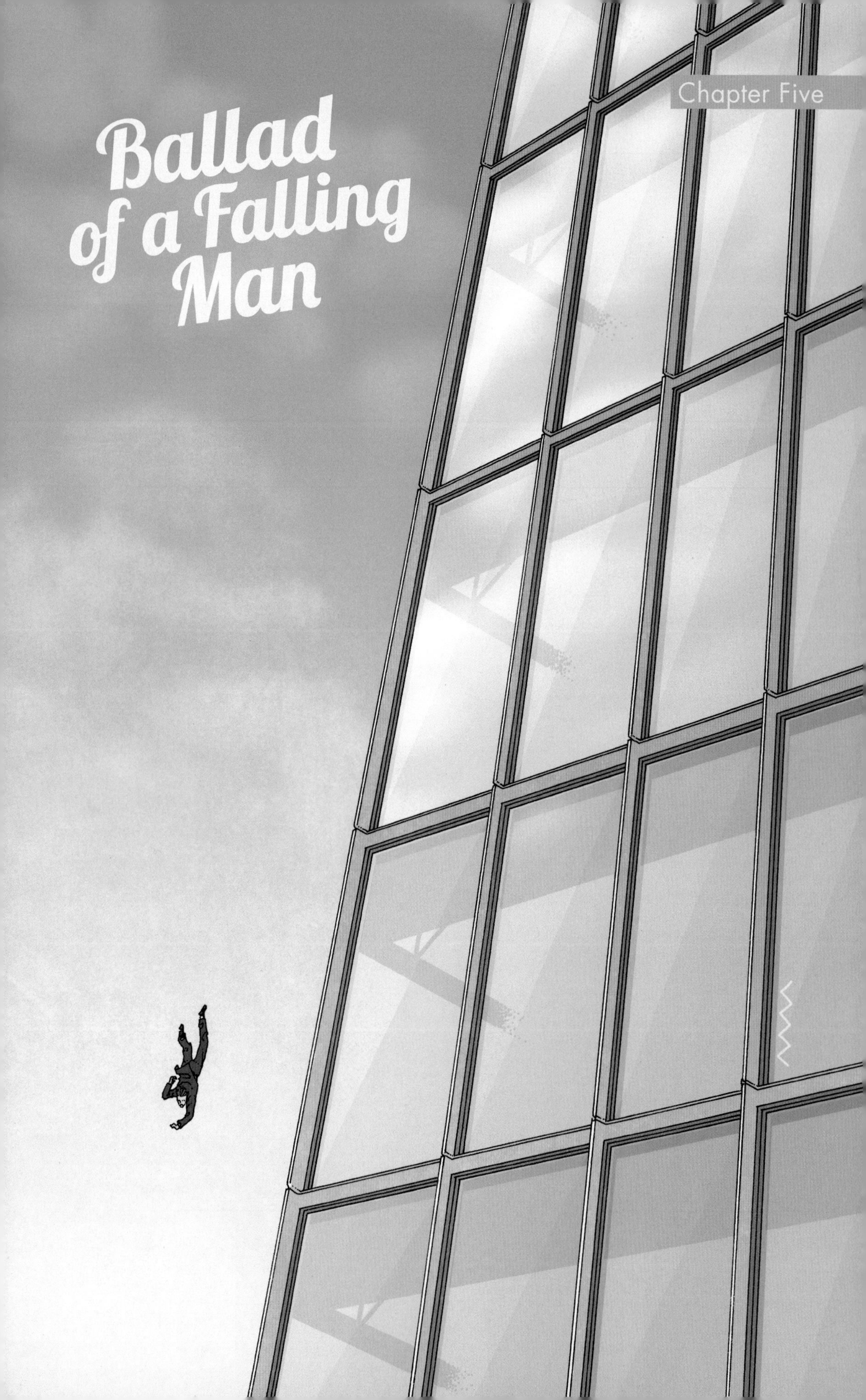

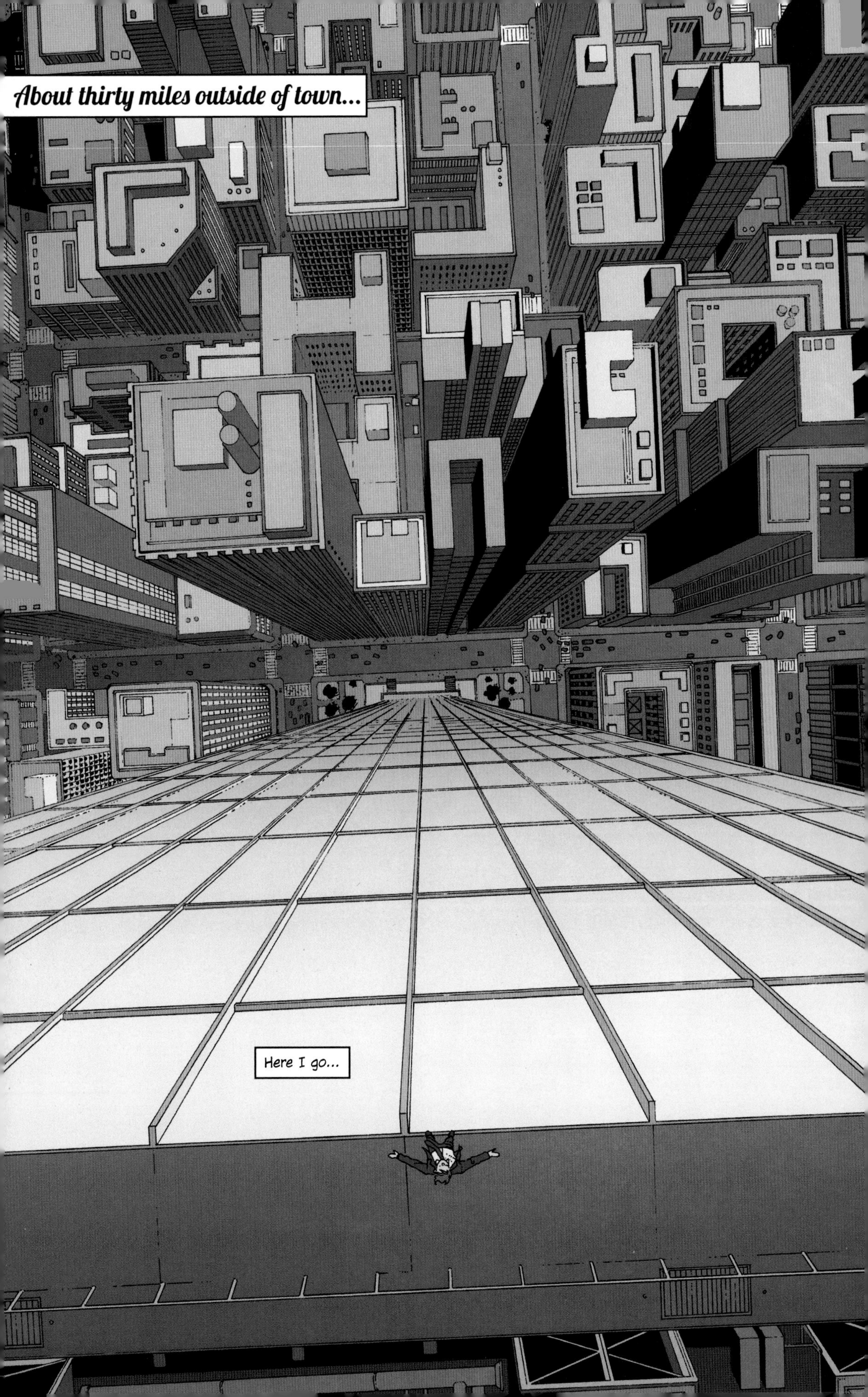
About thirty miles outside of town...
Here I go...

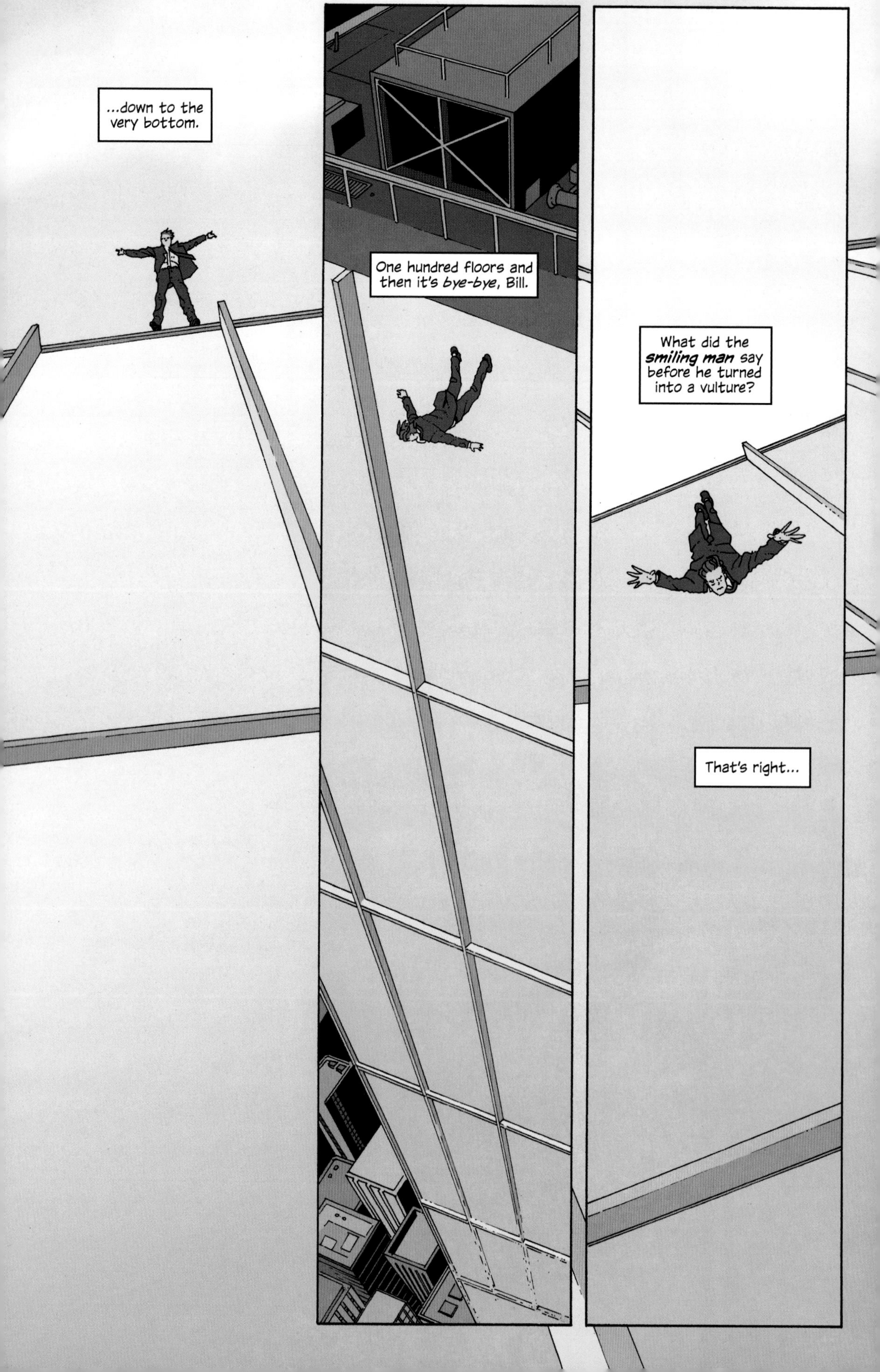
...down to the very bottom.
One hundred floors and then it's *bye-bye*, Bill.
What did the ***smiling man*** say before he turned into a vulture?
That's right...

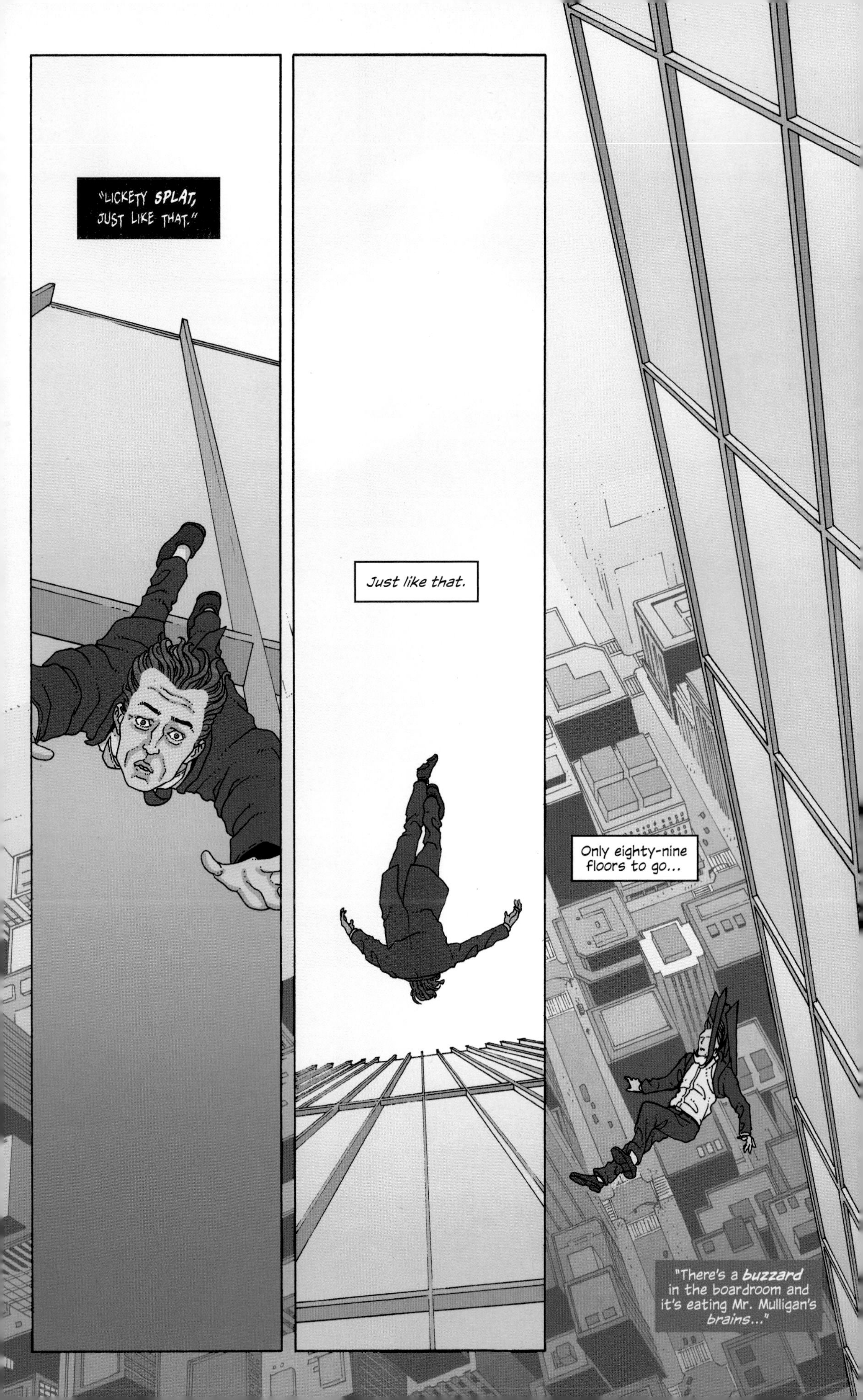
"LICKETY SPLAT, JUST LIKE THAT."
Just like that.
Only eighty-nine floors to go...
"There's a buzzard in the boardroom and it's eating Mr. Mulligan's brains..."

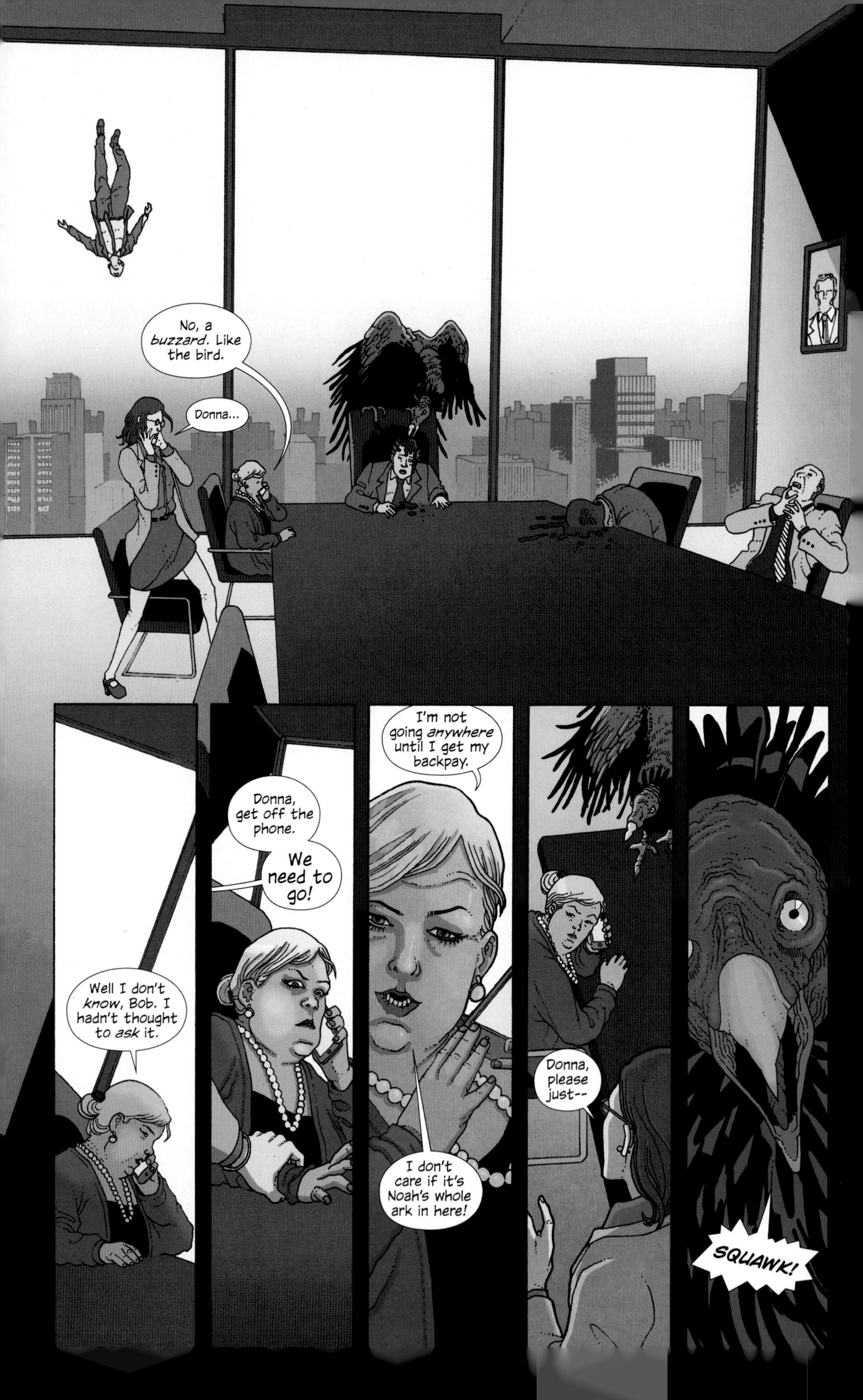
No, a *buzzard*. Like the bird.
Donna...
Well I don't *know*, Bob. I hadn't thought to *ask* it.
Donna, get off the phone.
We need to go!
I'm not going *anywhere* until I get my backpay.
I don't care if it's Noah's whole ark in here!
Donna, please just--
SQUAWK!

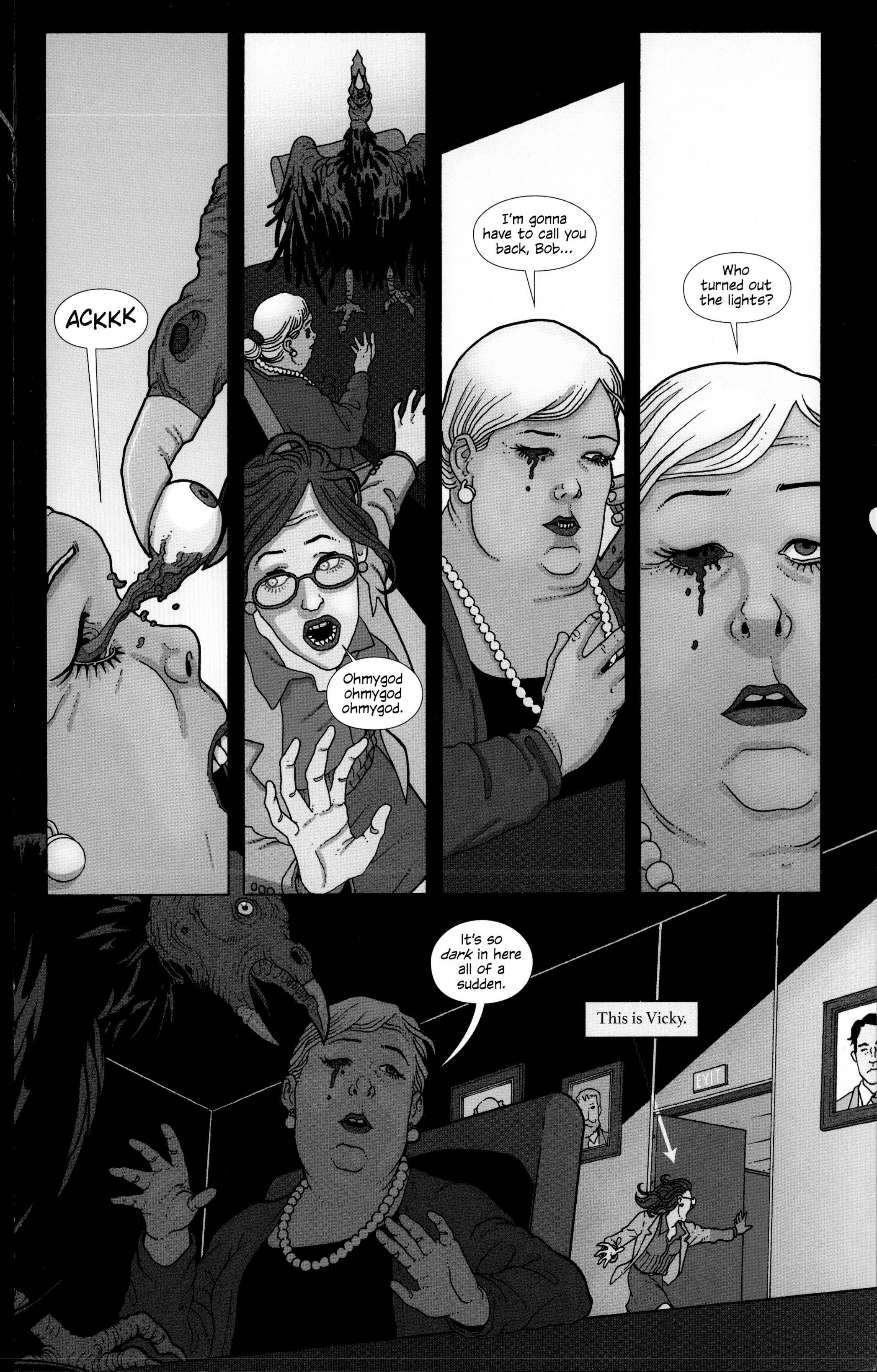
ACKKK
Ohmygod ohmygod ohmygod.
I'm gonna have to call you back, Bob...
Who turned out the lights?
It's so *dark* in here all of a sudden.
This is Vicky.
EXIT

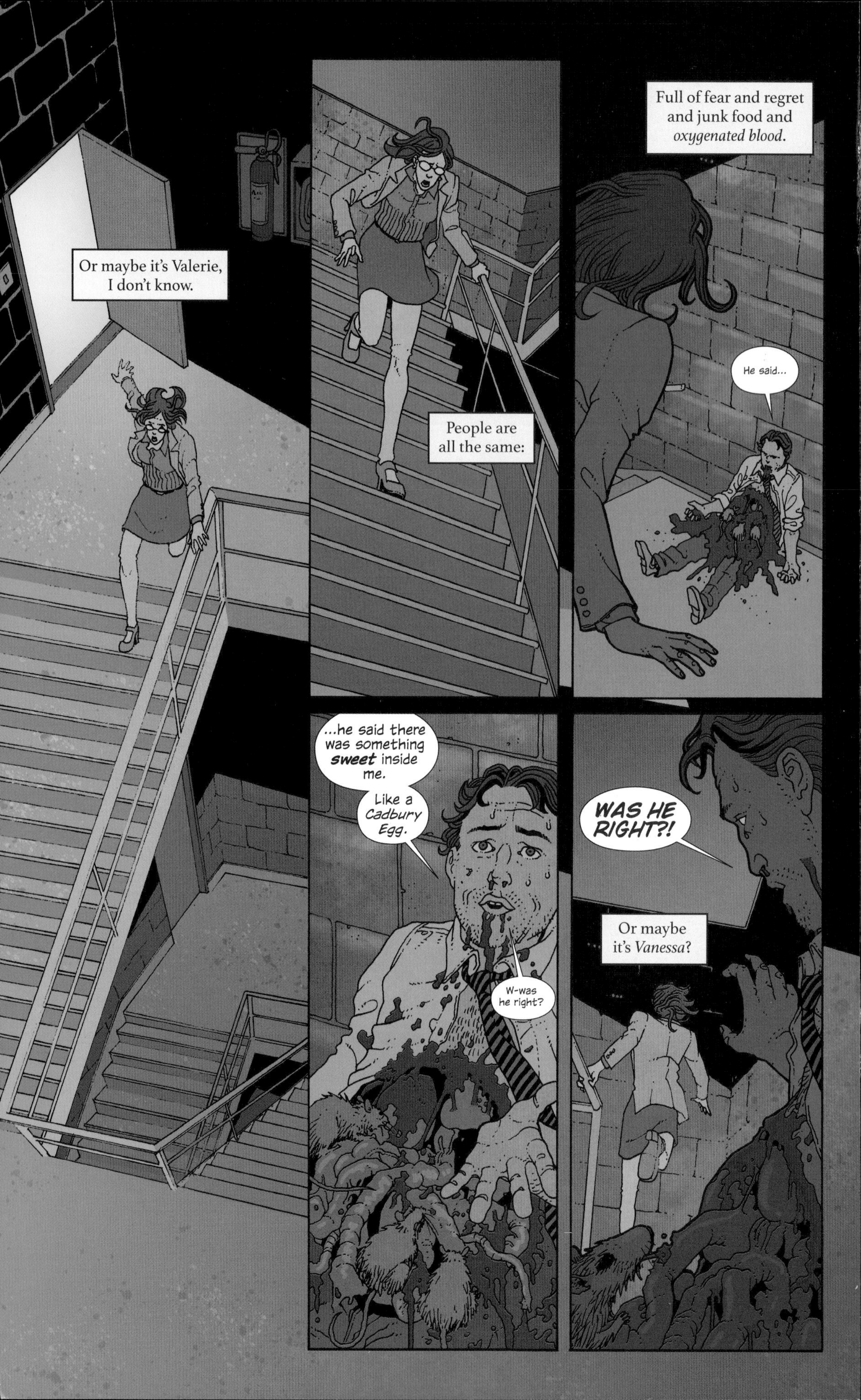

Or maybe it's Valerie,
I don't know.
People are
all the same:
Full of fear and regret
and junk food and
oxygenated blood.
He said...
...he said there
was something
sweet inside
me.
Like a
Cadbury
Egg.
W-was
he right?
WAS HE
RIGHT?!
Or maybe
it's *Vanessa*?

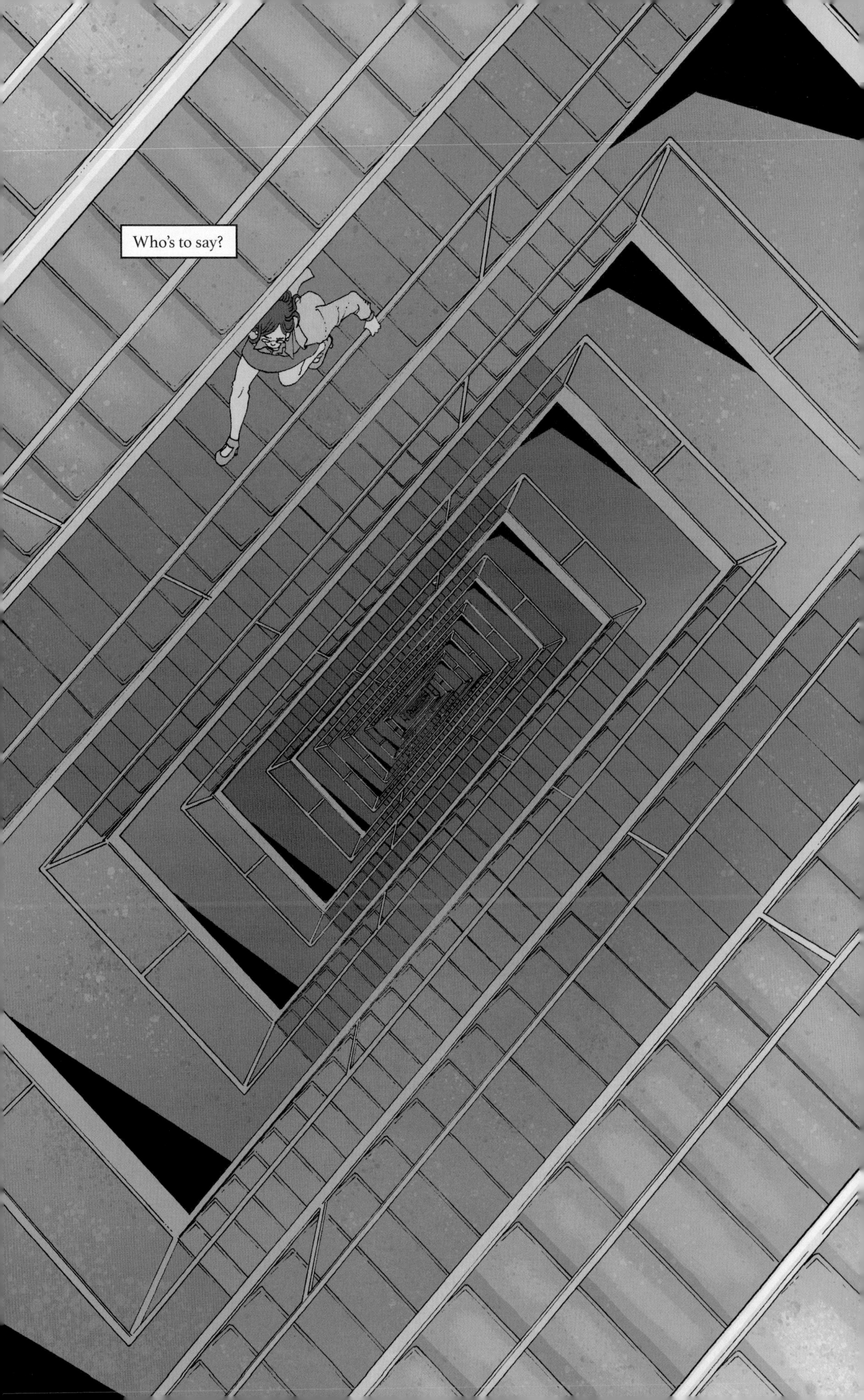
Who's to say?

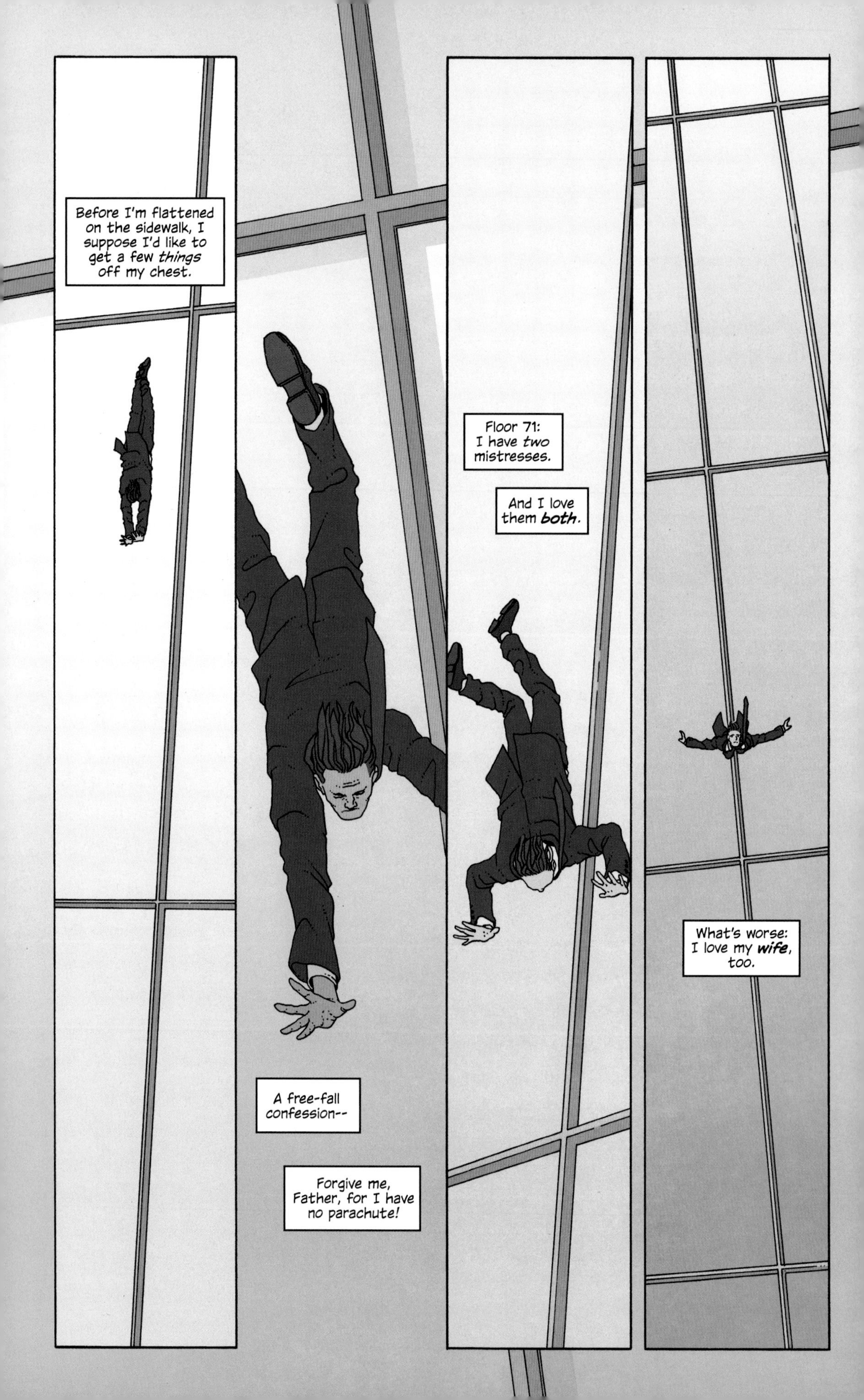
Before I'm flattened on the sidewalk, I suppose I'd like to get a few *things* off my chest.
A free-fall confession--
Forgive me, Father, for I have no parachute!
Floor 71: I have *two* mistresses.
And I love them ***both***.
What's worse: I love my ***wife***, too.

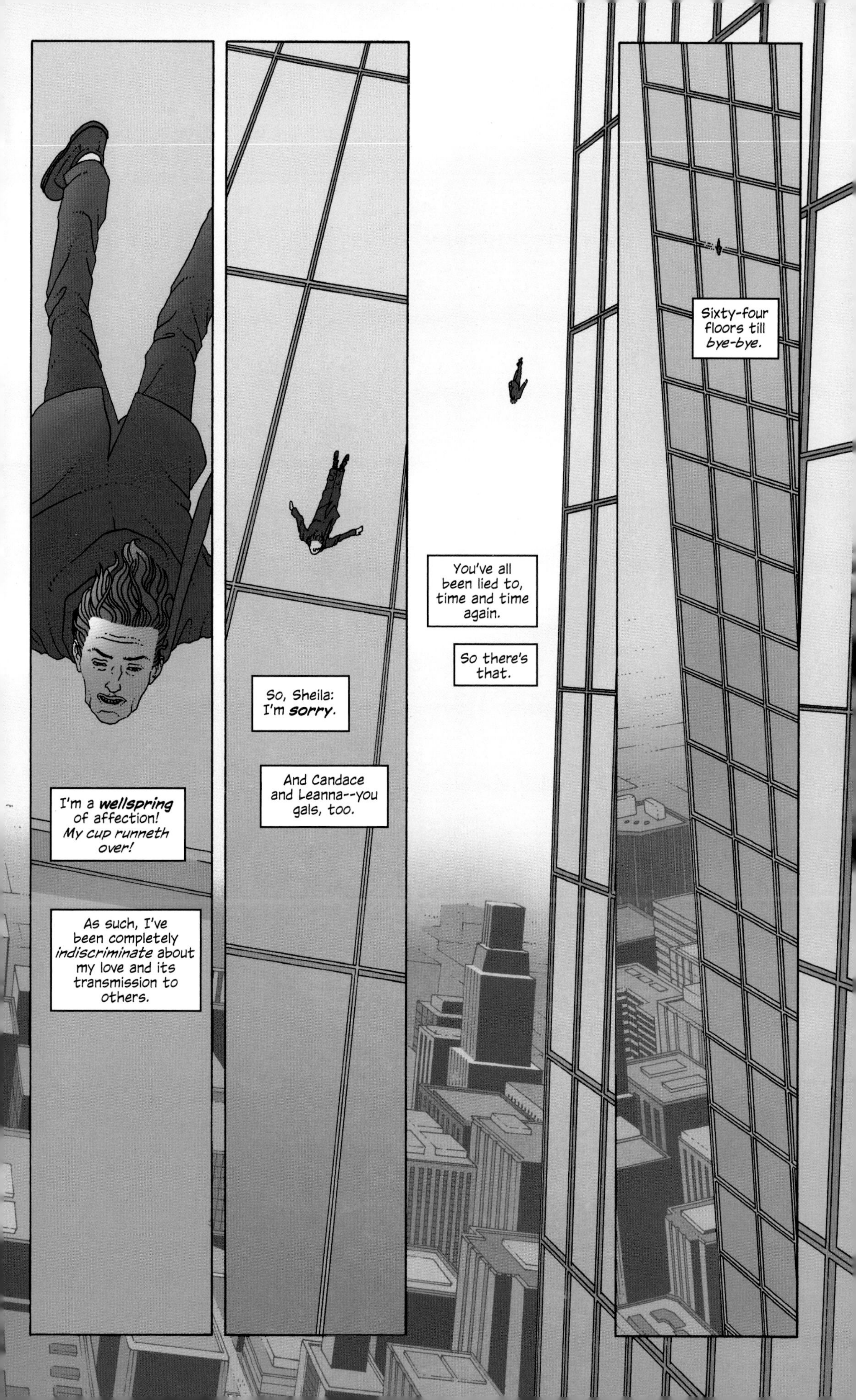
I'm a **wellspring** of affection! *My cup runneth over!*
As such, I've been completely *indiscriminate* about my love and its transmission to others.
So, Sheila: I'm ***sorry***.
And Candace and Leanna--you gals, too.
You've all been lied to, time and time again.
So there's that.
Sixty-four floors till *bye-bye*.

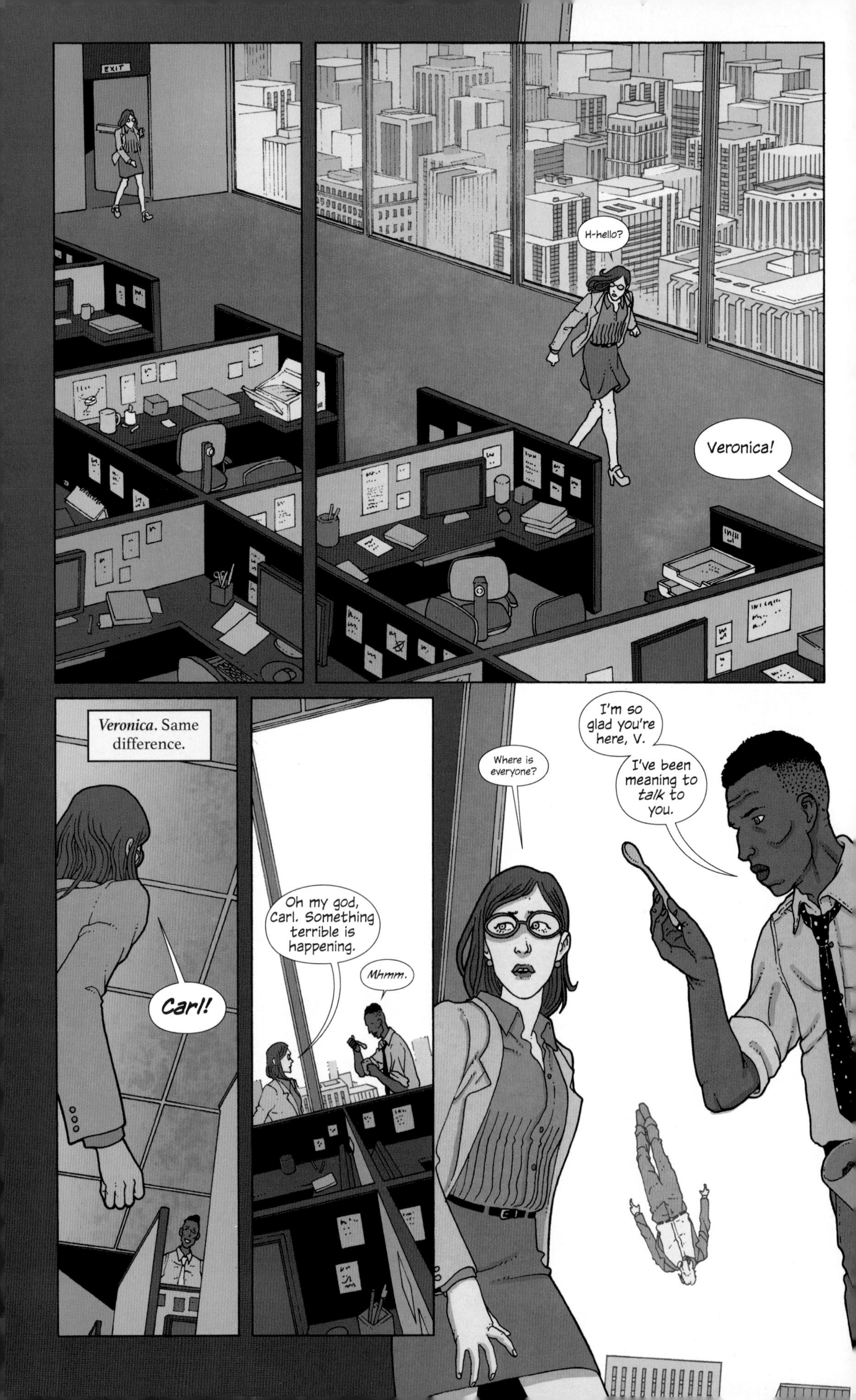
EXIT
H-hello?
Veronica!
Veronica. Same difference.
Carl!
Oh my god, Carl. Something terrible is happening.
Mhmm.
Where is everyone?
I'm so glad you're here, V.
I've been meaning to *talk* to you.

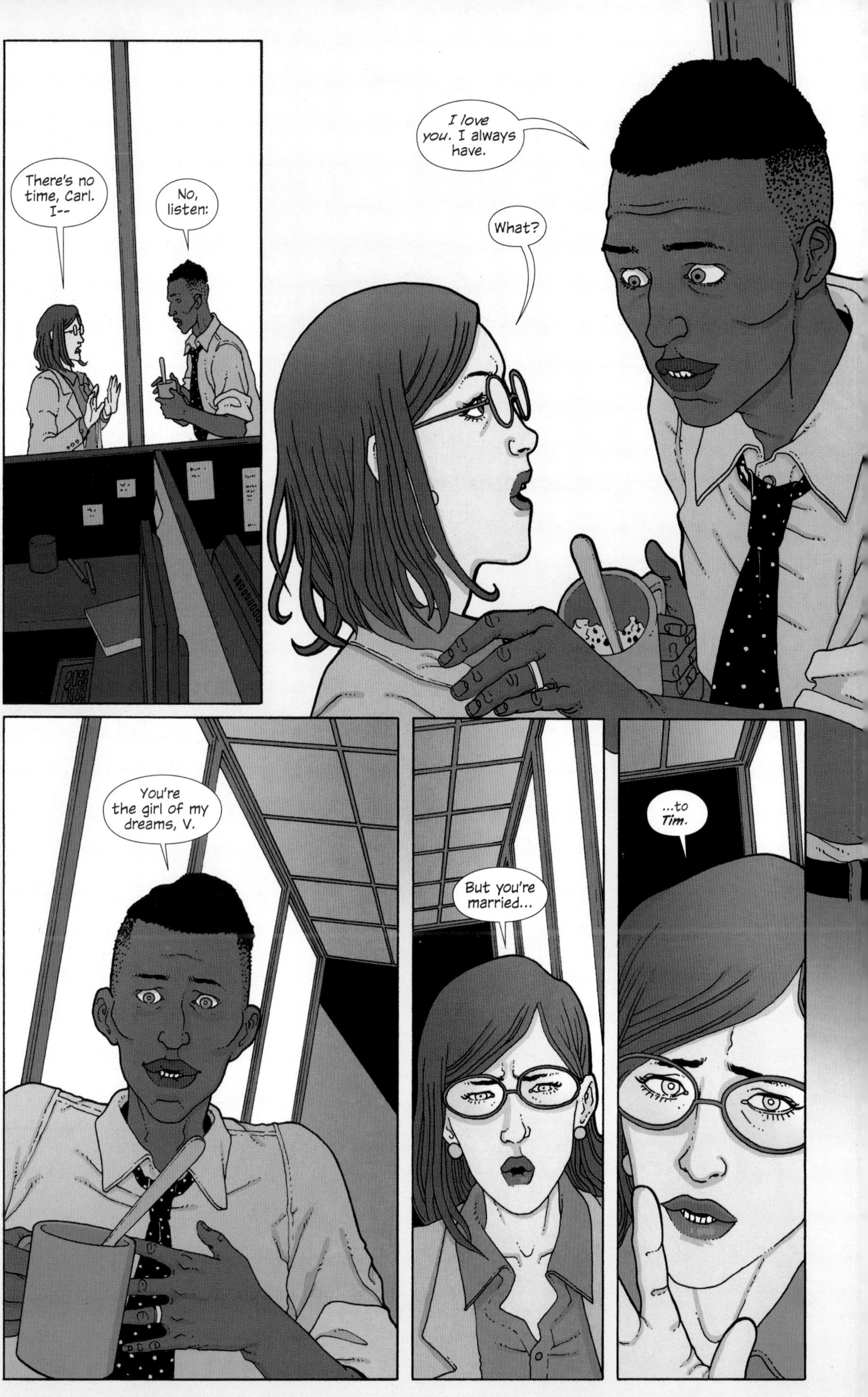
There's no time, Carl. I--
No, listen:
I love you. I always have.
What?
You're the girl of my dreams, V.
But you're married...
...to Tim.

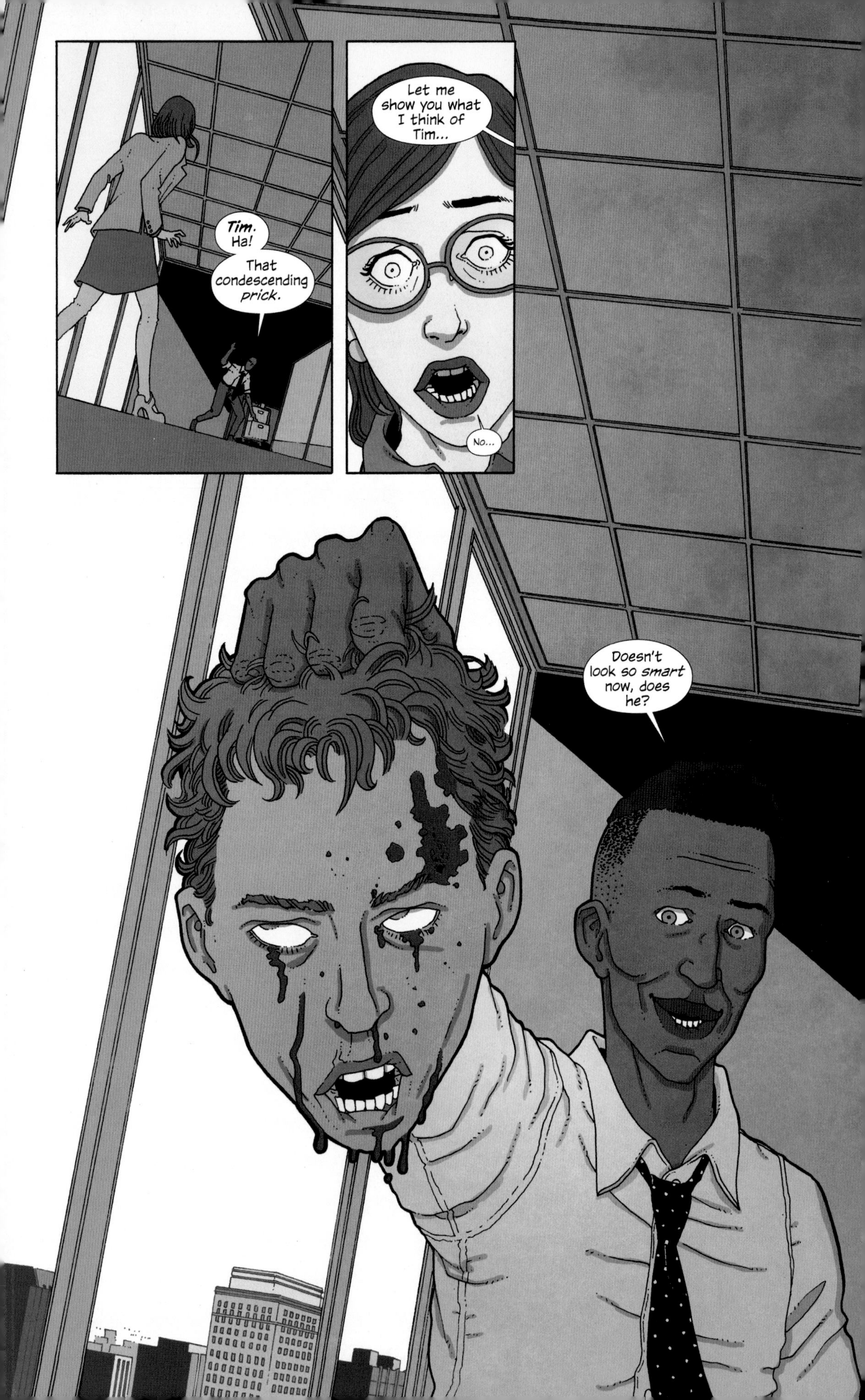

Tim. Ha!
That condescending *prick*.
Let me show you what I think of Tim...
No...
Doesn't look so *smart* now, does he?

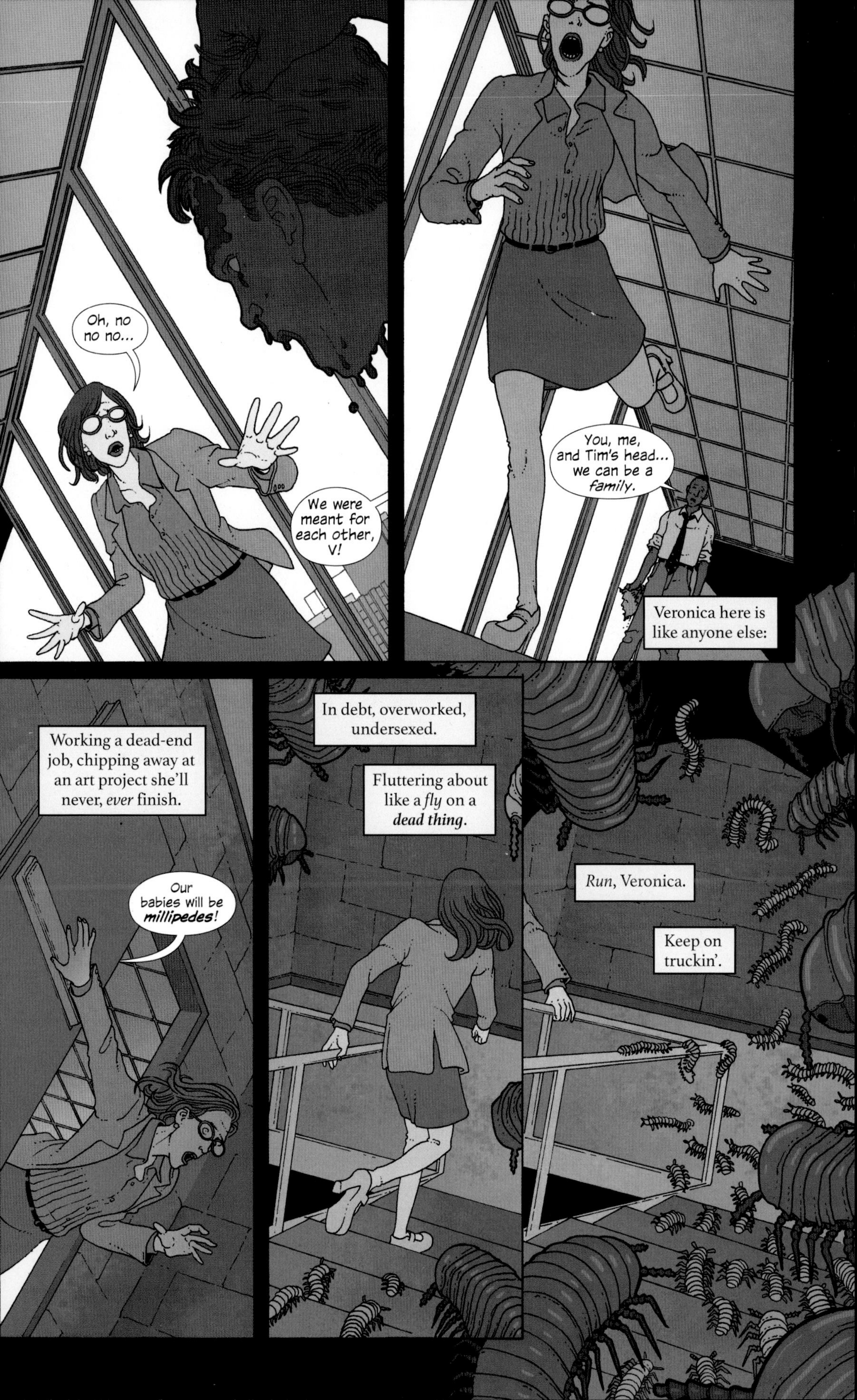

Oh, no no no...
We were meant for each other, V!
You, me, and Tim's head... we can be a *family*.
Veronica here is like anyone else:
Working a dead-end job, chipping away at an art project she'll never, *ever* finish.
Our babies will be ***millipedes***!
In debt, overworked, undersexed.
Fluttering about like a *fly* on a ***dead thing***.
Run, Veronica.
Keep on truckin'.

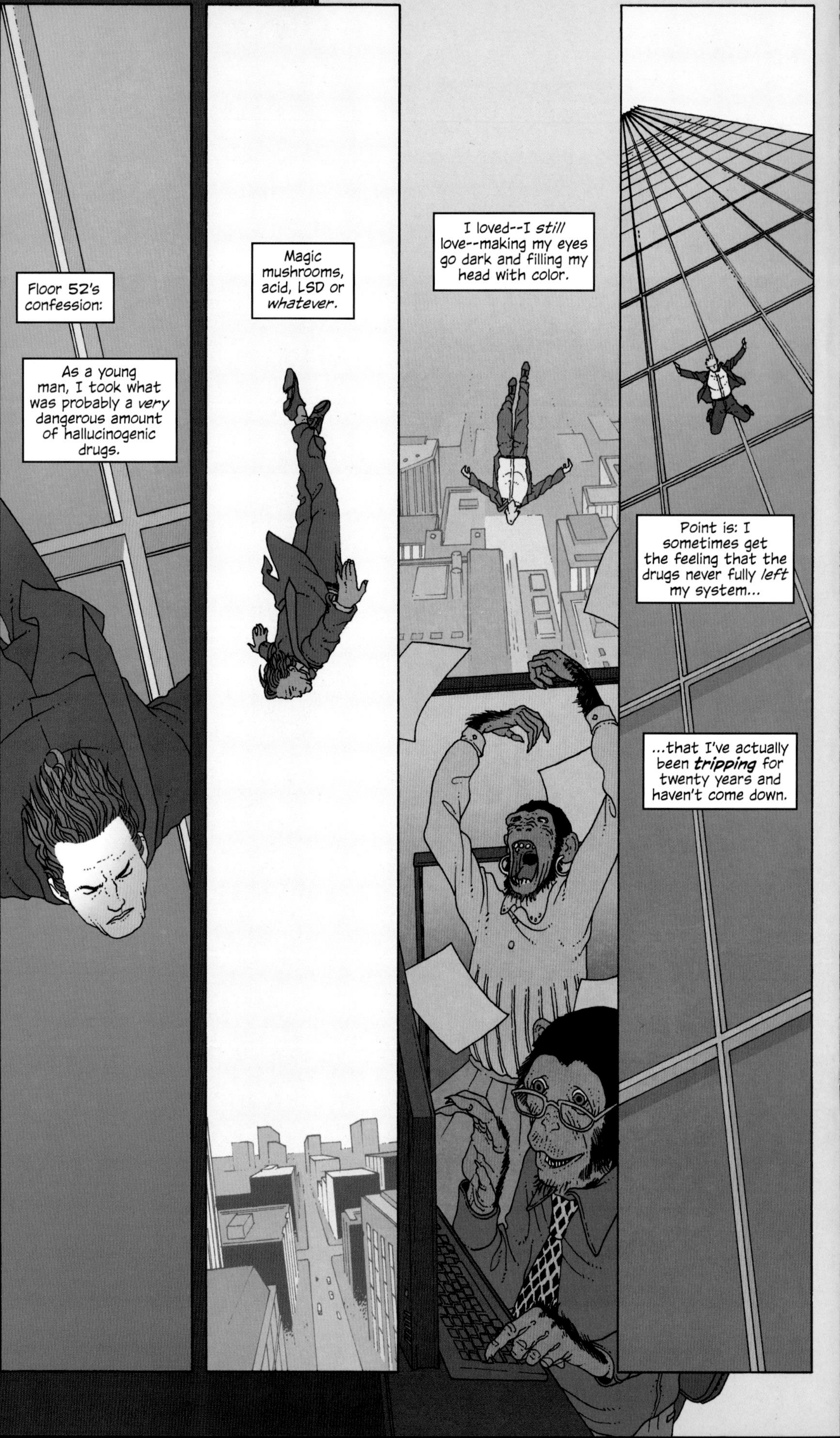
Floor 52's confession:
As a young man, I took what was probably a *very* dangerous amount of hallucinogenic drugs.
Magic mushrooms, acid, LSD or *whatever.*
I loved--I *still* love--making my eyes go dark and filling my head with color.
Point is: I sometimes get the feeling that the drugs never fully *left* my system...
...that I've actually been ***tripping*** for twenty years and haven't come down.

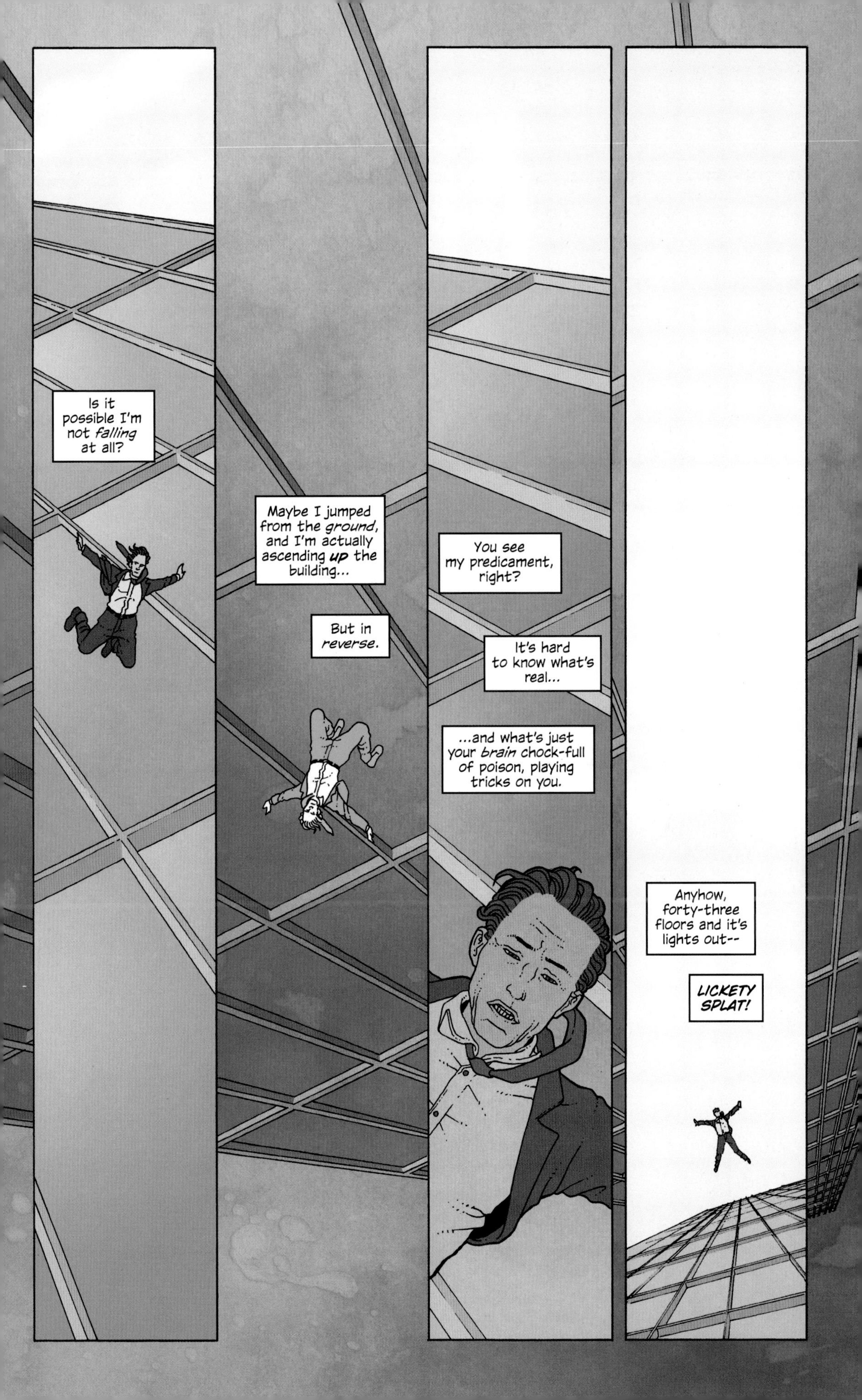
Is it possible I'm not *falling* at all?
Maybe I jumped from the *ground*, and I'm actually ascending ***up*** the building...
But in *reverse.*
You see my predicament, right?
It's hard to know what's real...
...and what's just your *brain* chock-full of poison, playing tricks on you.
Anyhow, forty-three floors and it's lights out--
LICKETY SPLAT!

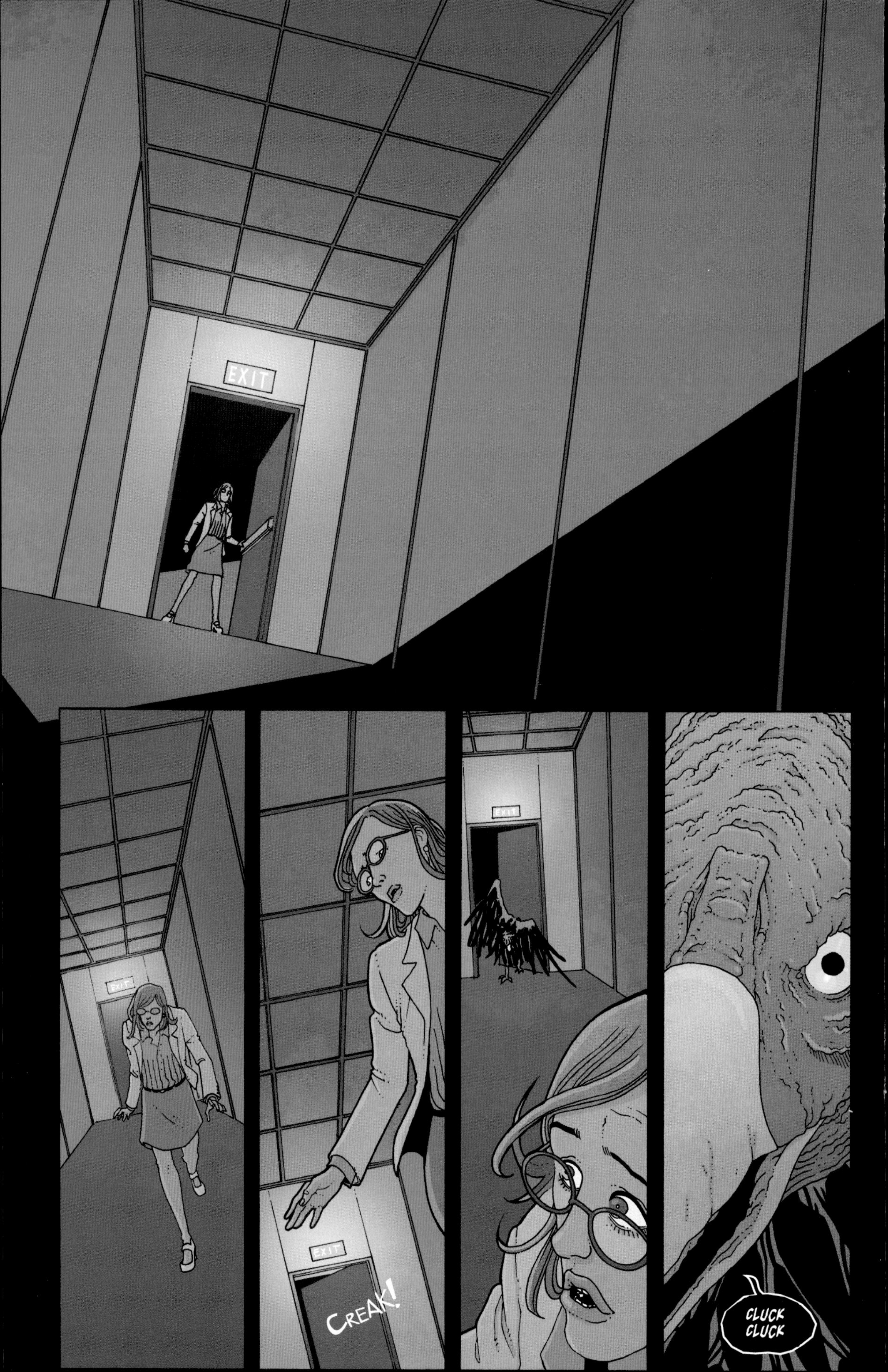
EXIT
EXIT
EXIT
EXIT
CREAK!
CLUCK
CLUCK

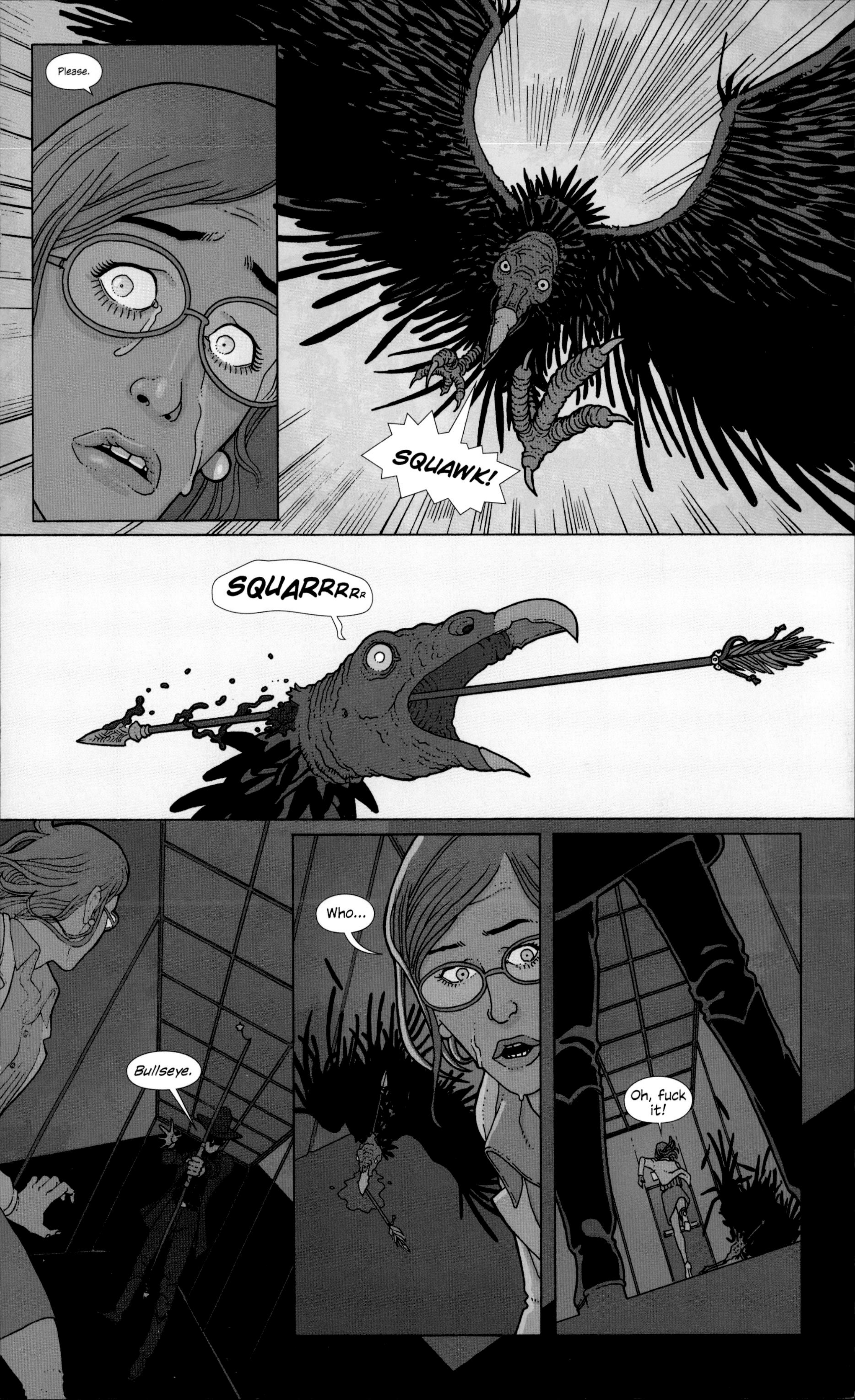
Please.
SQUAWK!
SQUARRRRR
Bullseye.
Who...
Oh, fuck it!

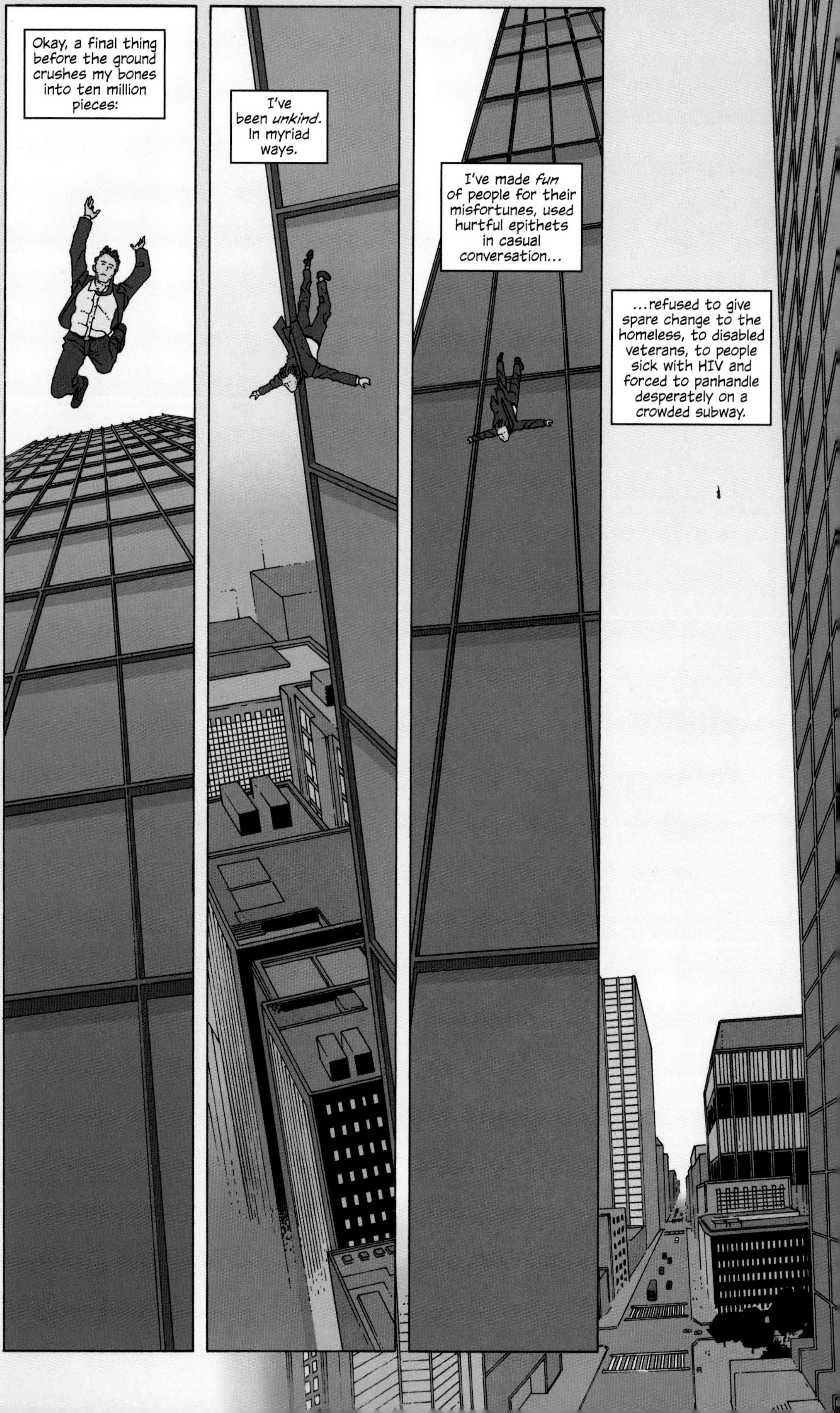
Okay, a final thing before the ground crushes my bones into ten million pieces:
I've been *unkind*. In myriad ways.
I've made *fun* of people for their misfortunes, used hurtful epithets in casual conversation...
...refused to give spare change to the homeless, to disabled veterans, to people sick with HIV and forced to panhandle desperately on a crowded subway.

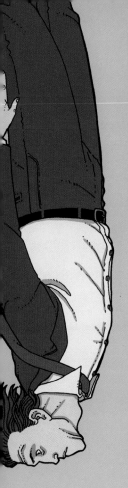

And why? I...

I have no idea.

Maybe I'm a *bad* person.

But the thing is: I don't *feel* like a bad person.

There's an abiding compassion within me, deep down...

Either way, know this:

I'm sorry.

I'd do it different if I got a second chance.

That's all.

Bill over and out.

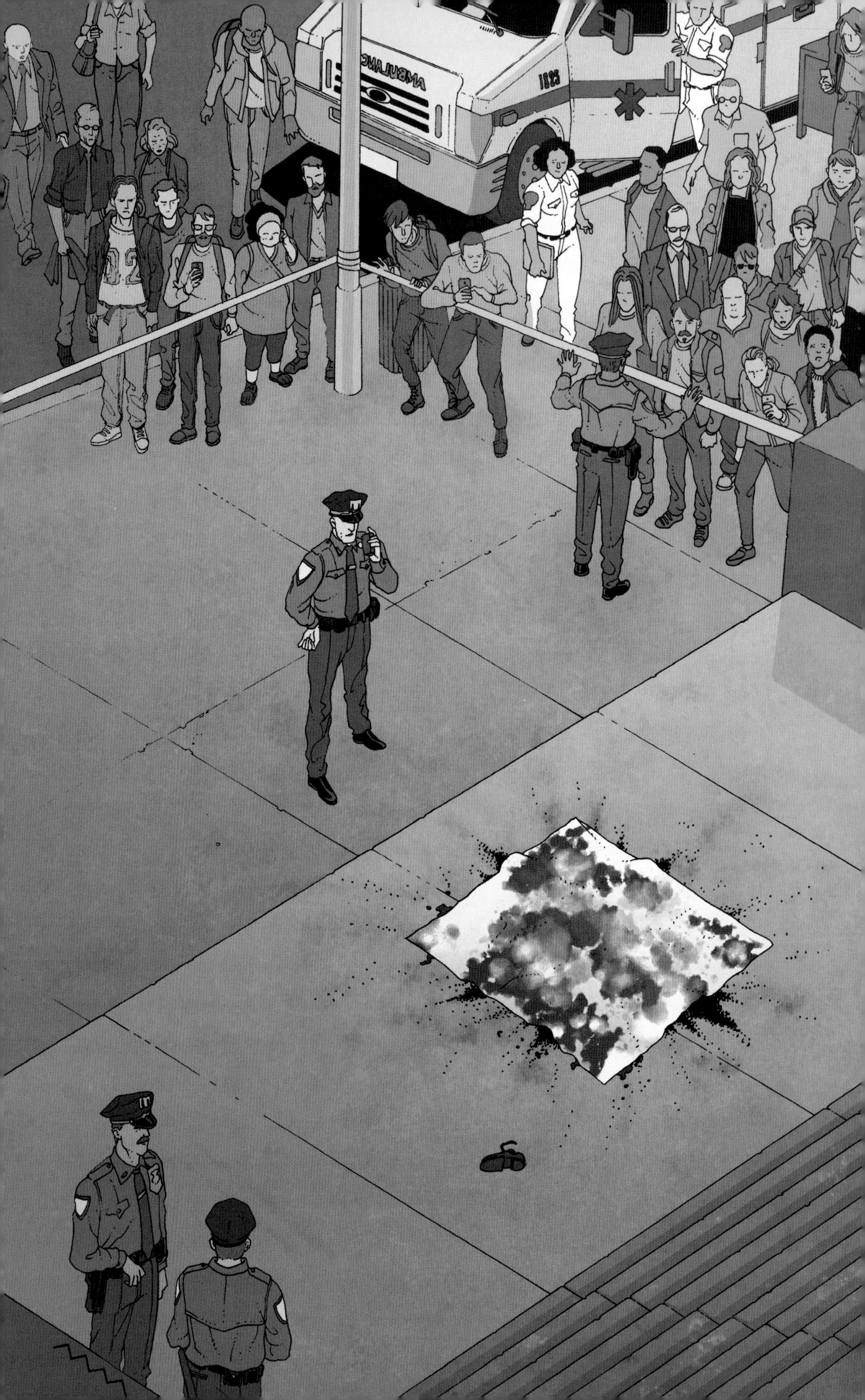

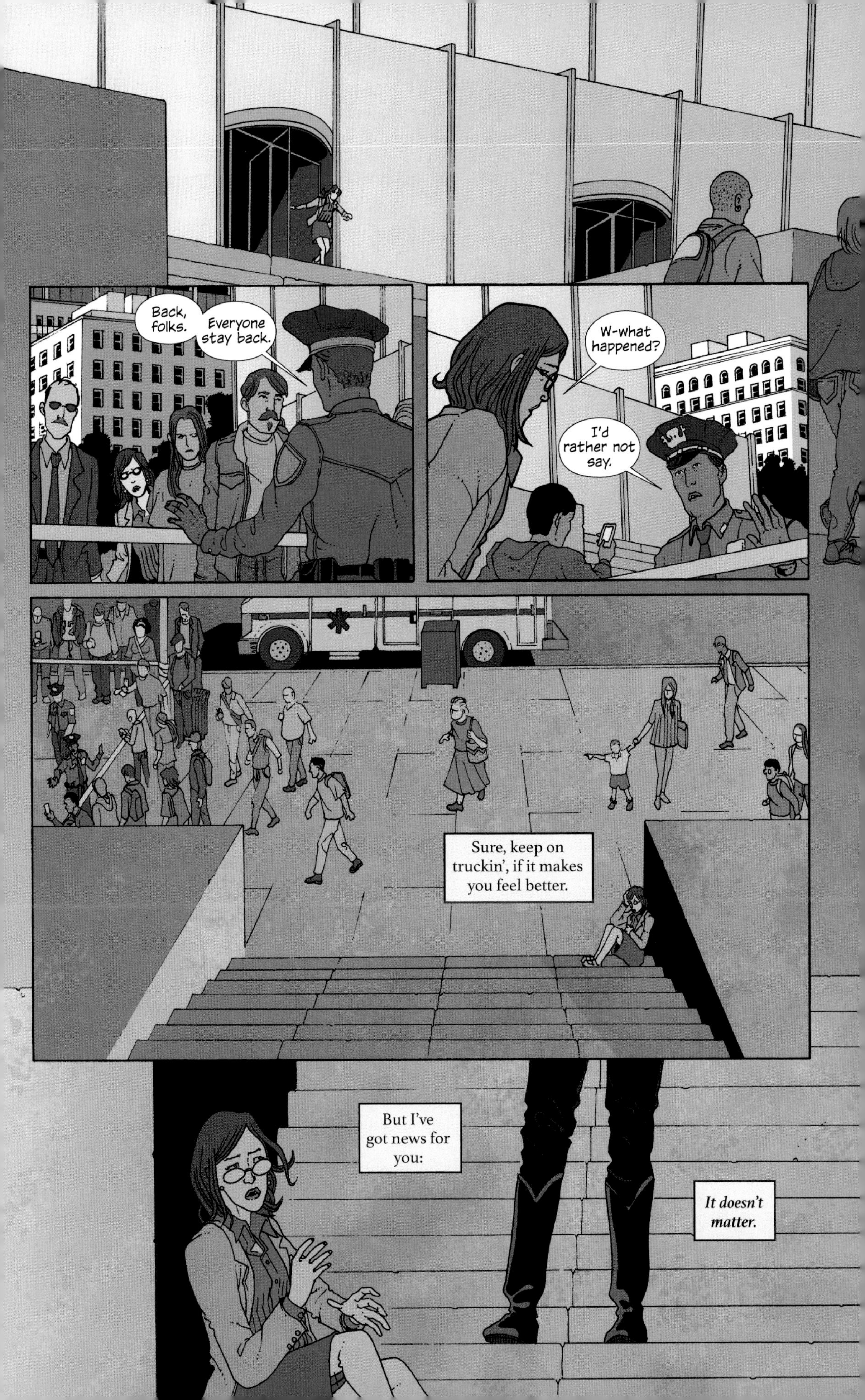
Back, folks.
Everyone stay back.
W-what happened?
I'd rather not say.
Sure, keep on truckin', if it makes you feel better.
But I've got news for you:
It doesn't matter.

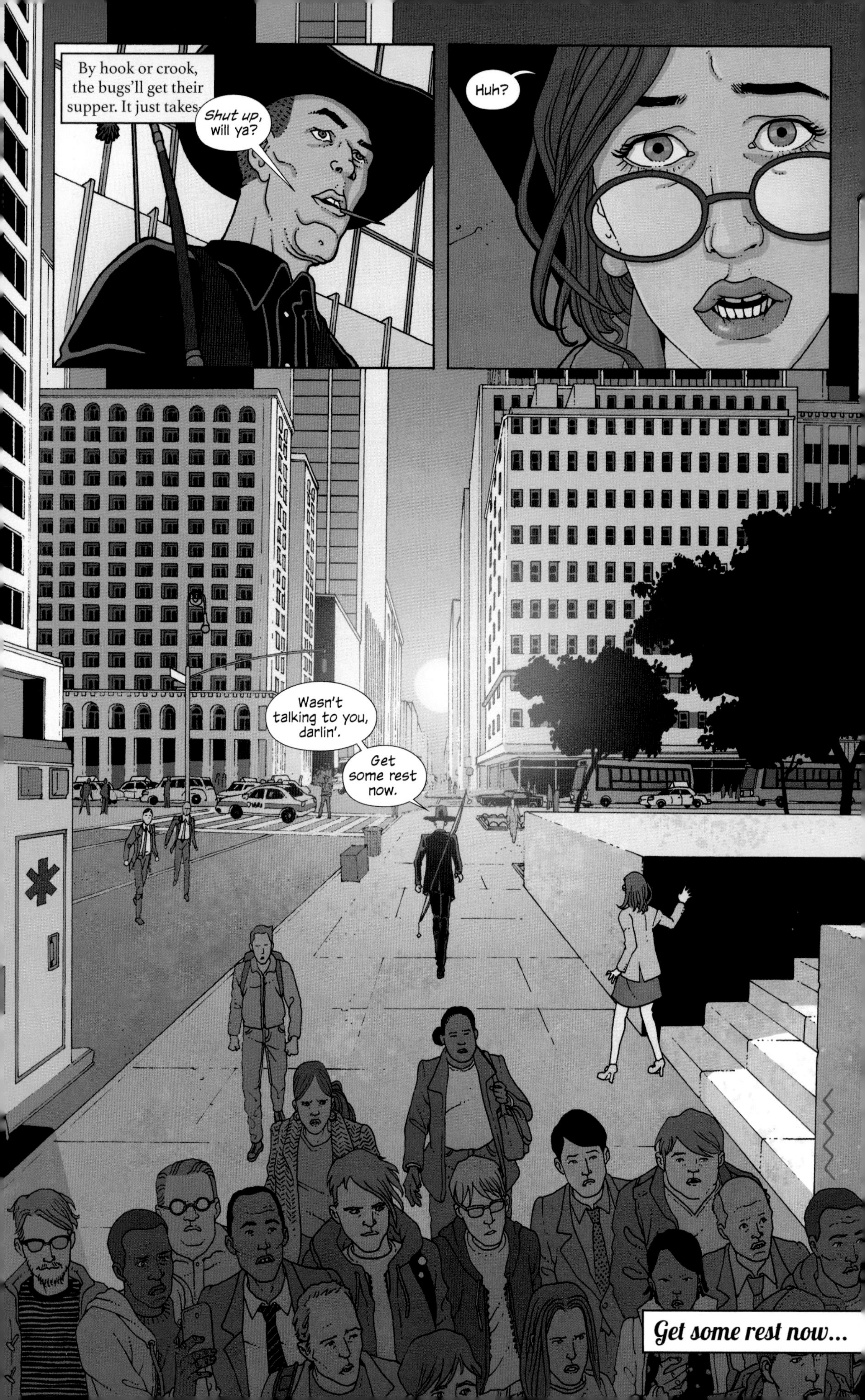
By hook or crook, the bugs'll get their supper. It just takes
Shut up, will ya?
Huh?
Wasn't talking to you, darlin'.
Get some rest now.
Get some rest now...

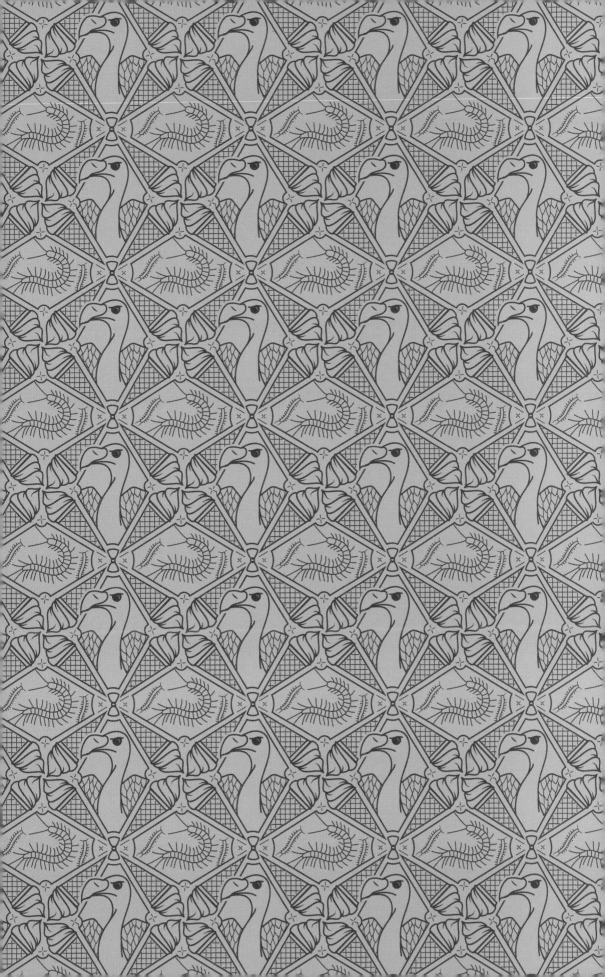

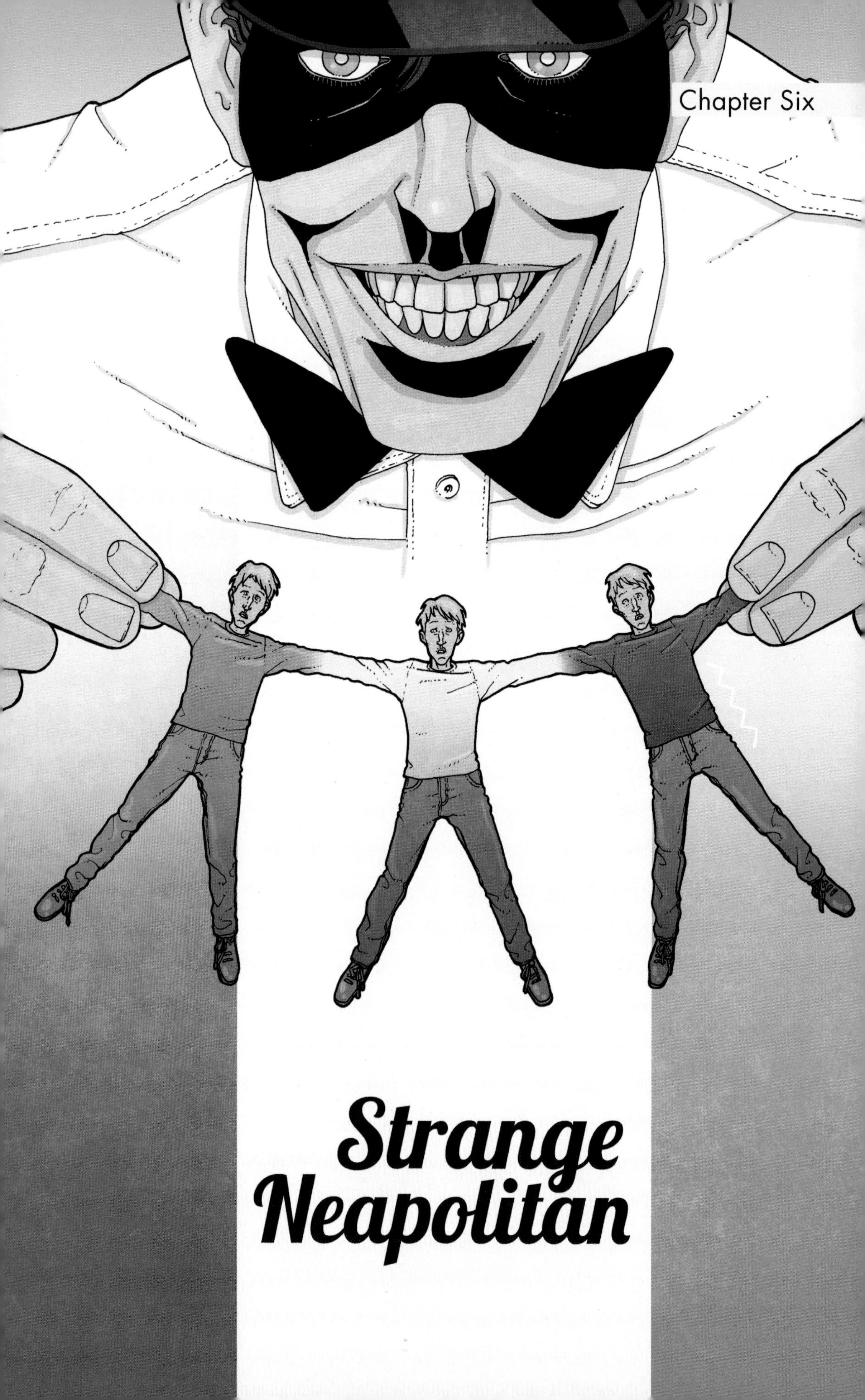
Chapter Six
Strange
Neapolitan

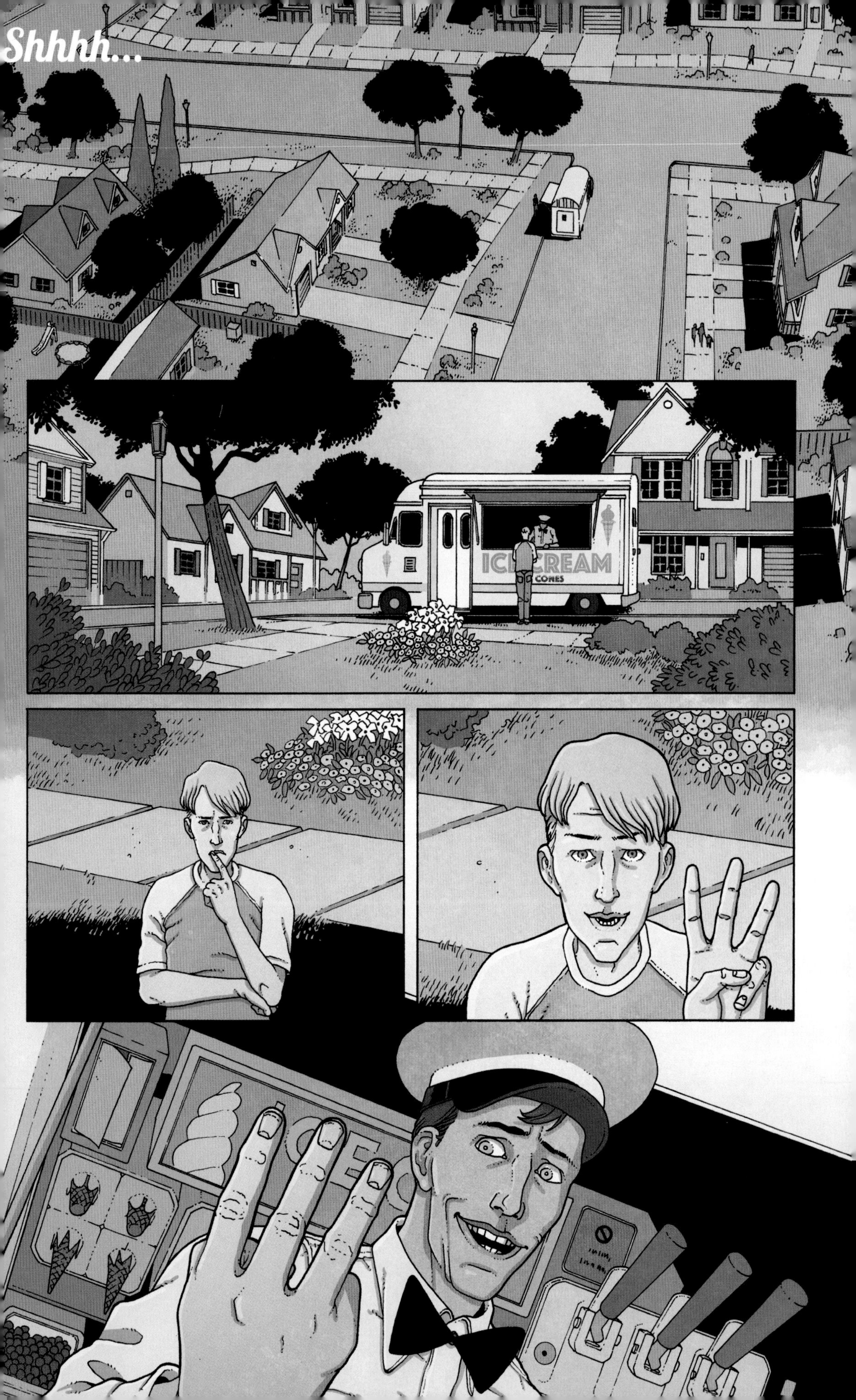
Shhhh...

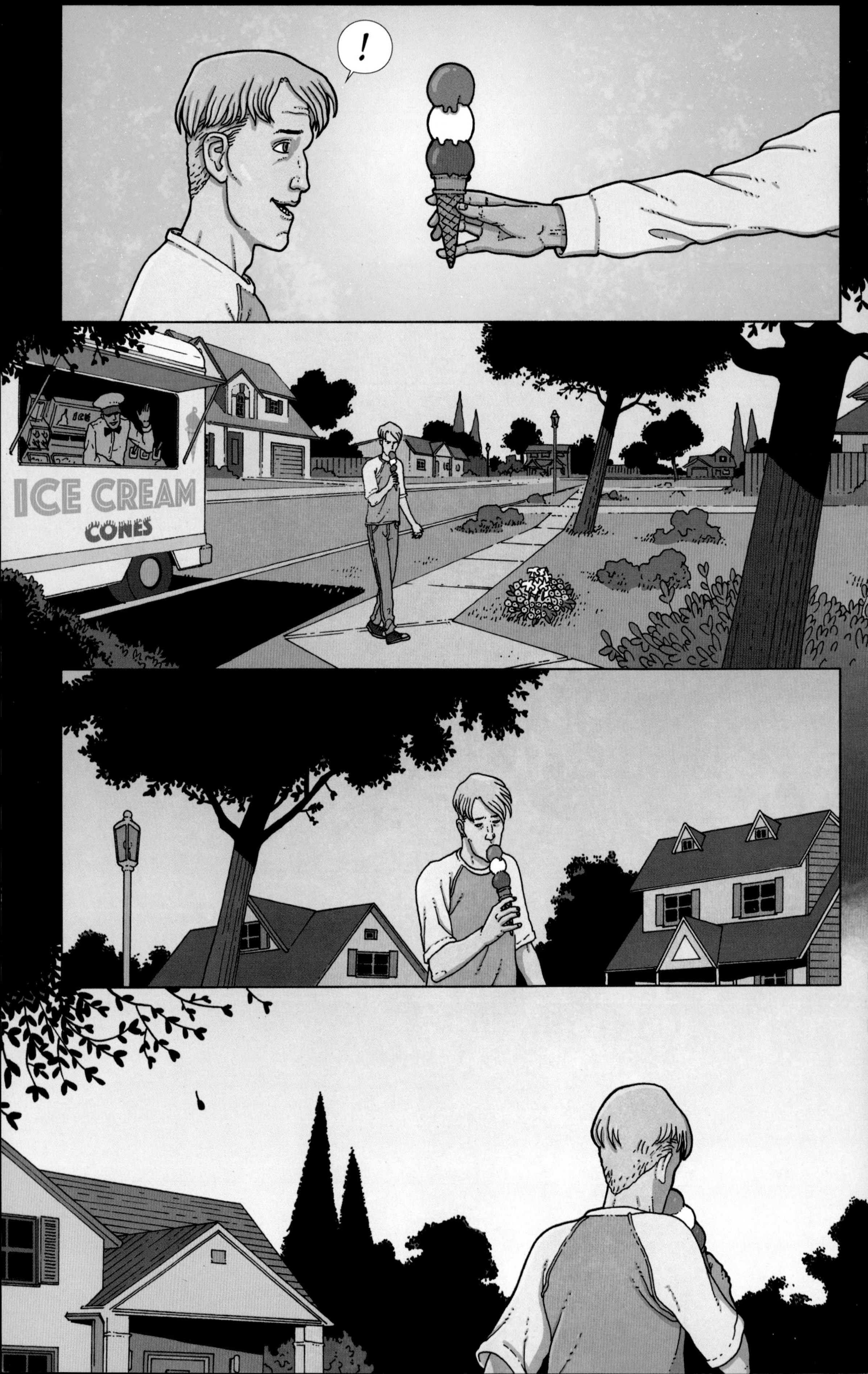
!
ICE
ICE CREAM
CONES

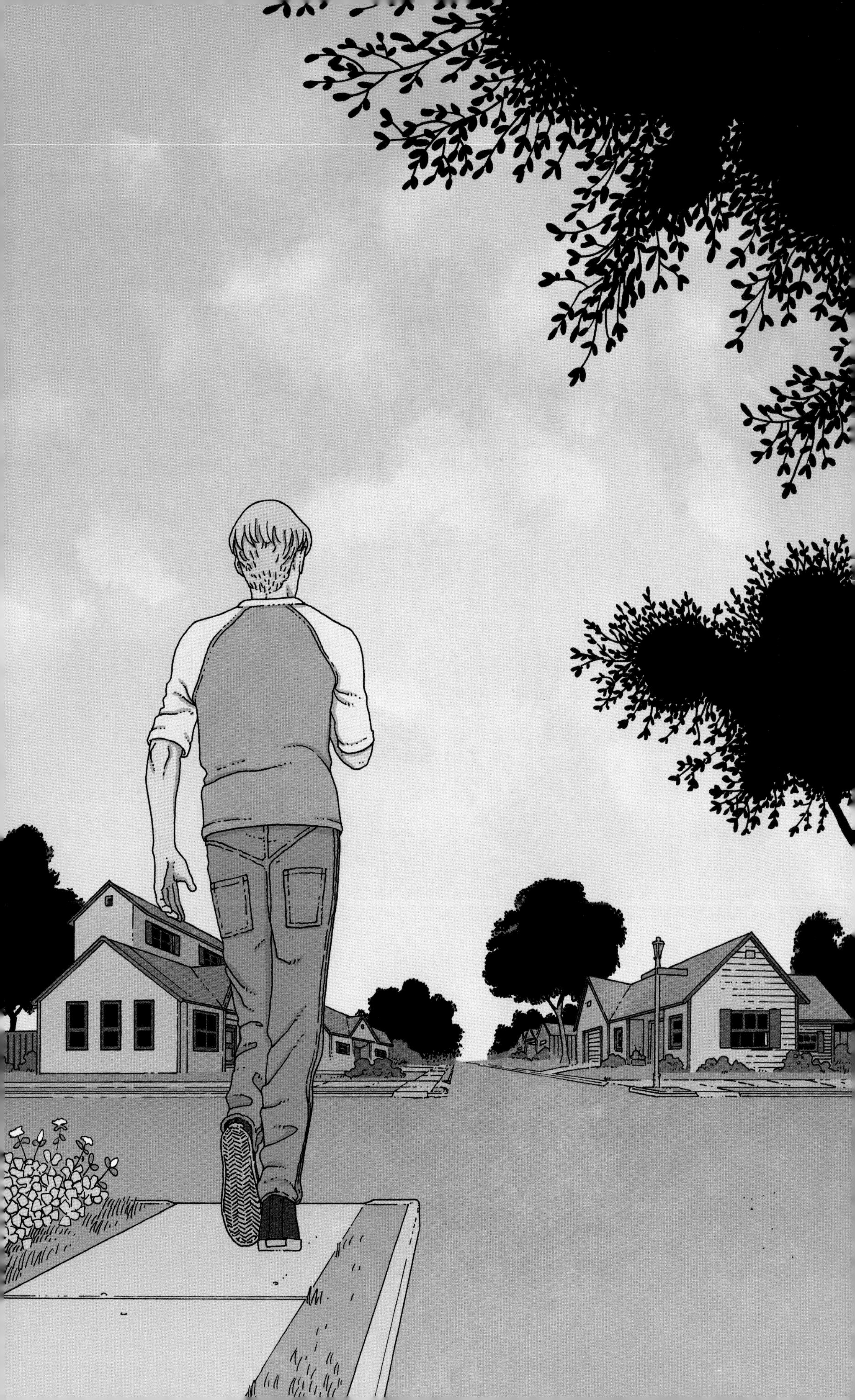

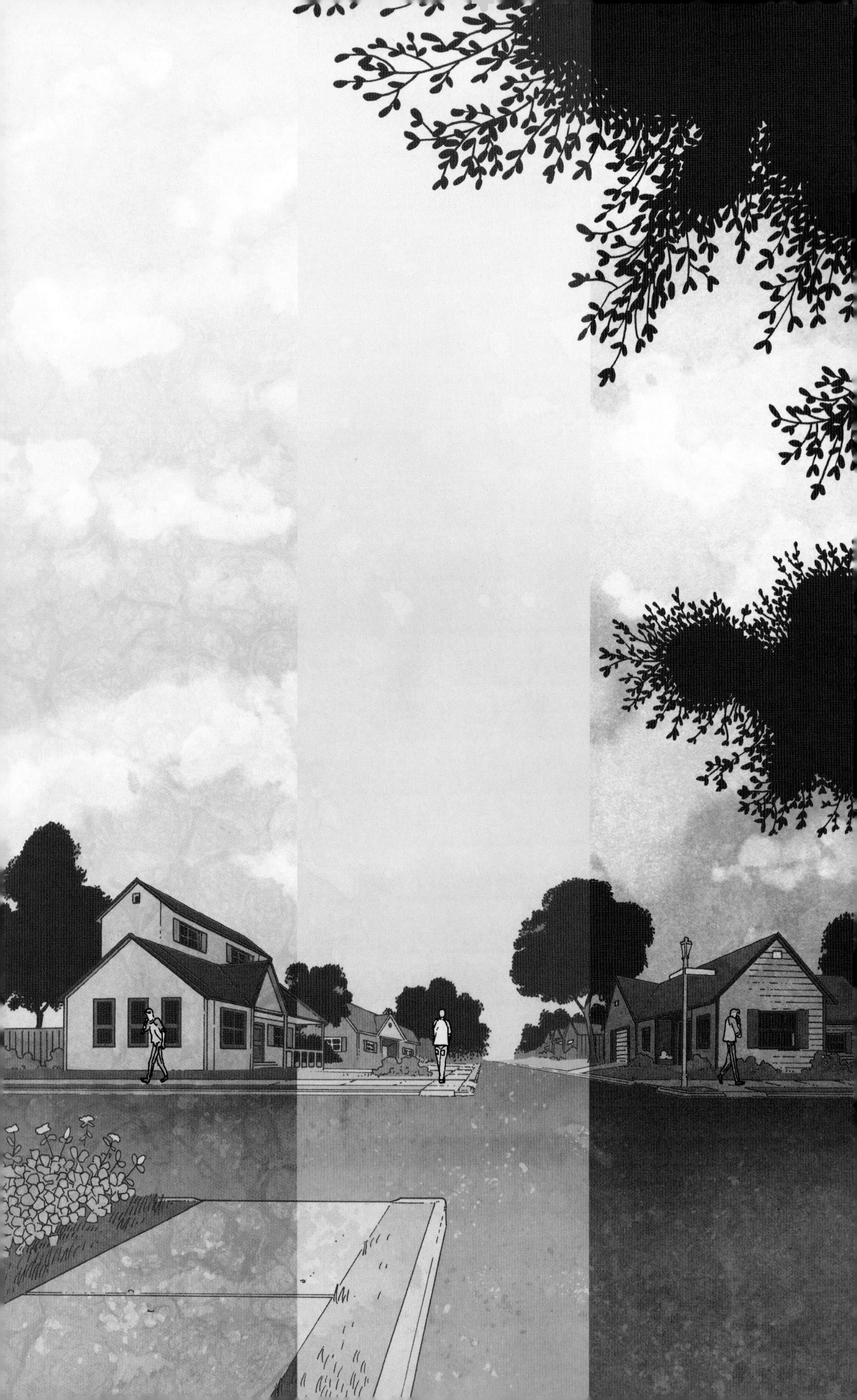

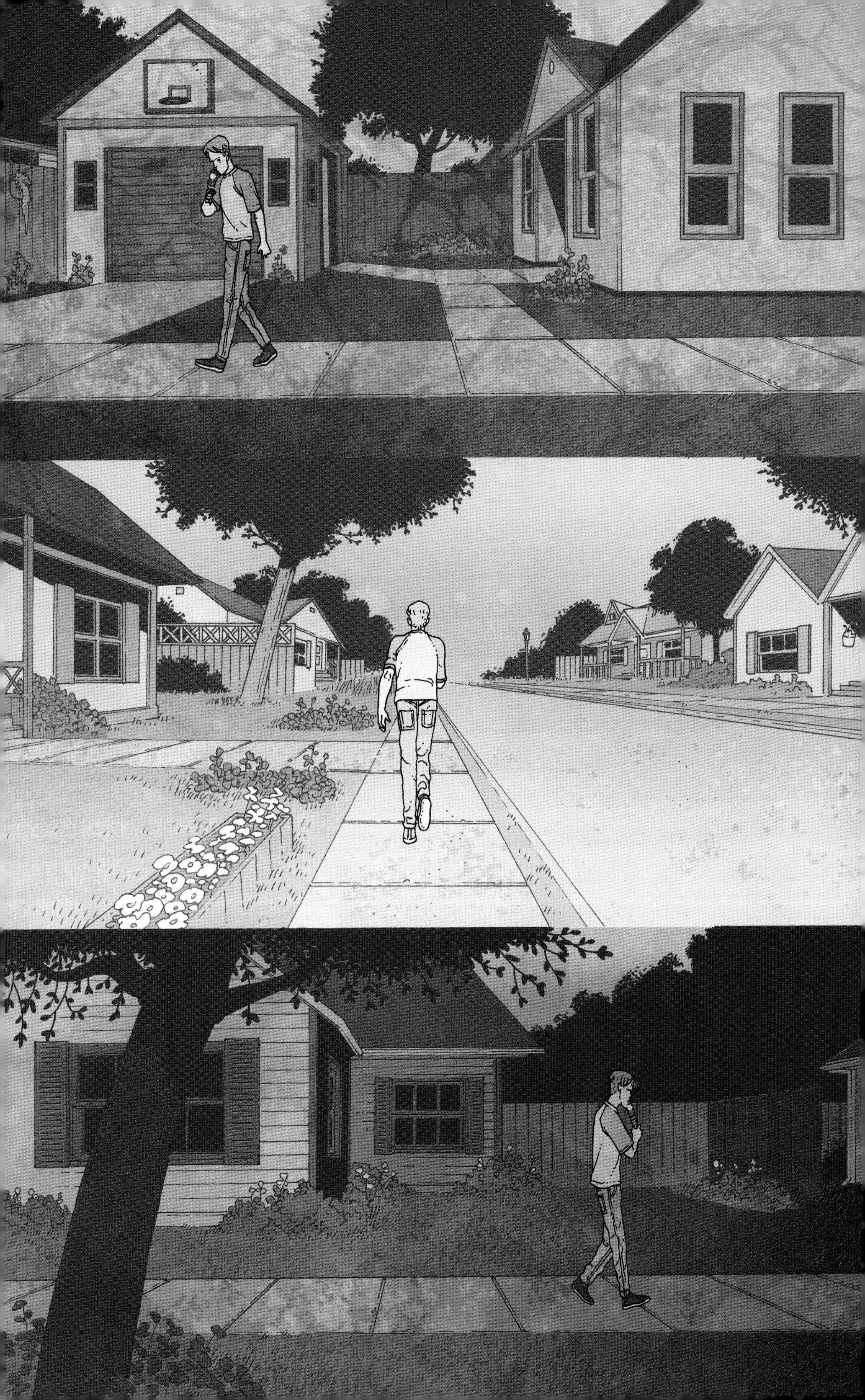

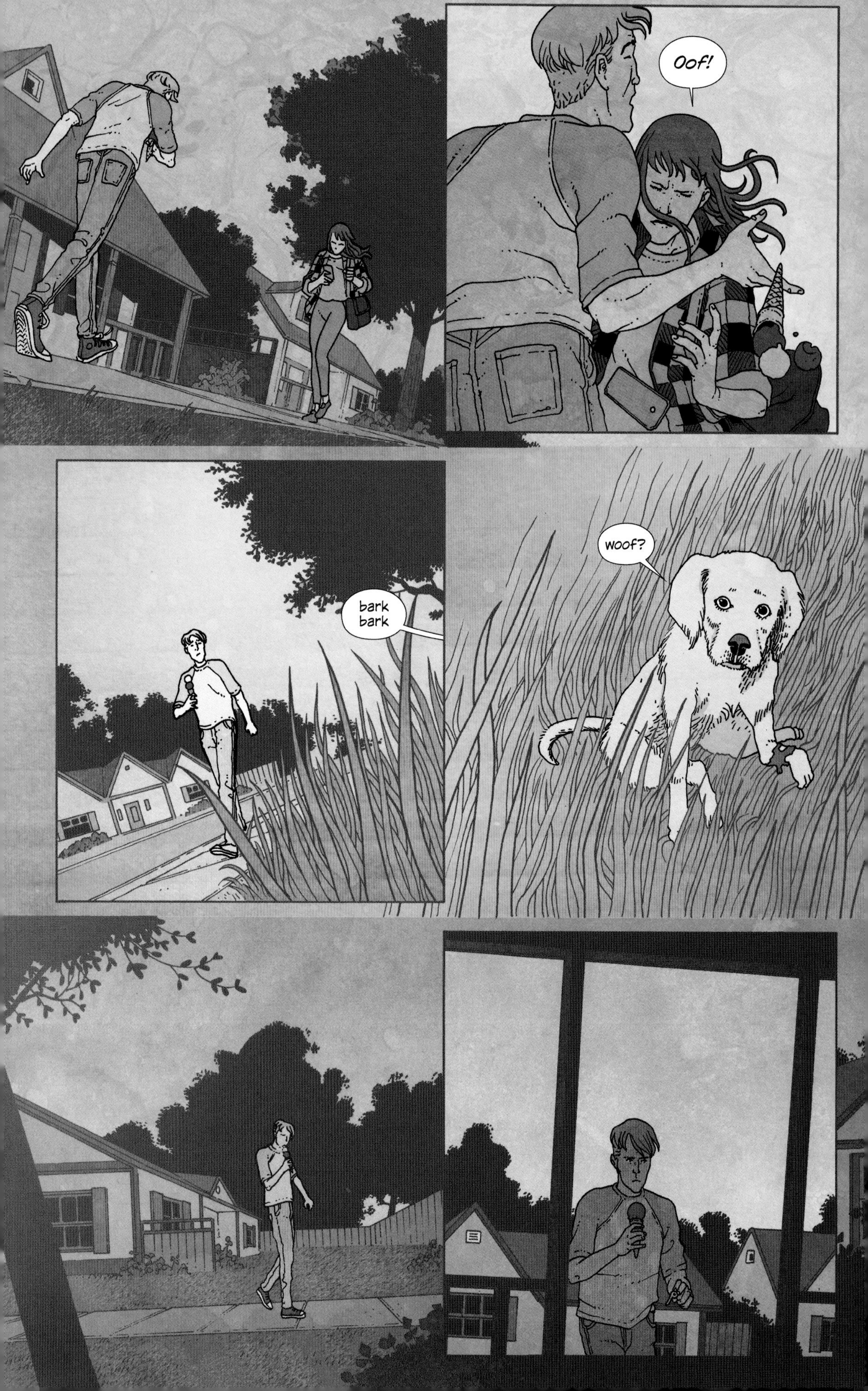
Oof!
bark
bark
woof?

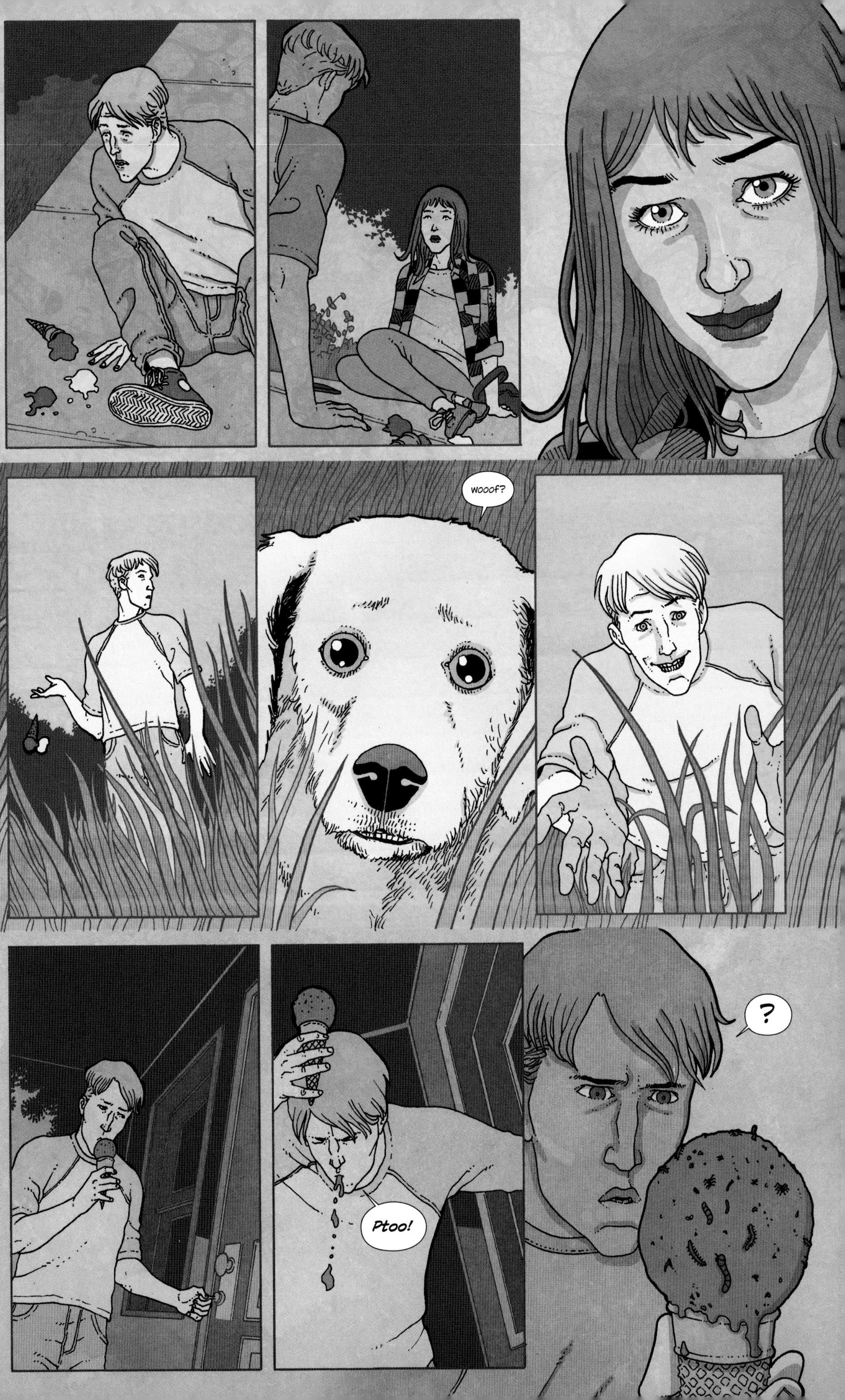
wooof?
Ptoo!
?

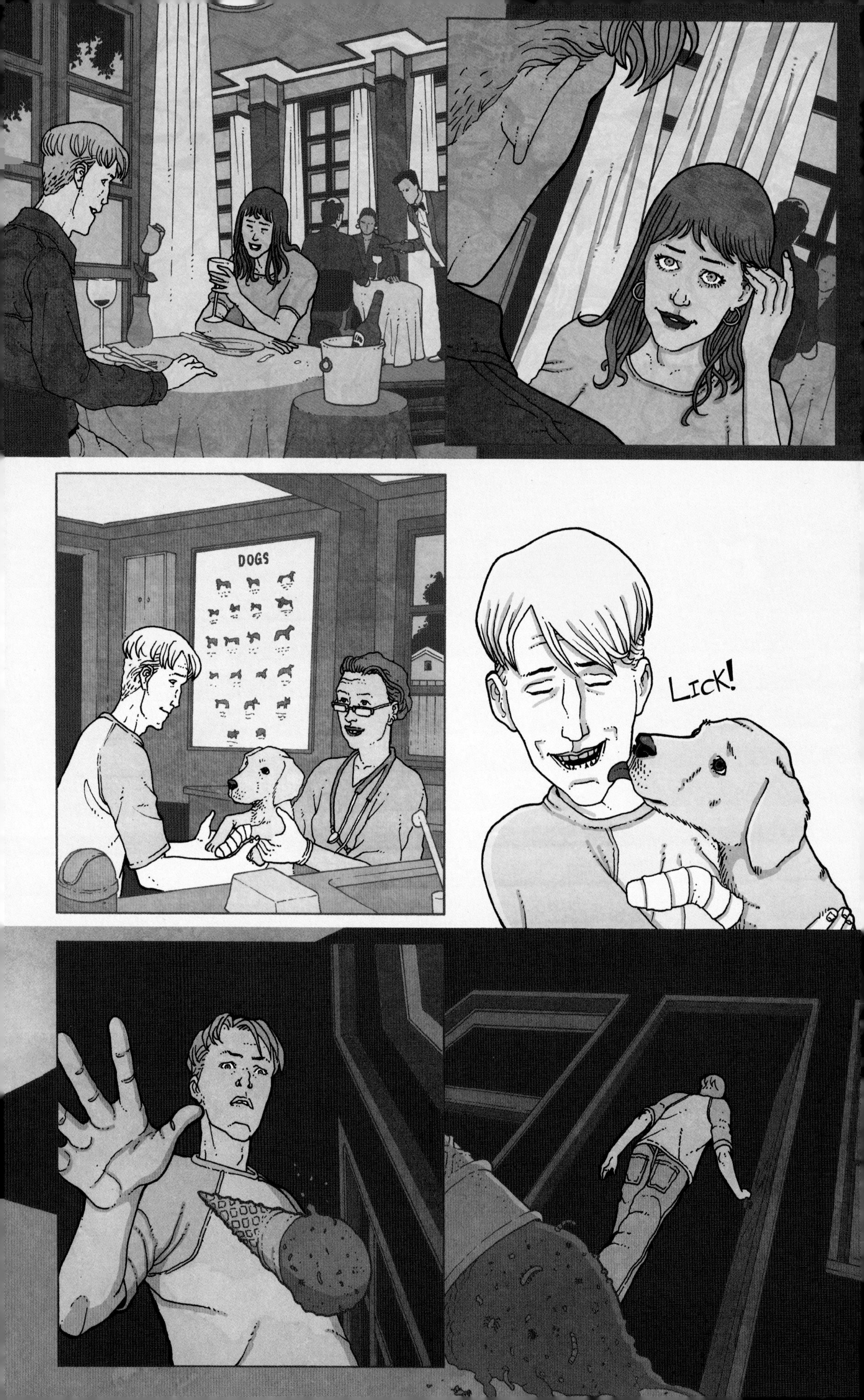
DOGS
LICK!

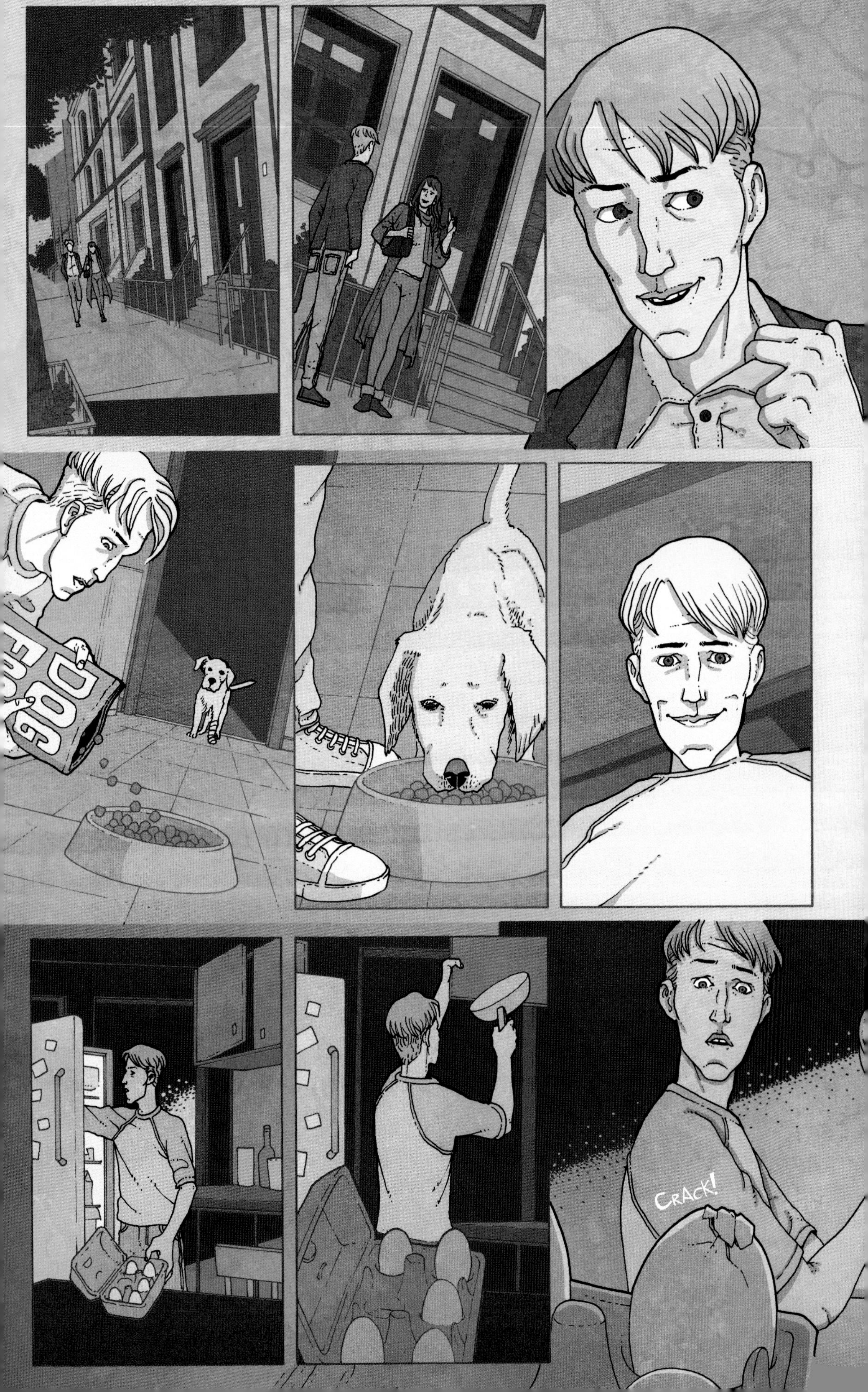
DOG
CRACK!

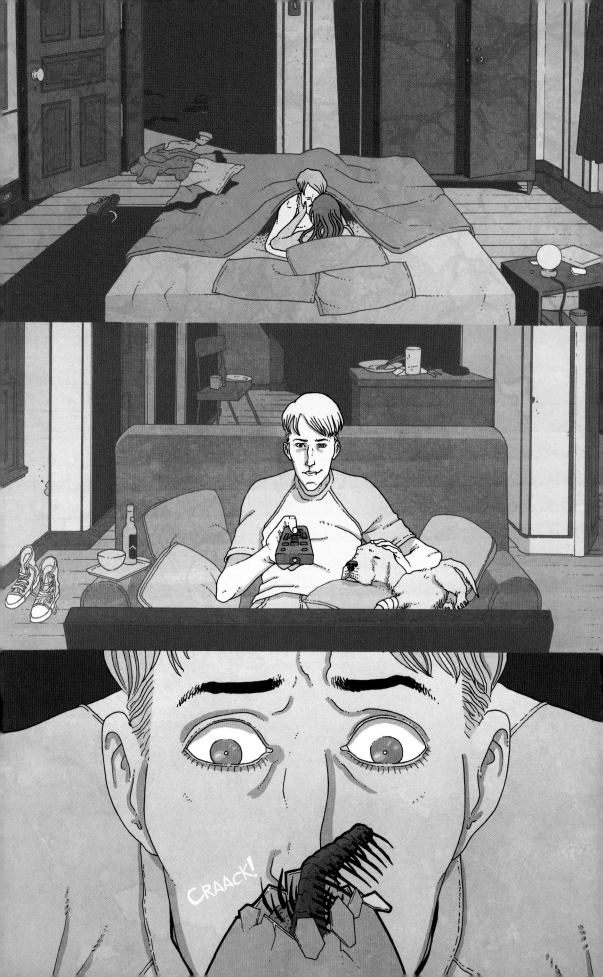

CRAACK!

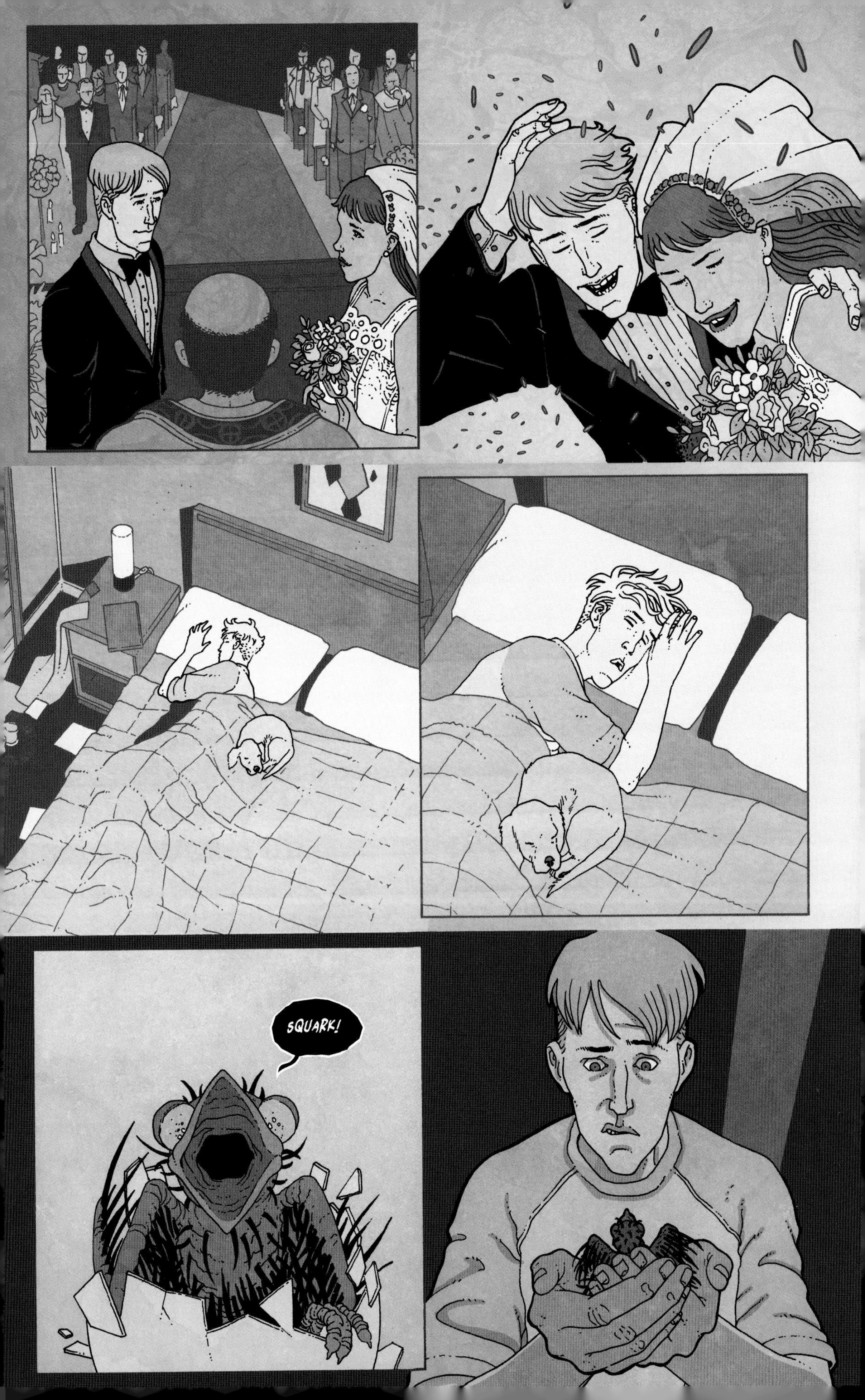
SQUARK!

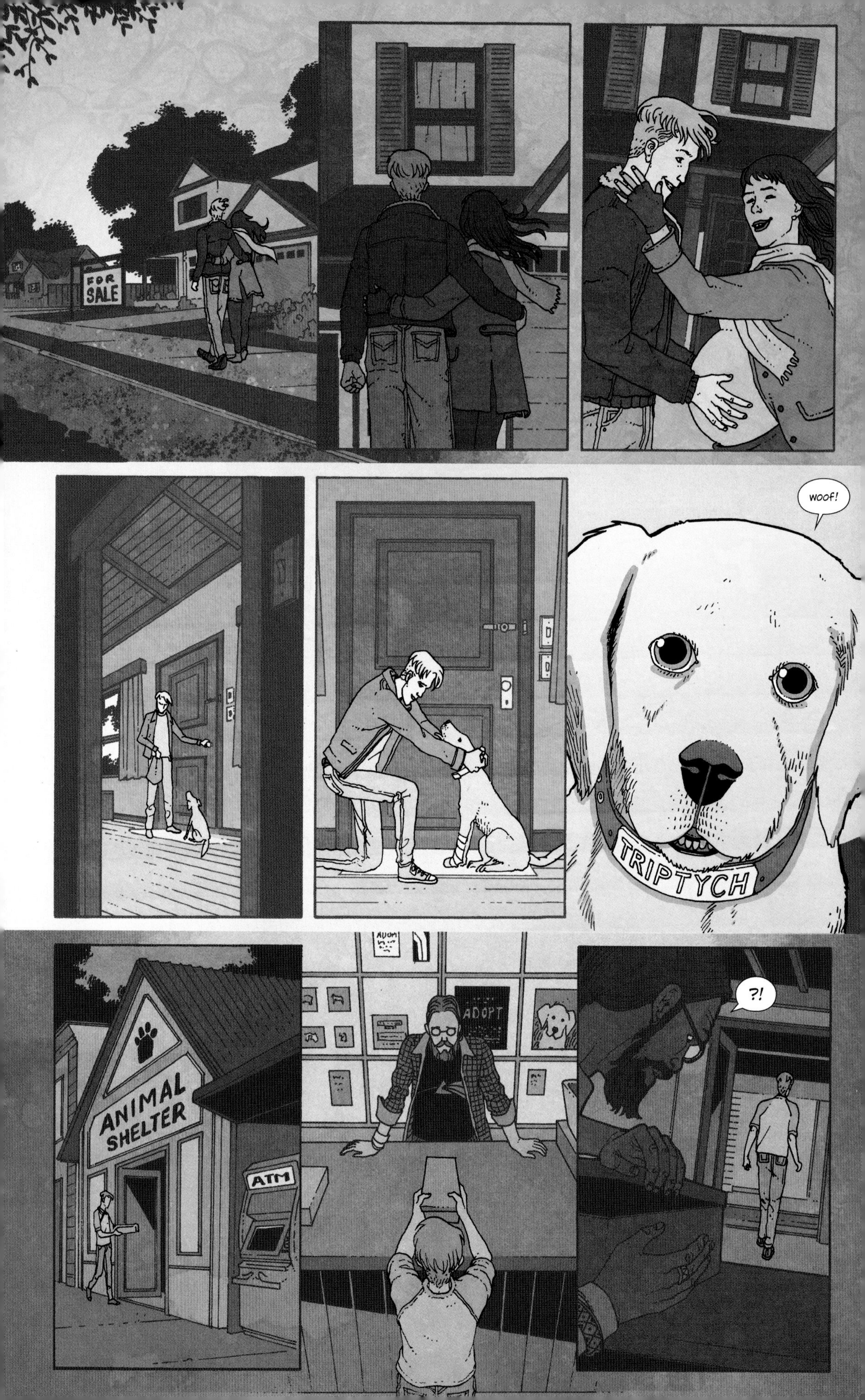

FOR SALE
WOOF!
TRIPTYCH
ANIMAL SHELTER
ATM
ADOPT
?!

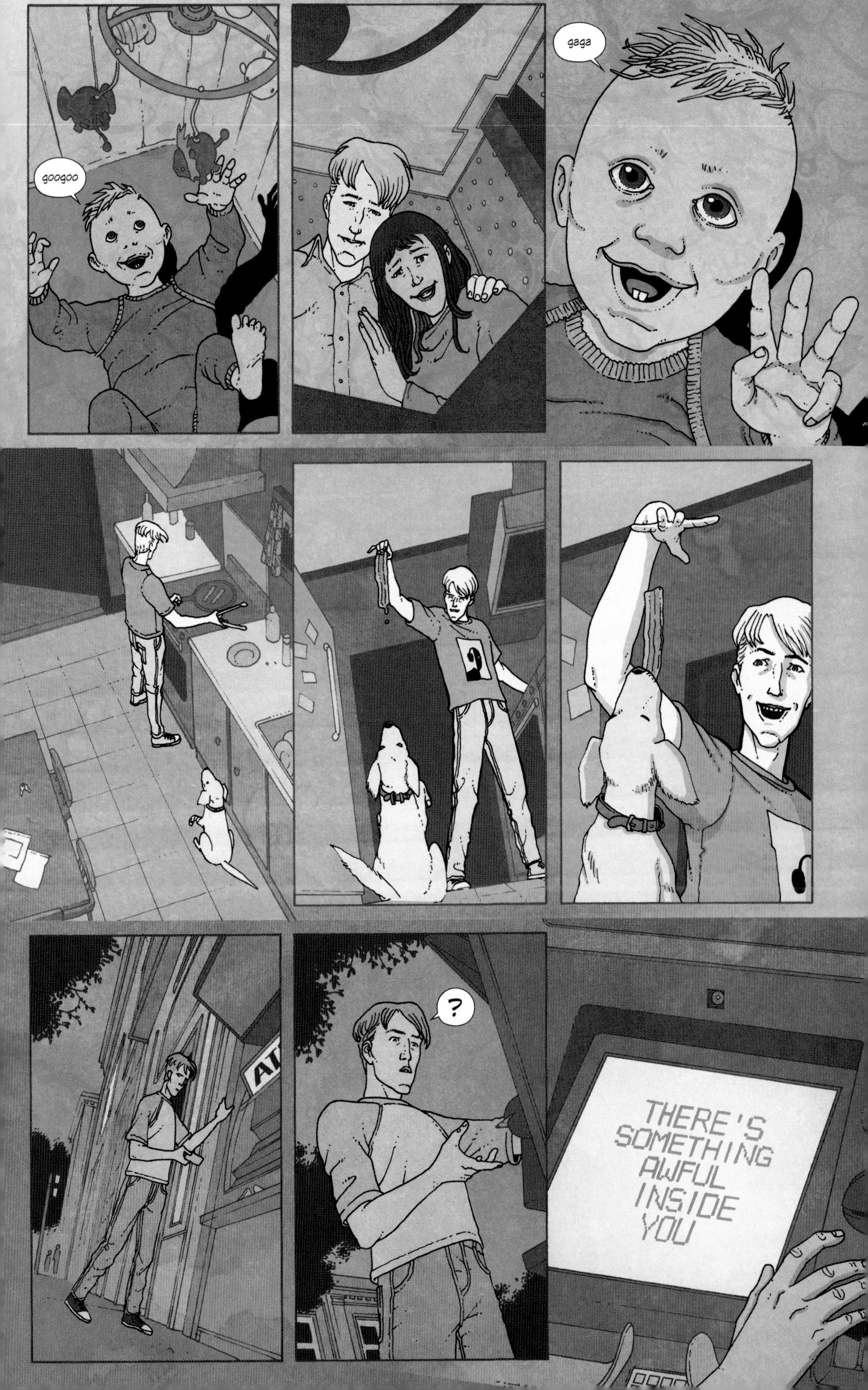
googoo
gaga
?
AT
THERE'S SOMETHING AWFUL INSIDE YOU

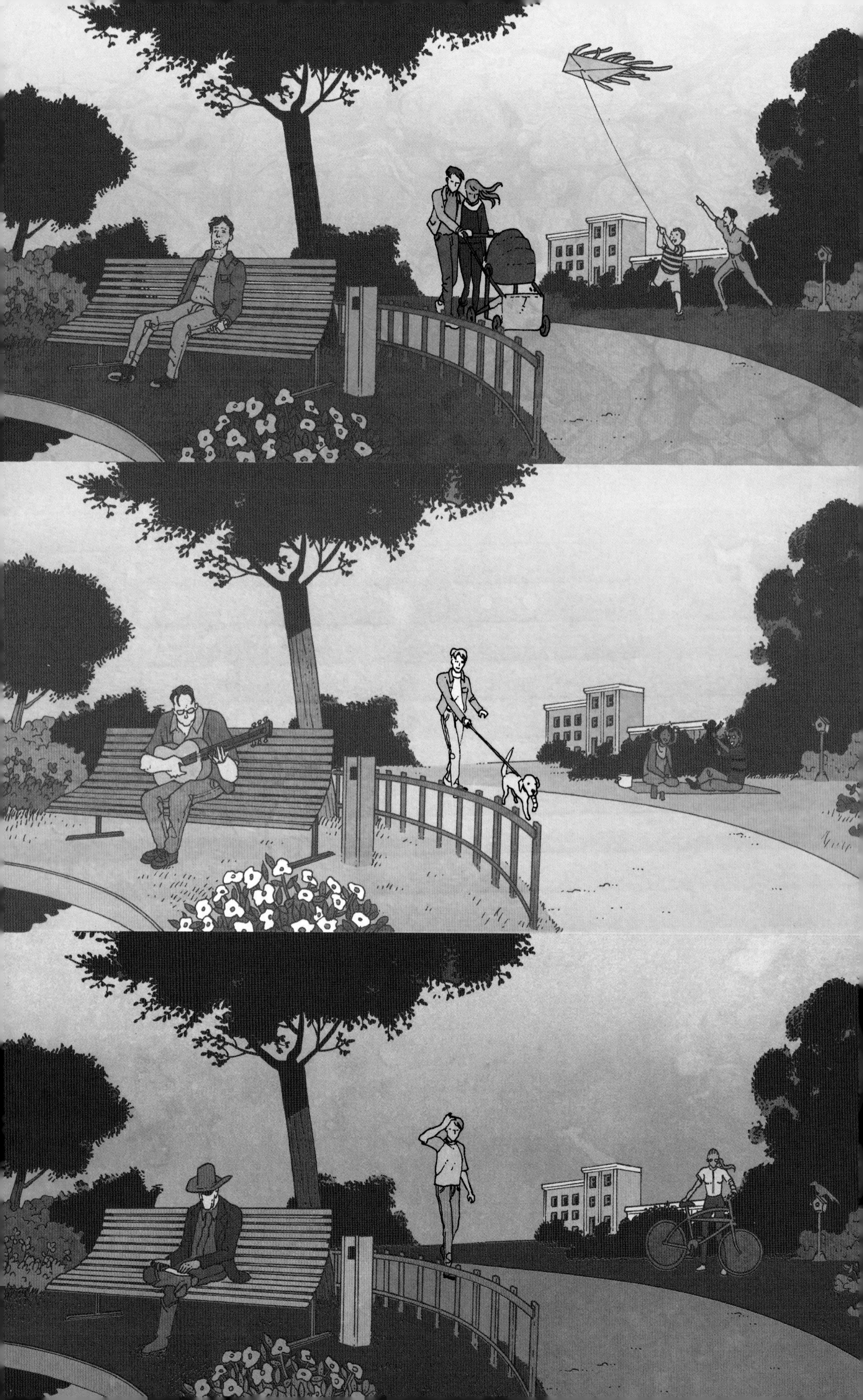

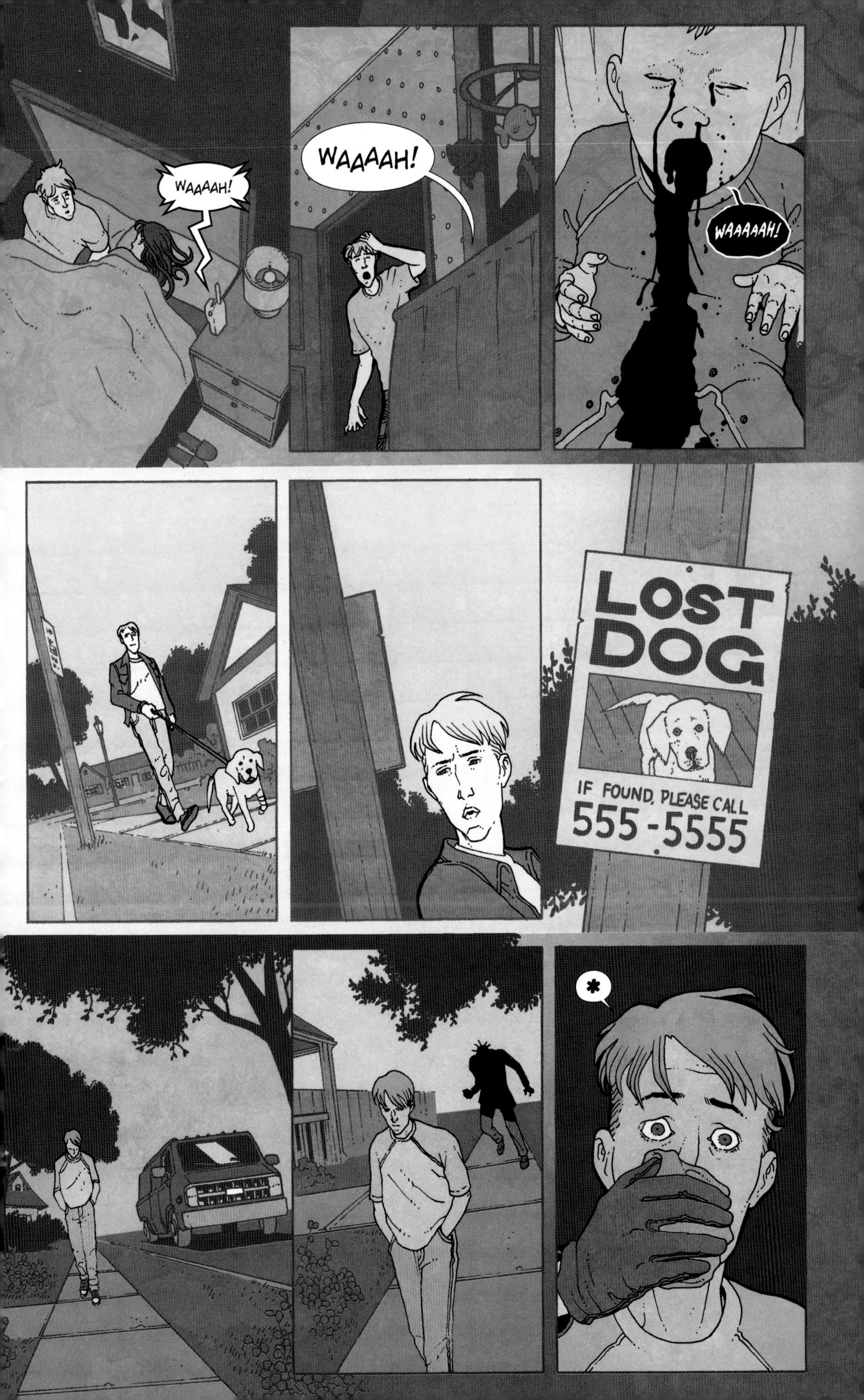
WAAAAH!
WAAAAH!
WAAAAAH!
LOST DOG
IF FOUND, PLEASE CALL
555-5555
*

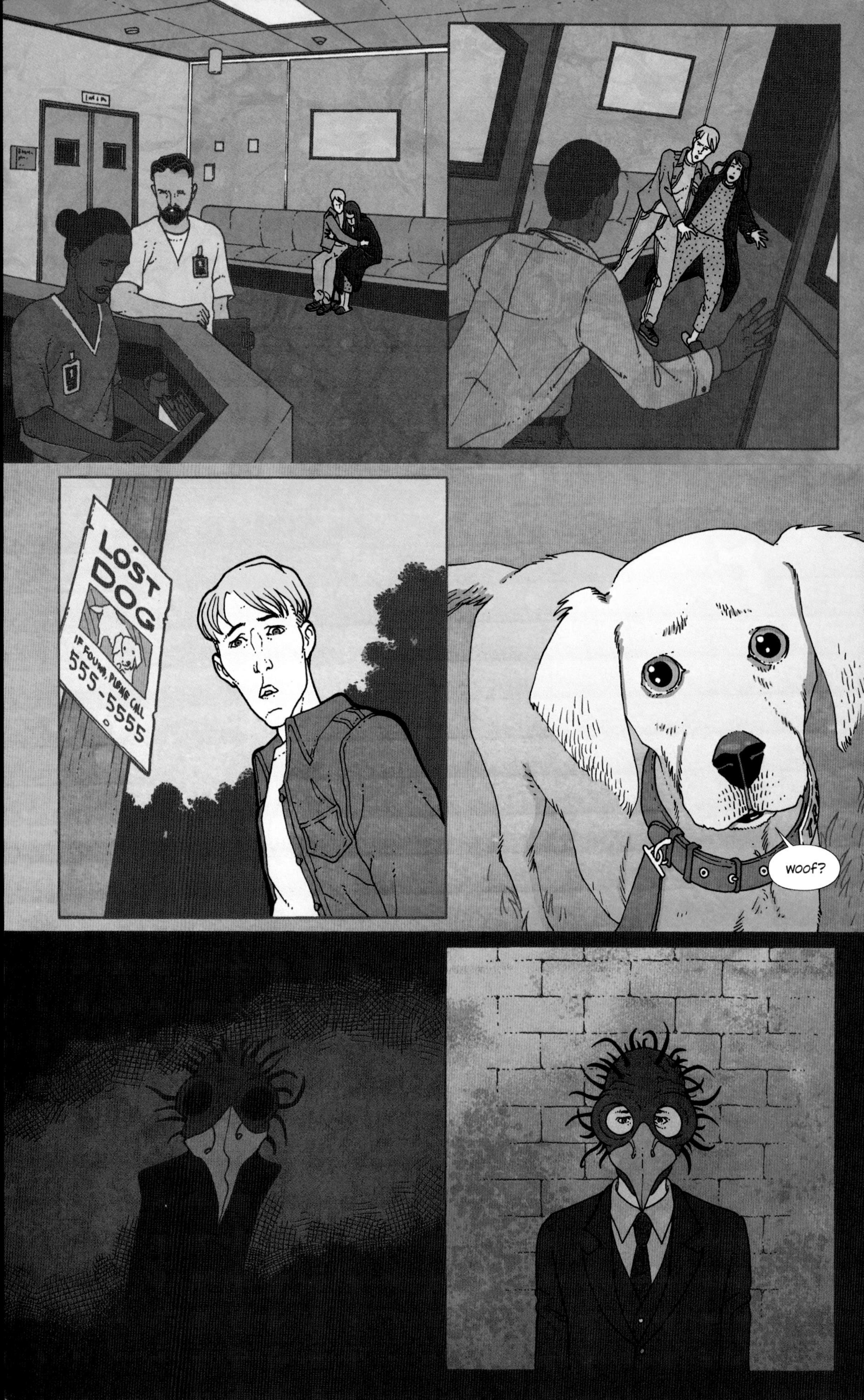
LOST DOG
IF FOUND, PLEASE CALL
555-5555
WOOF?

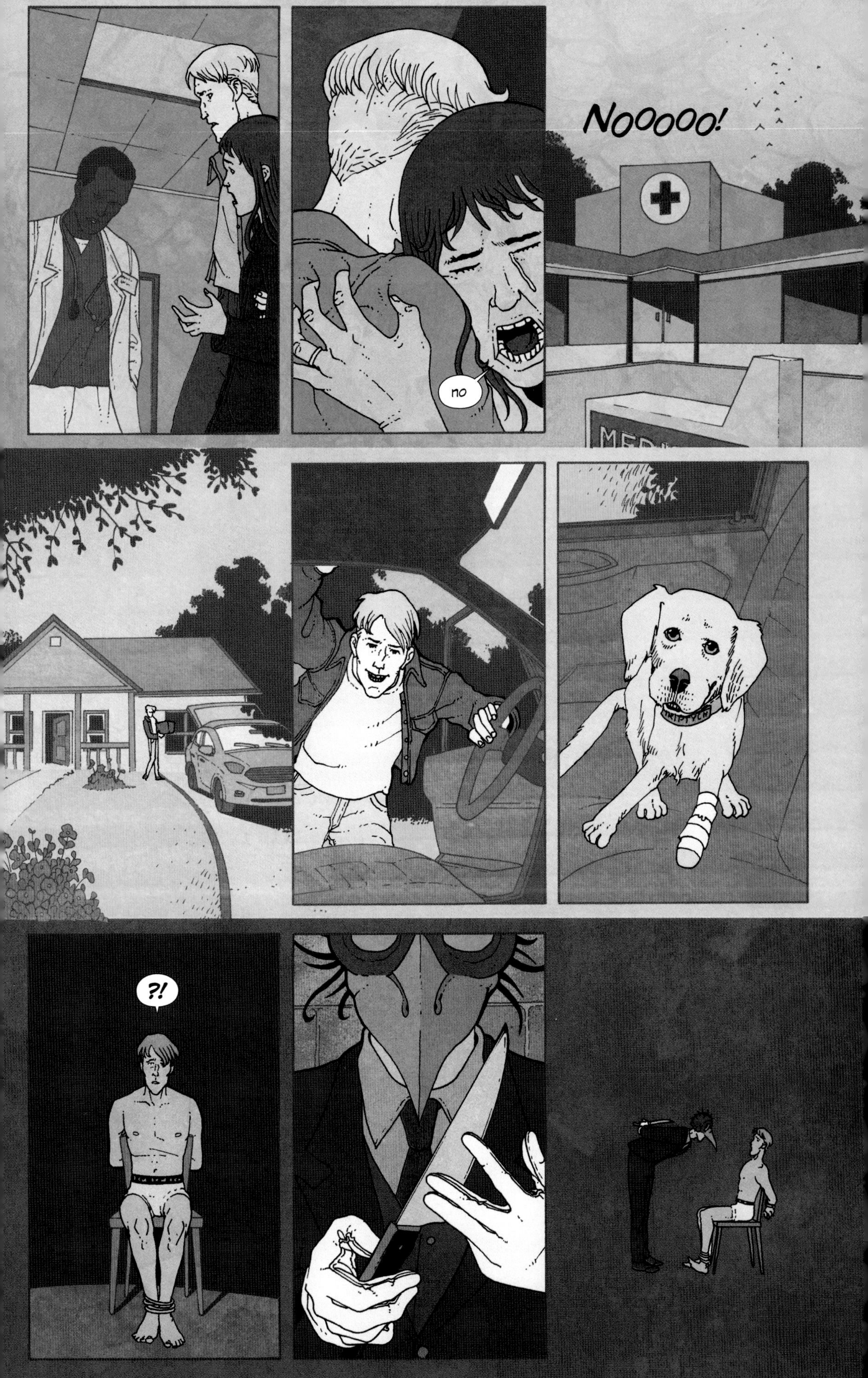
no
NOOOOO!
?!

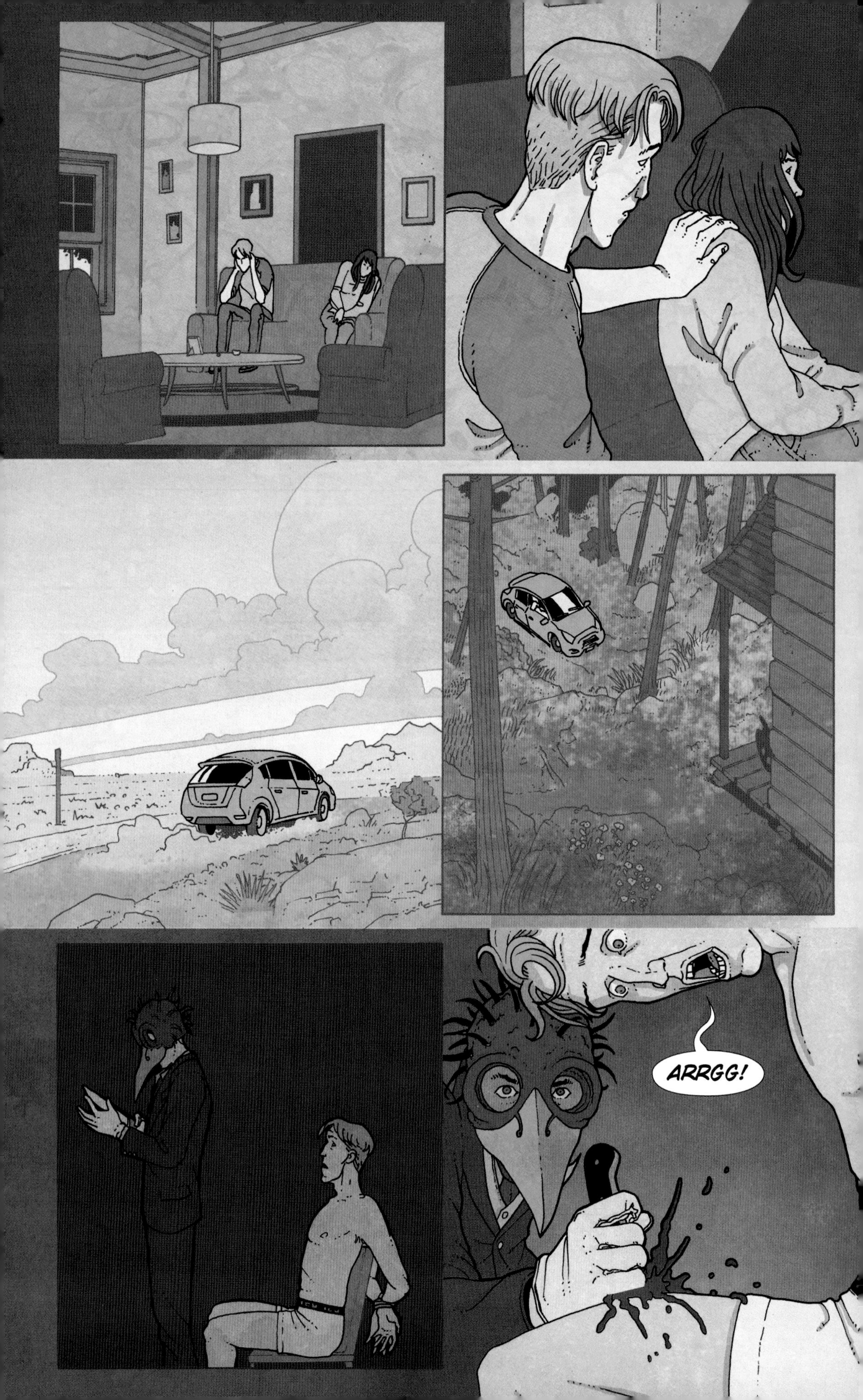
ARRGG!

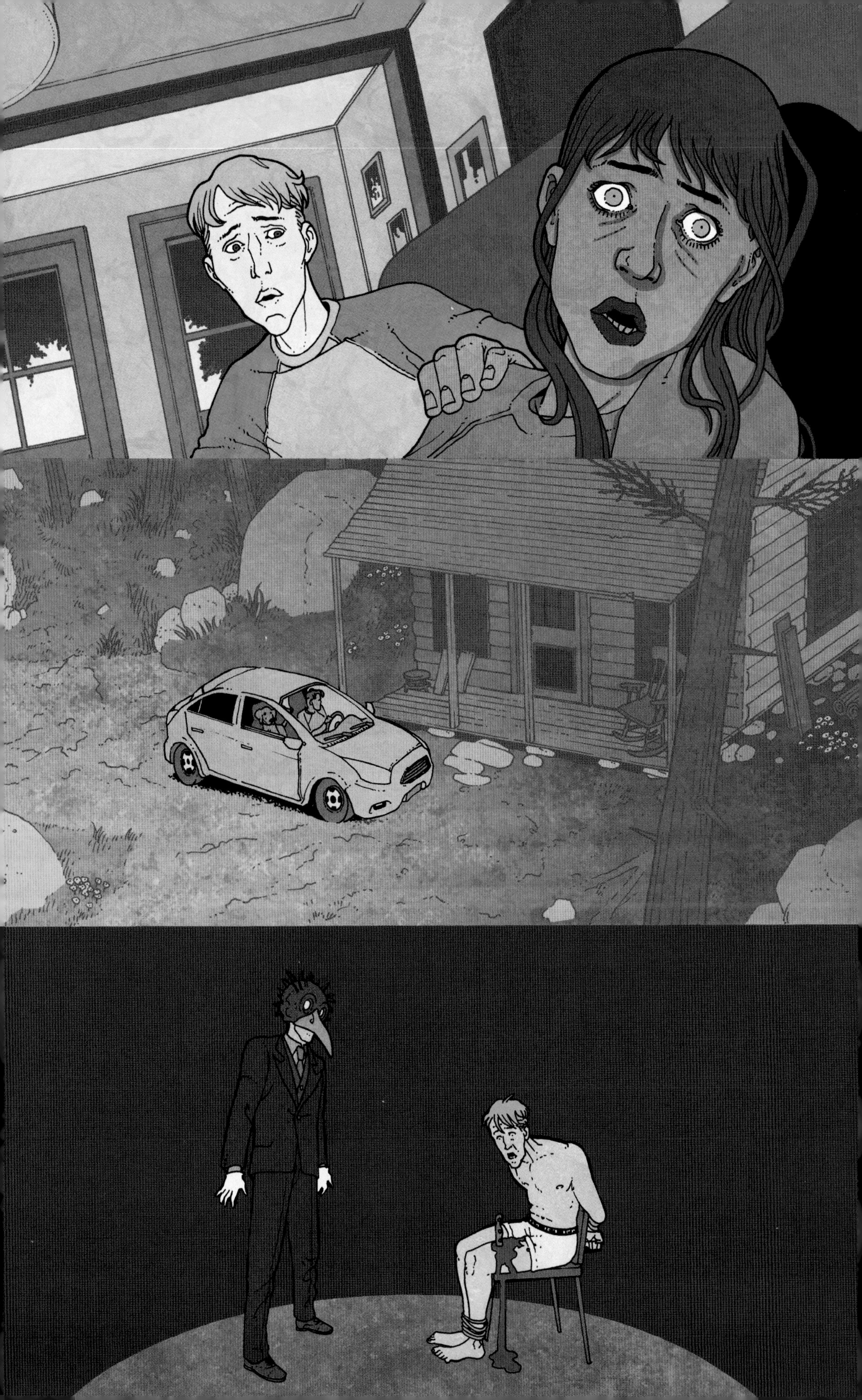

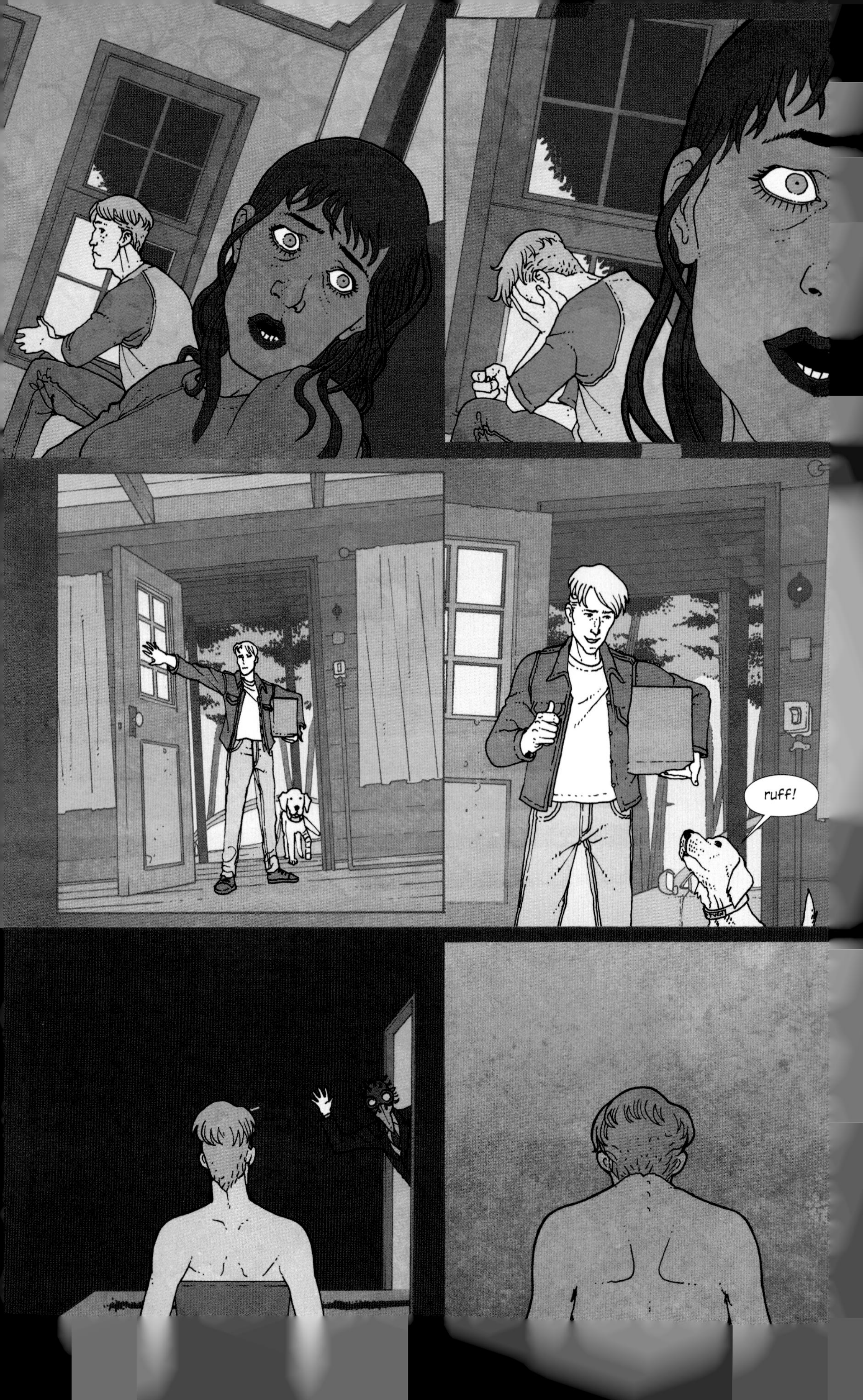
ruff!

Months...

Years...

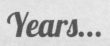

Days...

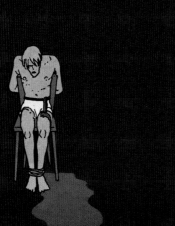

Nnngg

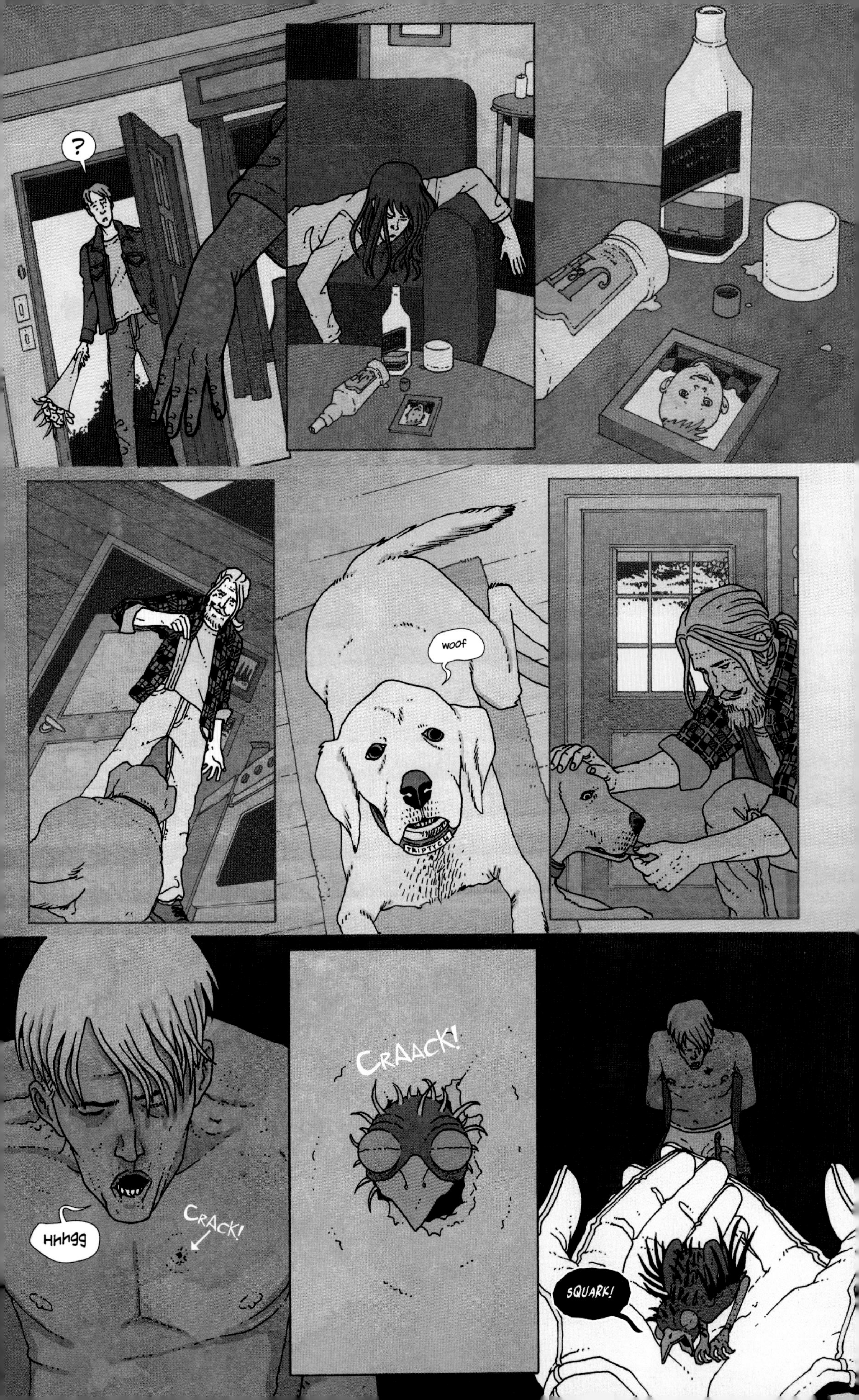
?
woof
TRIPTYCH
Hhhgg
CRACK!
CRAACK!
SQUARK!

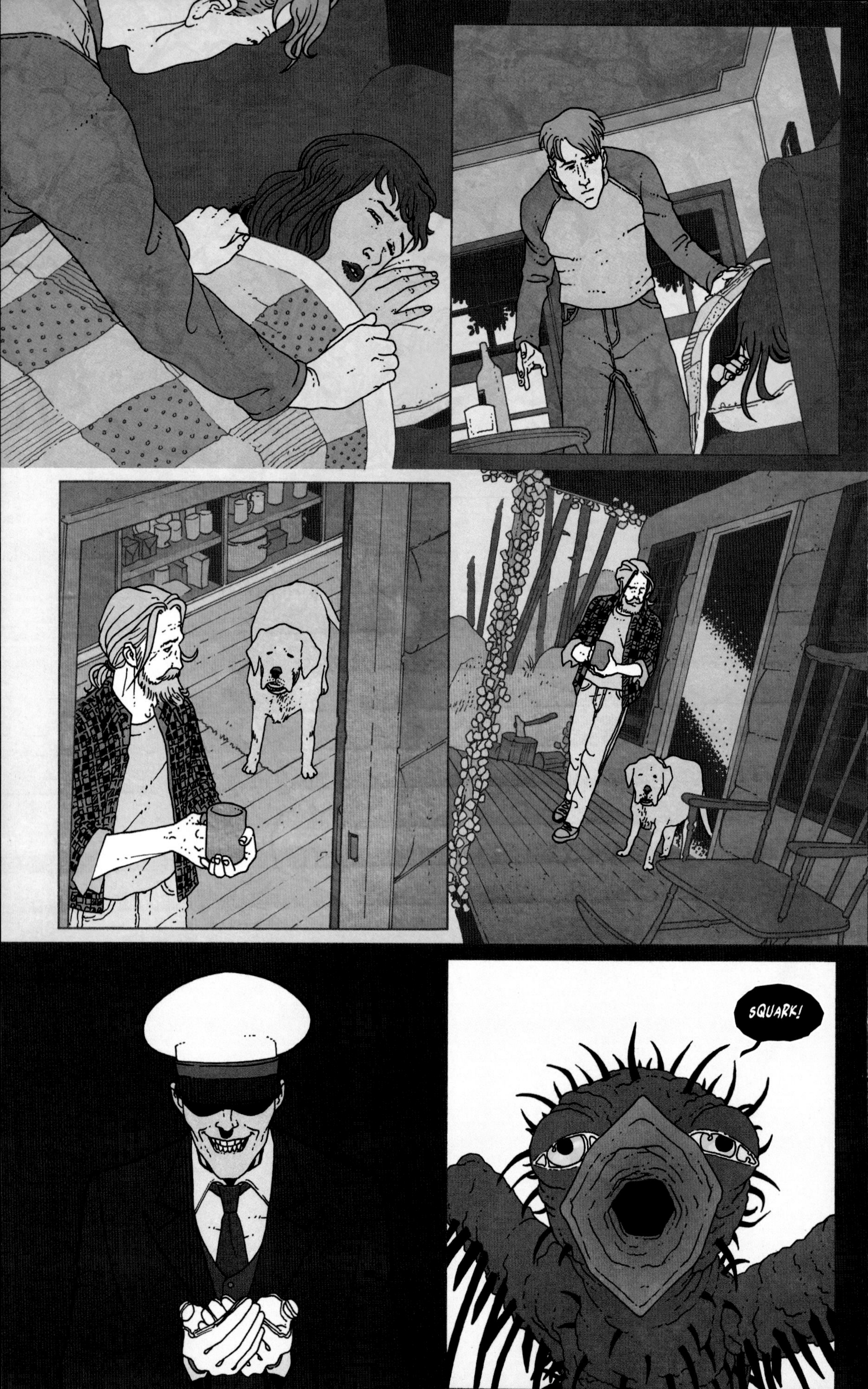
SQUARK!

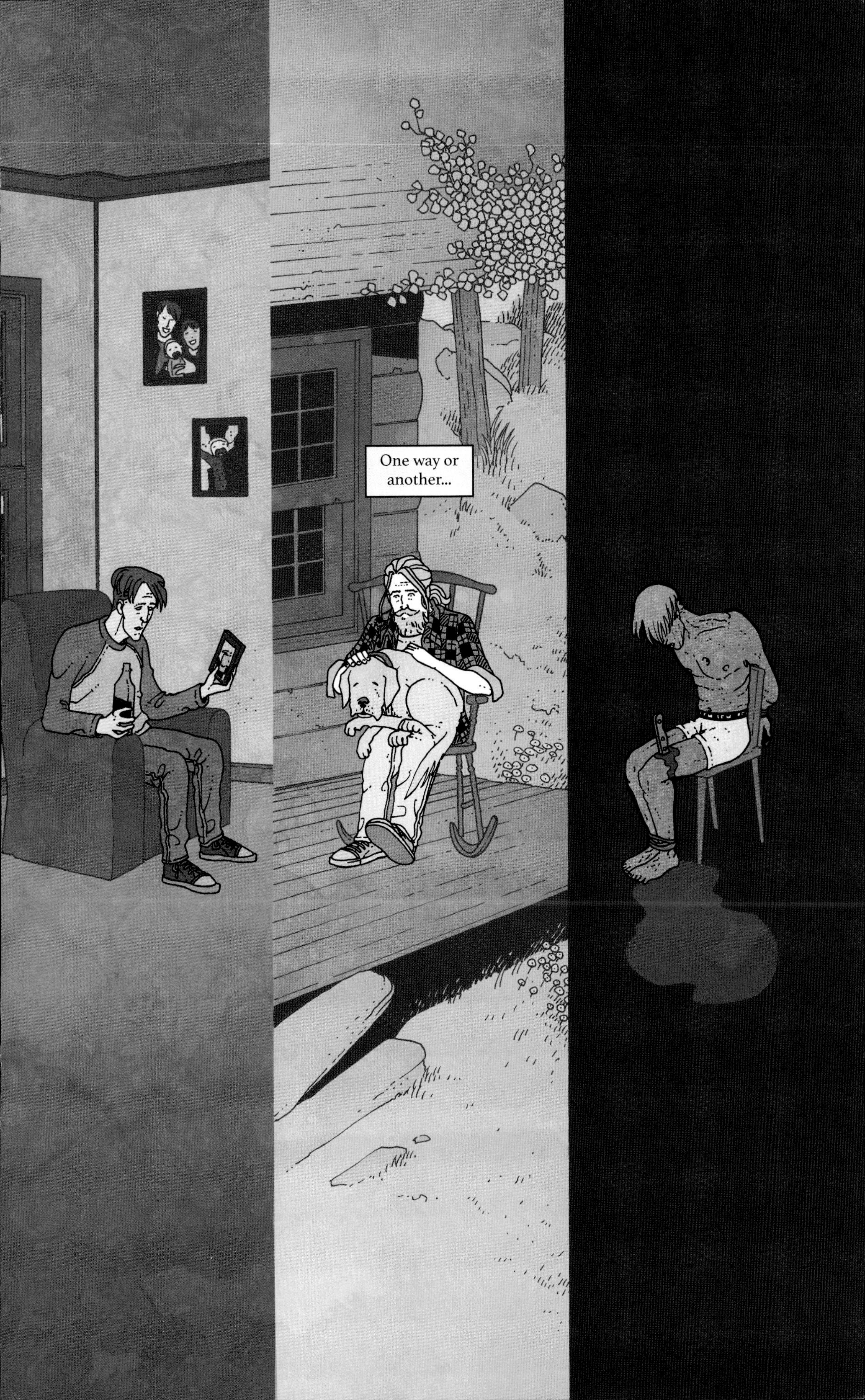
One way or another...

Chapter Seven

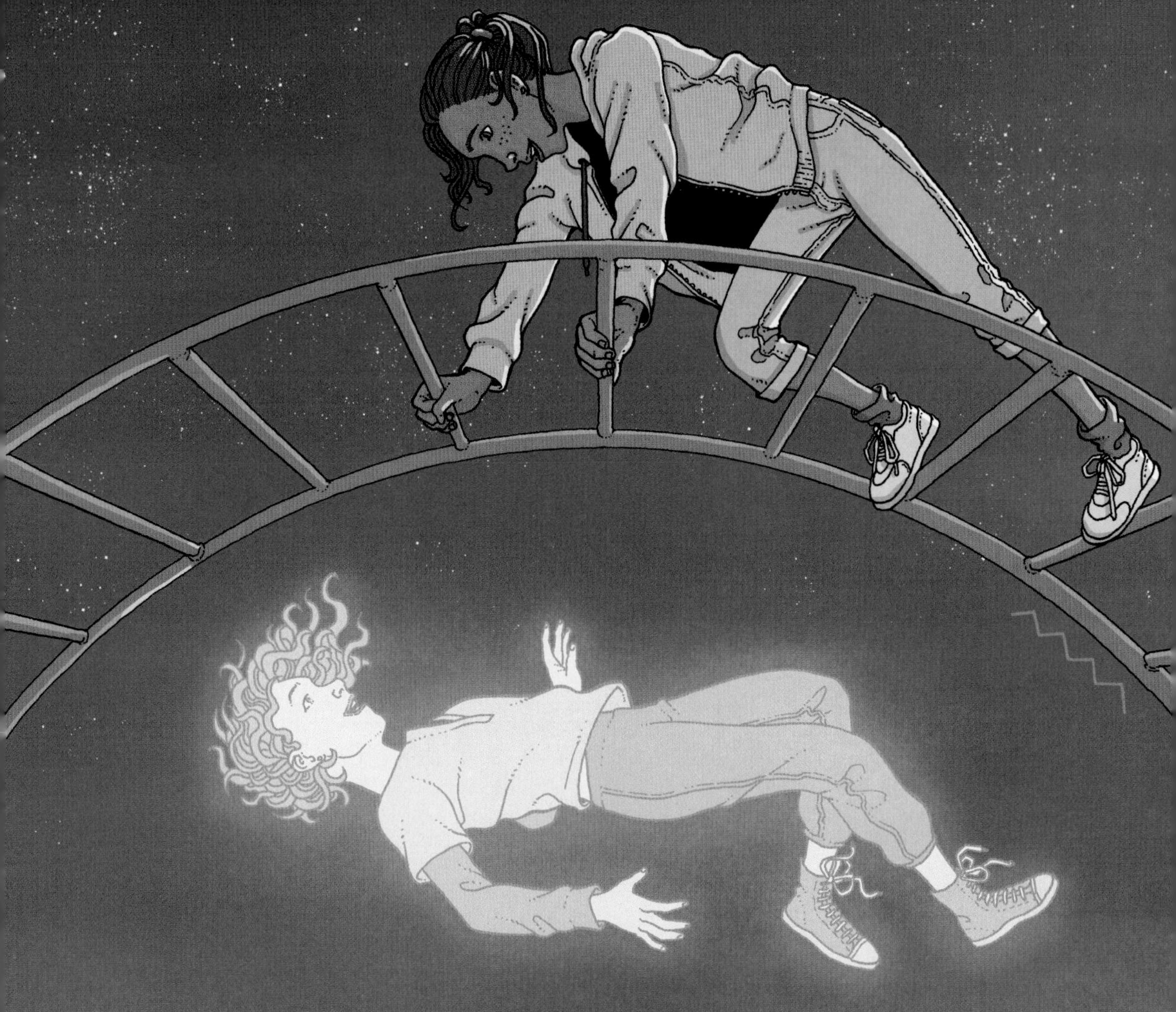

My Little Poltergeist

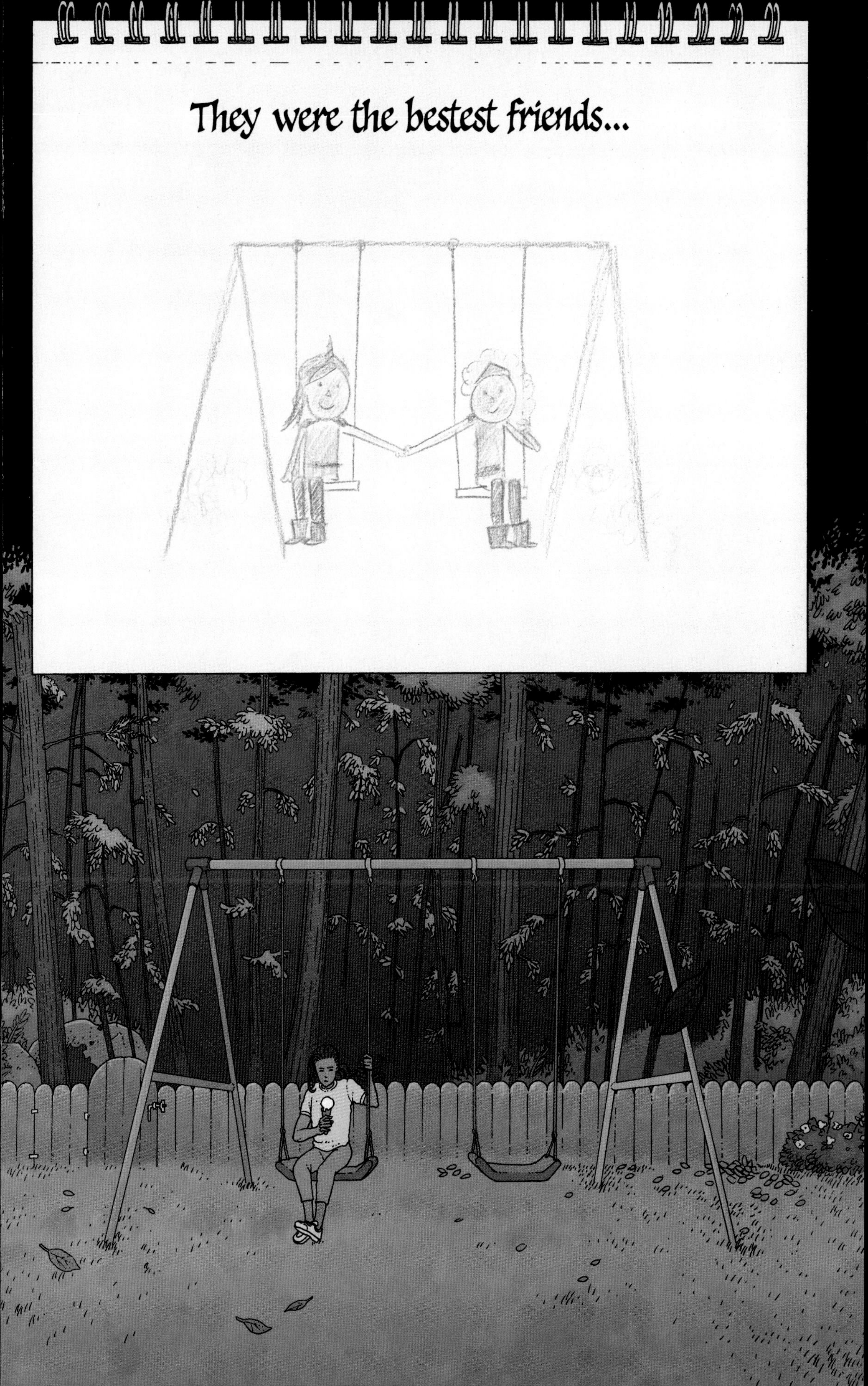
They were the bestest friends...

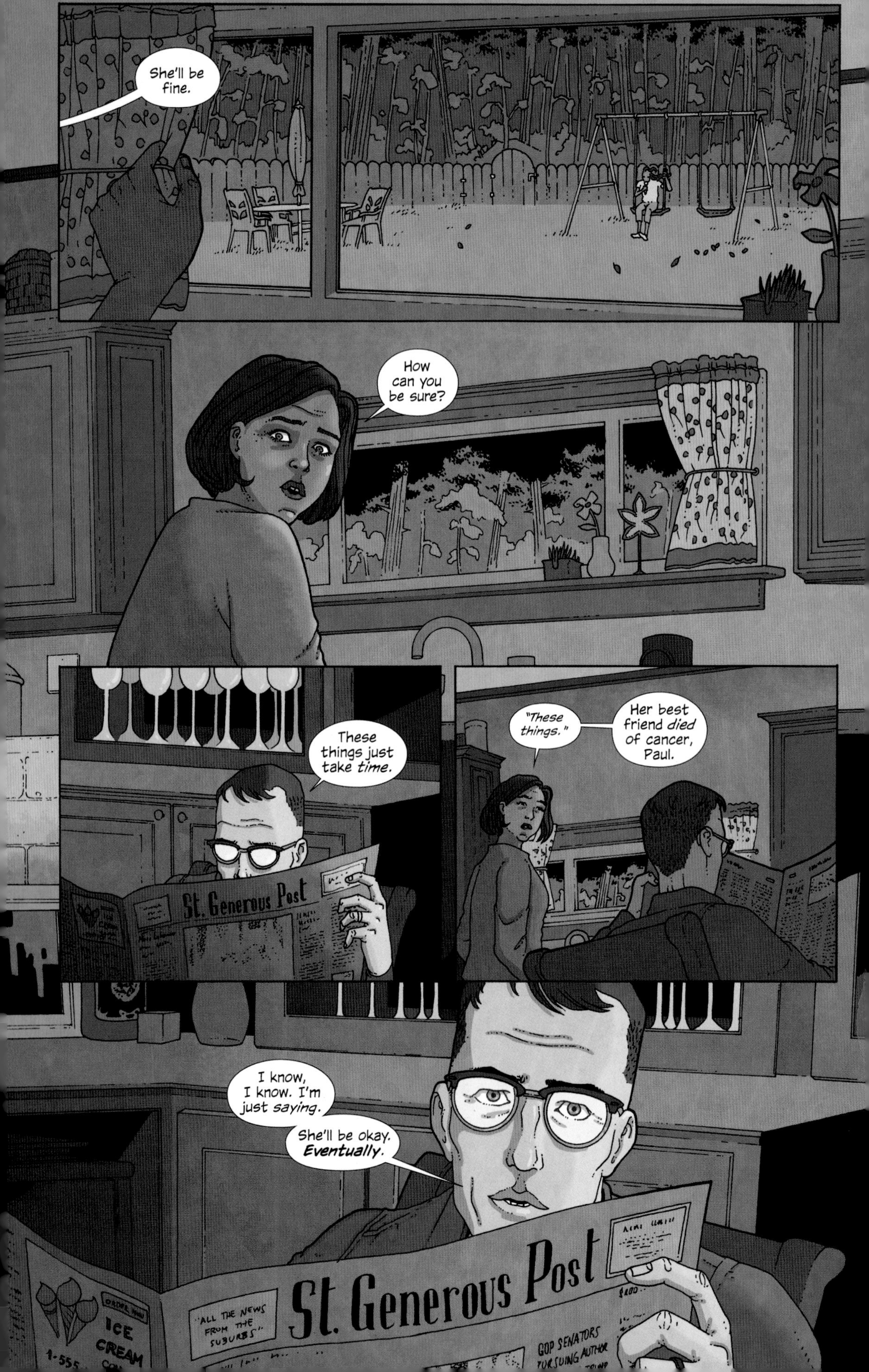

She'll be fine.
How can you be sure?
These things just take *time*.
St. Generous Post
"These things."
Her best friend *died* of cancer, Paul.
I know, I know. I'm just *saying*.
She'll be okay. ***Eventually***.
St. Generous Post
"ALL THE NEWS FROM THE SUBURBS"
ICE CREAM
GOP SENATORS PURSUING AUTHOR

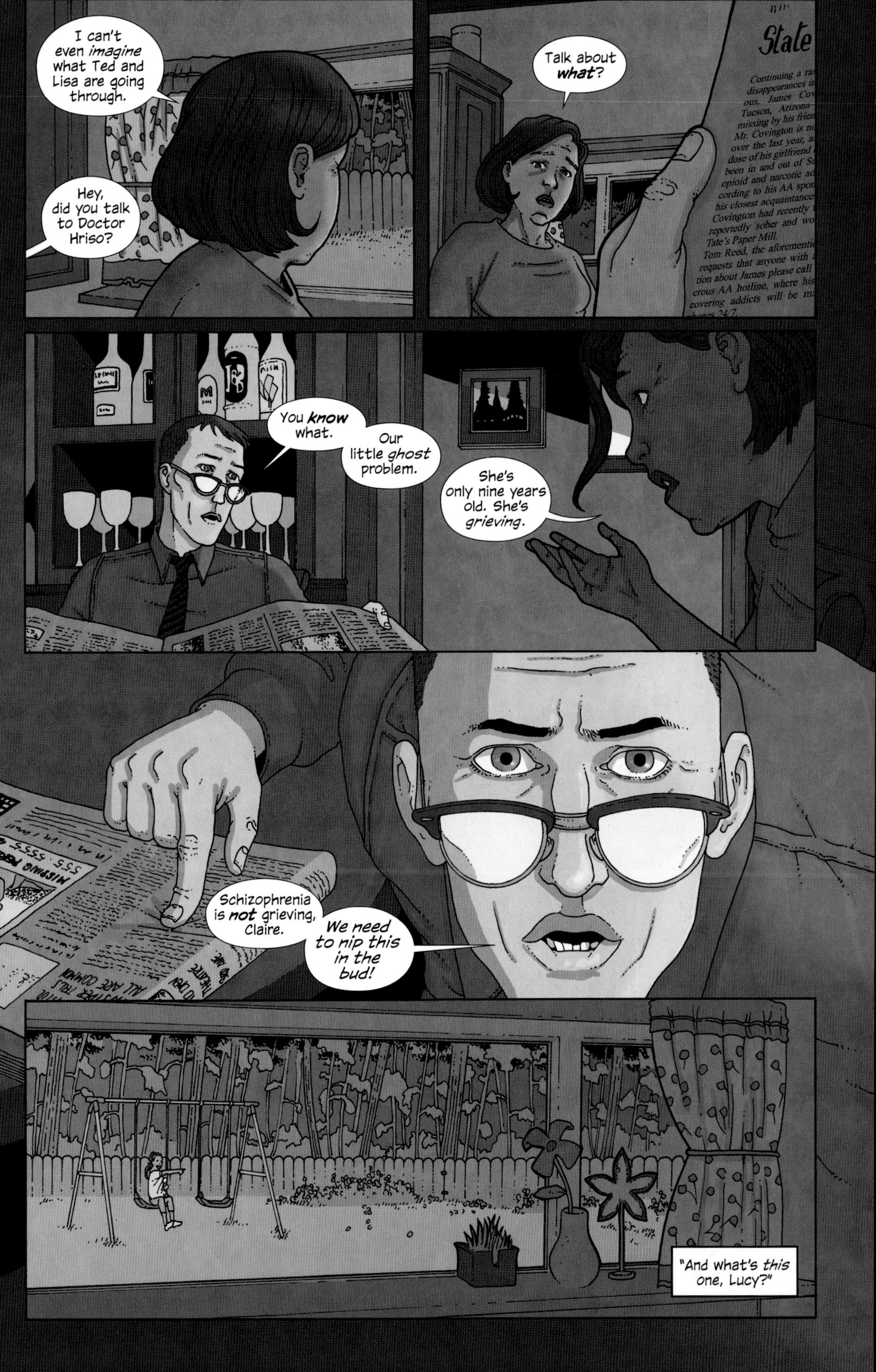
I can't even *imagine* what Ted and Lisa are going through.
Hey, did you talk to Doctor Hriso?
Talk about ***what***?
State
You ***know*** what.
Our little *ghost* problem.
She's only nine years old. She's *grieving*.
Schizophrenia is ***not*** grieving, Claire.
We need to nip this in the bud!
"And what's *this* one, Lucy?"

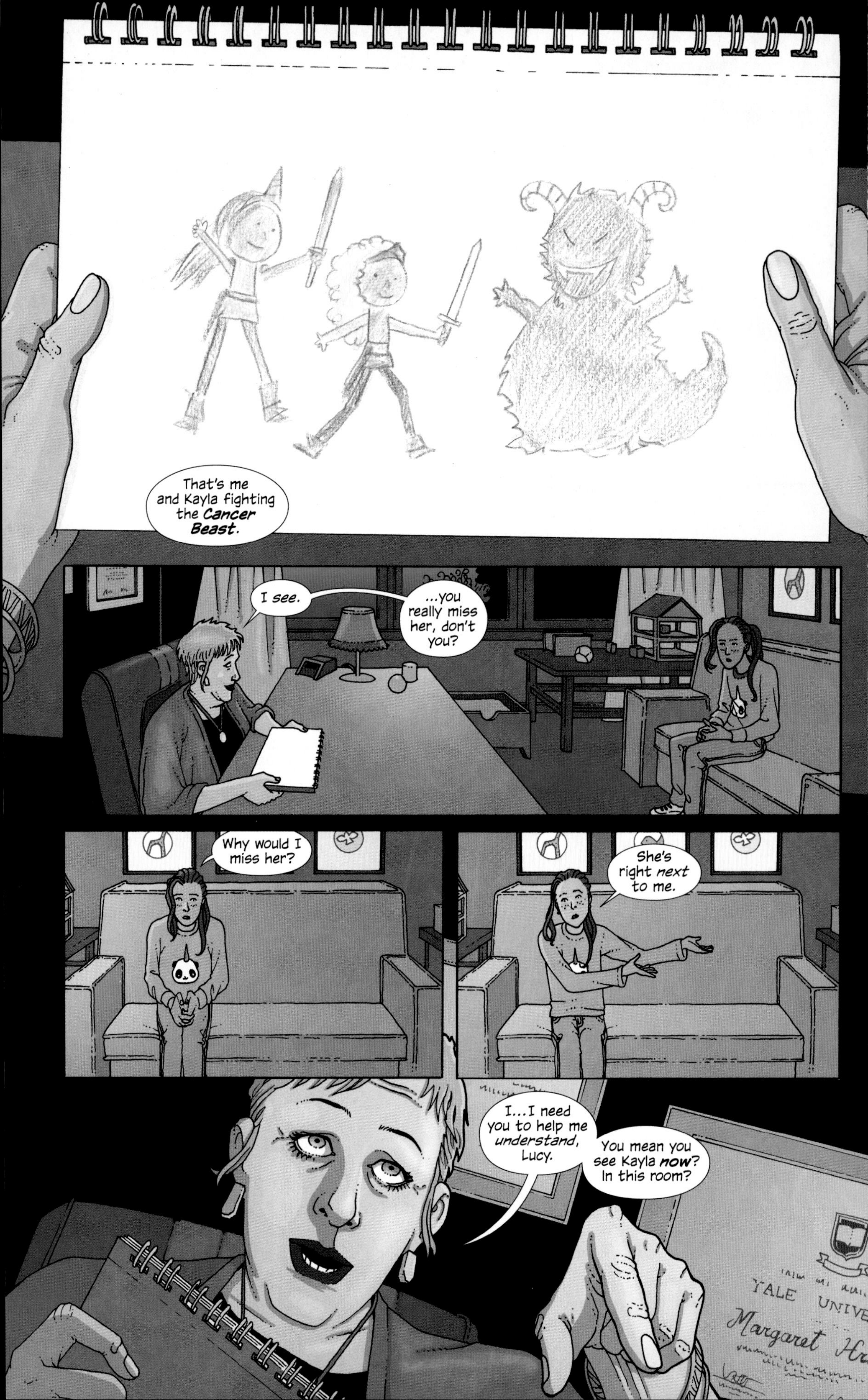
That's me and Kayla fighting the *Cancer Beast*.
I see.
...you really miss her, don't you?
Why would I miss her?
She's right *next* to me.
I...I need you to help me *understand*, Lucy.
You mean you see Kayla ***now***? In this room?

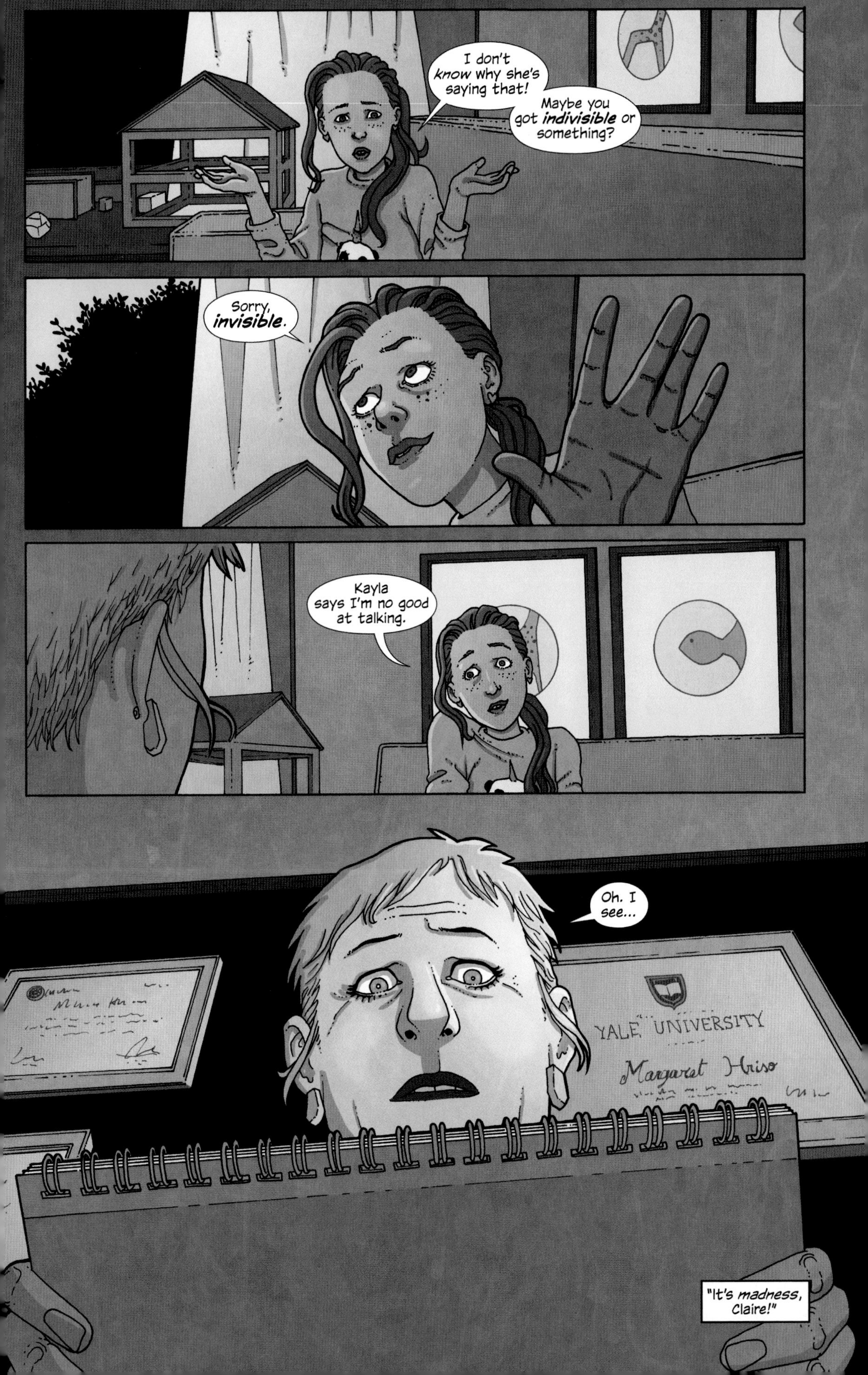

I don't *know* why she's saying that!
Maybe you got ***indivisible*** or something?
Sorry, ***invisible***.
Kayla says I'm no good at talking.
Oh. I see...
YALE UNIVERSITY
Margaret Hriso
"It's *madness*, Claire!"

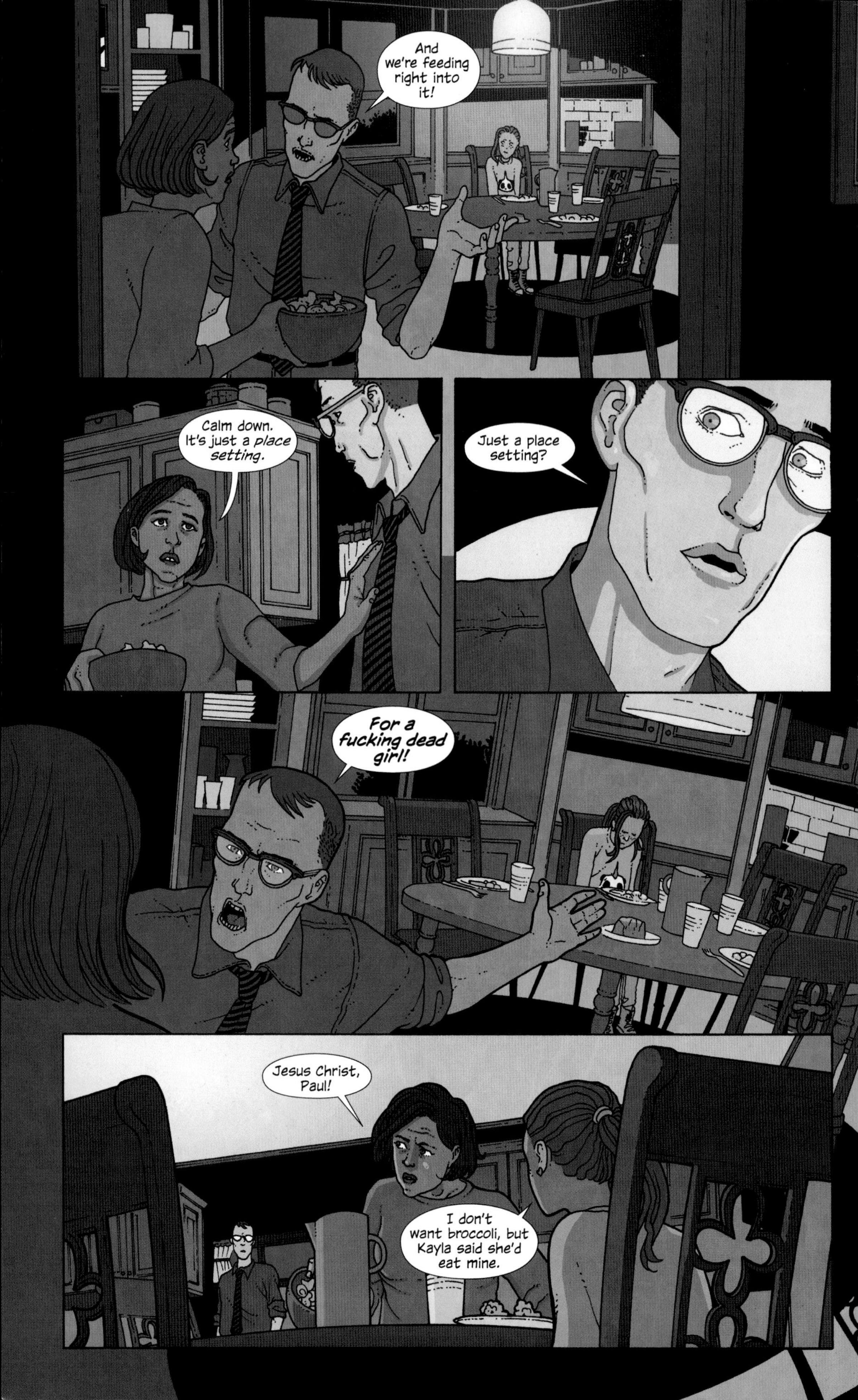
And we're feeding right into it!
Calm down. It's just a *place setting*.
Just a place setting?
For a fucking dead girl!
Jesus Christ, Paul!
I don't want broccoli, but Kayla said she'd eat mine.

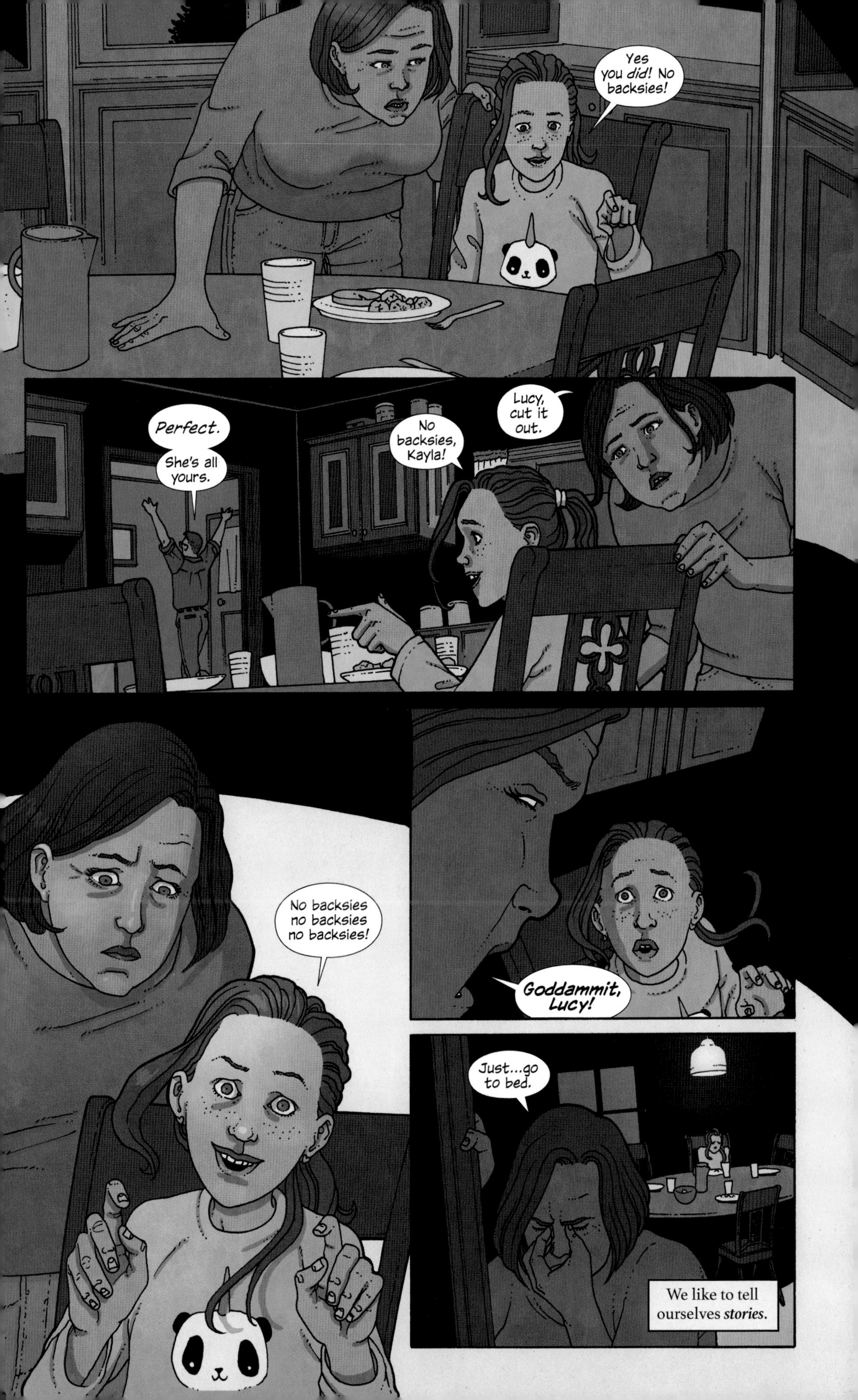
Yes you *did*! No backsies!
Perfect.
She's all yours.
No backsies, Kayla!
Lucy, cut it out.
No backsies no backsies no backsies!
Goddammit, Lucy!
Just...go to bed.
We like to tell ourselves *stories*.

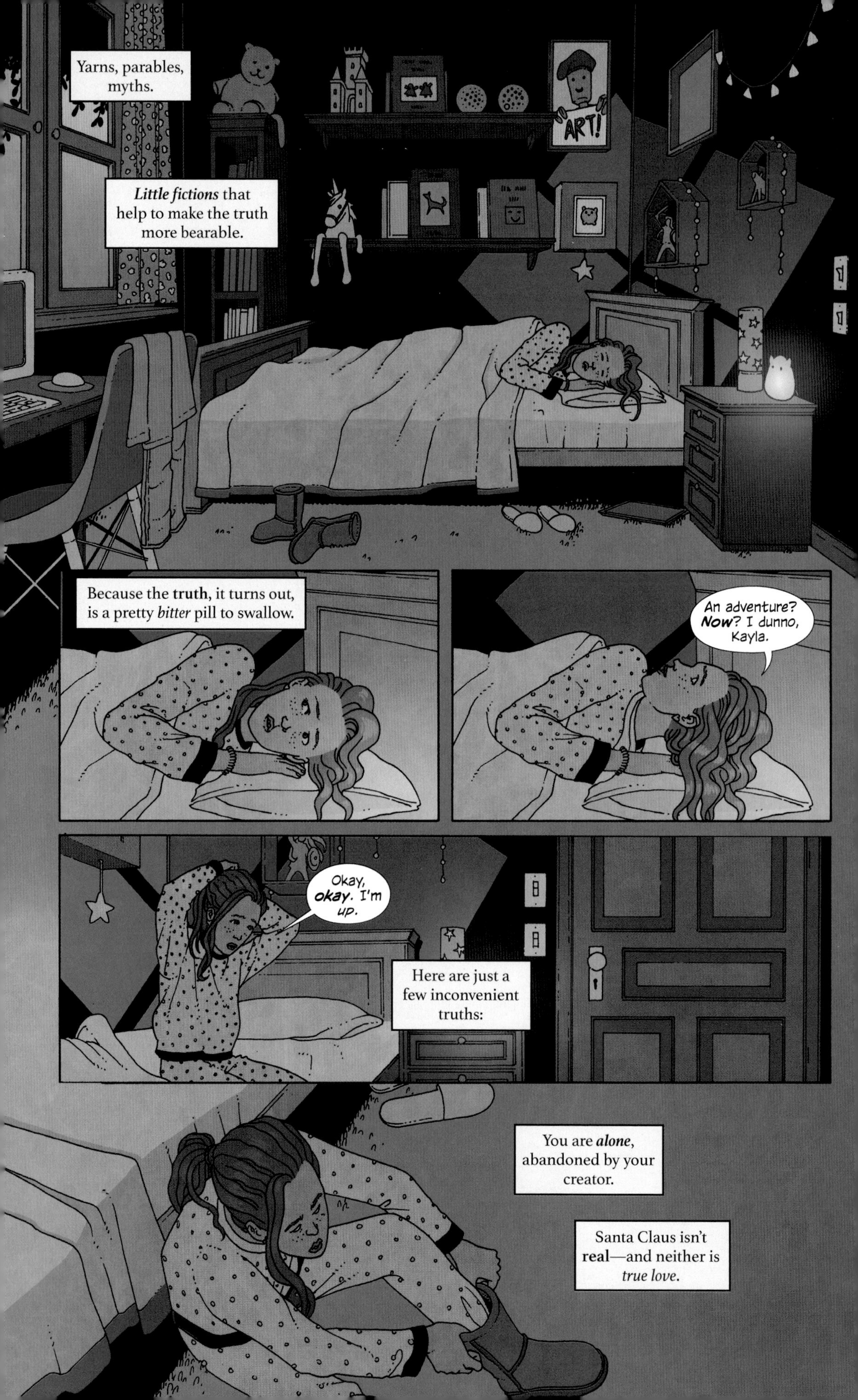
Yarns, parables, myths.
ART!
Little fictions that help to make the truth more bearable.
Because the **truth**, it turns out, is a pretty *bitter* pill to swallow.
An adventure? **Now**? I dunno, Kayla.
Okay, **okay**. I'm up.
Here are just a few inconvenient truths:
You are ***alone***, abandoned by your creator.
Santa Claus isn't **real**—and neither is *true love*.

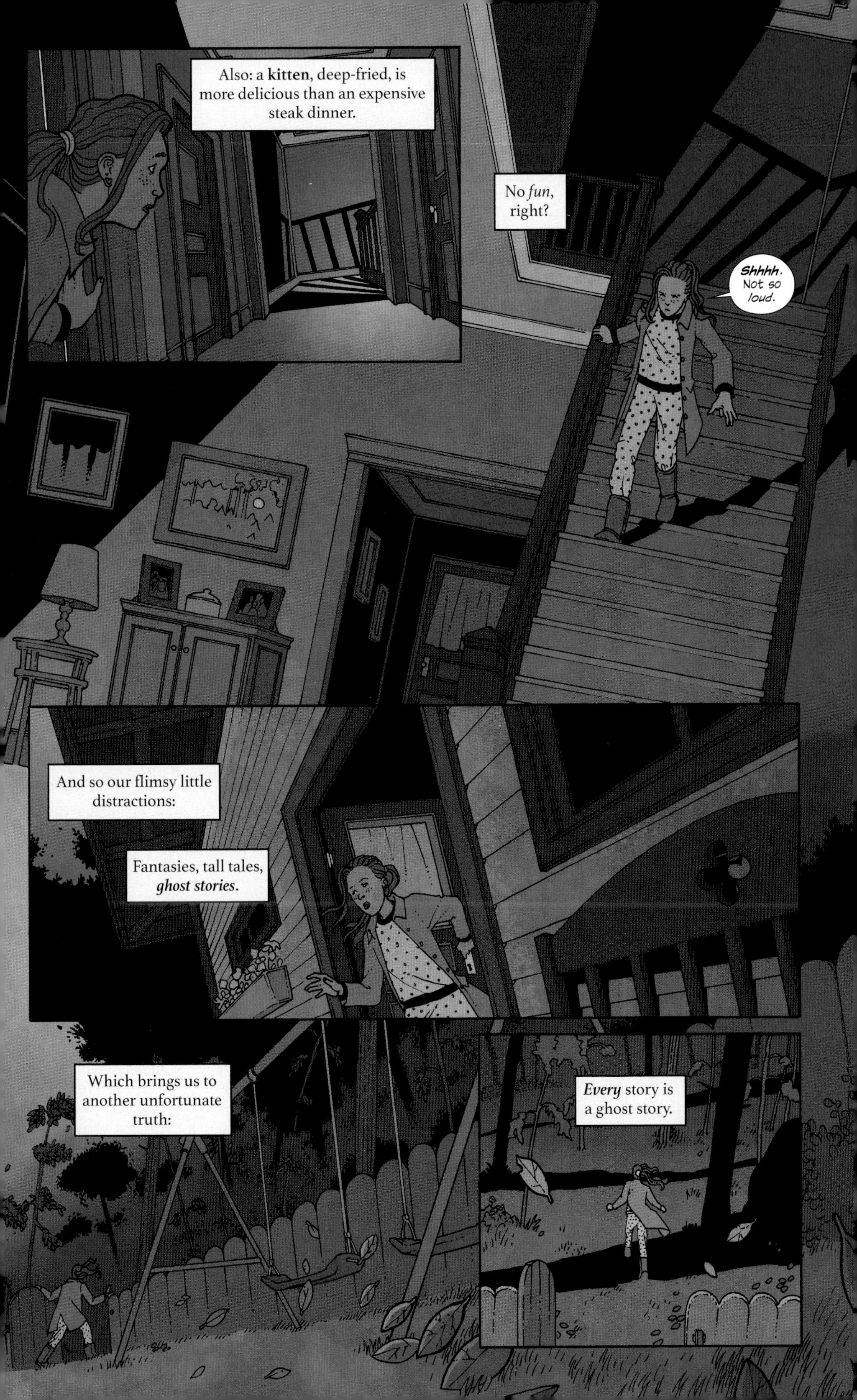
Also: a **kitten**, deep-fried, is more delicious than an expensive steak dinner.
No *fun*, right?
Shhhh. Not so loud.
And so our flimsy little distractions:
Fantasies, tall tales, ***ghost stories***.
Which brings us to another unfortunate truth:
Every story is a ghost story.

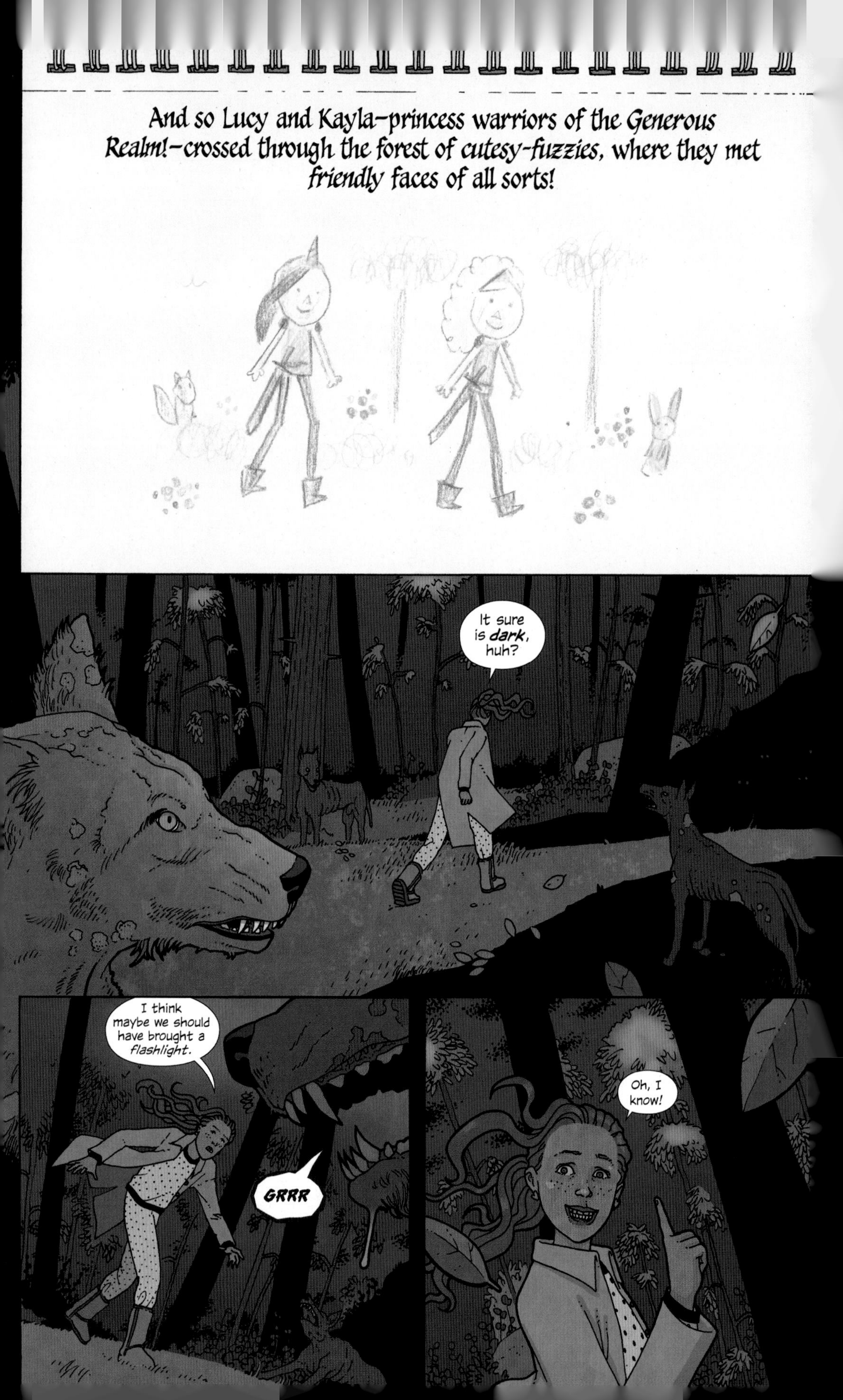
And so Lucy and Kayla–princess warriors of the Generous Realm!–crossed through the forest of cutesy-fuzzies, where they met friendly faces of all sorts!
It sure is dark, huh?
I think maybe we should have brought a flashlight.
GRRR
Oh, I know!

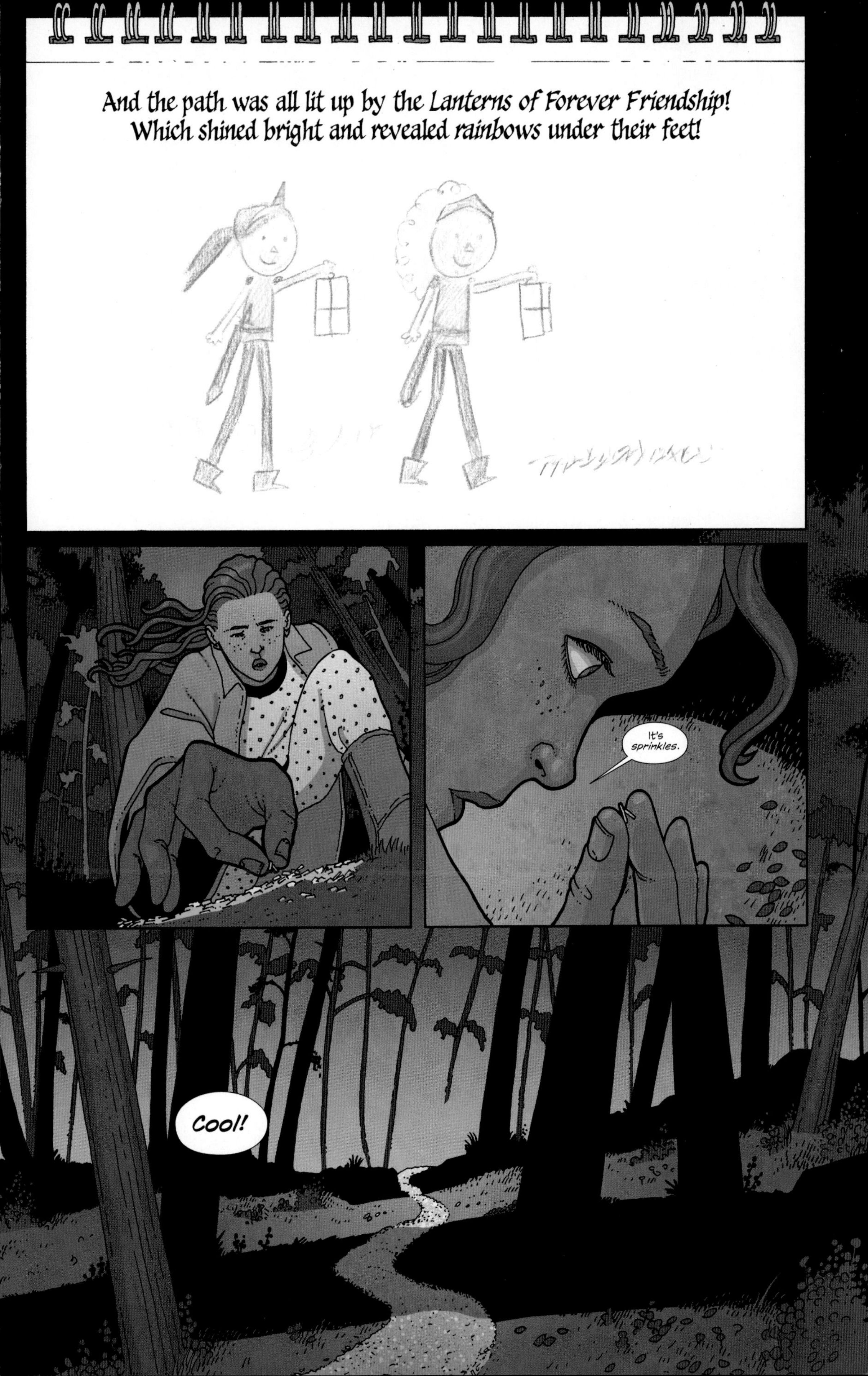
And the path was all lit up by the *Lanterns of Forever Friendship!*
Which shined bright and revealed *rainbows* under their feet!
It's sprinkles.
Cool!

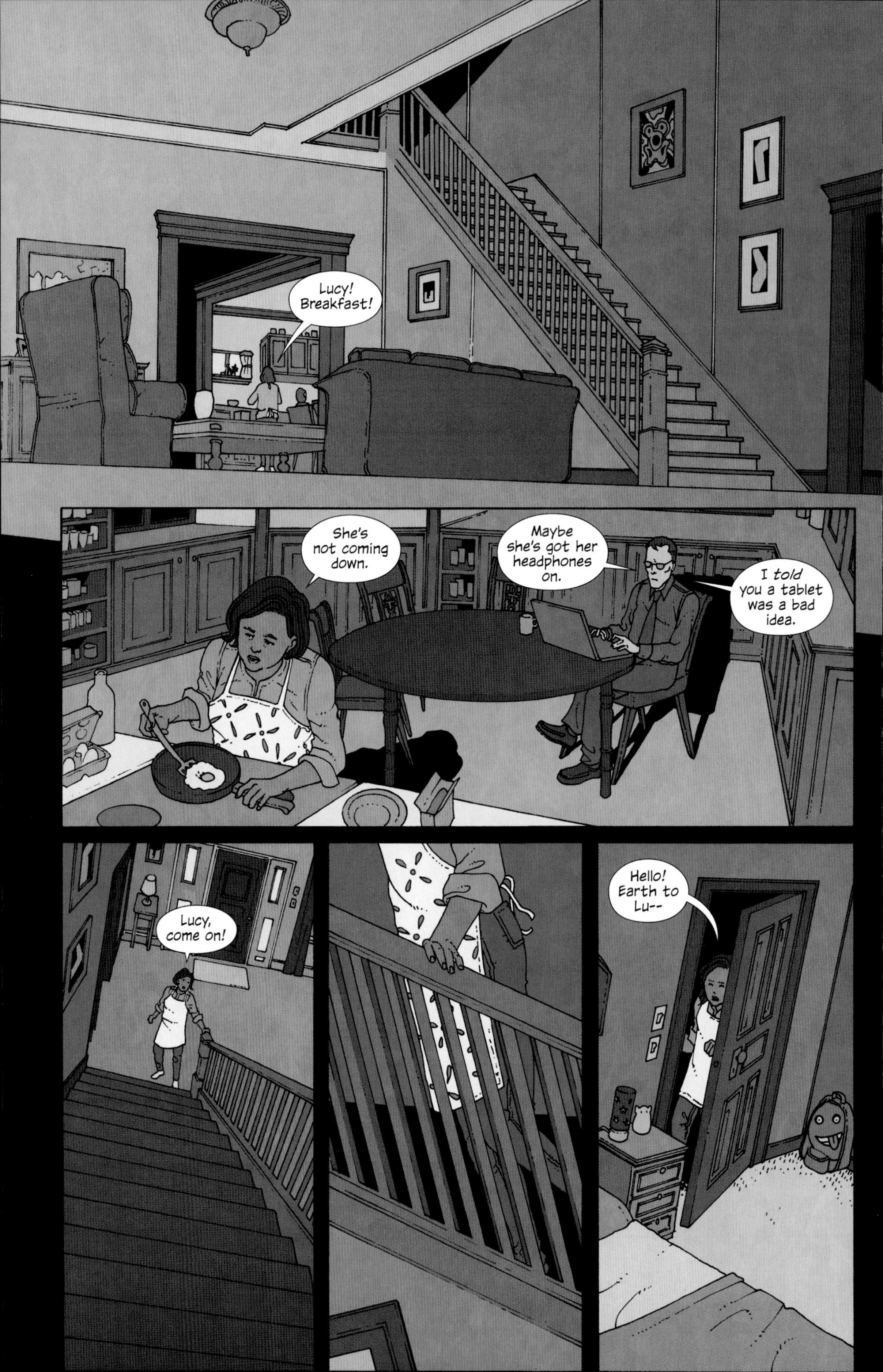
Lucy! Breakfast!
She's not coming down.
Maybe she's got her headphones on.
I *told* you a tablet was a bad idea.
Lucy, come on!
Hello! Earth to Lu--

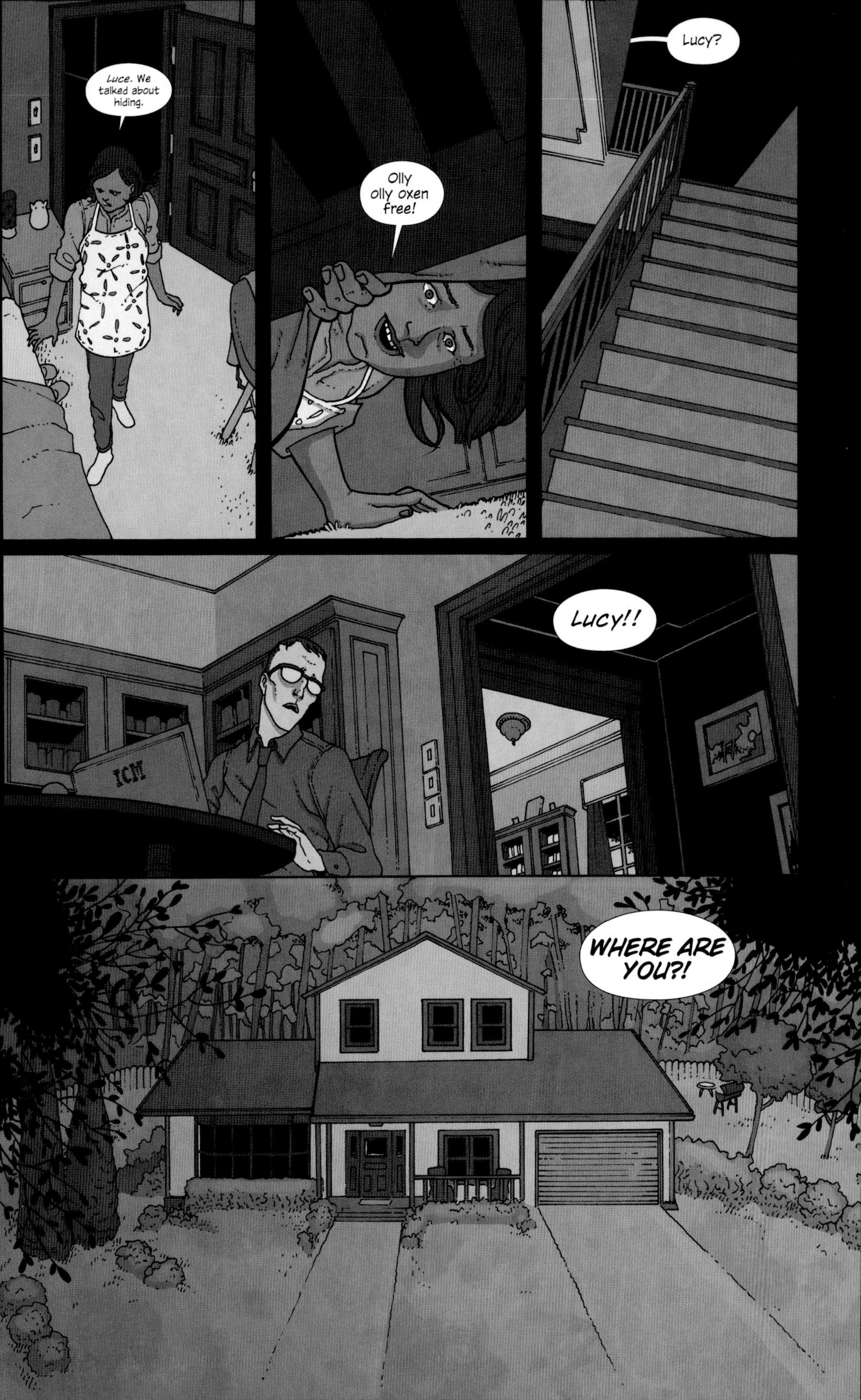
Luce. We talked about hiding.
Olly olly oxen free!
Lucy?
Lucy!!
WHERE ARE YOU?!

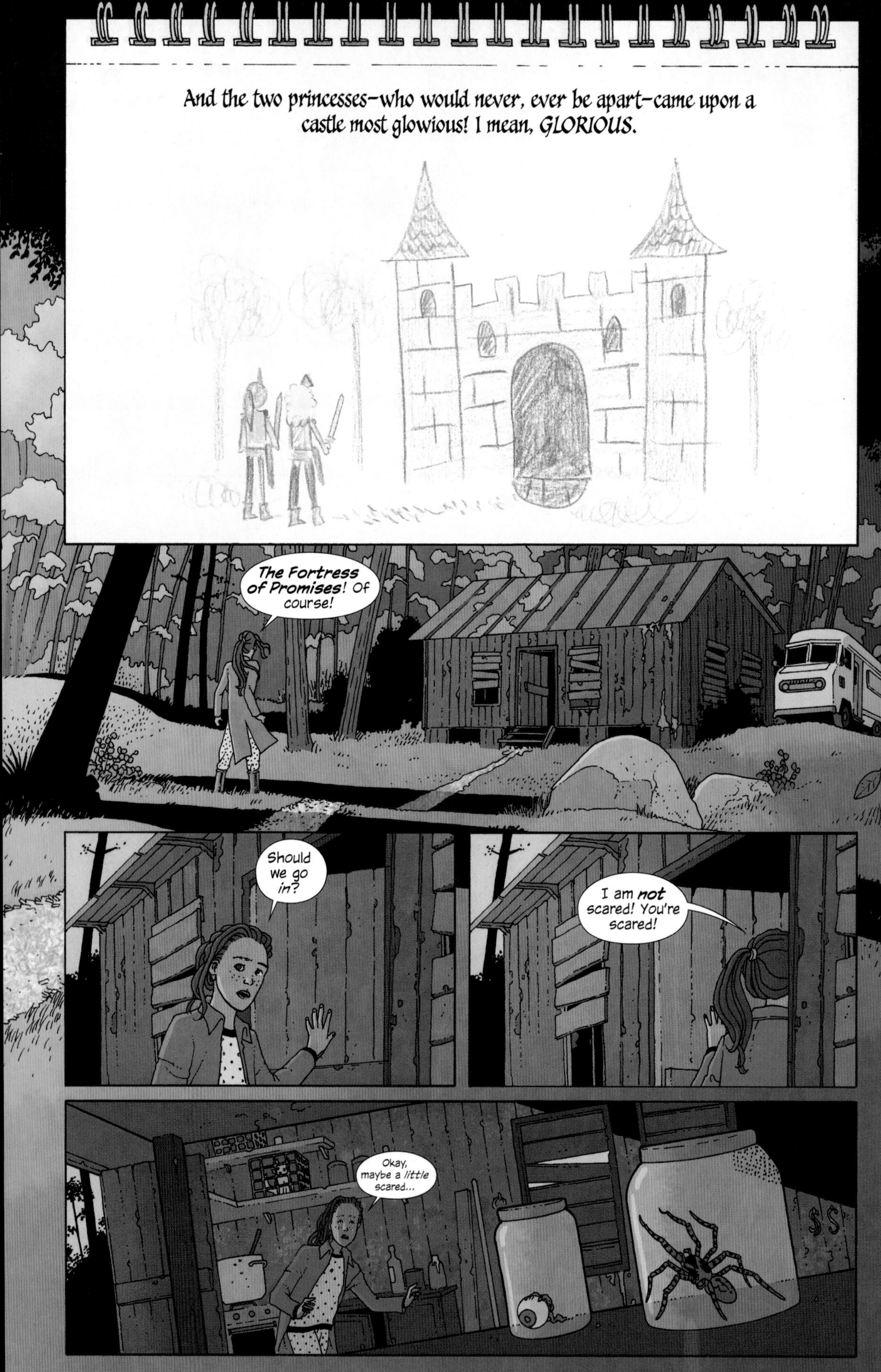
And the two princesses–who would never, ever be apart–came upon a castle most glowious! I mean, GLORIOUS.
The Fortress of Promises! Of course!
Should we go in?
I am not scared! You're scared!
Okay, maybe a little scared...

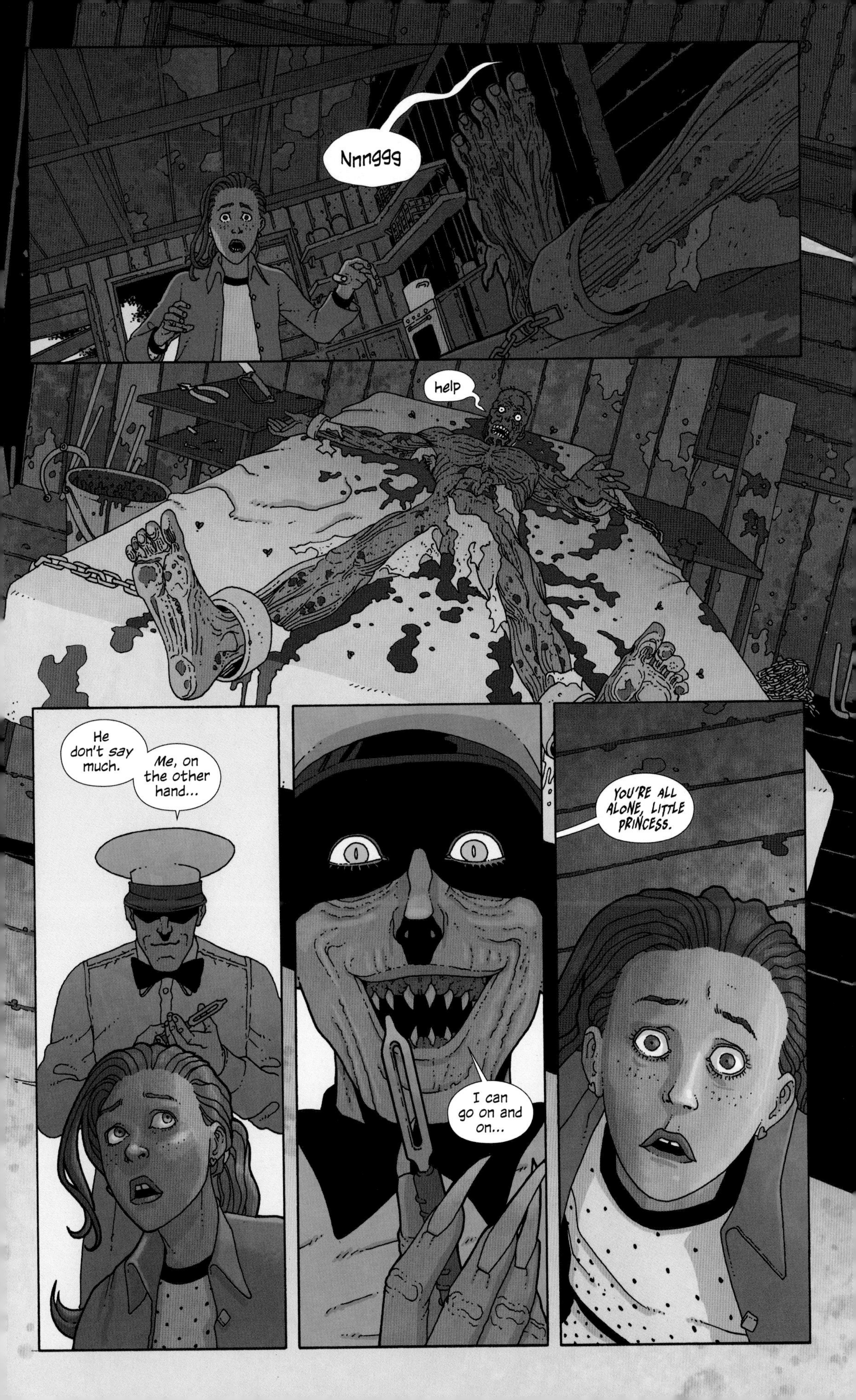
Nnnggg
help
He don't say much.
Me, on the other hand...
I can go on and on...
YOU'RE ALL ALONE, LITTLE PRINCESS.

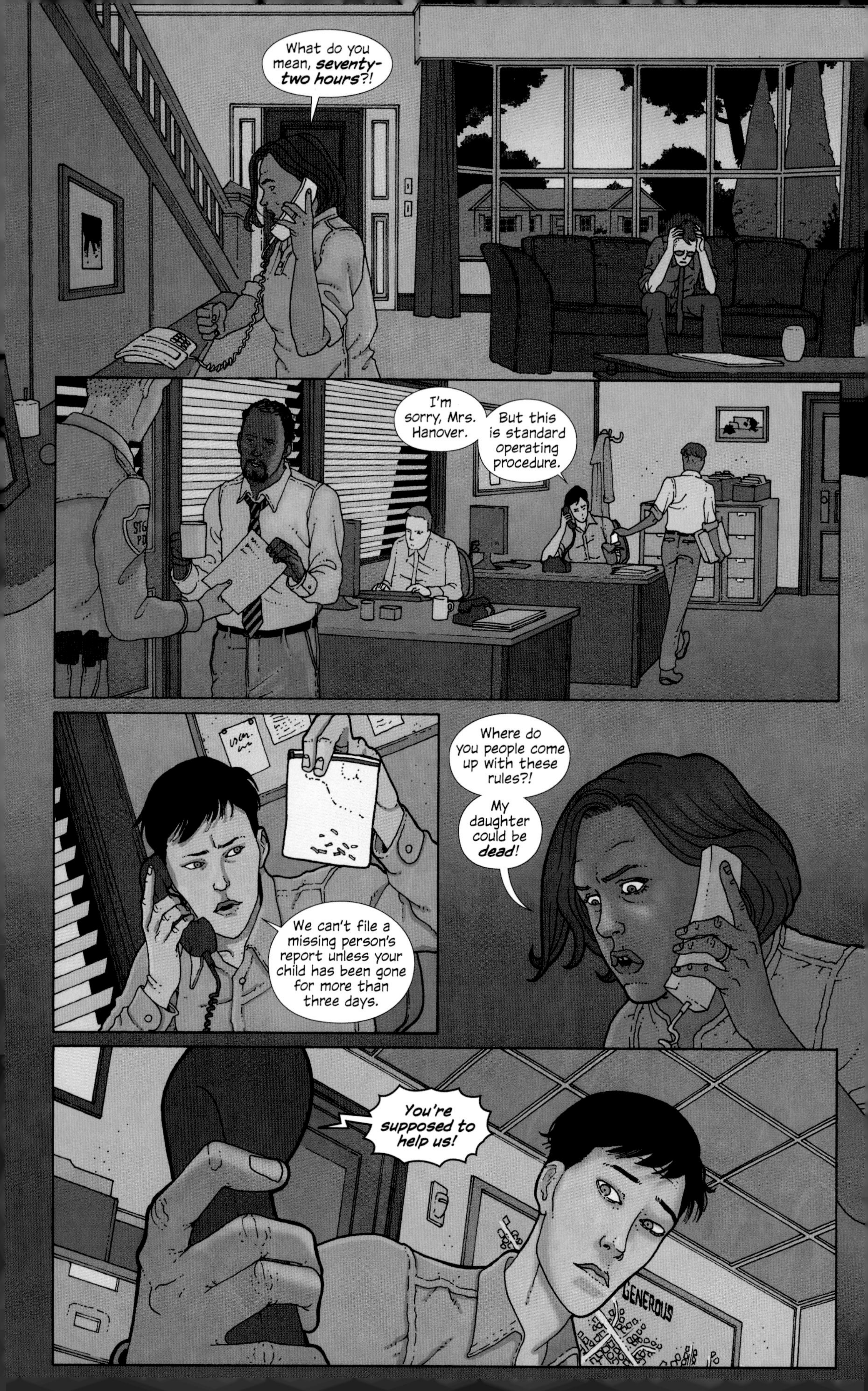
What do you mean, *seventy-two hours*?!
I'm sorry, Mrs. Hanover.
But this is standard operating procedure.
We can't file a missing person's report unless your child has been gone for more than three days.
Where do you people come up with these rules?!
My daughter could be *dead*!
You're supposed to help us!
GENEROUS

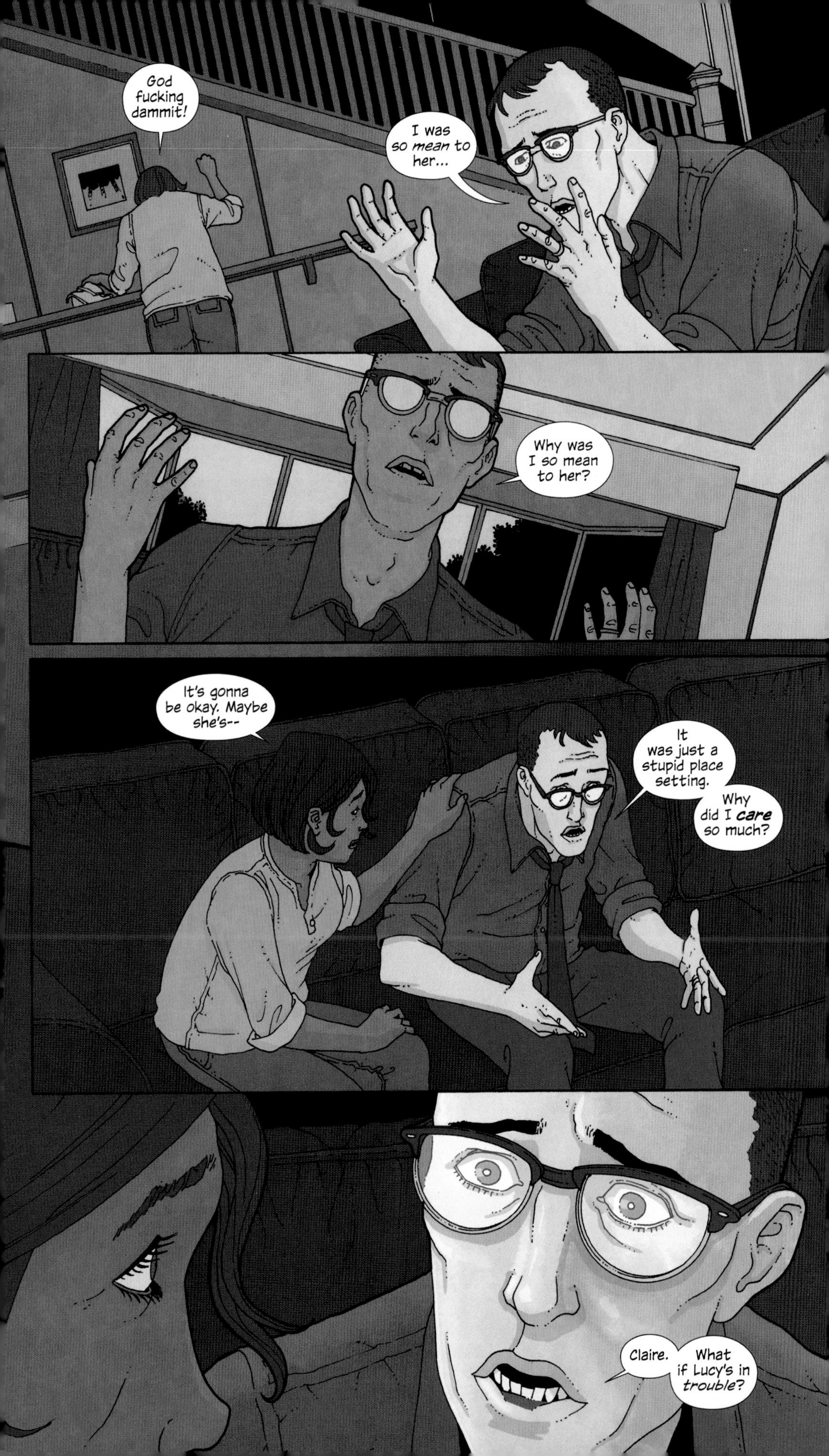
God fucking dammit!
I was so *mean* to her...
Why was I so mean to her?
It's gonna be okay. Maybe she's--
It was just a stupid place setting.
Why did I ***care*** so much?
Claire.
What if Lucy's in *trouble*?

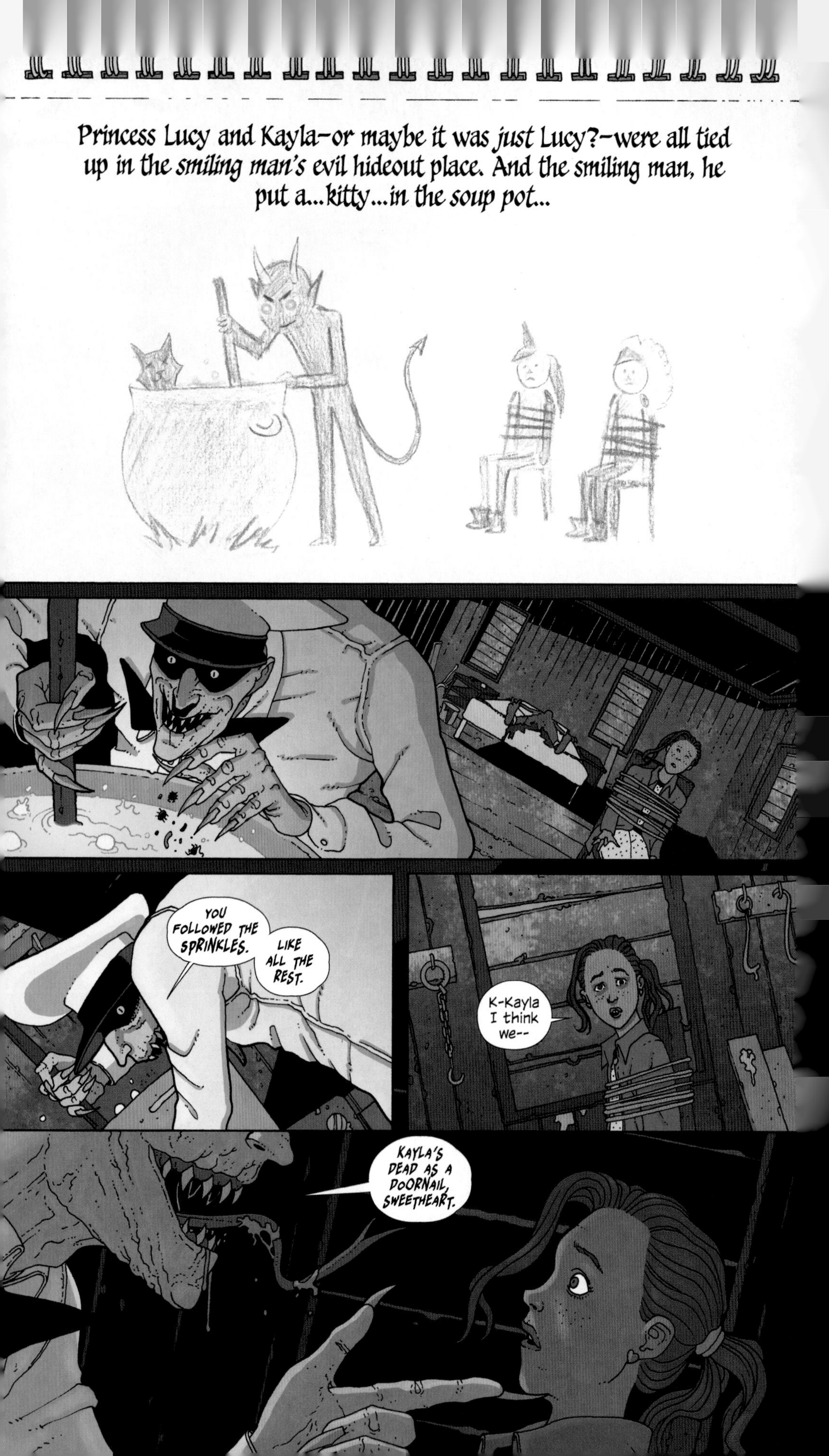

Princess Lucy and Kayla—or maybe it was *just* Lucy?—were all tied up in the *smiling man's* evil hideout place. And the smiling man, he put a...kitty...in the *soup pot*...
YOU FOLLOWED THE SPRINKLES.
LIKE ALL THE REST.
K-Kayla I think we--
KAYLA'S DEAD AS A DOORNAIL, SWEETHEART.

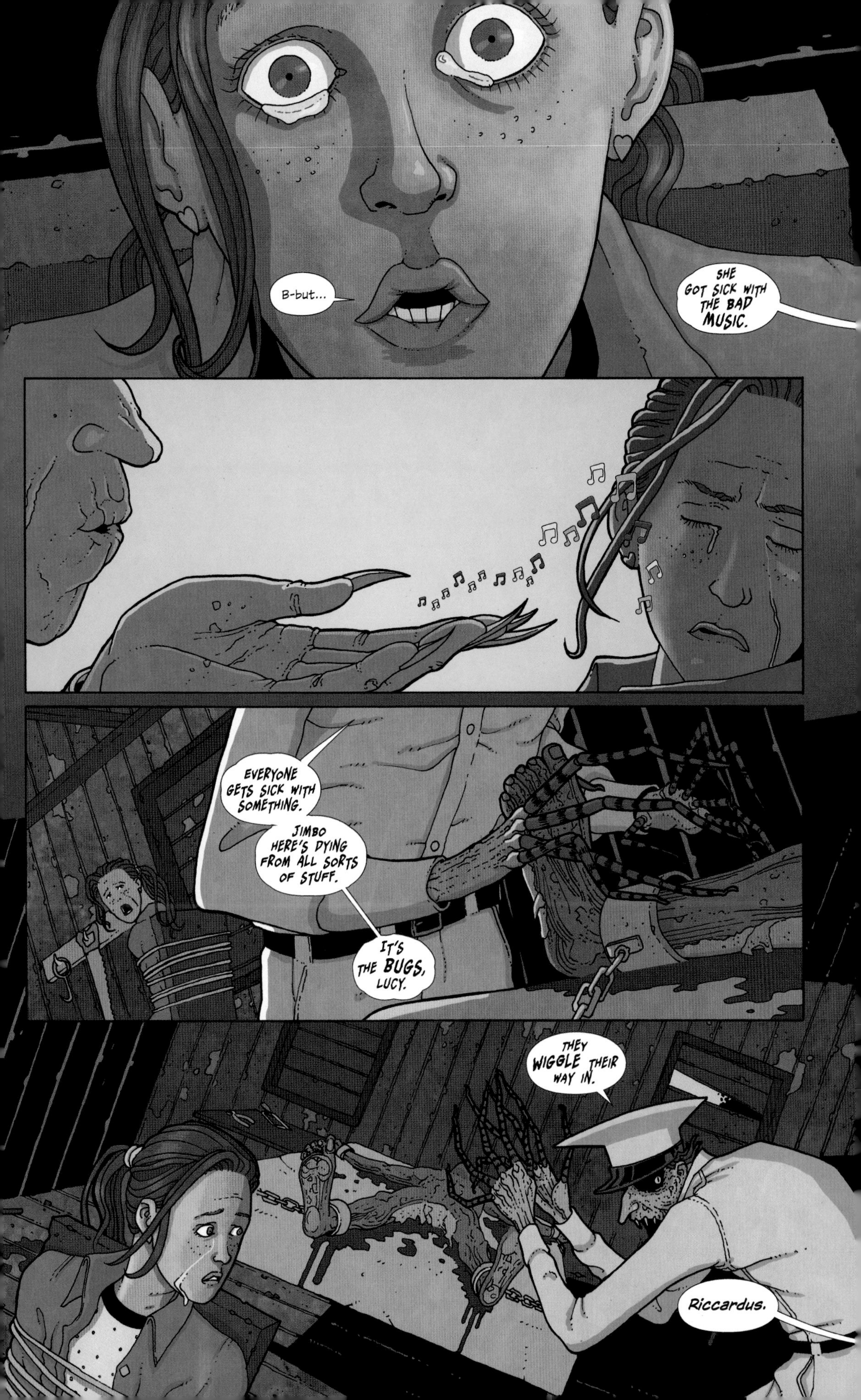
B-but...
SHE GOT SICK WITH THE BAD MUSIC.
EVERYONE GETS SICK WITH SOMETHING.
JIMBO HERE'S DYING FROM ALL SORTS OF STUFF.
IT'S THE BUGS, LUCY.
THEY WIGGLE THEIR WAY IN.
Riccardus.

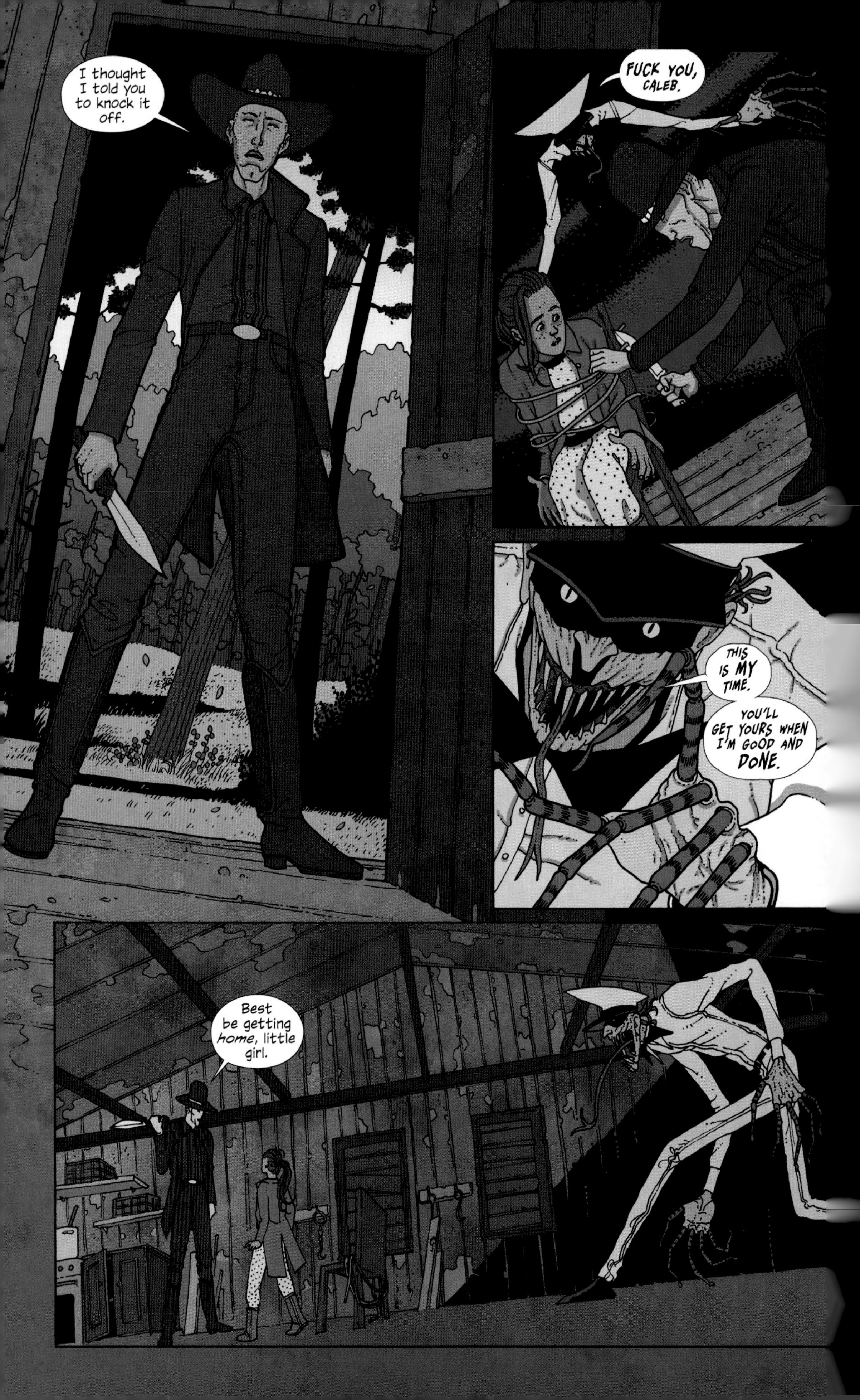

I thought I told you to knock it off.
FUCK YOU, CALEB.
THIS IS MY TIME.
YOU'LL GET YOURS WHEN I'M GOOD AND DONE.
Best be getting *home*, little girl.

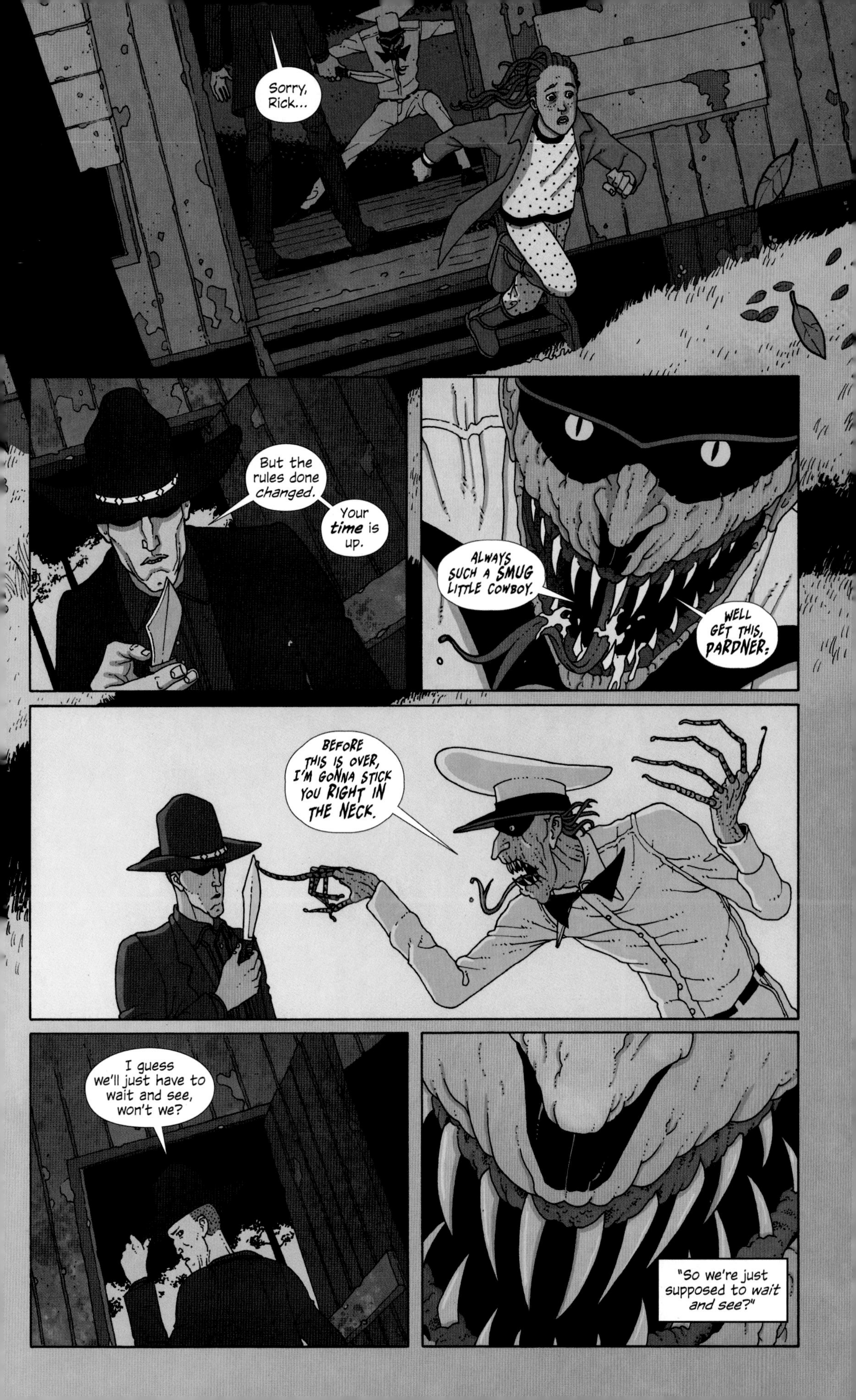
Sorry, Rick...
But the rules done changed.
Your time is up.
ALWAYS SUCH A SMUG LITTLE COWBOY.
WELL GET THIS, PARDNER:
BEFORE THIS IS OVER, I'M GONNA STICK YOU RIGHT IN THE NECK.
I guess we'll just have to wait and see, won't we?
"So we're just supposed to wait and see?"

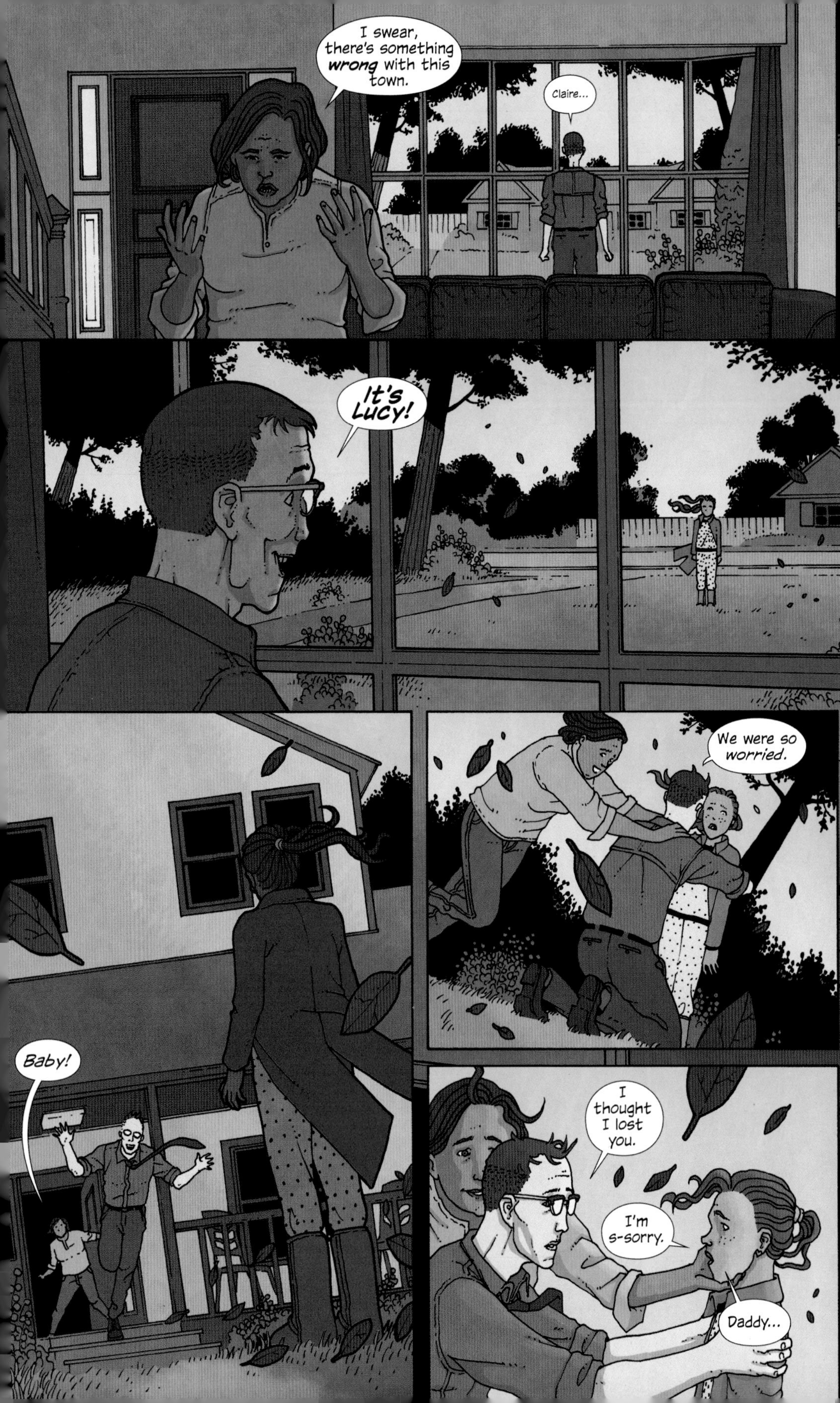
I swear, there's something *wrong* with this town.
Claire...
It's Lucy!
Baby!
We were so worried.
I thought I lost you.
I'm s-sorry.
Daddy...

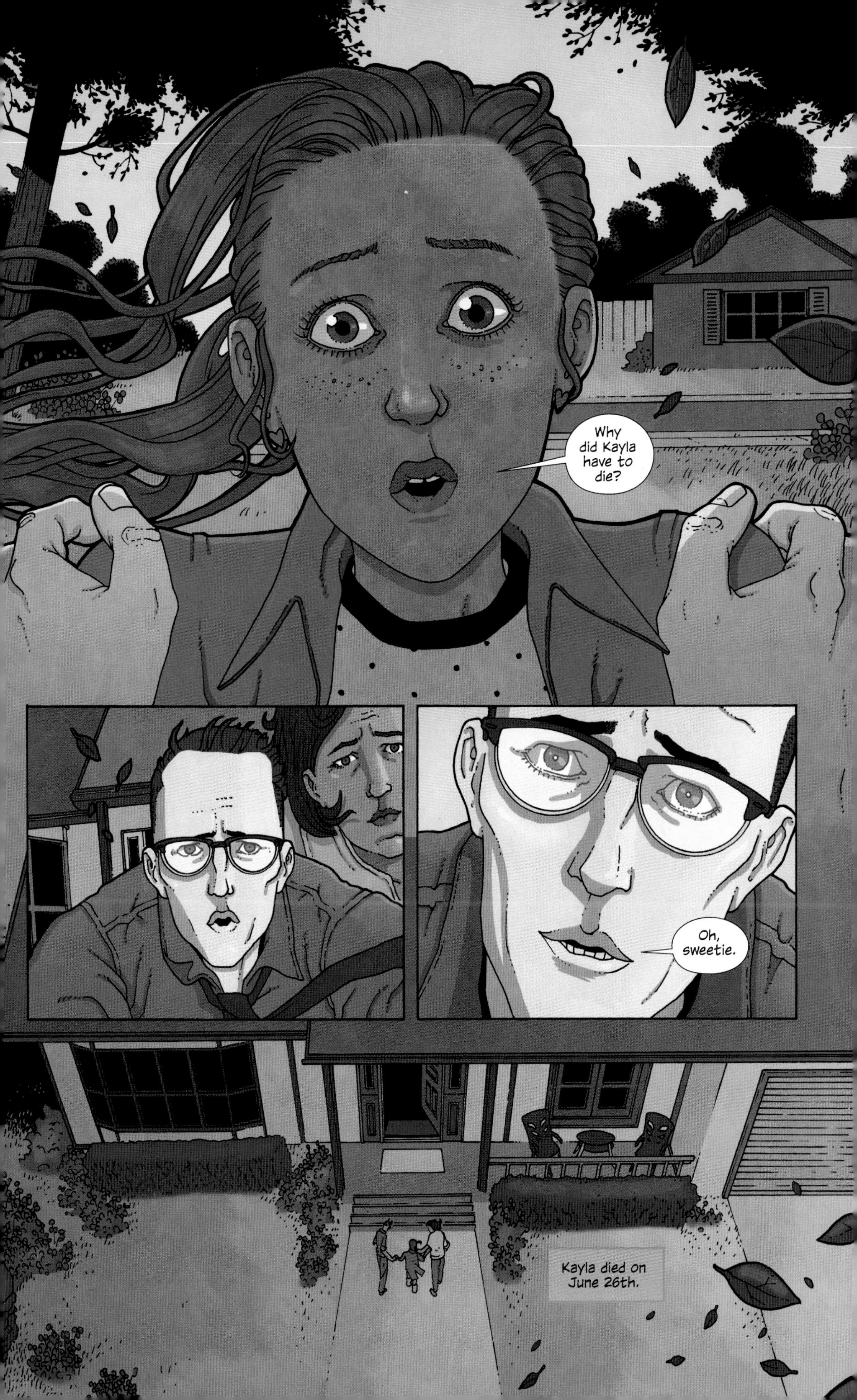
Why did Kayla have to die?
Oh, sweetie.
Kayla died on June 26th.

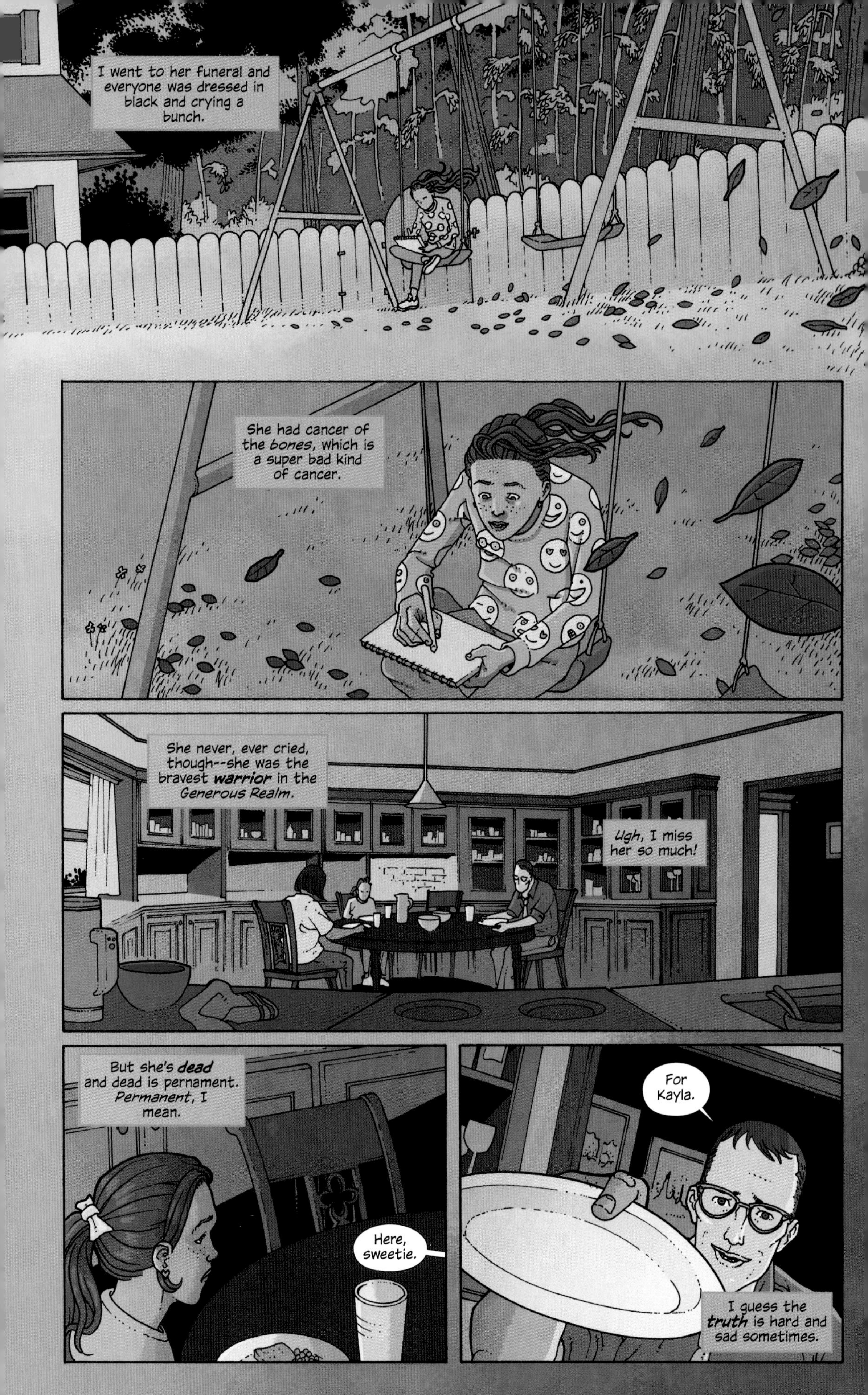
I went to her funeral and everyone was dressed in black and crying a bunch.
She had cancer of the *bones*, which is a super bad kind of cancer.
She never, ever cried, though--she was the bravest **warrior** in the *Generous Realm*.
Ugh, I miss her so much!
But she's **dead** and dead is pernament. *Permanent*, I mean.
Here, sweetie.
For Kayla.
I guess the **truth** is hard and sad sometimes.

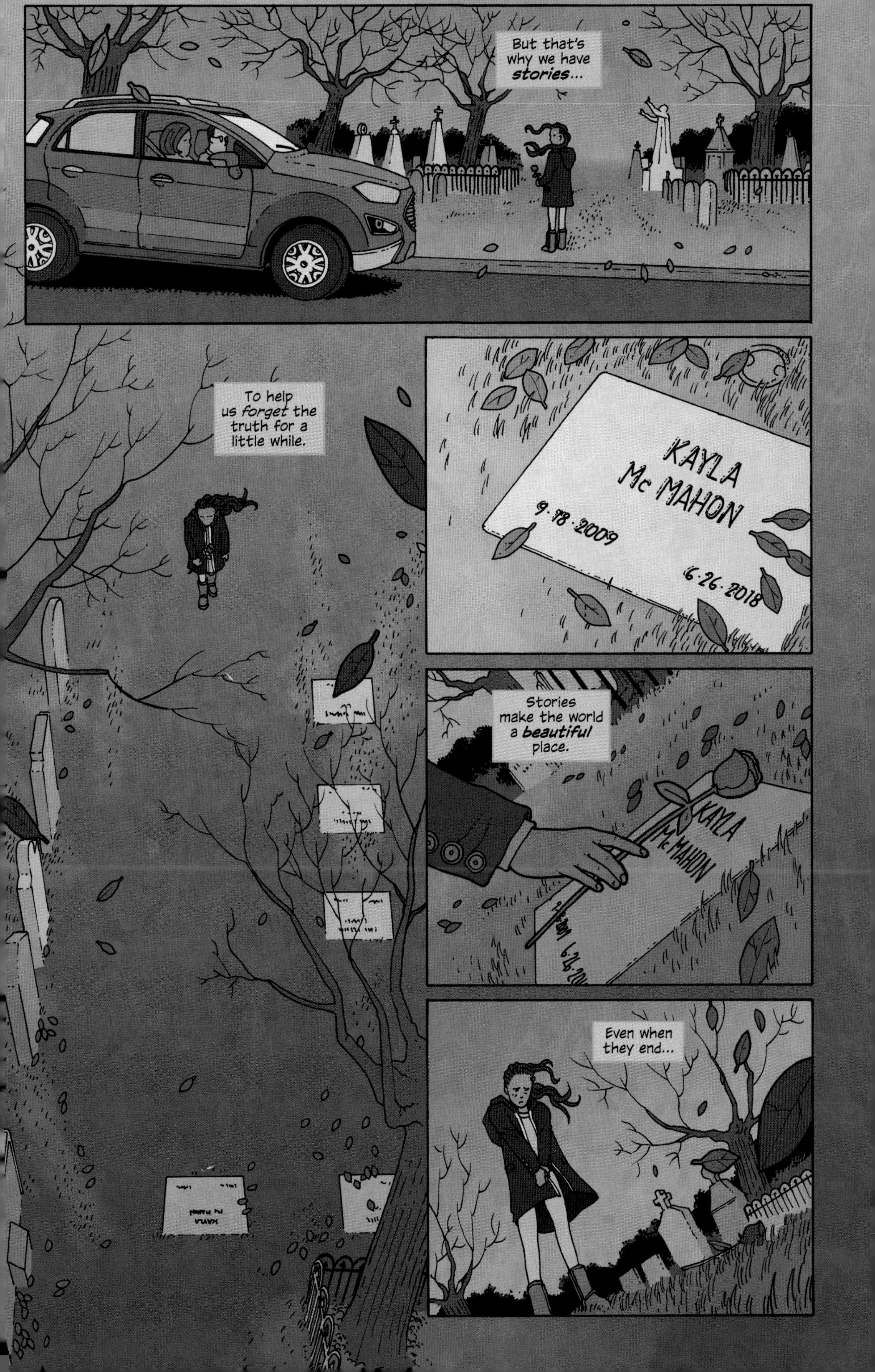
But that's why we have *stories*...
To help us *forget* the truth for a little while.
KAYLA
Mc MAHON
9·18·2009
6·26·2018
Stories make the world a *beautiful* place.
Even when they end...

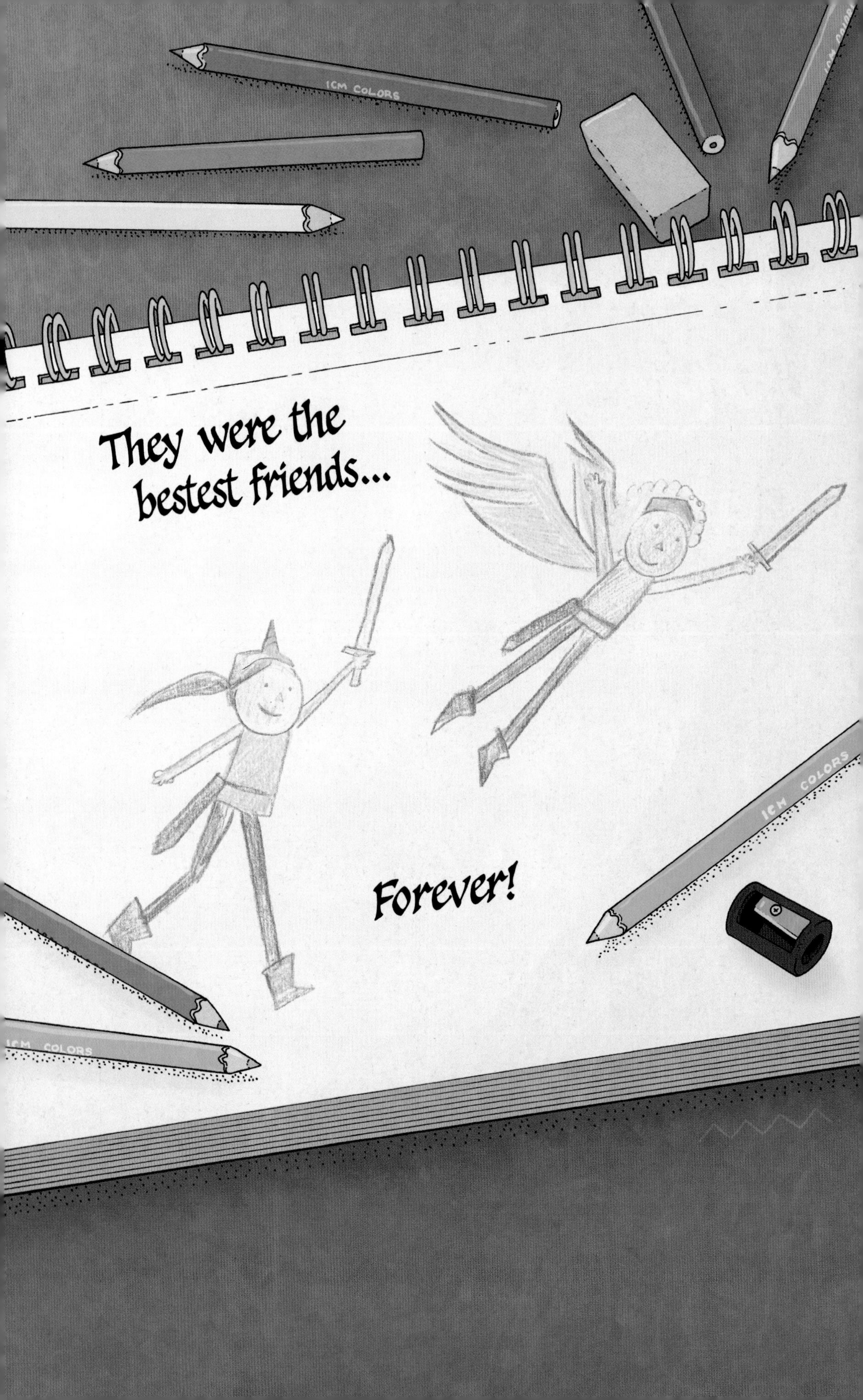
They were the bestest friends...
Forever!
ICM COLORS
ICM COLORS
ICM COLORS
ICM COLORS

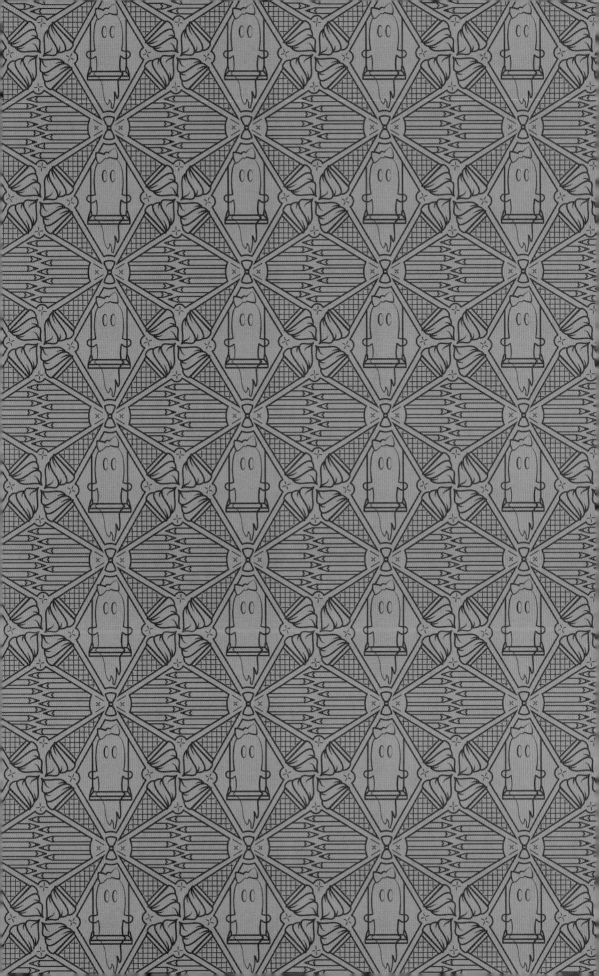

Chapter Eight

Emergencies

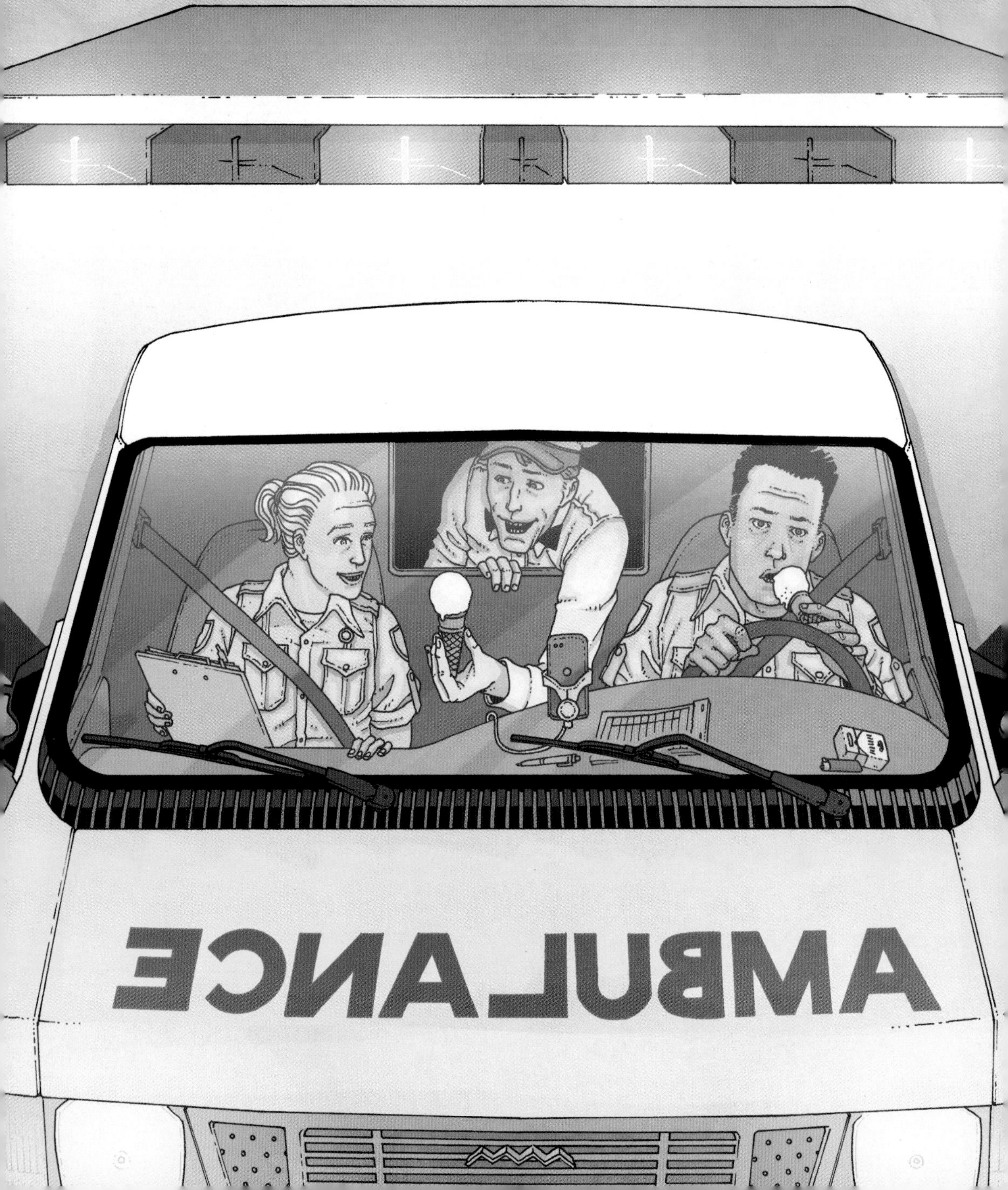
AMBULANCE

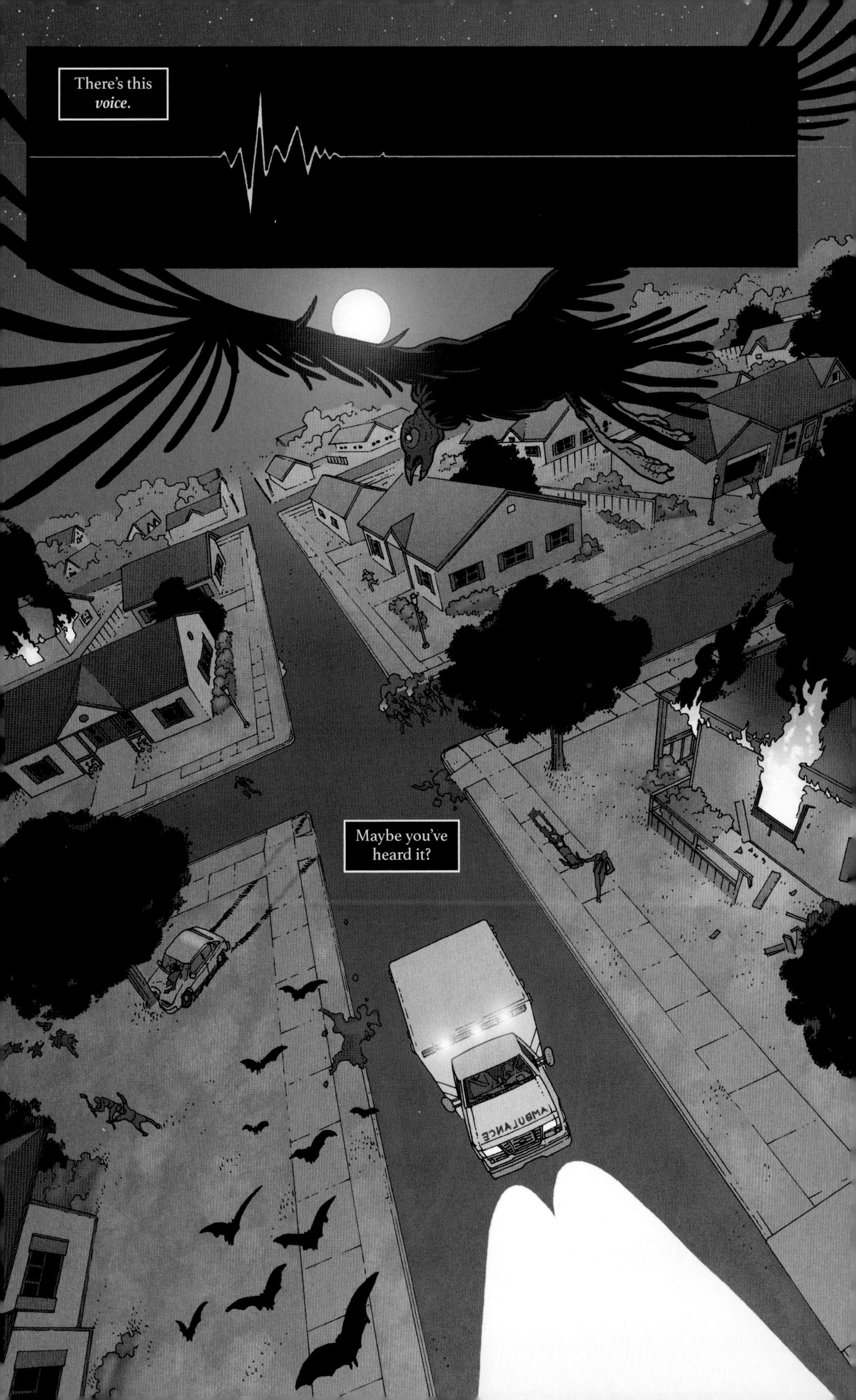
There's this *voice.*
Maybe you've heard it?
AMBULANCE

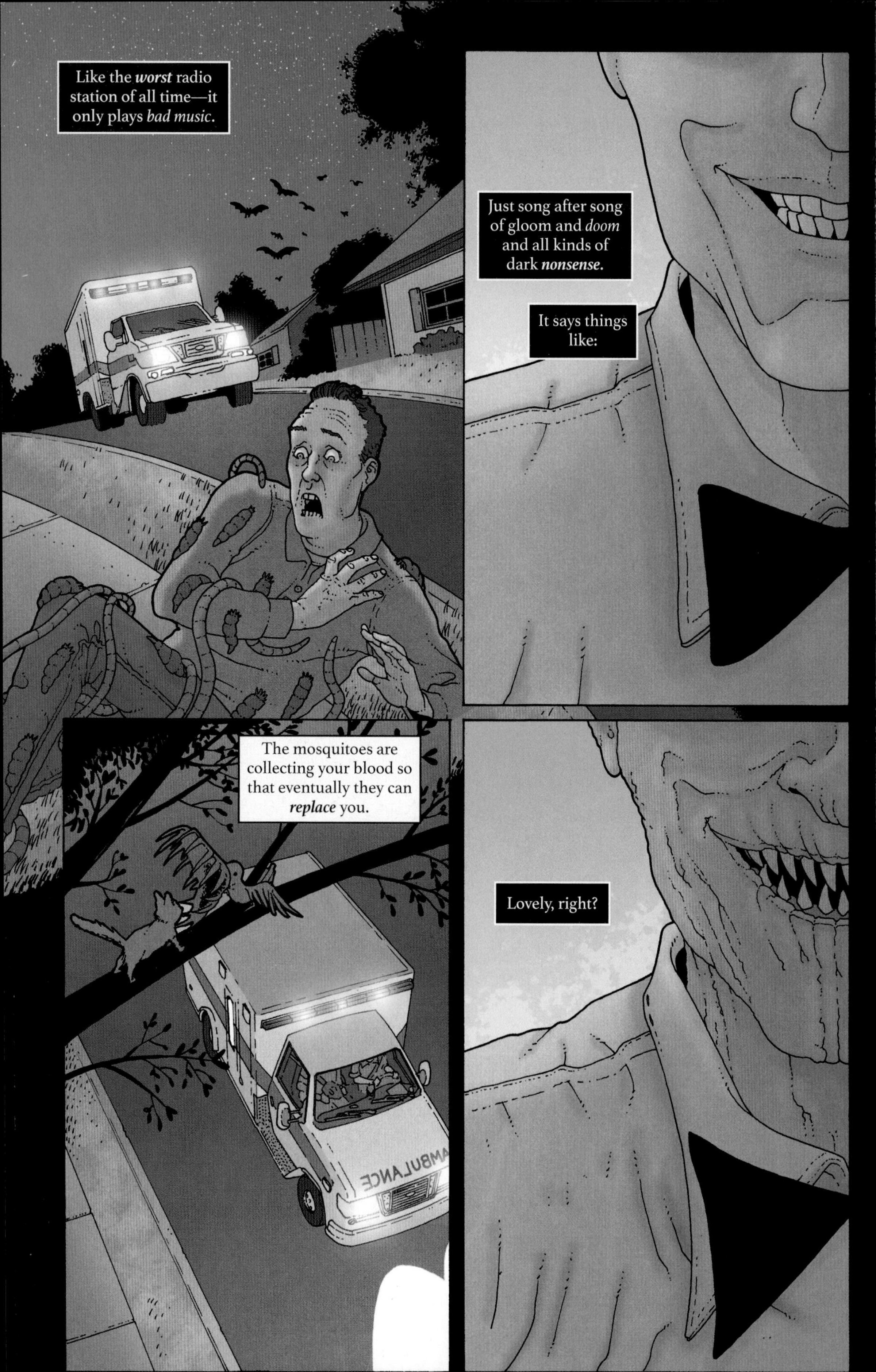
Like the *worst* radio station of all time—it only plays *bad music*.
Just song after song of gloom and *doom* and all kinds of dark *nonsense*.
It says things like:
The mosquitoes are collecting your blood so that eventually they can *replace* you.
Lovely, right?
AMBULANCE

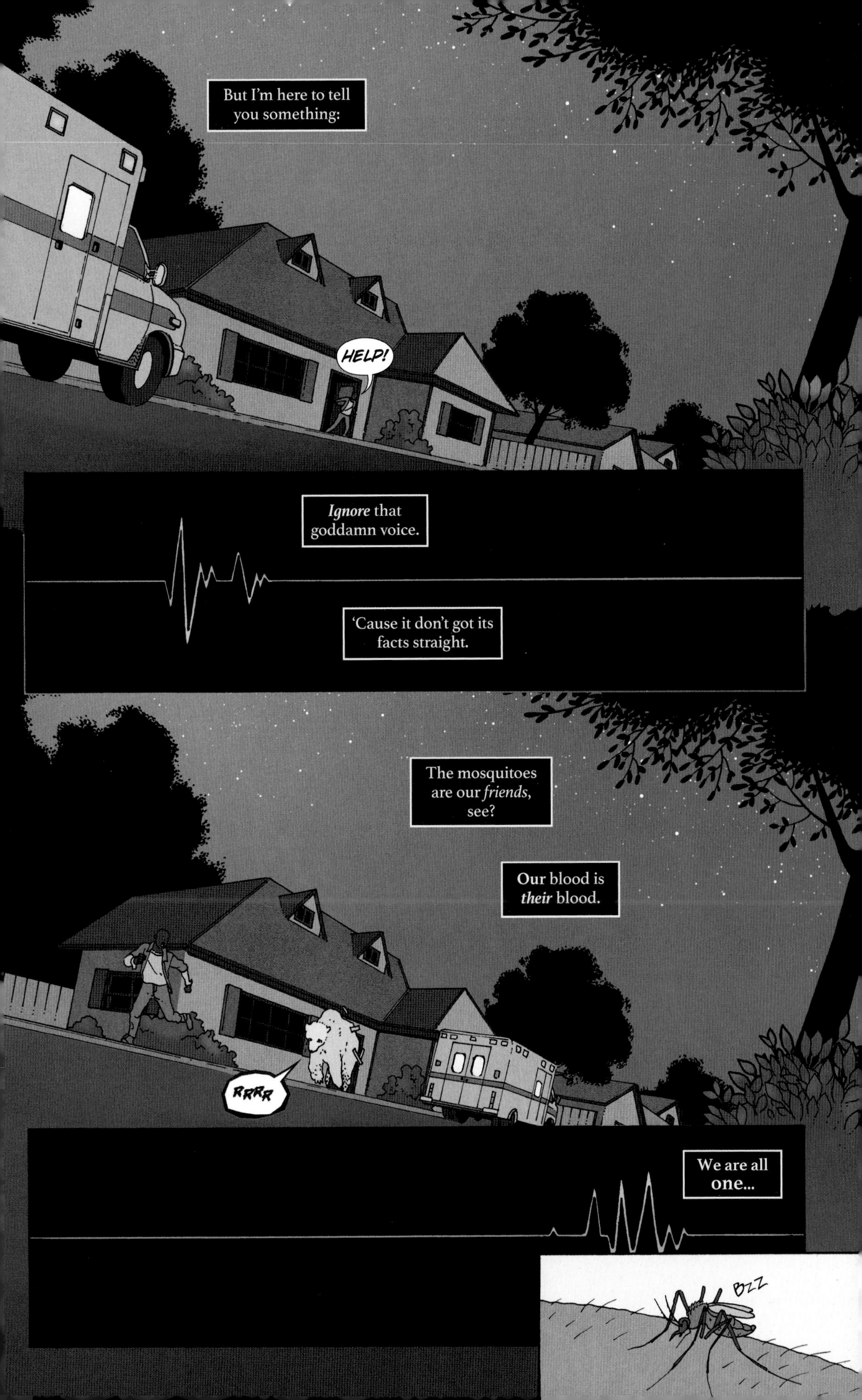
But I'm here to tell you something:
HELP!
Ignore that goddamn voice.
'Cause it don't got its facts straight.
The mosquitoes are our *friends*, see?
Our blood is *their* blood.
RRRR
We are all one...
BZZ

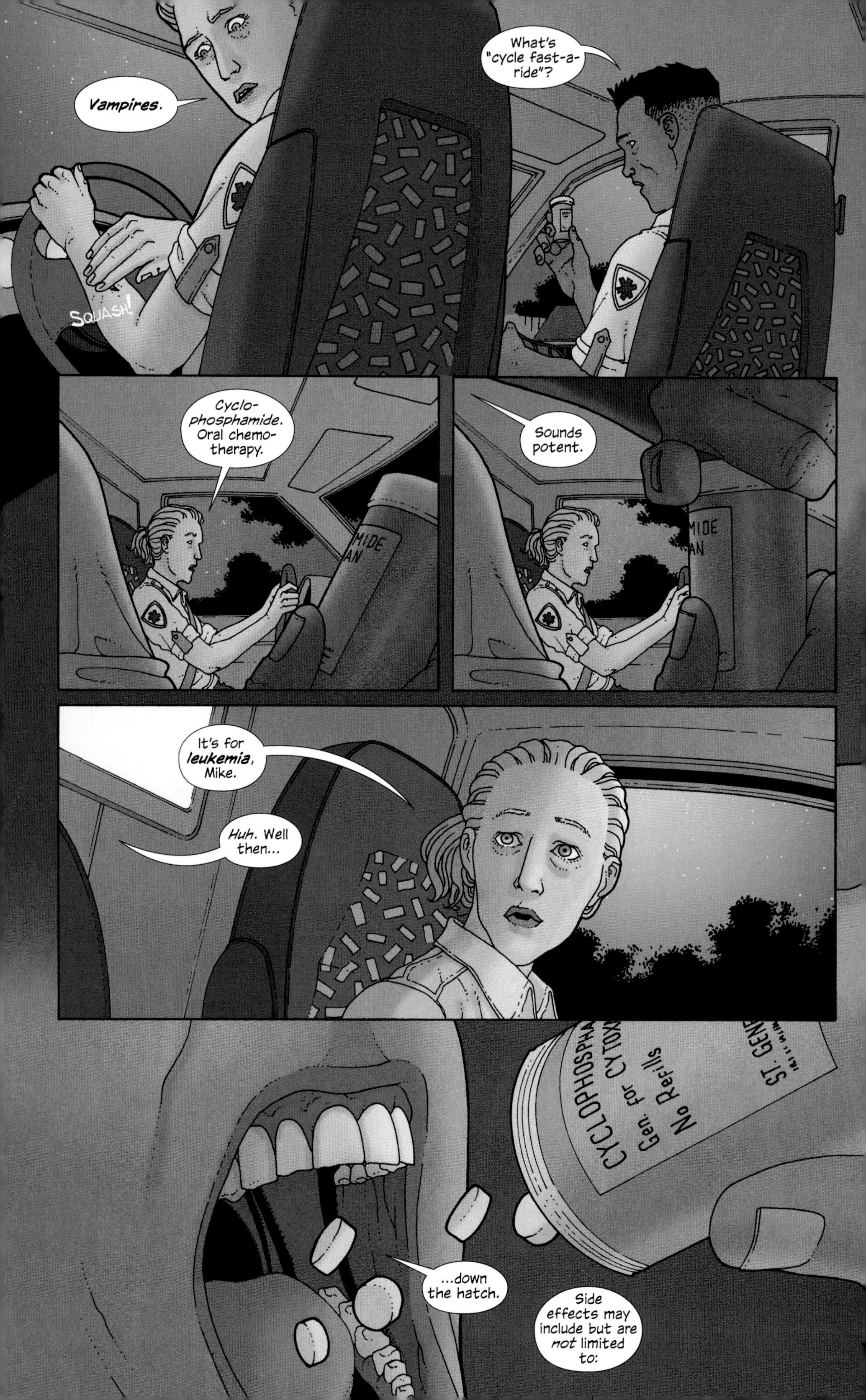
Vampires.
What's "cycle fast-a-ride"?
SQUASH!
Cyclo-phosphamide. Oral chemo-therapy.
Sounds potent.
MIDE
AN
It's for *leukemia*, Mike.
Huh. Well then...
CYCLOPHOSPHA
Gen. for CYTOX
No Refills
ST. GENE
...down the hatch.
Side effects may include but are *not* limited to:

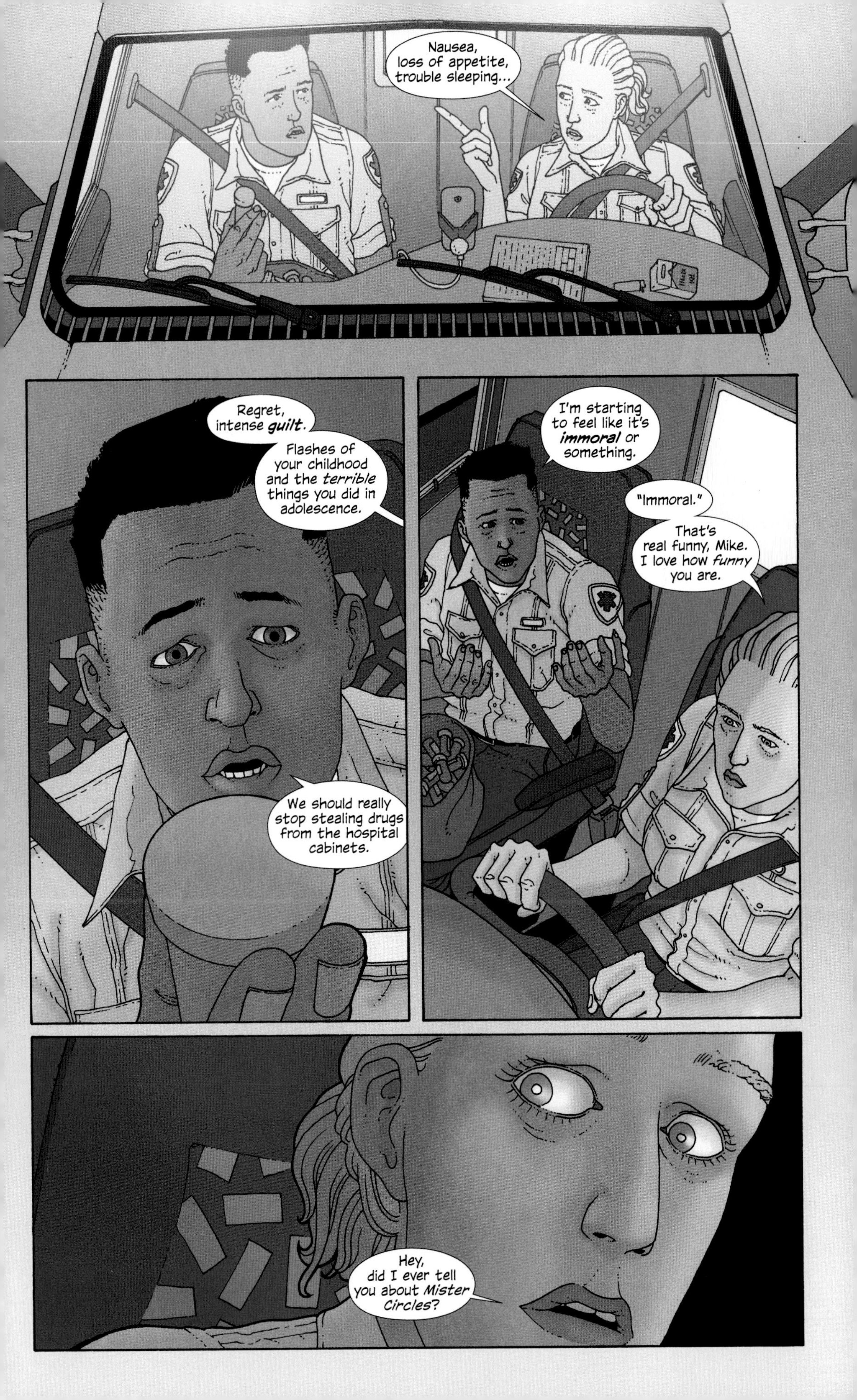
Nausea, loss of appetite, trouble sleeping...
Regret, intense *guilt*.
Flashes of your childhood and the *terrible* things you did in adolescence.
We should really stop stealing drugs from the hospital cabinets.
I'm starting to feel like it's *immoral* or something.
"Immoral."
That's real funny, Mike. I love how *funny* you are.
Hey, did I ever tell you about *Mister Circles*?

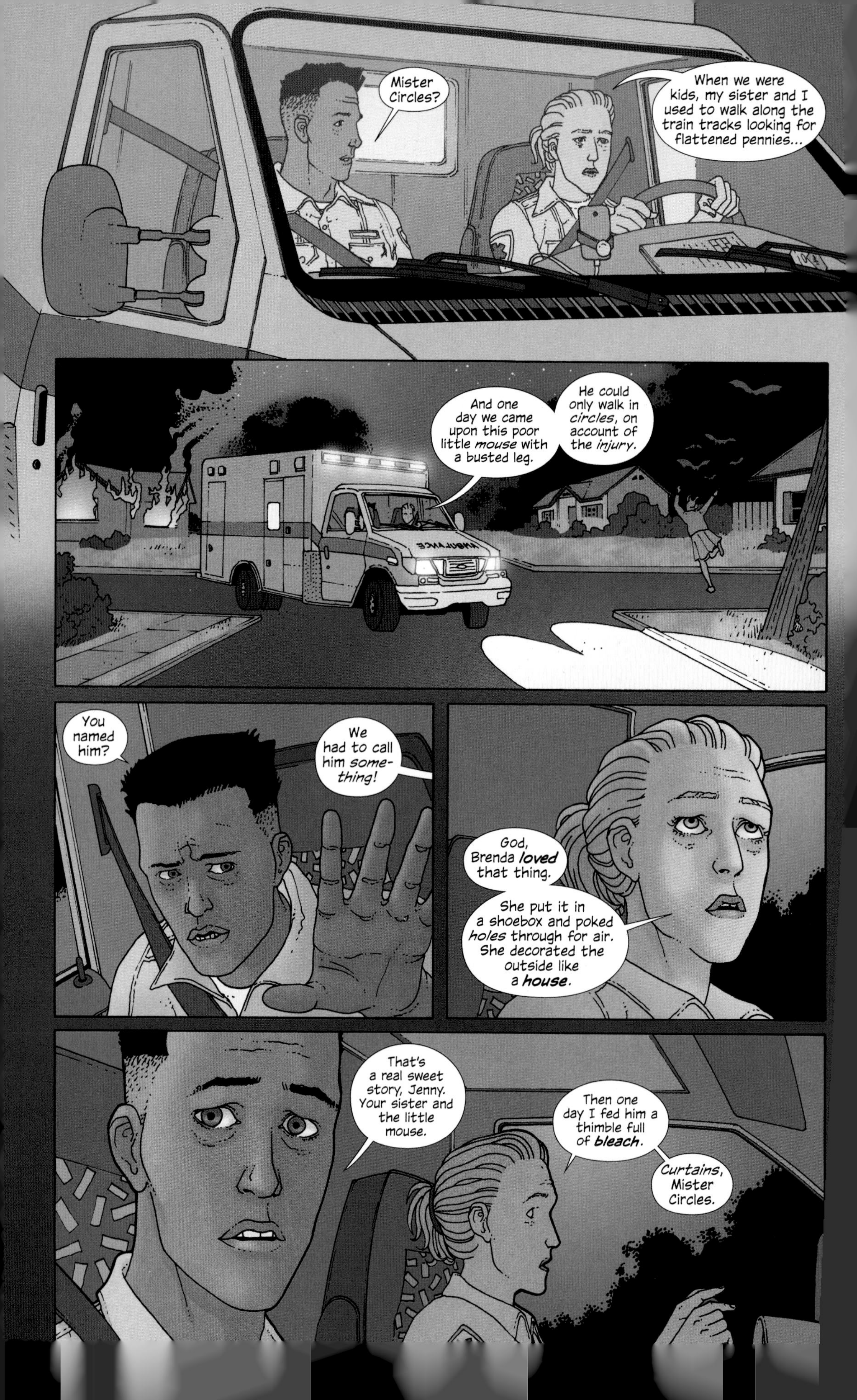
Mister Circles?
When we were kids, my sister and I used to walk along the train tracks looking for flattened pennies...
And one day we came upon this poor little *mouse* with a busted leg.
He could only walk in *circles*, on account of the *injury*.
AMBULANCE
You named him?
We had to call him *some-thing*!
God, Brenda ***loved*** that thing.
She put it in a shoebox and poked *holes* through for air. She decorated the outside like a ***house***.
That's a real sweet story, Jenny. Your sister and the little mouse.
Then one day I fed him a thimble full of ***bleach***.
Curtains, Mister Circles.

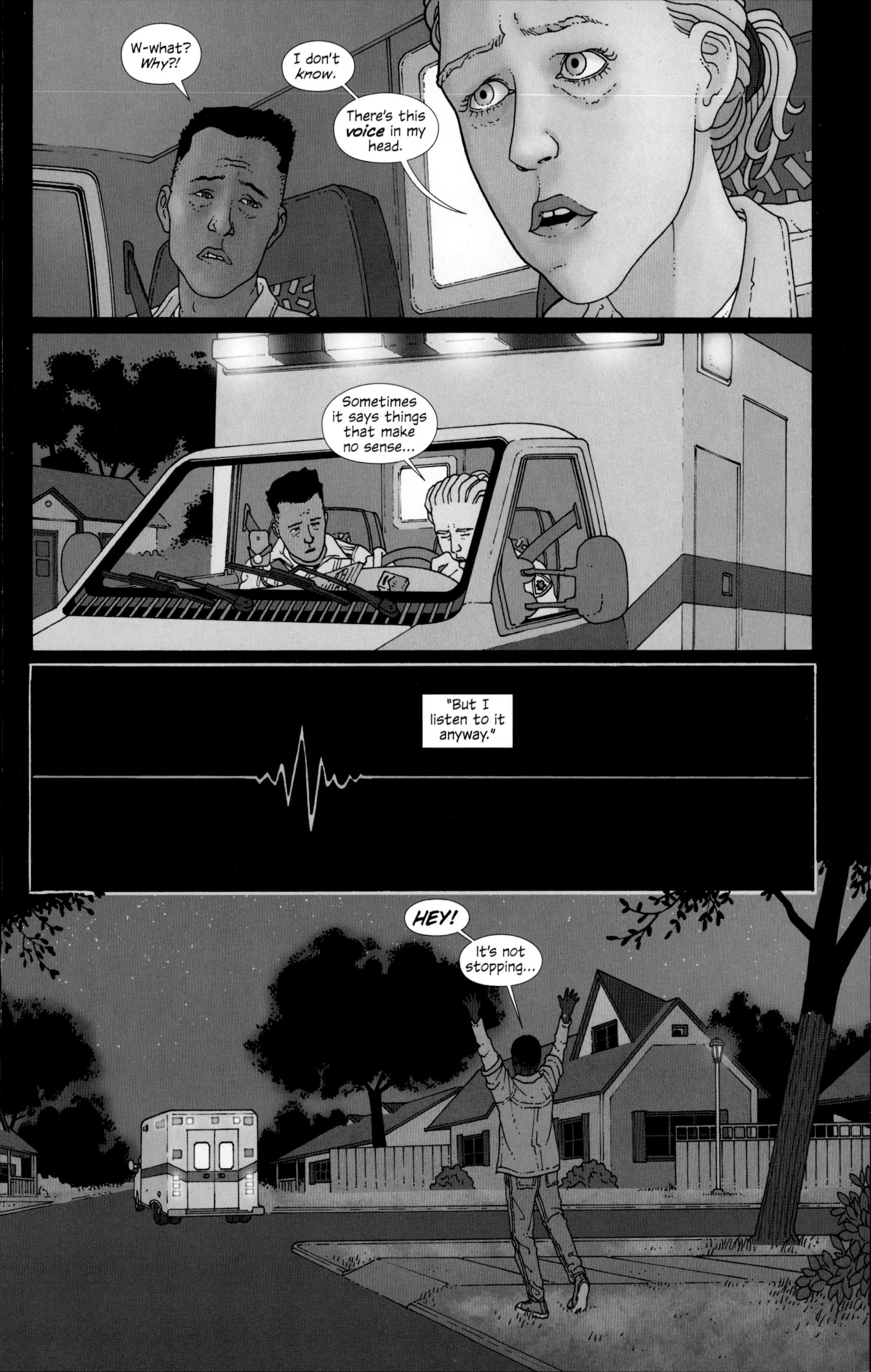
W-what? Why?!
I don't know.
There's this voice in my head.
Sometimes it says things that make no sense...
"But I listen to it anyway."
HEY!
It's not stopping...

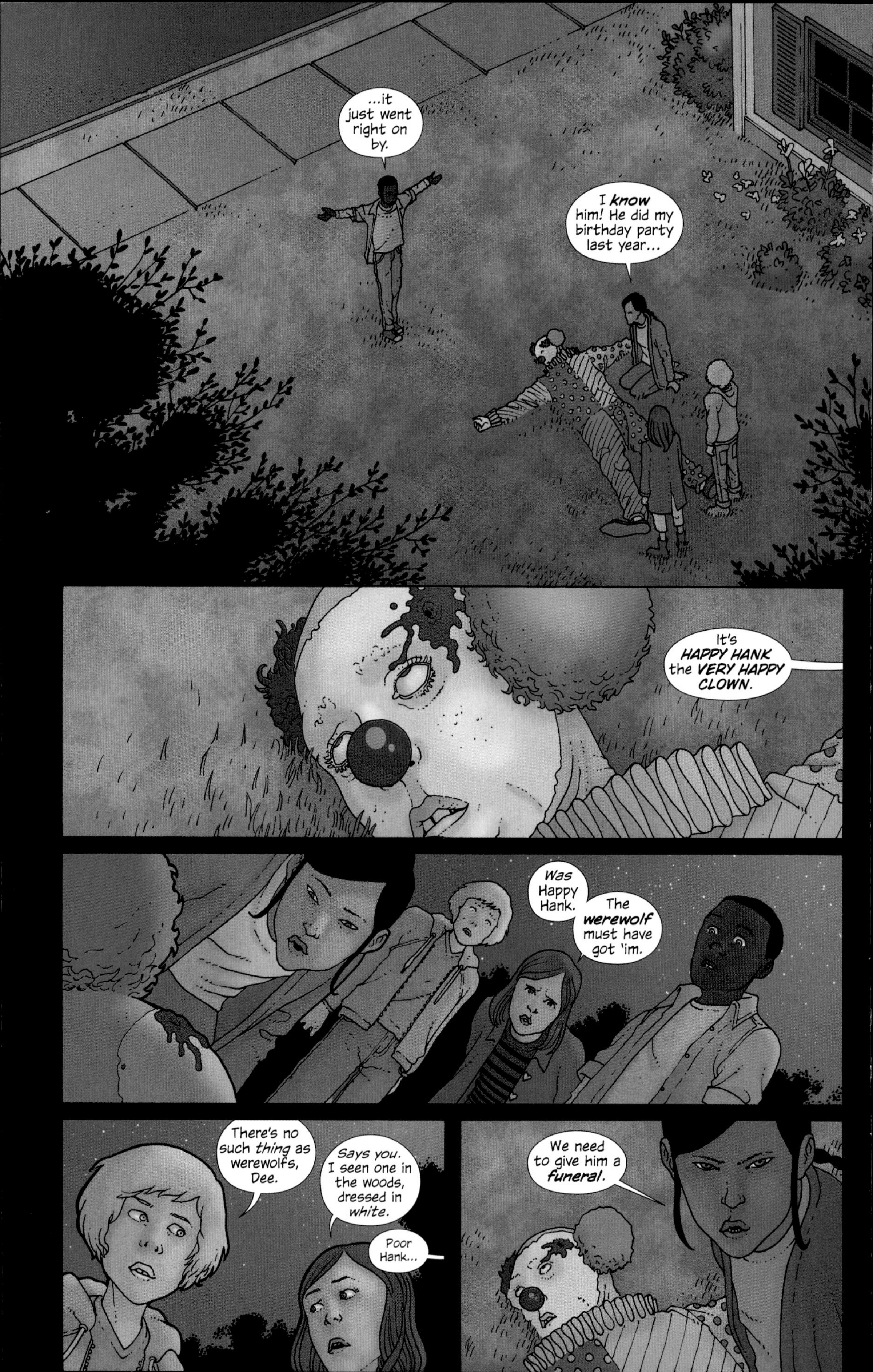
...it just went right on by.
I *know* him! He did my birthday party last year...
It's *HAPPY HANK* the *VERY HAPPY CLOWN*.
Was Happy Hank.
The *werewolf* must have got 'im.
There's no such *thing* as werewolfs, Dee.
Says you. I seen one in the woods, dressed in *white*.
Poor Hank...
We need to give him a *funeral*.

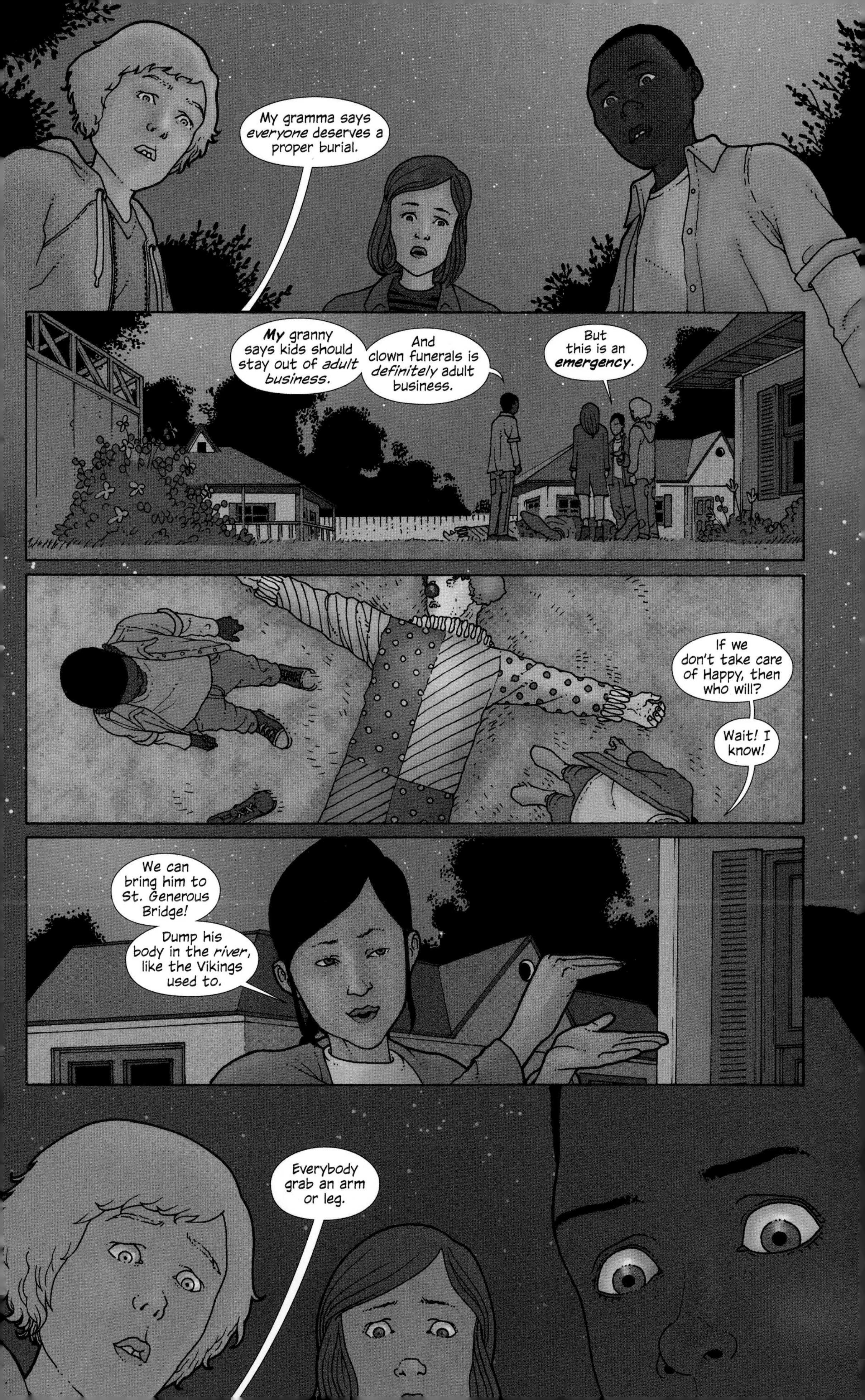

My gramma says *everyone* deserves a proper burial.
My granny says kids should stay out of *adult business.*
And clown funerals is *definitely* adult business.
But this is an ***emergency***.
If we don't take care of Happy, then who will?
Wait! I know!
We can bring him to St. Generous Bridge!
Dump his body in the *river*, like the Vikings used to.
Everybody grab an arm or leg.

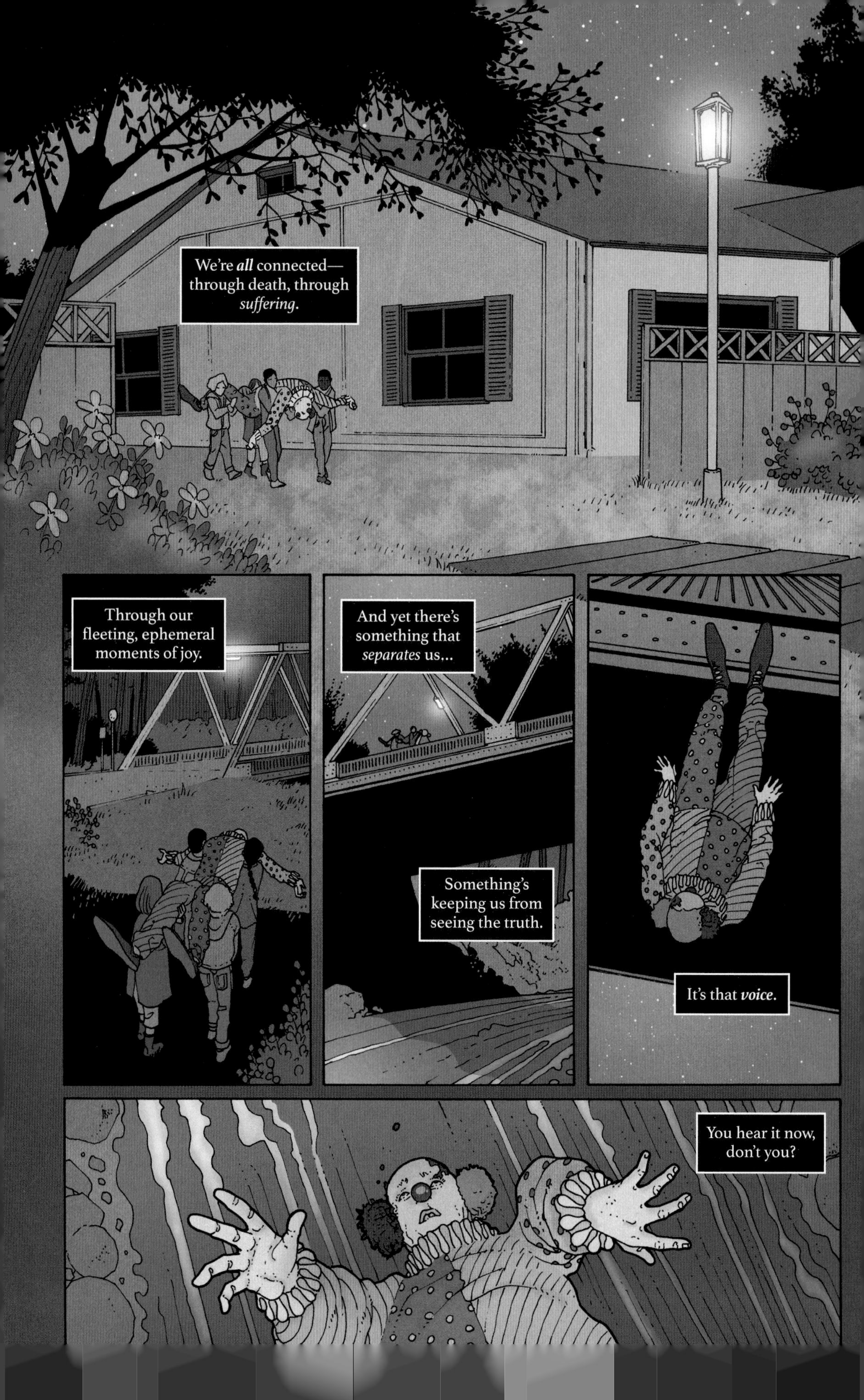
We're *all* connected—through death, through *suffering*.
Through our fleeting, ephemeral moments of joy.
And yet there's something that *separates* us...
Something's keeping us from seeing the truth.
It's that *voice*.
You hear it now, don't you?

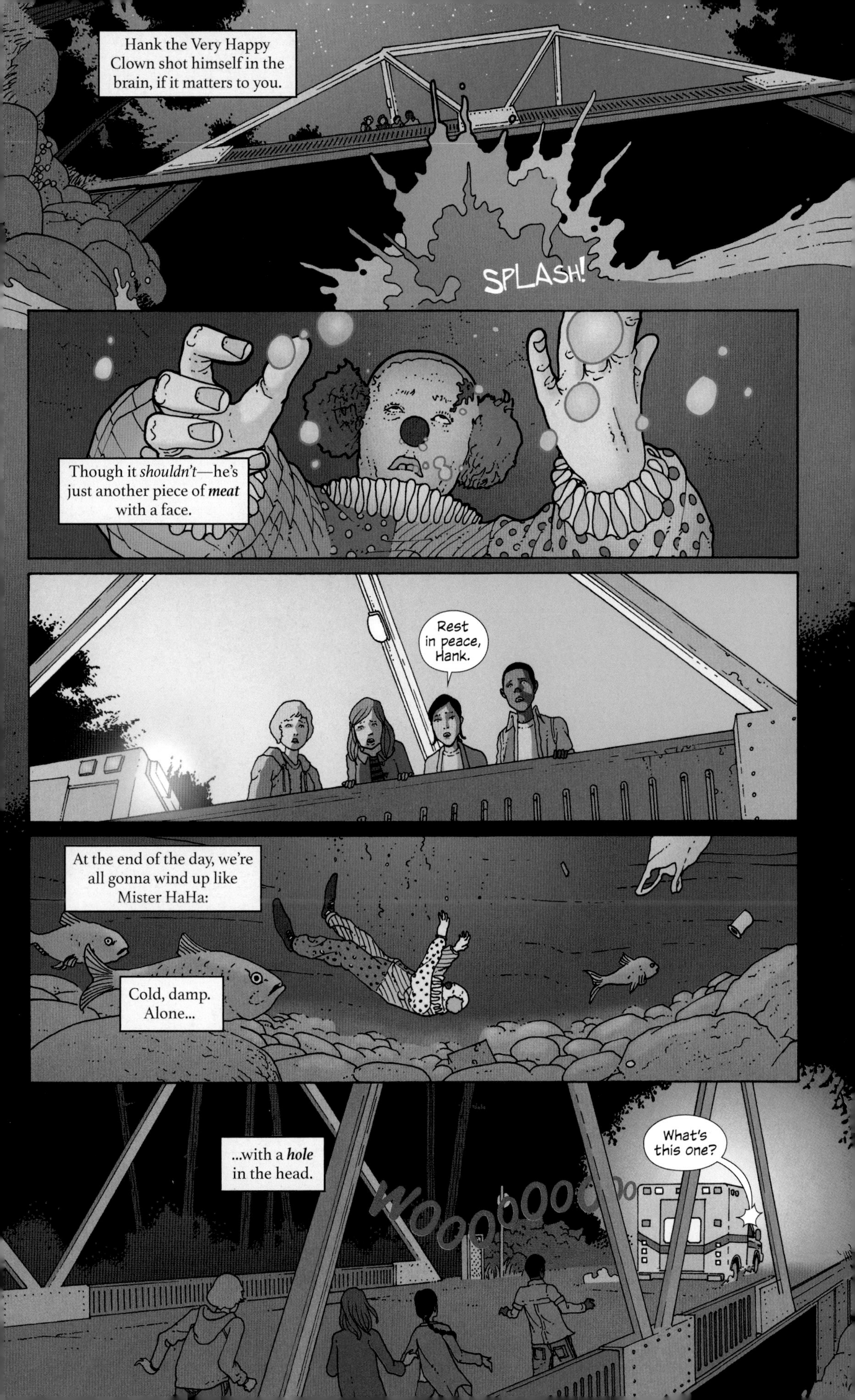
Hank the Very Happy Clown shot himself in the brain, if it matters to you.
SPLASH!
Though it *shouldn't*—he's just another piece of ***meat*** with a face.
Rest in peace, Hank.
At the end of the day, we're all gonna wind up like Mister HaHa:
Cold, damp. Alone...
...with a ***hole*** in the head.
WOOOOOOOO
What's this one?

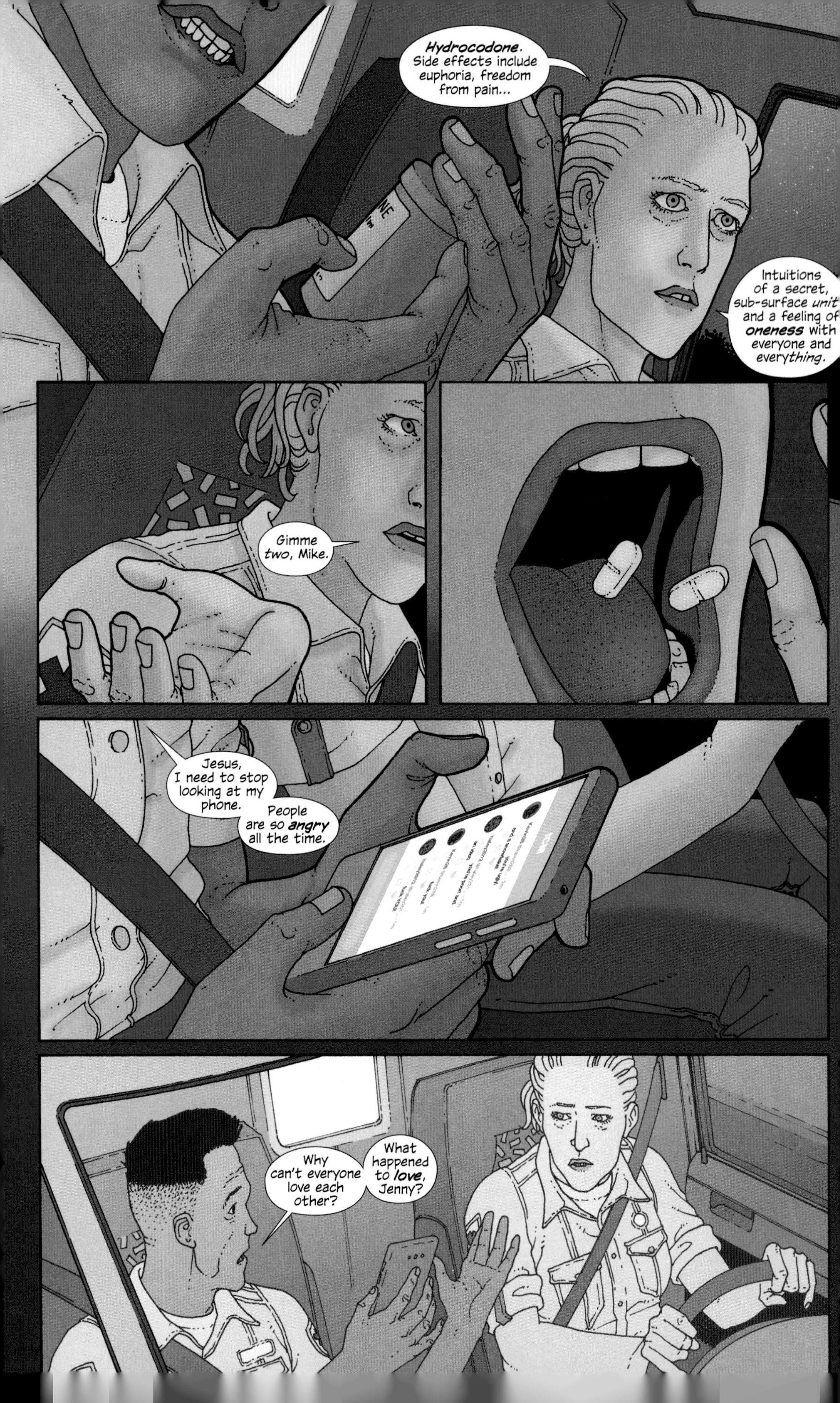

Hydrocodone. Side effects include euphoria, freedom from pain...
Intuitions of a secret, sub-surface *unit* and a feeling of ***oneness*** with everyone and every*thing*.
Gimme *two*, Mike.
Jesus, I need to stop looking at my phone.
People are so ***angry*** all the time.
Why can't everyone love each other?
What happened to ***love***, Jenny?

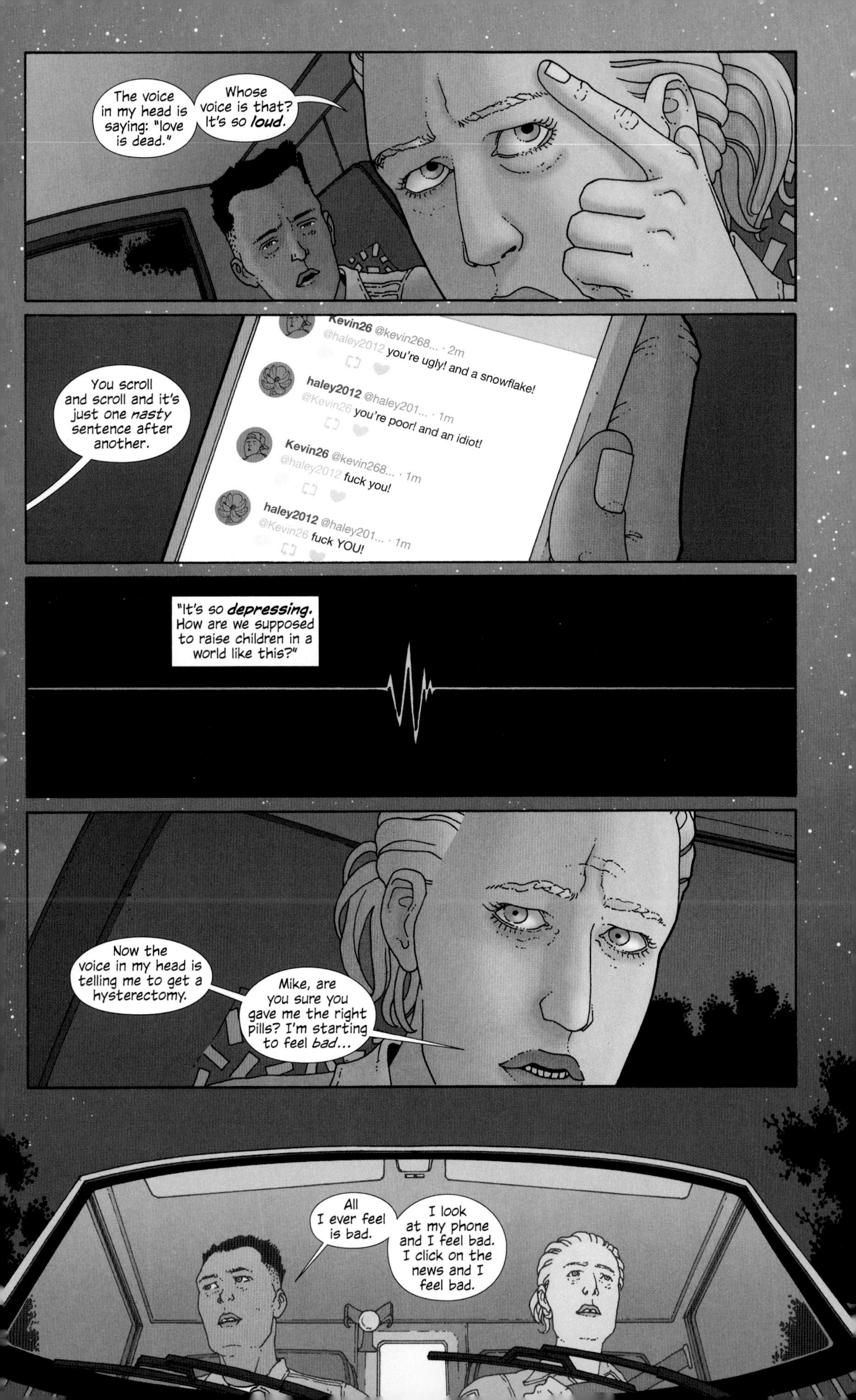

The voice in my head is saying: "love is dead."
Whose voice is that? It's so *loud*.
You scroll and scroll and it's just one *nasty* sentence after another.
Kevin26 @kevin268... · 2m
@haley2012 you're ugly! and a snowflake!
haley2012 @haley201... · 1m
@Kevin26 you're poor! and an idiot!
Kevin26 @kevin268... · 1m
@haley2012 fuck you!
haley2012 @haley201... · 1m
@Kevin26 fuck YOU!
"It's so *depressing*. How are we supposed to raise children in a world like this?"
Now the voice in my head is telling me to get a hysterectomy.
Mike, are you sure you gave me the right pills? I'm starting to feel *bad*...
All I ever feel is bad.
I look at my phone and I feel bad. I click on the news and I feel bad.

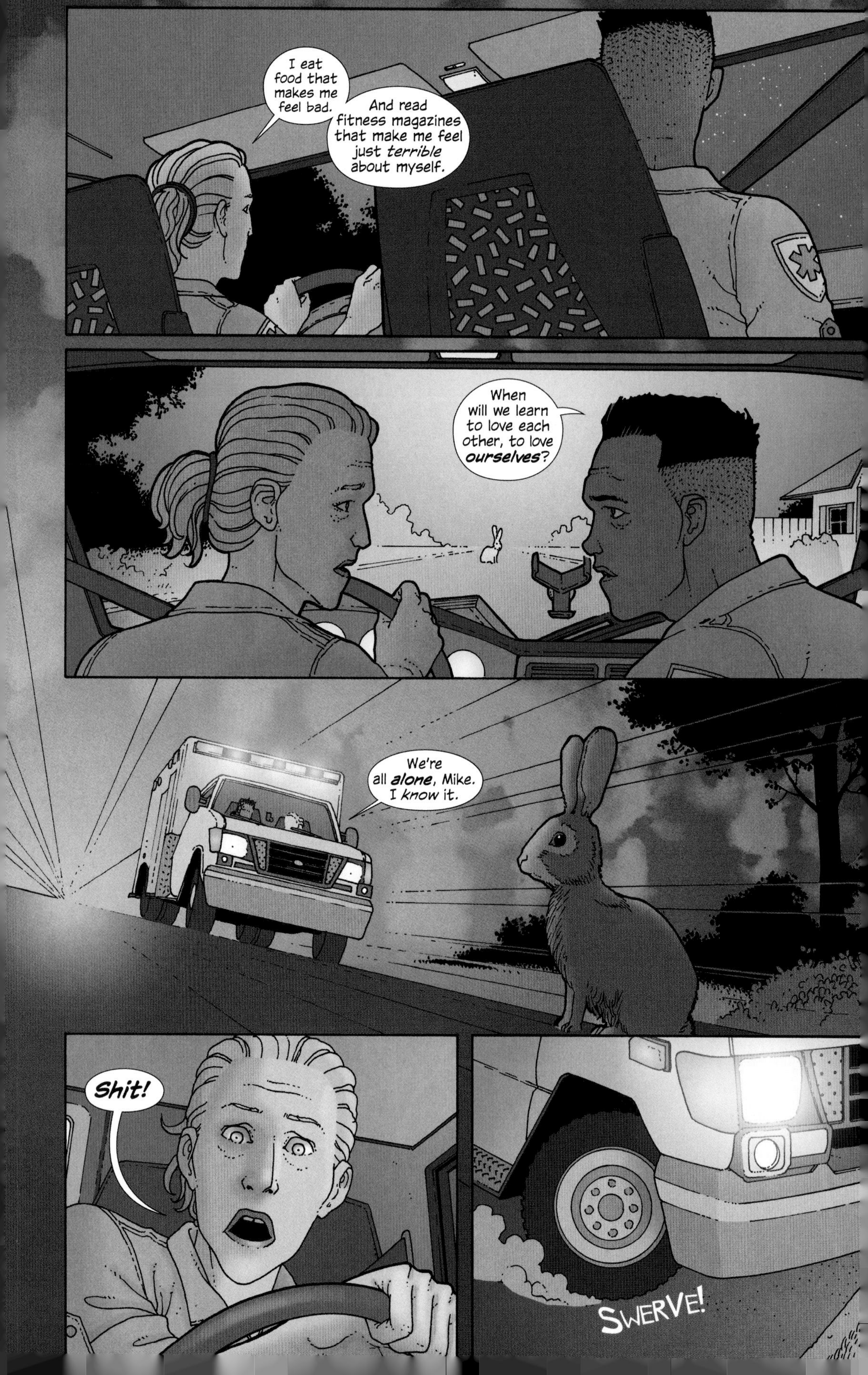
I eat food that makes me feel bad.
And read fitness magazines that make me feel just *terrible* about myself.
When will we learn to love each other, to love ***ourselves***?
We're all ***alone***, Mike. I *know* it.
Shit!
SWERVE!

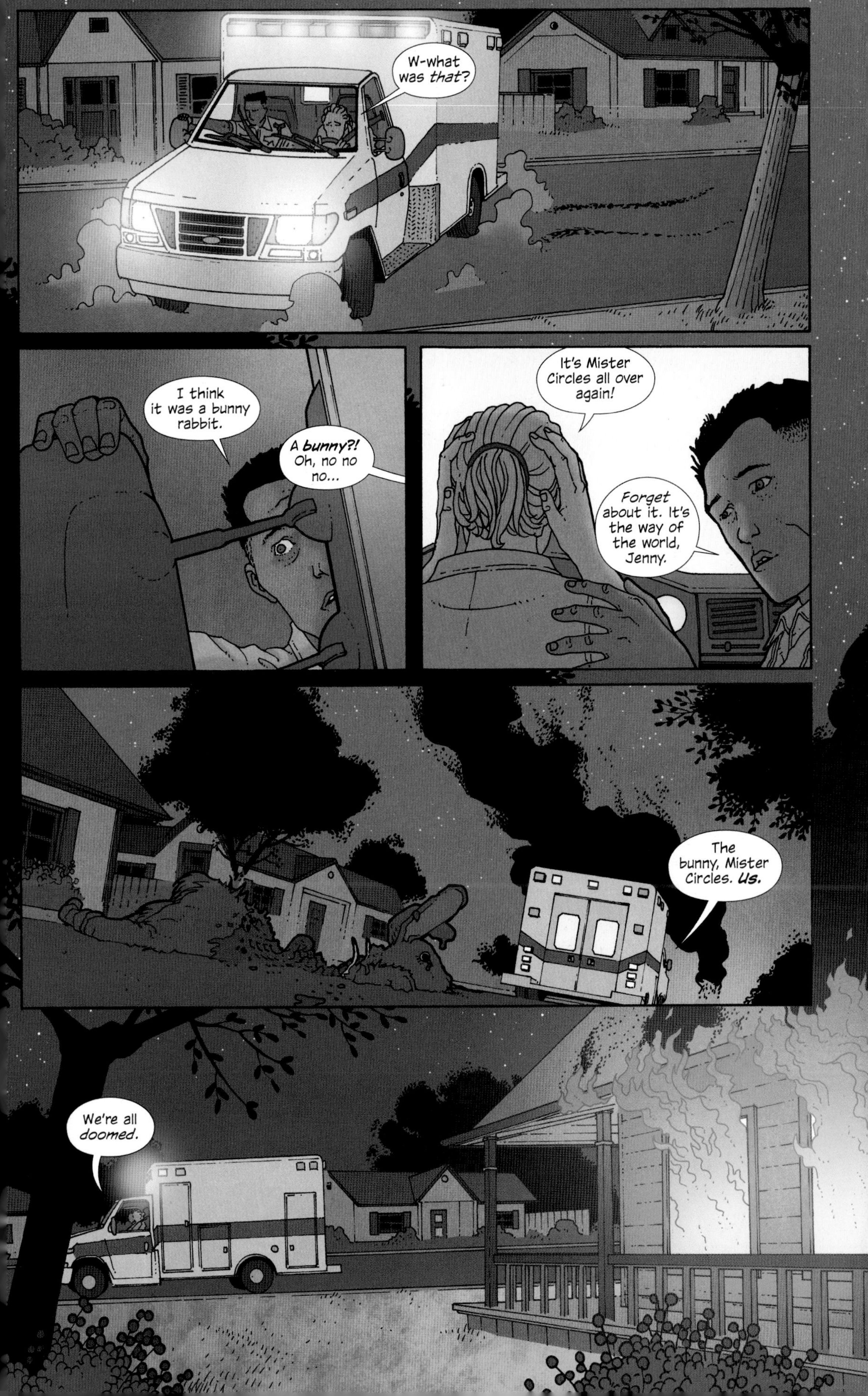
W-what was *that*?
I think it was a bunny rabbit.
A ***bunny?!*** Oh, no no no...
It's Mister Circles all over again!
Forget about it. It's the way of the world, Jenny.
The bunny, Mister Circles. ***Us.***
We're all *doomed.*

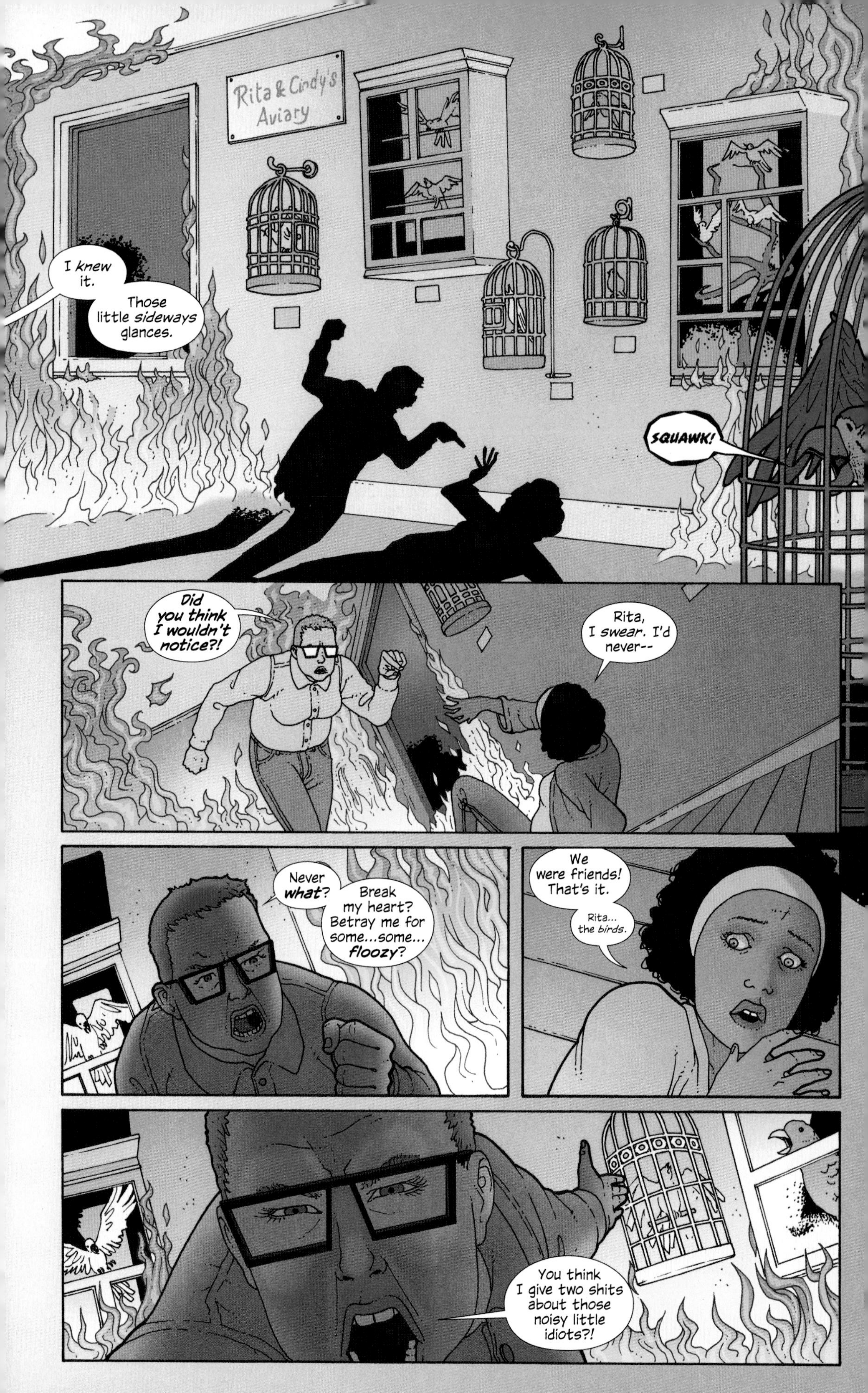
Rita & Cindy's Aviary
I *knew* it.
Those little *sideways* glances.
SQUAWK!
Did you think I wouldn't notice?!
Rita, I *swear*. I'd never--
Never *what*?
Break my heart? Betray me for some...some... *floozy*?
We were friends! That's it.
Rita... the *birds*.
You think I give two shits about those noisy little idiots?!

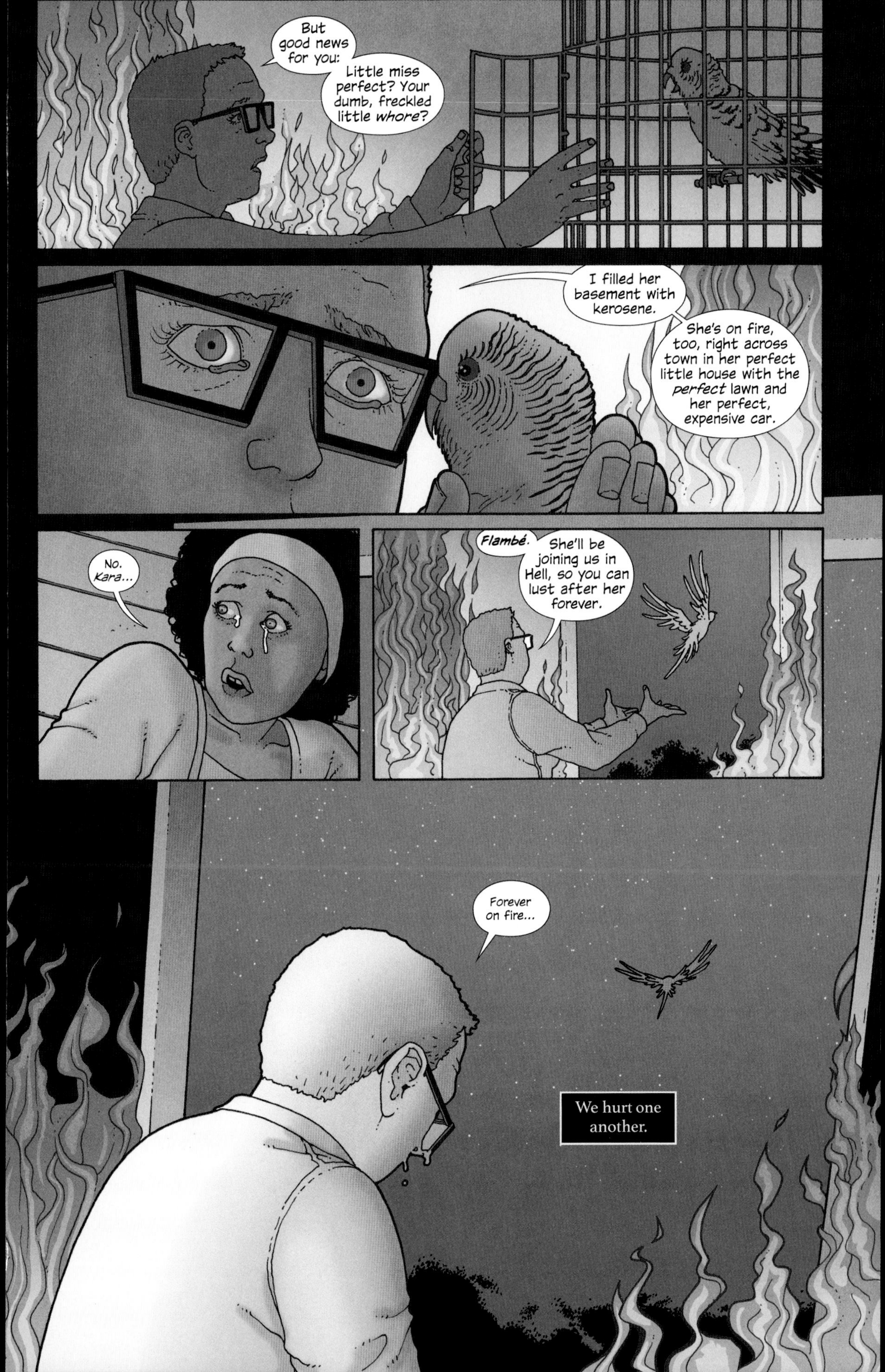
But good news for you:
Little miss perfect? Your dumb, freckled little *whore*?
I filled her basement with kerosene.
She's on fire, too, right across town in her perfect little house with the *perfect* lawn and her perfect, expensive car.
No. *Kara*...
Flambé.
She'll be joining us in Hell, so you can lust after her forever.
Forever on fire...
We hurt one another.

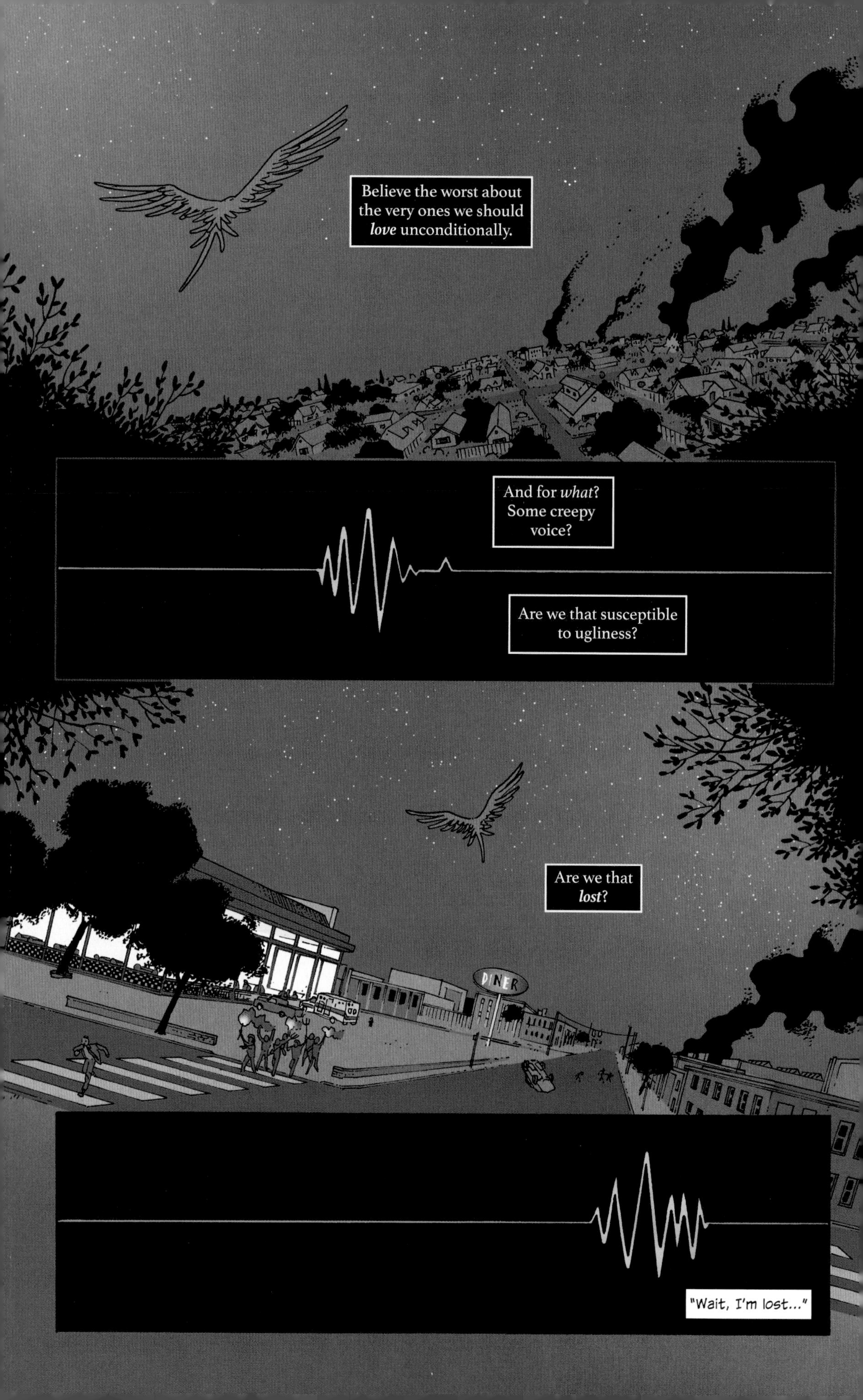

Believe the worst about the very ones we should *love* unconditionally.
And for *what*? Some creepy voice?
Are we that susceptible to ugliness?
Are we that *lost*?
DINER
"Wait, I'm lost..."

It's simple...

You take two eszopiclone, one escitalopram, then *chug* a cup of coffee...

...and you *hallucinate* for like fifteen minutes.

I don't feel anything...

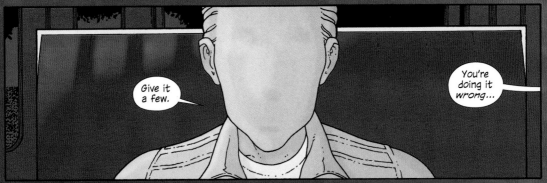

Give it a few.

You're doing it *wrong*...

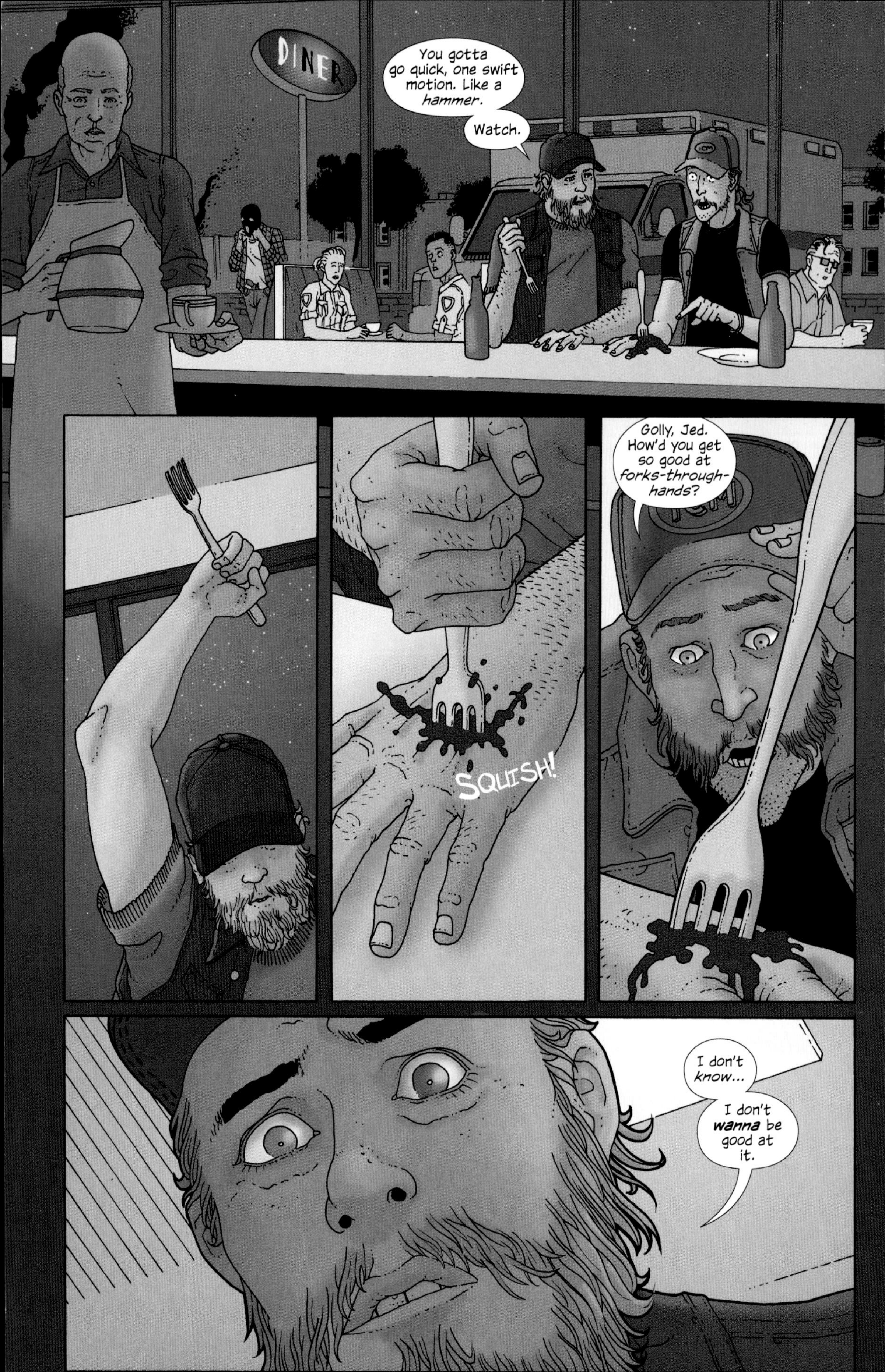

DINER
You gotta go quick, one swift motion. Like a *hammer*.
Watch.
SQUISH!
Golly, Jed. How'd you get so good at *forks-through-hands*?
I don't *know*...
I don't ***wanna*** be good at it.

Why do we do this?

Do what?

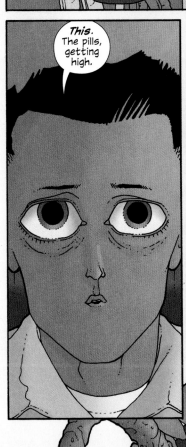

This. The pills, getting high.

It doesn't take a psychology degree.

It's the same reason anyone does anything.

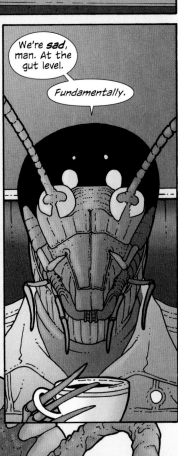

We're sad, man. At the gut level.

Fundamentally.

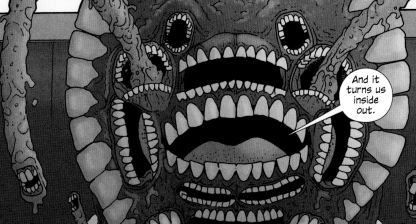

And it turns us inside out.

You don't gotta do this, kid.

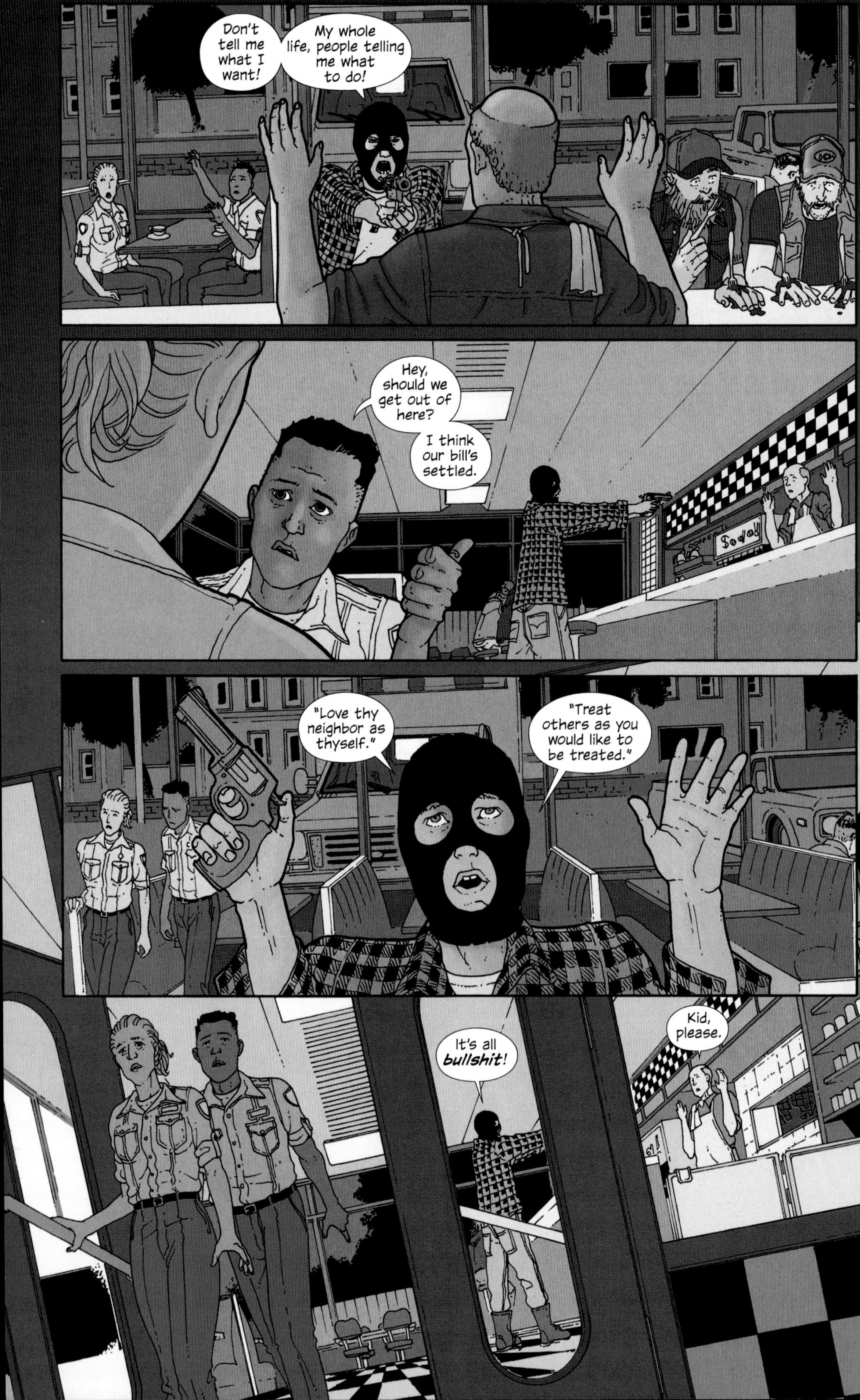
Don't tell me what I want!
My whole life, people telling me what to do!
Hey, should we get out of here?
I think our bill's settled.
"Love thy neighbor as thyself."
"Treat others as you would like to be treated."
It's all *bullshit*!
Kid, please.

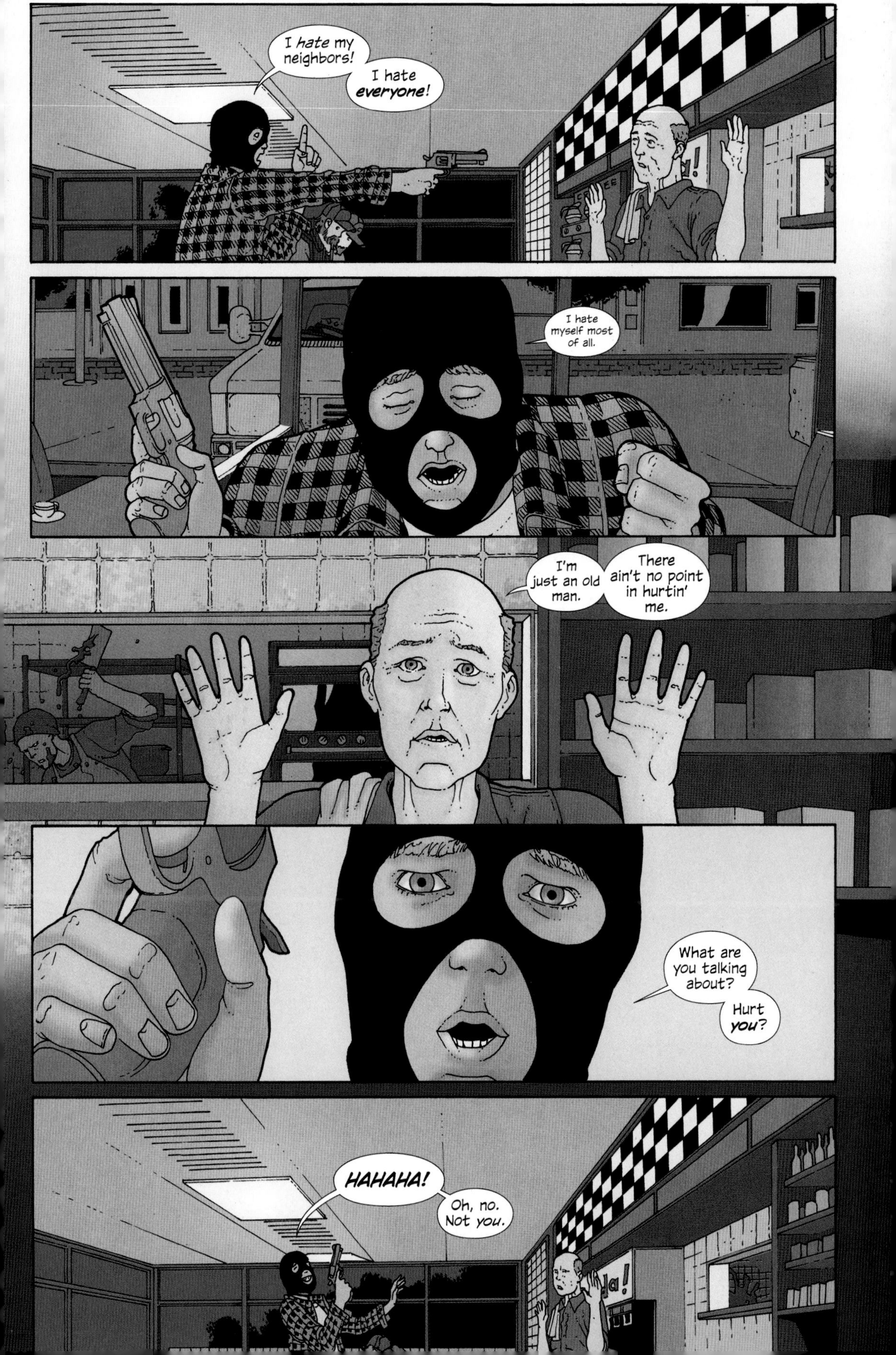
I *hate* my neighbors!
I hate ***everyone***!
I hate myself most of all.
I'm just an old man.
There ain't no point in hurtin' me.
What are you talking about?
Hurt ***you***?
HAHAHA!
Oh, no. Not *you*.

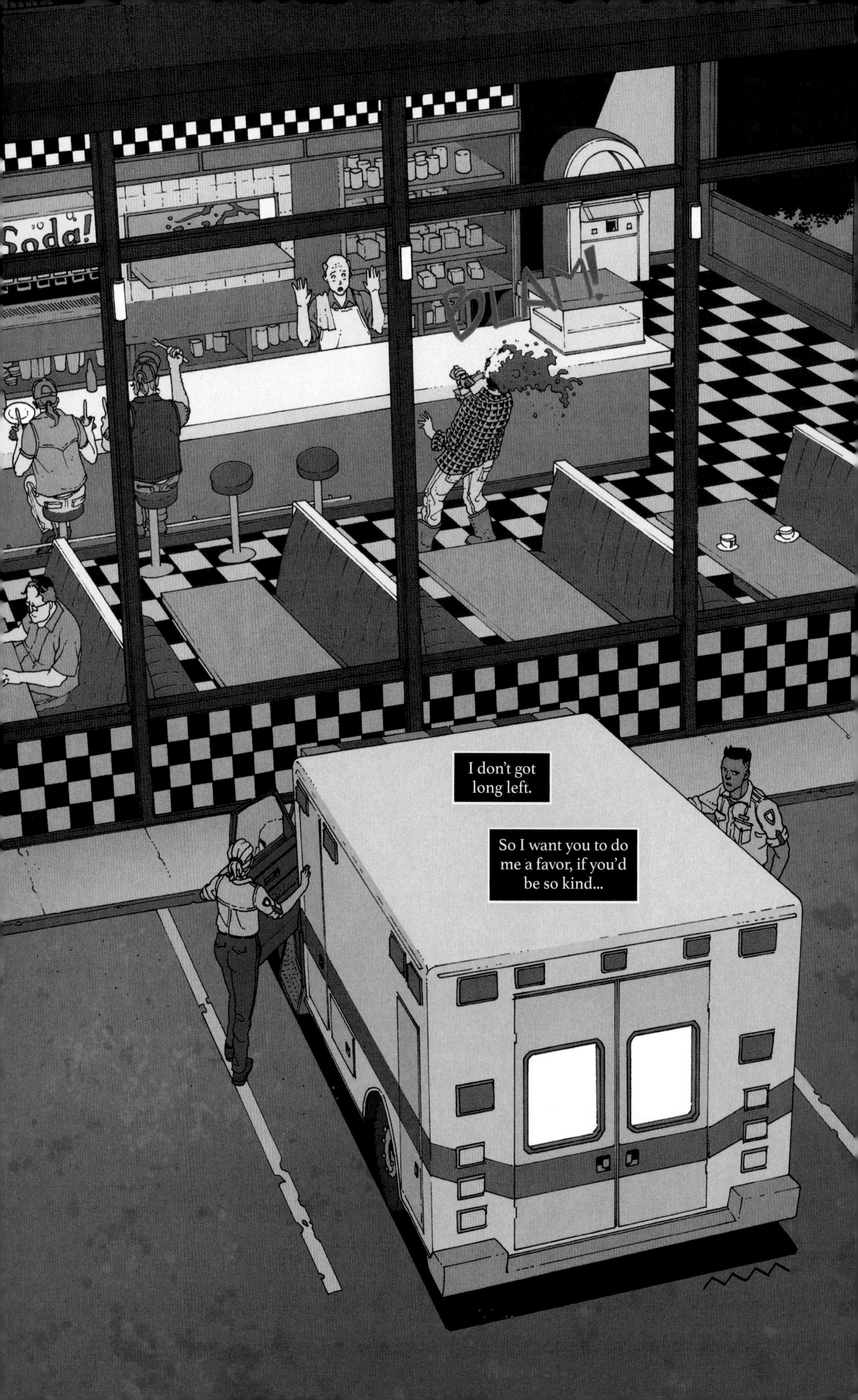
Soda!
BLAM!
I don't got long left.
So I want you to do me a favor, if you'd be so kind...

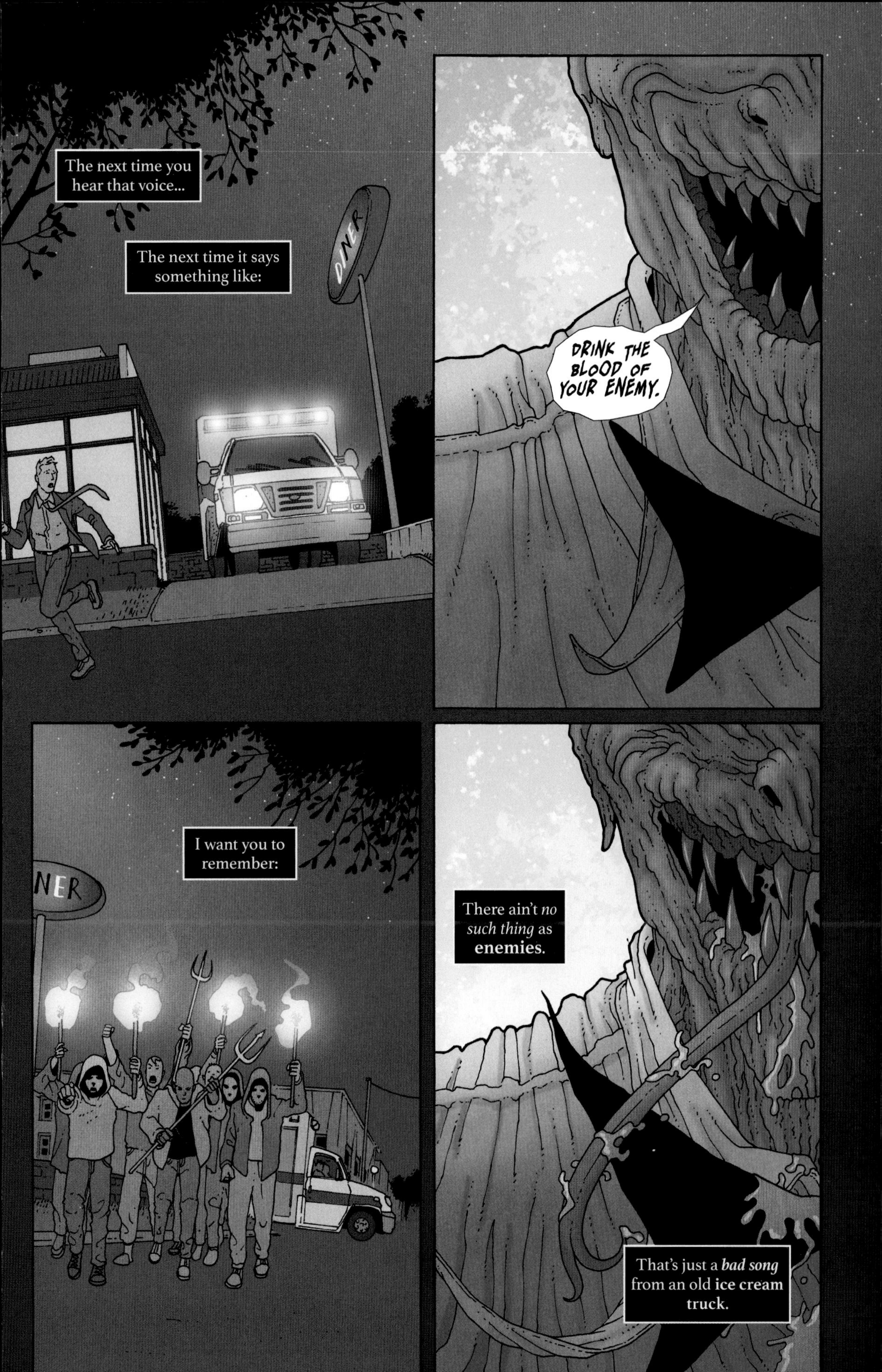
The next time you hear that voice...
DINER
The next time it says something like:
DRINK THE BLOOD OF YOUR ENEMY.
I want you to remember:
NER
There ain't *no such thing* as **enemies**.
That's just a ***bad song*** from an old **ice cream truck**.

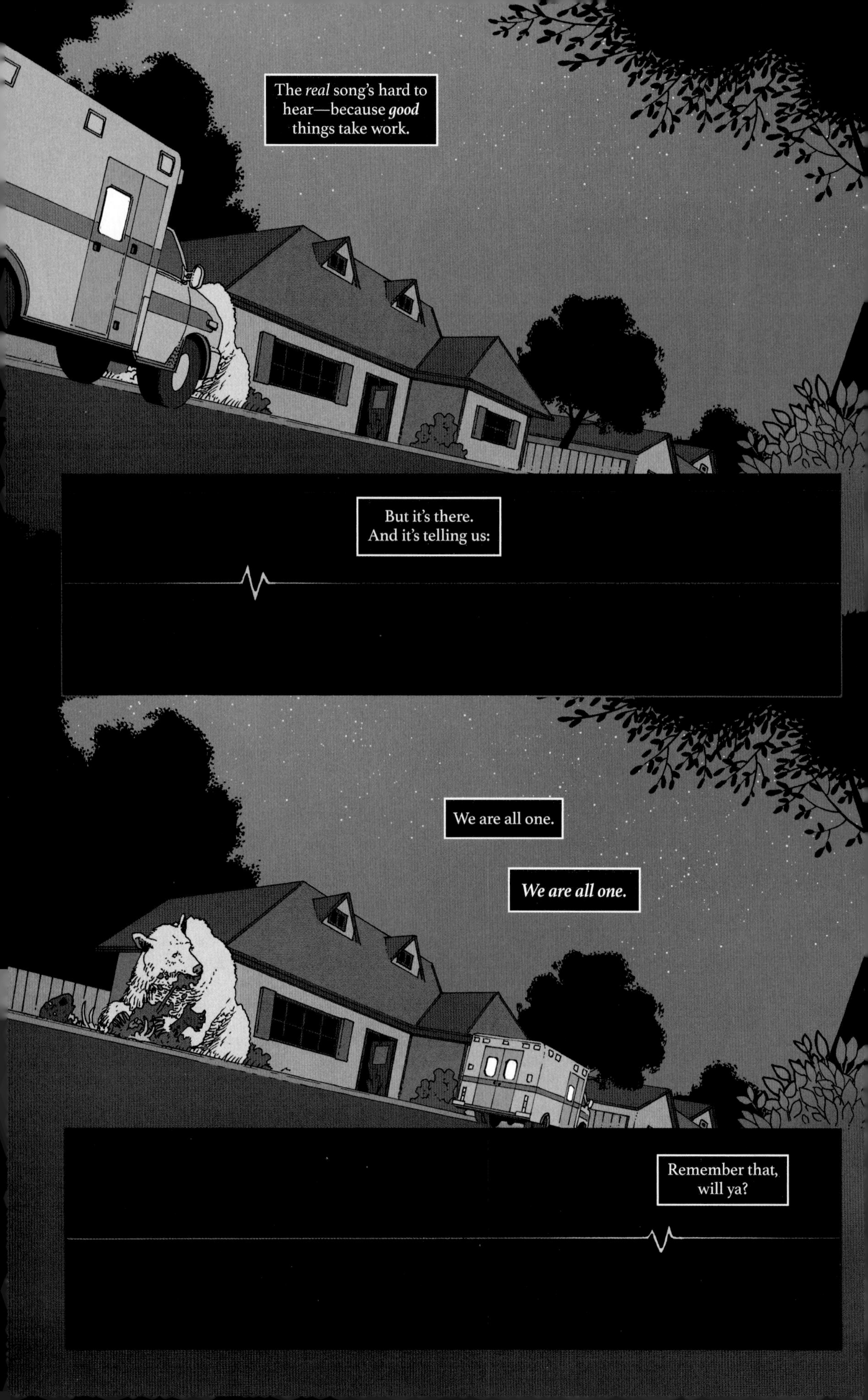
The *real* song's hard to hear—because ***good*** things take work.
But it's there. And it's telling us:
We are all one.
We are all one.
Remember that, will ya?

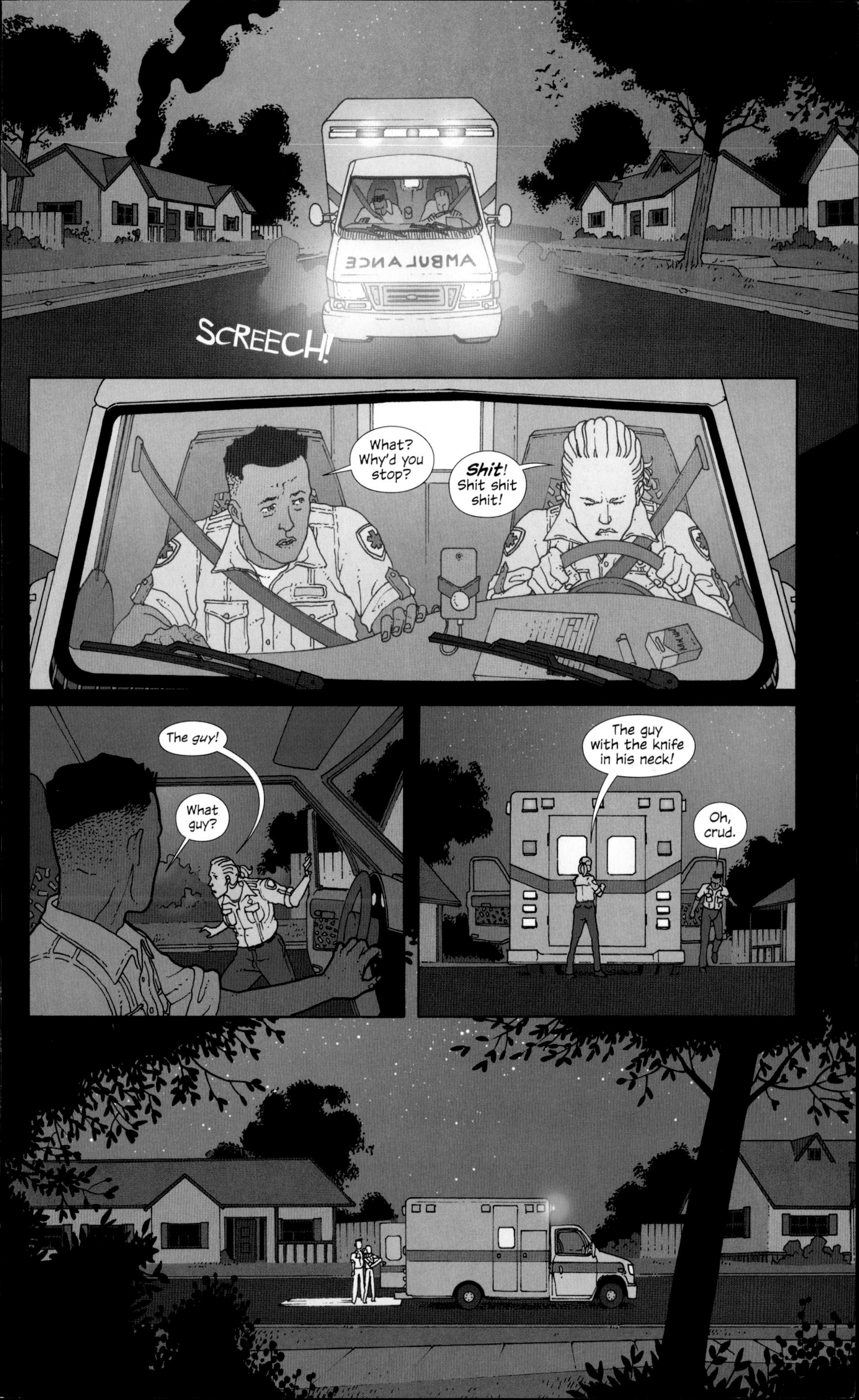
AMBULANCE
SCREECH!
What? Why'd you stop?
Shit! Shit shit shit!
The guy!
What guy?
The guy with the knife in his neck!
Oh, crud.

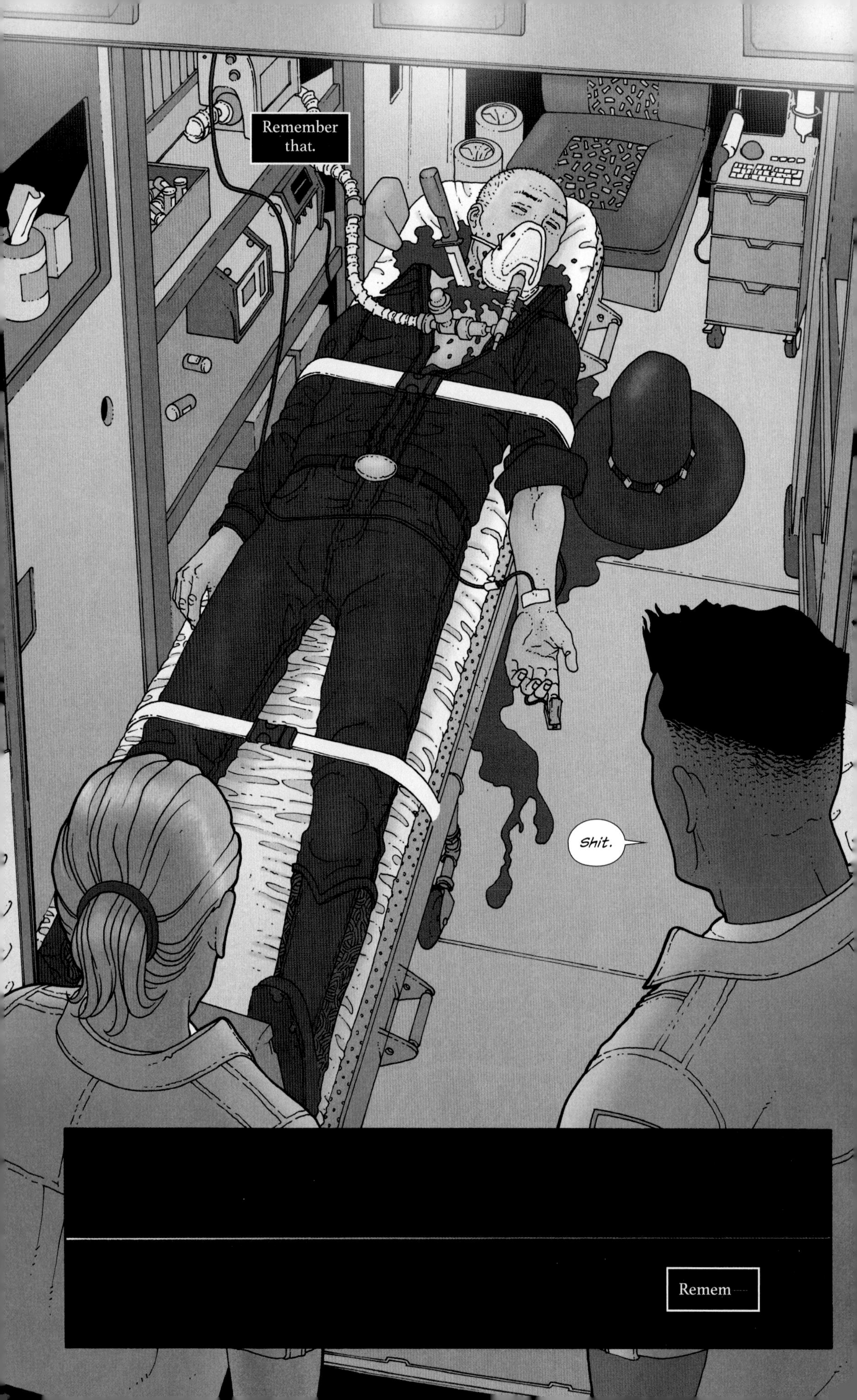
Remember that.
Shit.
Remem—

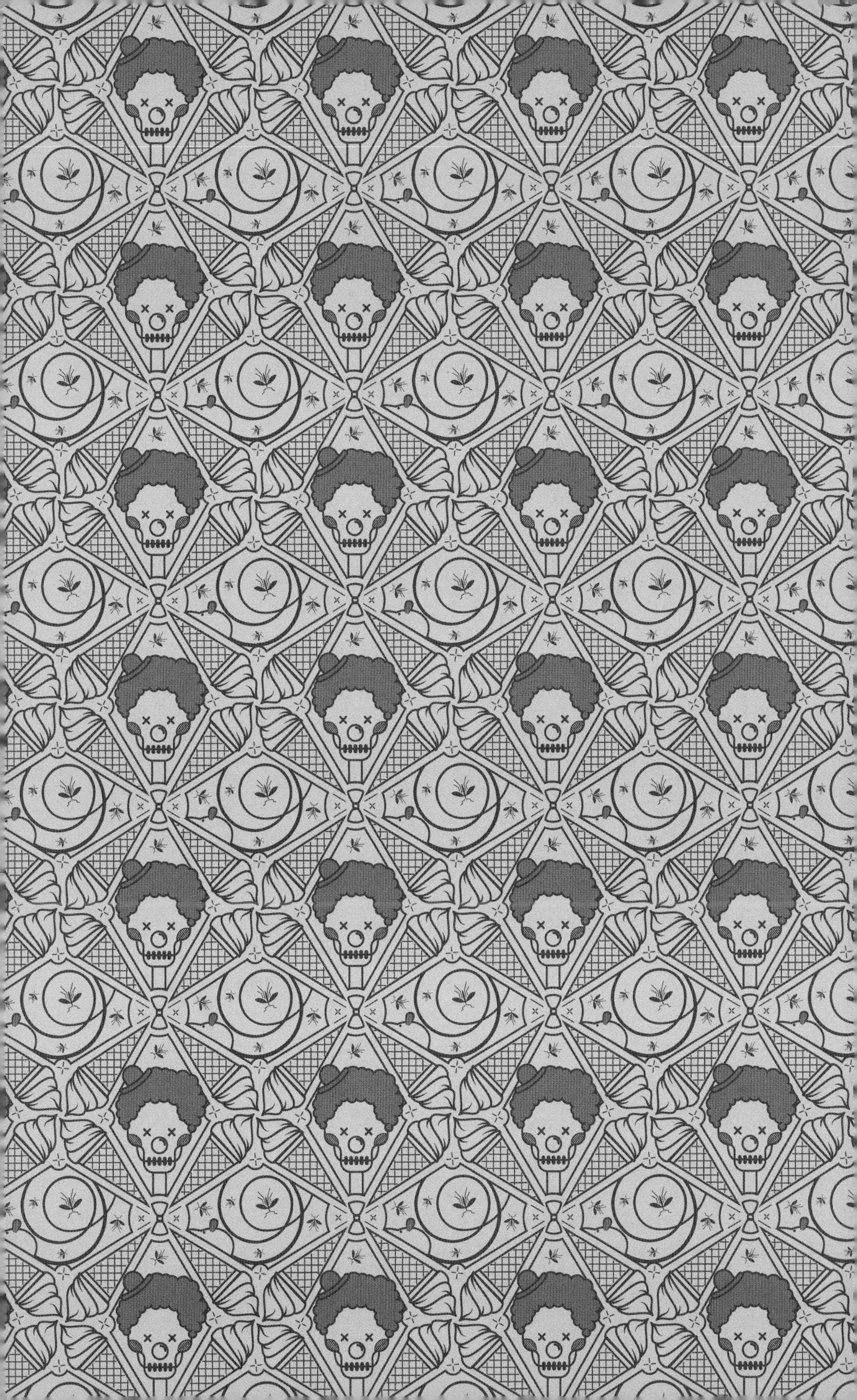

ADDED SUGAR

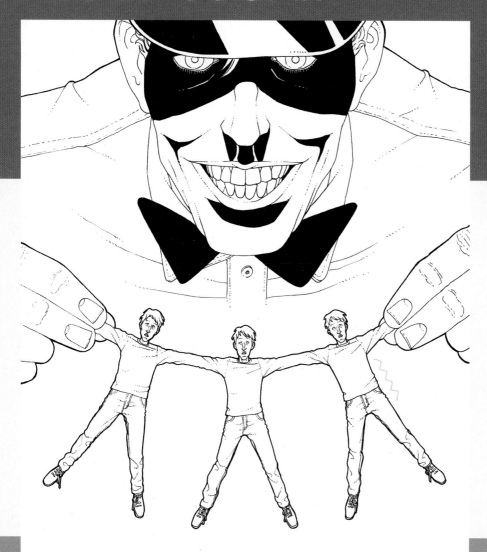

What follows are variant covers, sketches, and miscellania from the second volume of **ICE CREAM MAN**.

One way or another...

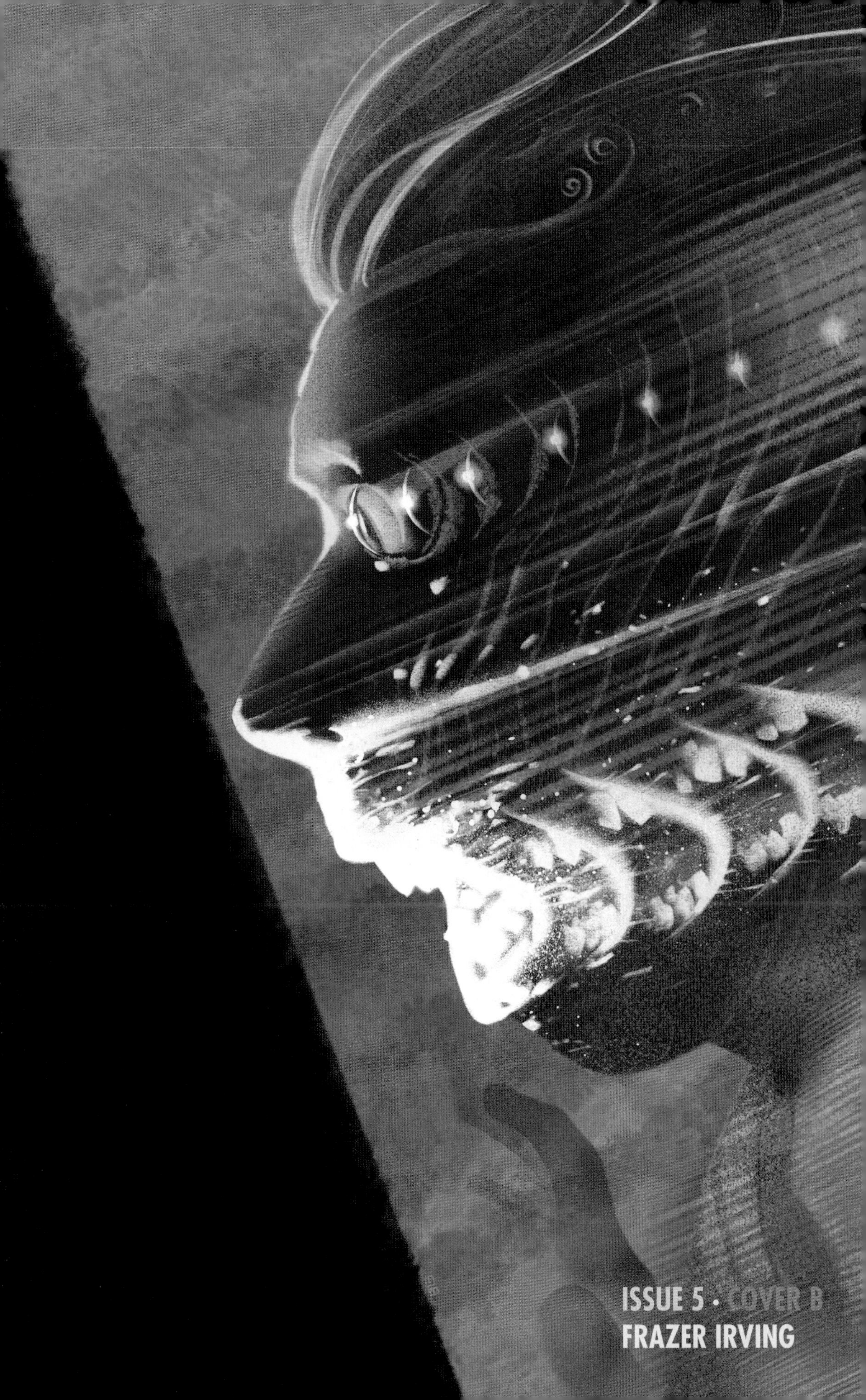

ISSUE 5 · COVER B
FRAZER IRVING

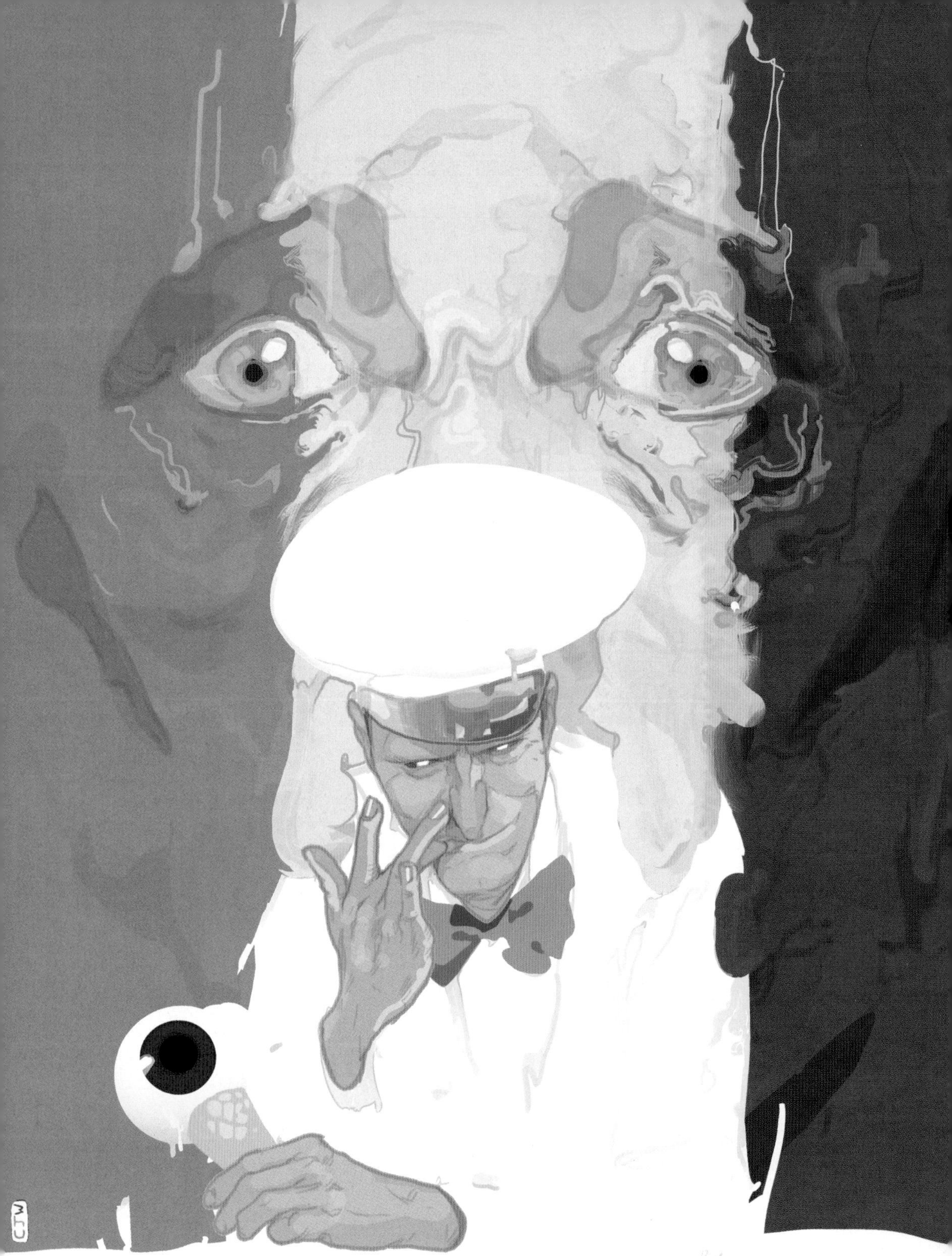
CJW

ISSUE 6 · COVER B
CHRISTIAN WARD

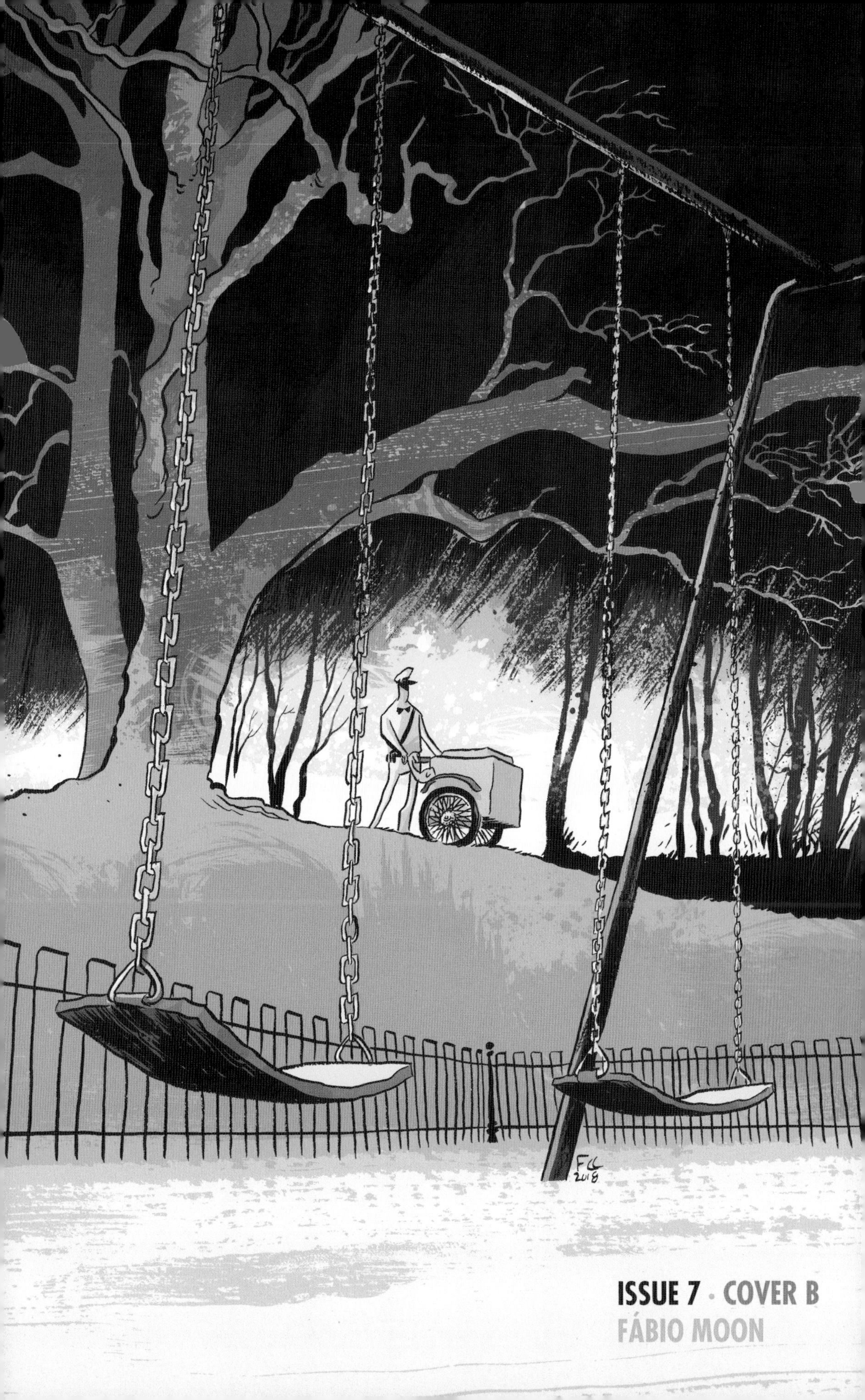

ISSUE 7 · COVER B
FÁBIO MOON

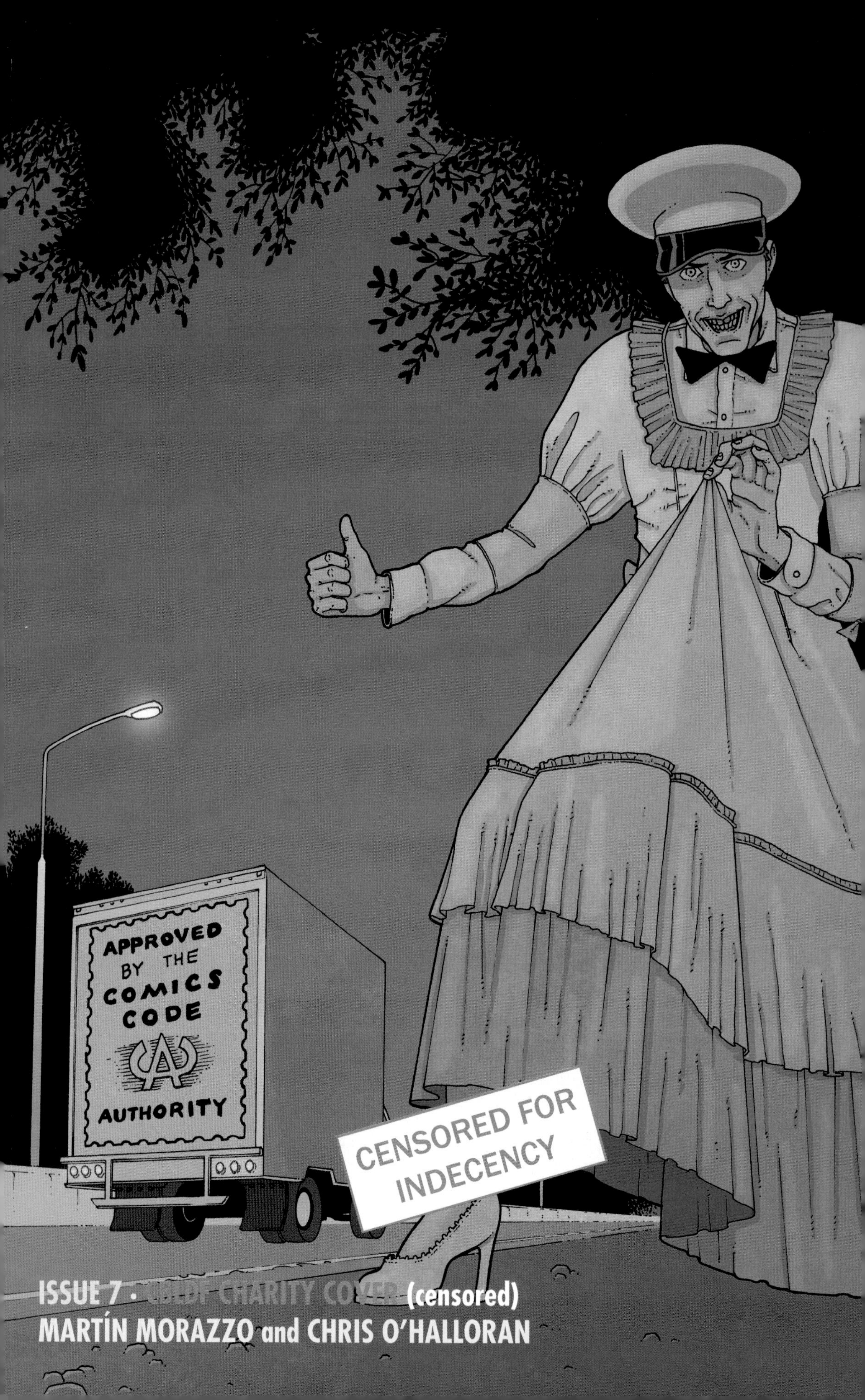
APPROVED
BY THE
COMICS
CODE
AUTHORITY
CENSORED FOR
INDECENCY

ISSUE 7 · CBLDF CHARITY COVER (censored)
MARTÍN MORAZZO and CHRIS O'HALLORAN

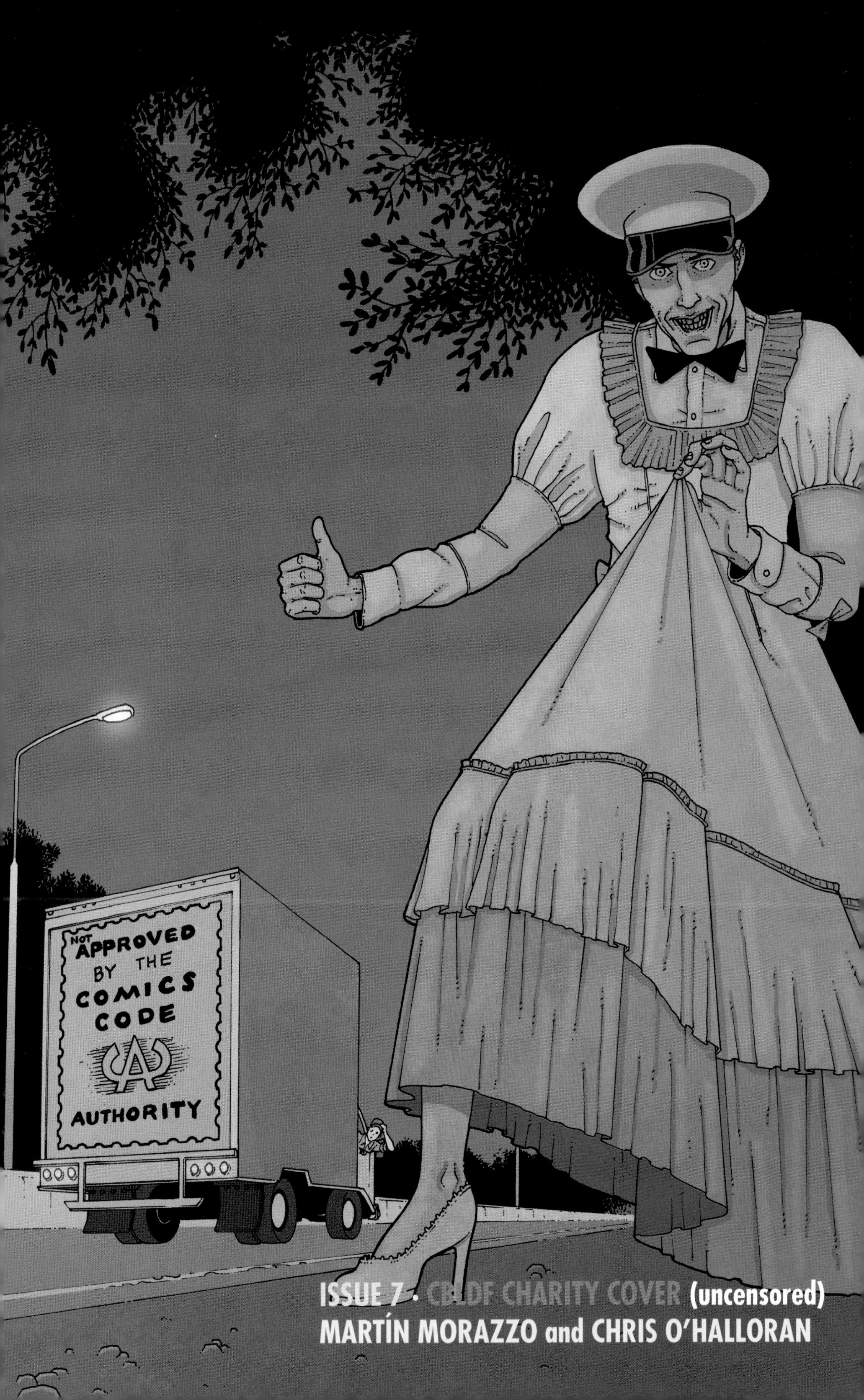
NOT APPROVED BY THE COMICS CODE AUTHORITY

ISSUE 7 · CBLDF CHARITY COVER (uncensored)
MARTÍN MORAZZO and CHRIS O'HALLORAN

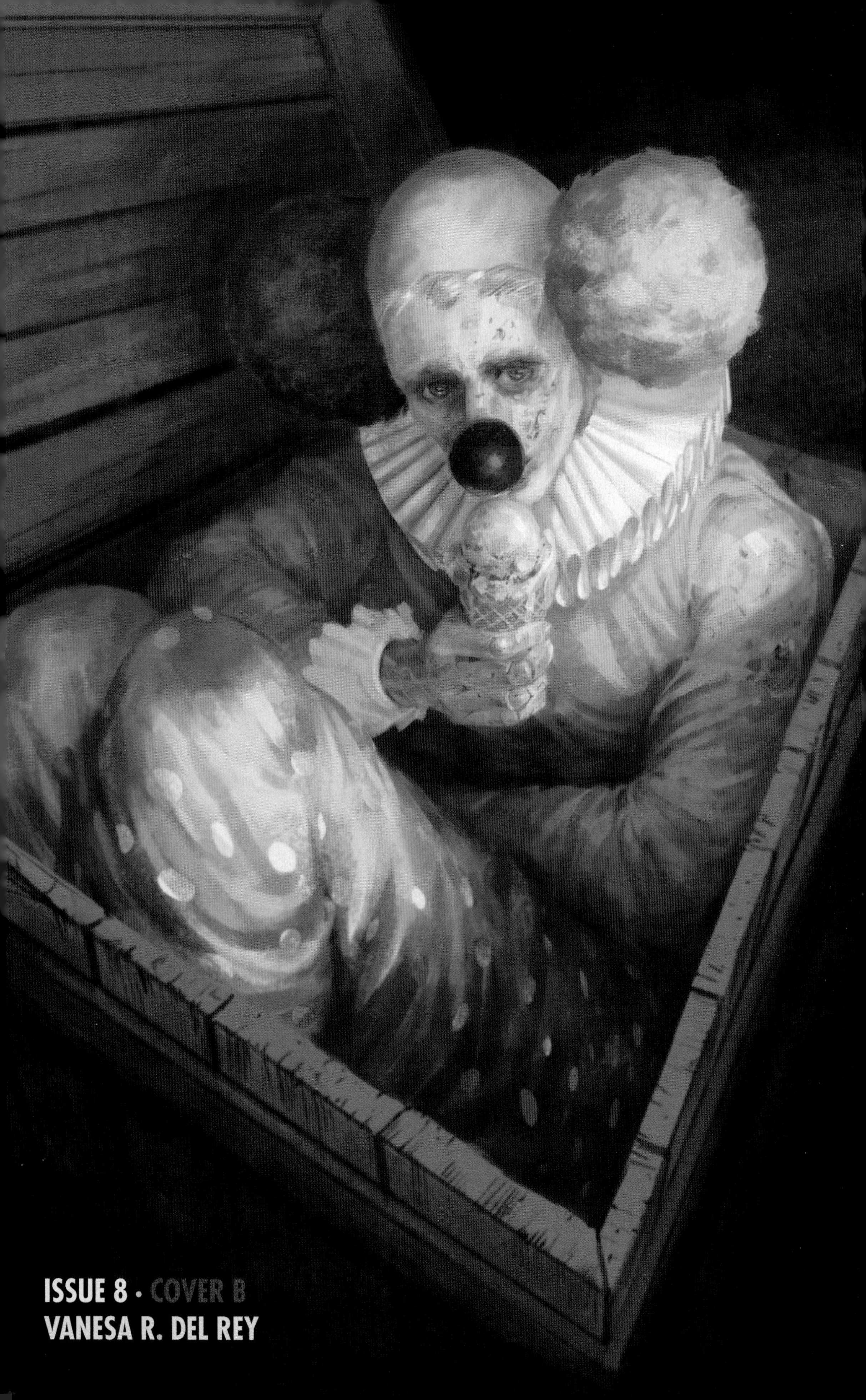

ISSUE 8 • COVER B
VANESA R. DEL REY

FUNNY FACES

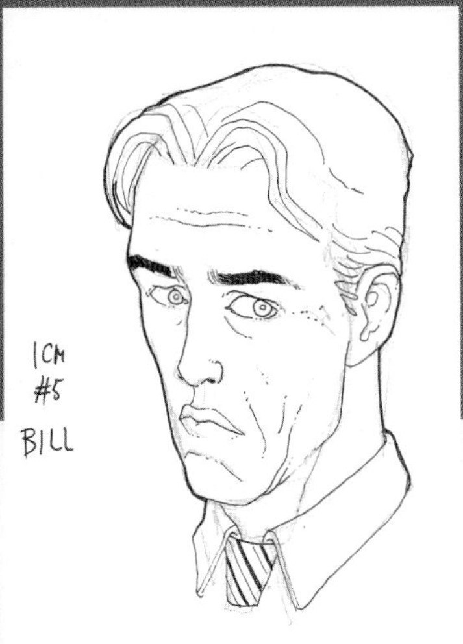
ICM
#5
BILL

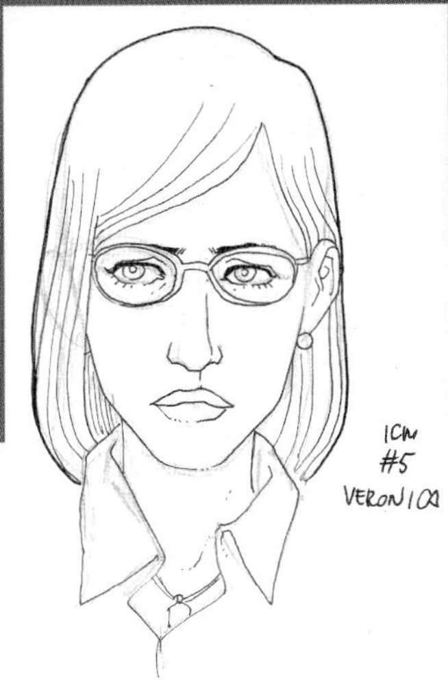
ICM
#5
VERONICA

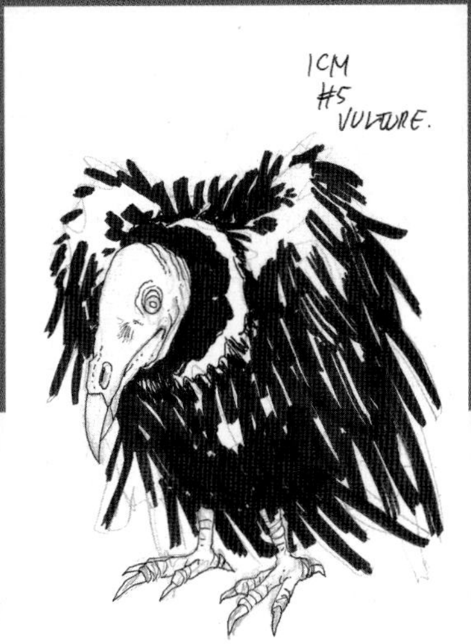
ICM
#5
VULTURE.

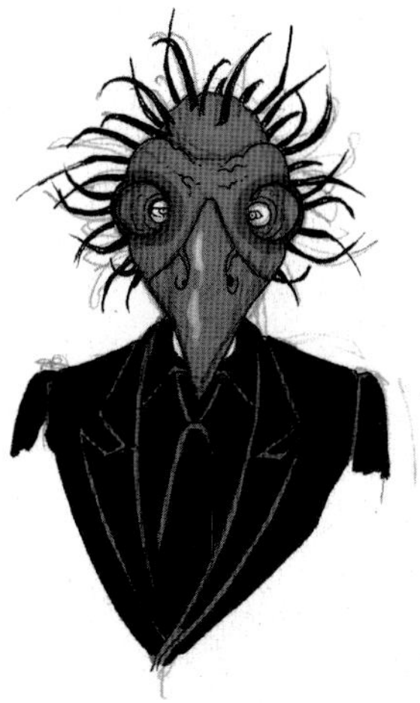

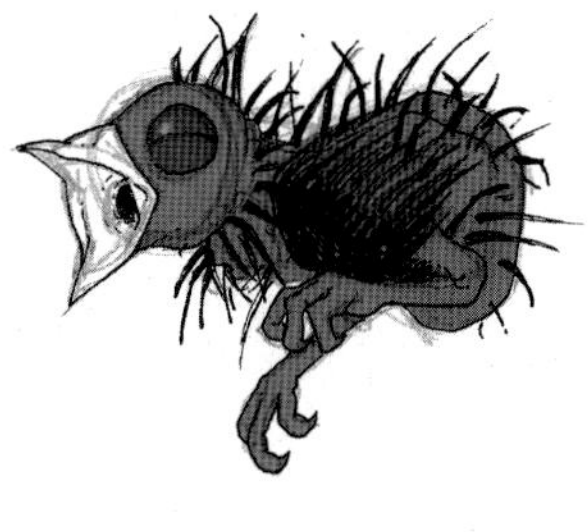

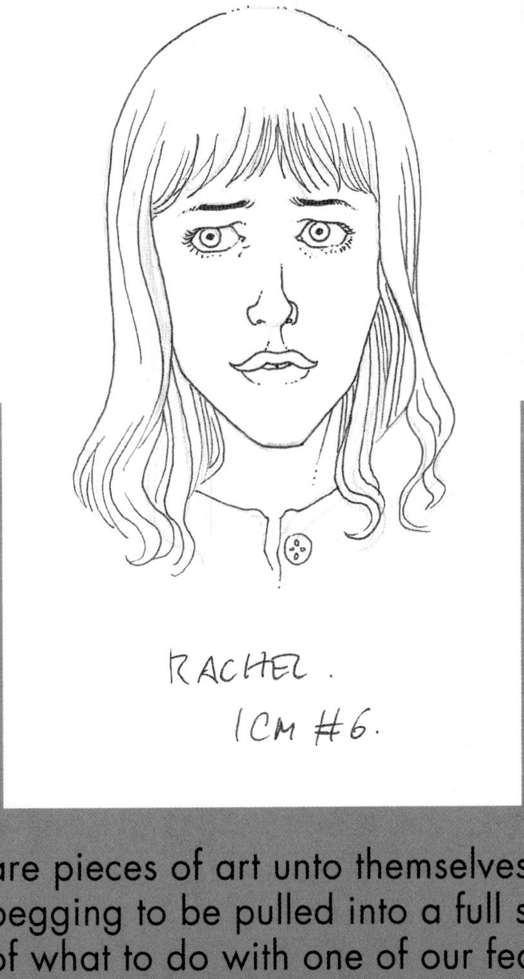
RACHEL.
ICM #6.

Martín's character sketches are pieces of art unto themselves—each one teems with personality, begging to be pulled into a full story. Occasionally, I'll be unsure of what to do with one of our featured players, and Martín's sketch will solve the problem, suggesting an entire narrative through only some loose ink against white space.

FACES, FUNNY

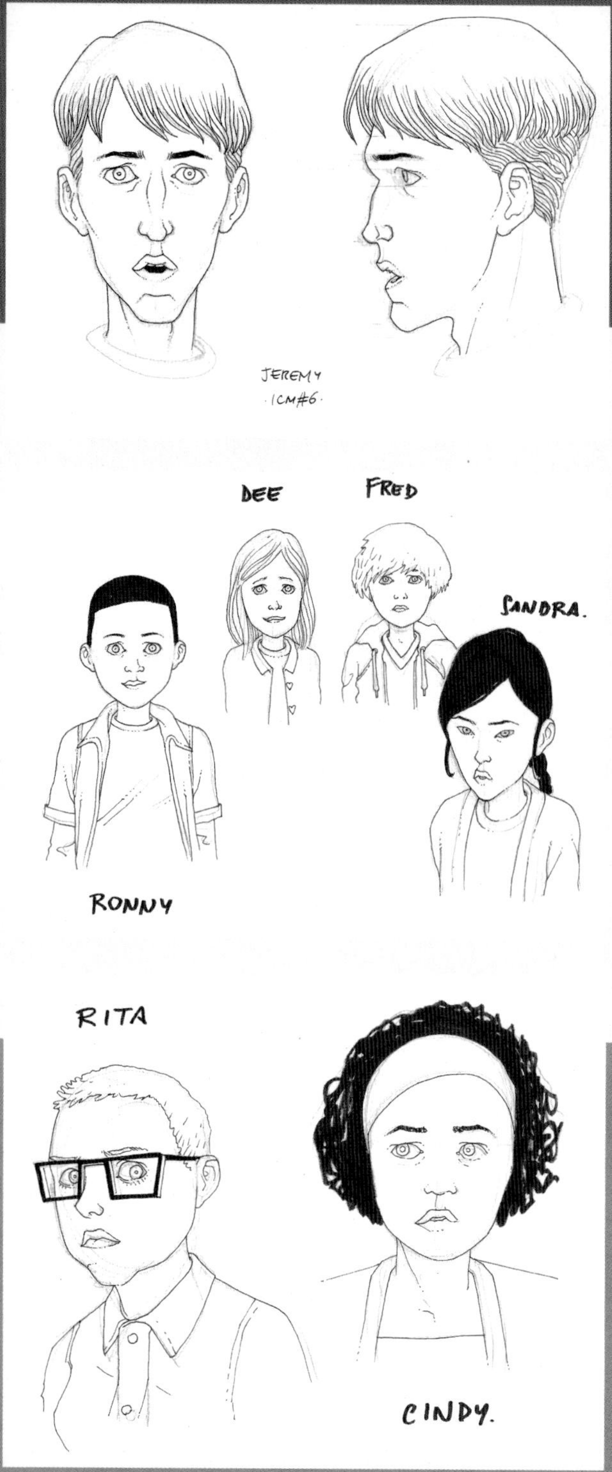
JEREMY
ICM#6.
DEE
FRED
SANDRA.
RONNY
RITA
CINDY.

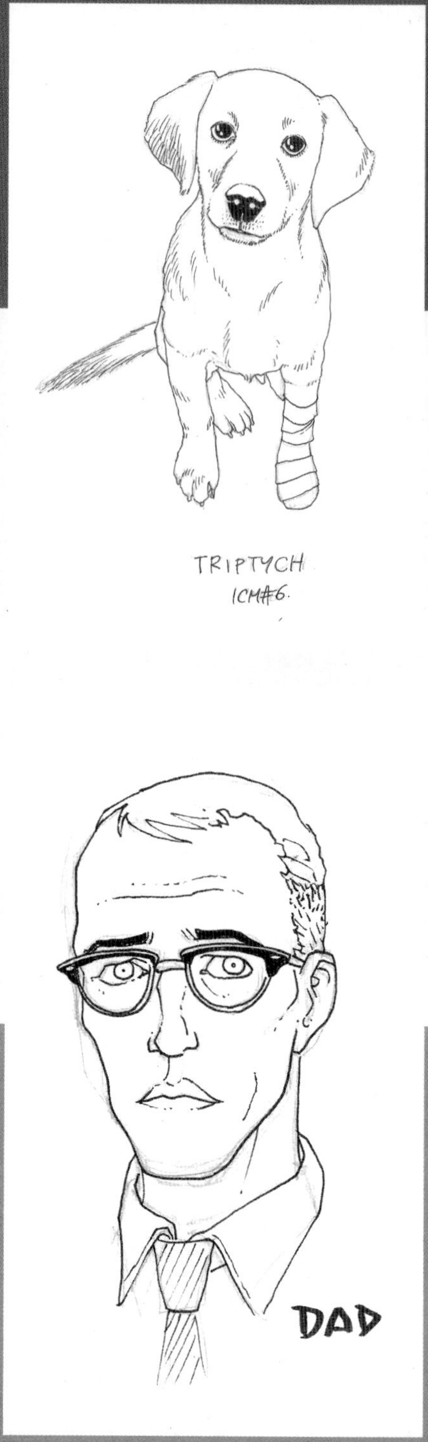
TRIPTYCH
ICM#6.
DAD

No, seriously. Just look.

PICK A FLAVOR, PART DEUX

ICE CREAM MAN #6 cover sketches

ICE CREAM MAN #7 cover sketches

Gaze here upon Martín's many marvelous mock-ups for his mischievous covers. Plus: some sketches by our murderers' row of variant artists.

CANDY COATING

ICE CREAM MAN #8 cover sketches

A

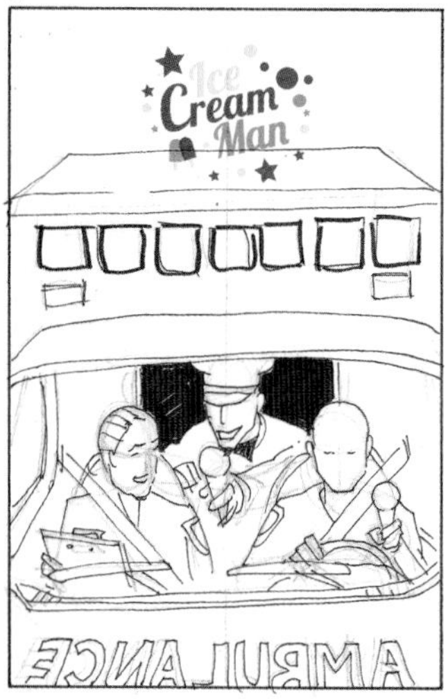
Ice Cream Man

B

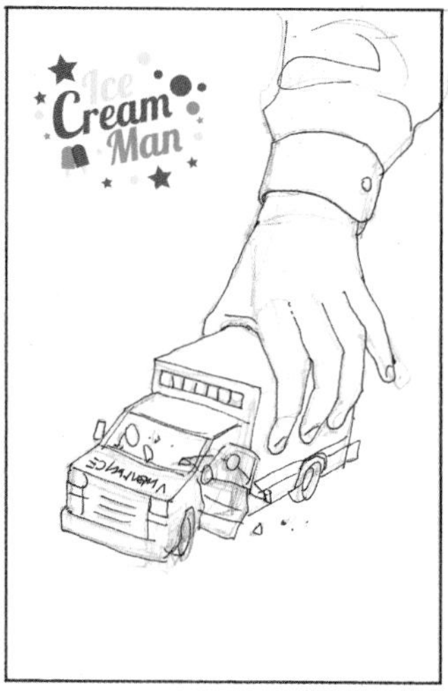
Ice Cream Man

C

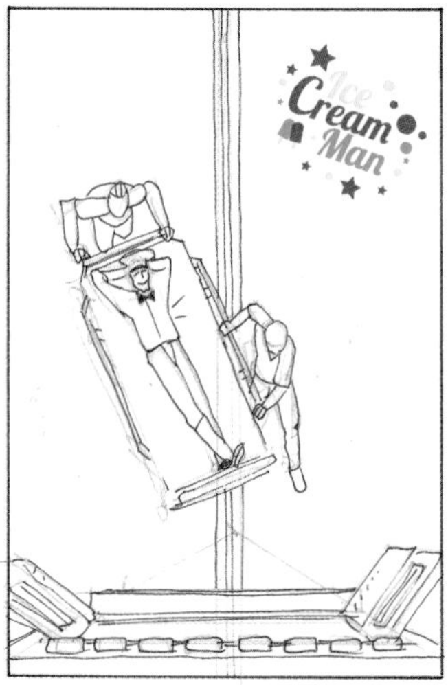
Ice Cream Man

D

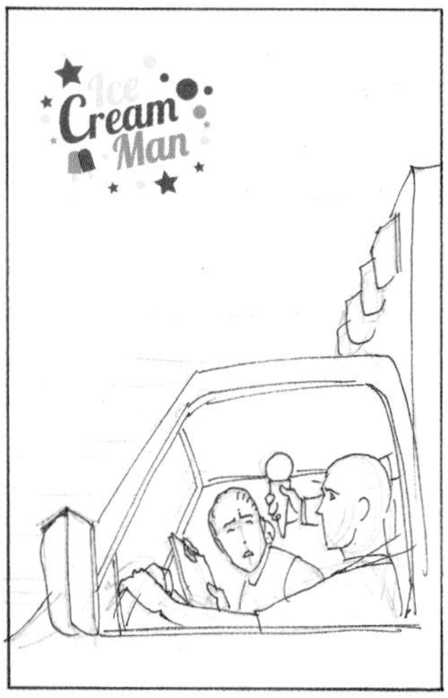
Ice Cream Man

E

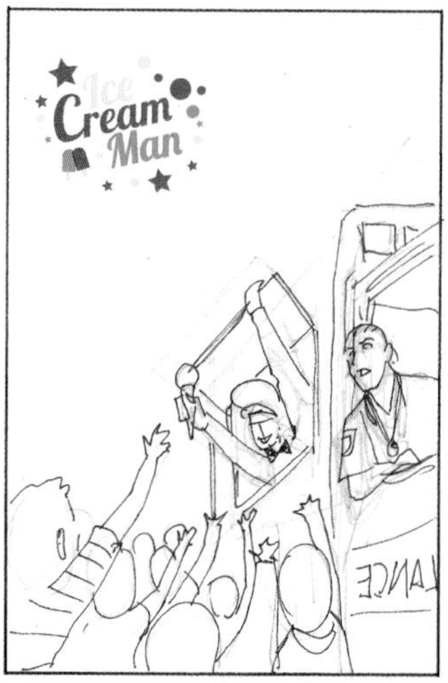
Ice Cream Man

F

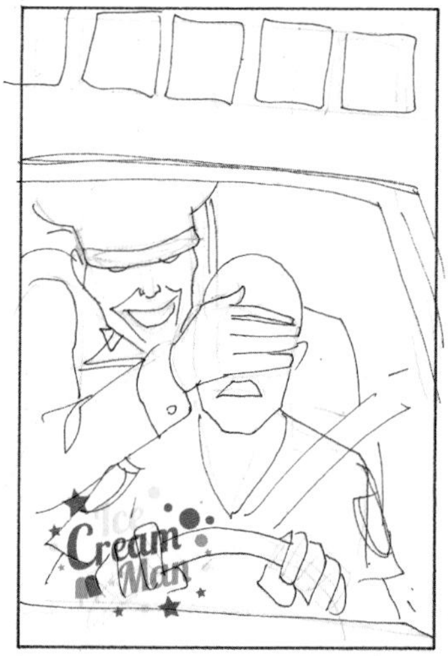
Ice Cream Man

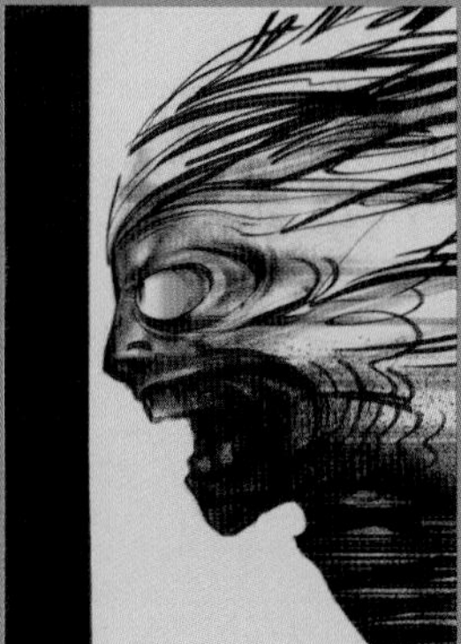

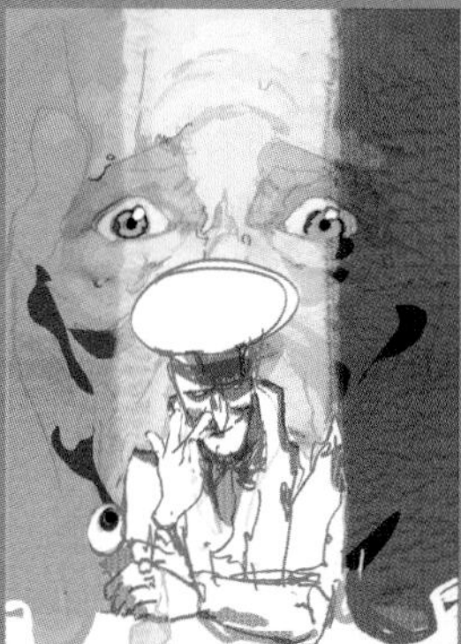

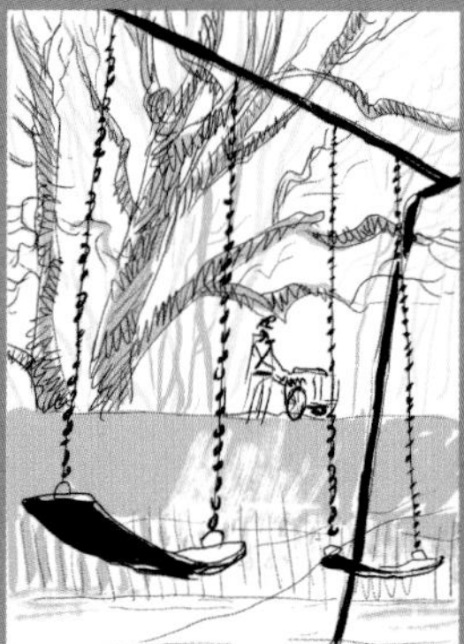

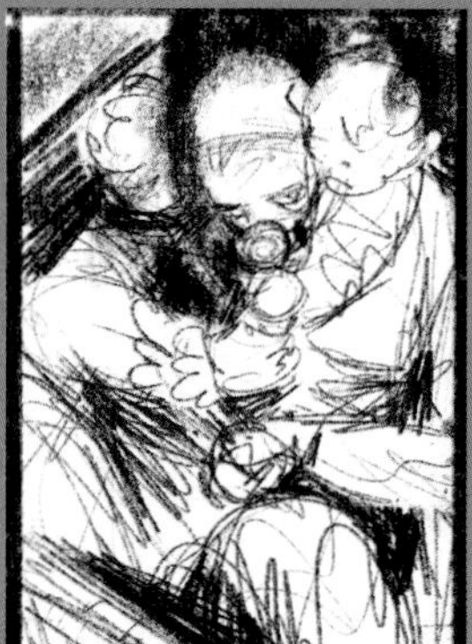

Golly.

MADDENING RECIPES
Herewith select script pages from Chapter 6, "Strange Neapolitan," to give you a sense of how the issue came together.

ICE CREAM MAN
Issue 6, "Strange Neapolitan"

Intro: Martín, Chris—this one's a doozy. It's a silent issue, but there's more: the gist here is that from pages 5-24, we'll be telling THREE different stories, all at the same time. Each story will be about the same guy—it's 3 different what-ifs, 3 different strands of possibility. Each strand will be colored in its own way (take note, Chris), to mimic the colors of Neapolitan Ice Cream. It should be clear to the reader, through these different treatments, that each tier is a different reality.

Pages 1-2 will be standard comics storytelling (so you can come up with the panel set-ups, Martín).

Pages 3-4 will be two versions of the same image, and I'll provide a mock-up of how those should generally look.

The rest of the issue will take this form:

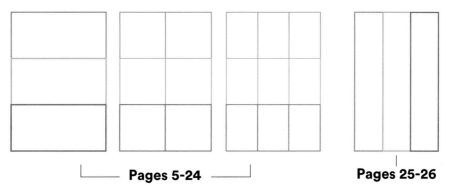

Pages 5-24   **Pages 25-26**

For pages with 3 panels, it takes form 1. For pages with 6 panels, form 2. And 9-panel pages take form 3. (Form 4 is only used at the end.)

I've color-coded the panel descriptions to make the different strands clear. To give you an idea of the three different stories we're telling:

Strand 1: Jeremy walks down a street, bumps into a girl, falls in love, and has a child. But the child dies, and Jeremy's life thus becomes a lot more complicated.

Strand 2: Jeremy walks down a street, finds an injured dog, takes care of it, discovers that it's a LOST dog and that its owners are looking for it, and so moves out of town to live a quiet life with the dog

Strand 3: Jeremy is alone, haunted by strange things, and is eventually kidnapped and killed by a mysterious figure.

Let me know if you have any questions—and sorry in advance!

ICE CREAM MAN
Issue 6, "Strange Neapolitan"

PAGE SEVEN

Panel 1: A shot of Jeremy on the ground, on his butt, using his hands and elbows to prop himself up. He's not looking at the woman quite yet—here, he's sort of just recovering from the shock of bumping into somebody.

Panel 2: A shot of the girl, also on the ground, but looking at Jeremy and smiling. She's got the cone on her head, ice cream dripping down her cheek. (Her eyes should be flirtatious.)

Panel 3: Back to Jeremy, who smiles in an embarrassed way, now realizing that he's experiencing a "meet-cute."

Panel 4: Jeremy, standing, looks around for the owner of the dog.

Panel 5: Back to the dog, who looks up at Jeremy, injured but with a dumb smile on his face.

Panel 6: Jeremy's reaction to this, smiling apprehensively at the dog.

Panel 7: Jeremy reaches for the doorknob, taking a bite of his ice cream.

Panel 8: Jeremy spits to his side as if he's eaten something awful.

Panel 9: Jeremy looks at the cone to find that it's covered with little bugs of all sorts.

PAGE EIGHT

Panel 1: Jeremy and the girl are now on a date, at a restaurant. They're sitting across from each other, laughing and having fun.

Panel 2: A little closer in, we can see that the girl is using a finger to put her hair behind her ears in a semi-sexual/flirtatious way.

Panel 3: We're at a veterinary office. A doctor is handing the dog over to Jeremy. (He's holding it with both hands—the dog's leg is now bandaged.)

Panel 4: Jeremy holds the dog and it licks his face.

Panel 5: Jeremy drops the cone on the ground in disgust.

Panel 6: A shot from the ground. In the foreground, the upside cone is covered with crawling bugs. In the background, we can see Jeremy's feet advancing through his house. (He's headed toward the kitchen.)

ICE CREAM MAN
Issue 6, "Strange Neapolitan"

PAGE FIFTEEN

Panel 1: Aerial view of Jeremy and Rachel's bed. Rachel is sleeping, but Jeremy is awake, looking over at the baby monitor on Rachel's bedside table—it's making noise.

Panel 2: A shot from next to the crib. The corner of the crib is in the foreground (we can't see the baby inside), and in the background Jeremy opens the door of the baby's room, looking curiously toward the baby's crib.

Panel 3: A shot of the baby inside the crib. He's sitting up, crying, and black goop is falling from its eyes, out of its nose, out of its ears. The goop pools on the crib sheets.

Panel 4: Jeremy is walking the dog down one of our suburban streets. He passes a telephone pole, which has a sign pasted on it that we can't see.

Panel 5: Jeremy stops in his tracks, looking back at the sign on the pole.

Panel 6: We reveal the sign: It says "Lost Dog" and shows a picture of Triptych. Underneath the picture, it says "If found, please call 555-5555"

Panel 7: A side shot of Jeremy walking down one of our suburban streets. In the road next to him, a white van with no windows is driving along slowly.

Panel 8: As Jeremy walks, a dark figure comes out of the van's side door. We can't make out too many detail yet—all-black "robber" clothing, maybe a black ski mask. He's got a rag in one hand.

Panel 9: The figure comes from behind Jeremy and puts the rag over his mouth, causing Jeremy to pass out.

ICE CREAM MAN
Issue 6, "Strange Neapolitan"

PAGE TWENTY-FOUR

Panel 1: Jeremy pulls a blanket over his drunk wife. He loves her.

Panel 2: Same shot, but the blanket is on Rachel, and Jeremy stands over her, half-smiling, half-frowning.

Panel 3: A shot from the ground, from behind: Jeremy walks through the cabin, holding a cup of coffee, heading toward the open front door. At his feet, the almost-dead Triptych follows slowly behind him.

Panel 4: A shot of the cabin again. This time, we can see Jeremy exiting from the front door, making his way to the wooden rocking chair on the porch.

Panel 5: The bird man is holding the bird in his hands, looking at it and smiling. BUT, he's no longer wearing the mask here—he's revealed to be the ICM (wearing his hat), grinning down at the little creature. The bird here is just staring right back a him.

Panel 6: Same basic shot, but the bird SQUAWKS.

PAGE TWENTY-FIVE
Note: This page is 3 equal-sized VERTICAL panels, going from left to right. They're all going to show Jeremy "sitting."

Panel 1: Jeremy in the lounge chair next to the couch. He's got the bottle of whiskey in one hand, and the picture of the baby in the other, sort of laying it on his lap.

Panel 2: Jeremy in the rocking chair, the old dog curled up in his lap, its eyes closed. He rubs the dog's neck.

Panel 3: Jeremy still tied up in the chair, dead as a doornail with a hole in his chest and leg/thigh.

TEXT (across all): ONE WAY OR ANOTHER

PAGE TWENTY-SIX
Once again, 3 equal-sized VERTICAL panels, but they're just filled with solid colors—representative of our 3 different "timelines."